SHADOW WIZARD

BY
JEFFE KENNEDY

Spy, manipulator, traitor... He might be her only salvation.

Lady Seliah Phel can't escape feeling like she's one of those fairytale princesses awakened from a long slumber—except that her life is no romantic story and there's no happy ending in sight. Though she has her magic and she's been rescued from the depths of madness that consumed her since adolescence, Selly finds that the years she lost aren't so easily recovered. Everyone treats her like the child they remember. To prove something—perhaps only to herself—she's recklessly volunteered to stave off a host of monsters with only the enigmatically alluring, cuttingly sarcastic, and probably deceitful wizard Jadren El-Adrel for company.

Jadren isn't the heroic type. In fact, he's not much of anything. Relentlessly groomed into a shadow of a man by his sadistic mother, he's the perfect spy and tool, with no real will of his own. When he's stranded in the wilderness with Seliah Phel, he figures the outcome is immaterial. Live or die, it's all the same to him. But Seliah is a different story and she isn't like anyone else. Though he reminds himself she's basically a child in a woman's body, he finds it increasingly difficult to resist her artless charms and relentless curiosity.

As their predicament goes from dire to disastrous, Jadren realizes his many failures have jeopardized Selly's future, perhaps her very life. Far from home and trapped without resources, Selly has only Jadren to rely upon—the one person she can't possibly trust. There seems no possibility of rescue from their friends and family back home at House Phel, so Jadren and Selly must work together to survive... if they can.

DEDICATION

To Mary Robinette Kowal,

for conversations about story brain that helped me find the path into this book

and for providing me with a magical place to follow it.

ACKNOWLEDGMENTS

Thanks to my wonderful writing community who form the fabric of my days:

- Kelly Robson who's there daily with a good morning greeting, and who always knows what I'm working on. She gets a special star for coming up with the title for this book.
- Darynda Jones, there on the other side of the Zoom window with laughter and pithy insights.
- Grace Draven, who's always got helpful advice, good business sense, and the best gossip.
- Jennifer Estep who always provides interesting debates and business conversations—and who is totally not beta team.
- Carien Ubink, assistant, beta reader, and friend. I'd be a mess without you.

A round of coffee to the Writer Coffee peeps—Emily Mah, Jim Sorenson, and J. Barton Mitchell—for weekly doses of peopling. You all are awesome.

Shoutout to the staff, board, and key volunteers of SFWA. It's amazing to work with all of you who make my job so easy. Special thanks to John Murphy, Erin Hartshorn, and Kate Baker for handling stuff without me so I could get through the crunch on this book.

Love and margaritas to Megan Mulry, who never judges and is always there when I need her the most.

A moment of special hand-holding inspired parts of this book. Something I will forever treasure.

Love to David who is there every day and makes all things possible.

Thank you for reading!

Credits
Cover: Ravven (www.ravven.com)

SHADOW WIZARD

BY
JEFFE KENNEDY

J ADREN SQUINTED AT the onrushing horde of monsters, swinging his enchanted machete to limber up his muscles, and sighed to himself. He didn't know what had possessed him to volunteer to heroically sacrifice himself to play rear guard. Especially since he was no hero. Clearly being among the idealistic fools of House Phel had affected his sense and good judgment.

Well, that and a heavy dose of guilt on top of his inherent self-loathing. The people he'd offered to protect didn't trust him, which would be more upsetting if he could feel indignant about it. If he died, that would at least liberate him from the cage his darling maman had kept him in all his miserable life. Just because he was temporarily out of that cage didn't mean he'd fully escaped it.

"So," his lone companion drawled, "is your grand plan to stand here like an idiot and wait to be overrun?"

He glanced over at Selly, suppressing a rush of unwilling attraction. There was no way he should find the chit so compelling. Far too thin still from the magic stagnation that had very nearly killed her, Selly's face was mostly huge amber eyes and jutting cheekbones. It didn't help that she'd braided that tumbling mass of tangled black hair, the severe style making her look even younger, her piquant, heart-shaped face wistful, even sad in moments of repose, when she thought no one was watching. Her waifish mien made him want to cuddle and comfort her—not an urge he'd ever felt before in his emotionally stunted life. Fortunately that absurd impulse lasted only until she unleashed that sharp tongue of hers.

"No one asked you to stay," he observed. "Just the opposite, in fact. There's still time for you to flee, which would be the wise decision. Hop on your horsie and run along home."

"And strand you without magic reserves?" She huffed out a disgusted laugh. "You'd run out of your own magic in no time, leaving *you* without any way to defend yourself as we both know you're no fighter."

"You have no idea." Jadren set his teeth, turning away from her disdain to observe the river of hunters streaming from House Sammael and plunging through the valley straight for them. They moved like oily smoke, running on four legs, their long claws churning up a cloud of dust as they charged at full speed in their oddly loping stride, like a jackal's.

House Phel's small band of intrepid rescuers—like something out of the popular novels—had managed to rescue Lady Phel, but they wouldn't make it far if the hunters overtook them. Thus the rear-guard offer. It was true, though, that he'd never trained in hand-to-hand fighting. As a scion of House El-Adrel, he'd been expected to learn one thing and one thing only.

That one thing wasn't anything so menial as swinging a manual weapon.

He was beginning to appreciate the merits of edged weapons, however. He rather loved his enchanted machete. Made of silver that House Phel wizard ancestors had solidified from moonlight, then embedded with Gabriel Phel's living magic, the blade killed the otherwise unkillable hunters on contact. It was also satisfyingly heavy and, dare he say, proletariat. His maman would be appalled, which gave him a nice thrill of satisfaction.

The only fly in the ointment of his martyrdom was the stubborn familiar who'd insisted on staying with him. "Your virginal magic reserves won't do me any good, poppet," he informed her. "I can't lay waste to yon monstrous army from a distance like your rogue wizard brother. Unless you have a brilliant suggestion?"

She glared at him with glittering dislike that made her doelike amber eyes hard as faceted jewels. "You're the one educated in wizardry, Lord son-of-a-fancy Convocation high house. I've only been awake and in my right mind for a short time. Shouldn't *you* know what to do with the power I provide? As I understand it, I'm basically the fire in the stove while you're the expert chef doing the cooking."

He would've retorted, except the analogy was an apt one and, for the first time in his life, he'd lately begun to feel vaguely guilty about the status of familiars in the Convocation. Which made zero sense as it was hardly his fault that some people were born able to wield magic and others only to generate it. That was the way of the world, which sucked for everyone to a greater or lesser degree. "Yeah, well, this chef knows how to make enchanted artifacts, assorted widgets, and do a few other tricks. I'm not like Phel, able to bend rainstorms to my will and spin silver weapons out of thin air."

She hmphed in disgust. "Probably Gabriel should've stayed to stem the hunter tide while you took Nic home."

"What a brilliant plan," he snarled, stung despite himself. Dark arts knew he should be long past the sneers and thinly veiled insults about his inscrutable magic. "Except Nic isn't my familiar, is she? I know you're ignorant, but no wizard lets another wizard run off with their familiar."

"Do you wish she was?" Selly asked with innocent curiosity belied by the sly sparkle in her eyes. She seemed to have emerged from the oblivion of insanity raring to needle him to death.

He pointed the machete at the tide of hunters crossing the valley and closing far too rapidly on their vantage at the verge of the forest. "I'd love to have a conversation about my feelings—and lack thereof—for Lady Phel, not incidentally my employer, but I have hunters to kill."

Selly measured the distance with her gaze. "Since we're just standing here waiting for them to slaughter us, I figured we had time to chat."

"I am not 'just standing here,'" he snarled at her. "I am formulating a plan."

"Isn't that what I asked to begin with?" She batted her lashes, widening her eyes even more. "No need to get snippy."

He didn't dignify that with even a growl.

"Better formulate faster," she suggested, making it sound like an innovative idea, "or it's going to be slaughter for sure."

She sounded so blithely unconcerned about that eventuality that he eyed her. "Don't you care if you live or die?"

Shrugging, her expression went hard in a way that transformed her face from girlish to that of a woman three times her age.

Jadren waited, but she didn't answer the question. "Still more than a little insane, huh?" he asked with oozingly fake sympathy.

She fixed him with a blank stare that made the hairs on the back of his neck prickle. "You have no idea," she answered in a soft voice, flinging his words back at him with lethal accuracy.

Deciding to leave plumbing the psyche of the crazy girl for another time, he switched tactics. "How many arrows do you have left?"

"Between my quiver and the ones Iliana donated to our hopeless cause, just shy of a hundred."

"Plus my machete, the sword, and assorted daggers..." He estimated the number of hunters, considered the math. Even though they only needed to break skin on the hunters to melt them with the enchanted weapons, they still needed to make that essential contact. By the time the hunters came close enough for that, he and Selly would only be able to melt a small proportion before the sheer numbers overwhelmed them. Hopeless cause and slaughter were distressingly accurate descriptors. "How fast can you fire those arrows?"

"Not fast enough. And, you know, the thing with arrows is, once they're loosed, they're gone."

"It's not looking good for the hand-to-hand fighting thing then."

Selly nodded in wry sympathy. "This why I was hoping for

a feat of prodigious magic."

"I'm sure something will come to me," he muttered, mostly to himself.

She held out a slim hand. "Suck me dry, widget-maker."

If only. Then an idea struck him. "All right, my little woodstove—take up yon hatchet and start chopping up your arrows. Keep a few intact. A couple dozen or so. Chop the rest. Bitty pieces."

That got her. Surprise temporarily pierced her scorn. "Seriously?"

"A familiar never questions their wizard," he retorted, making it extra arrogant to repay her for the relentless needling. "You have a lot to learn, poppet."

"I am not *your* familiar, nor am I your puppet." She stalked away ungraciously before he could correct her misapprehension. She was following his instructions, however, muttering under her breath about Convocation wizards, their idiocy, their high-handed ways, and how—even if she *did* die—she didn't care because it was worth it to save Nic and Gabriel, it was just too bad she had to die with an arrogant fool.

"I can hear everything you're saying," he commented as he gathered up daggers of various sizes and constructed the enchantment in his mind.

"I figured those enormous flesh flaps on the sides of your head weren't just for decoration."

If they weren't slaughtered, he was going to kill her. Holding out a preemptory hand, he snapped his fingers. "To me, familiar. Bring the arrows."

"*Bits* of arrows," she corrected bitingly, but she complied—

dumping the arrow pieces in a pile next to the daggers and laying her hand in his. "I feel I should point out that the bow will be useless soon. You just destroyed our only long-distance weapon."

"Silence." He didn't smile at her scowl, but he really wanted to. Concentrating, more than a little leery of what he'd find, he drew on her magic. The first time he'd done this, she'd been a cesspool of magic so stagnant it had very nearly killed him, which would have been inconvenient. He still didn't quite understand what had possessed him to risk himself to help with that near-disastrous effort. Clearly the Phel contagion at work, with all this self-sacrifice. Pulling Selly out of the vortex of fetid, untapped magic and her resultant insanity had put Gabriel Phel out of commission for more than a week. If Nic hadn't leant Jadren her magic—and what a heady kick of the finest liquor that had been—he'd have been similarly dropped, or worse. It had helped immensely that Nic had the talent of a high-house daughter and the expertise of a Convocation education.

Conversely, Selly was worse than untrained: she knew just enough to make tapping her magic difficult. Nothing like working with an obstinate and untrained familiar under battlefield conditions, while attempting a meticulous spell he'd never before attempted. "Don't be so tense," he told her, shaking the hand he held hard enough to rattle her bones. "It's like sucking on a dried lemon rind trying to wring magic juice out of you."

"The hunters are getting closer," she replied tersely. "Just do whatever you're going to do."

He knew it. That characteristically oily mental feel of the hunters permeated his wizard senses. Despite his complaints, magic was flowing from Selly into him as he focused on extracting it, and it came as a welcome change of flavors. Far from hard or sour, her moon magic was bright and luminous, the water magic deeply cooling. Now that she'd been drained of that deadly backlog, healed, and was now producing new magic, she felt refreshing—and terribly addictive. *I am not* your *familiar.* Her words rang harsh in his mind. Selly was absolutely correct, although she had no idea how very true that was. He'd never have a familiar, never enjoy that mythical intimacy of that sort of magical relationship. He didn't dare, all thanks to his darling Maman.

Not that he had issues.

Having siphoned enough magic for the task, he forced himself to release Selly lest he succumb to the temptation to drink from her enticing flavor into oblivion. He let her go with a snap abrupt enough that she staggered back slightly. Without thinking, he reached to steady her. She was far too thin and frail still. Throttling back the impulse, he dropped his hand to his side. She'd be fine. He also had good cause to know she was more agile and resilient than she appeared.

"That's it?" she asked. Was it his imagination that she looked bereft?

"That's it." He bent his focus to the task, coaxing the arrow pieces to be sharp on one end, then bending his will to the daggers. He'd arranged them in a circle, points out, with the hilts touching just enough to leave a hole in the center. Extracting a coil of wire from the array of tools attached to his vest, he laid it on top of the center circle. Now to teach it all to work together. He'd never have thought to attempt something like this before, but Gabriel Phel had a way of inspiring innovation. Or of dragging everyone along with him into crazyland. *Could be both.*

"They're coming up the hill."

"Almost ready. Fetch me a stick."

"Woof." But she moved away.

Without Selly's distracting presence, he finished the enchantment and gazed at it critically. Ungainly and certainly unlovely, the dagger wheel would not be going into anyone's product line. But it just might keep them alive. He grunted when Selly thrust a stick at him. Not ideal, but none of this was. "Stand in front of me," he told her.

"So I can be your human shield? How gallant."

"Life isn't like in the novels, poppet."

"I told you, I'm not—"

"Less talking, more obeying," he interrupted, wrapping her fingers around the stick and threading the dagger wheel onto it. Then he scooped up a handful of the sharpened arrow pieces. Standing behind Selly, he laid a hand on her narrow shoulder, feeling as if he could break her in half if he squeezed too hard. It made him irrationally furious. Ignorant country folk to have let her deteriorate so far. He set it aside.

"They'll come through at that narrow point," he noted. At least they had the dubious advantage of a strategic position.

"What a brilliant observation."

He ignored her sarcasm; he was nervous, too. "Face it as squarely as you can."

"Fear my dagger wheel!" she shouted. "Rawr."

"Funny girl." But he nearly laughed. "Wait for it."

"Oh, I am," she assured him. "I cannot wait to see this. Especially as it will be my last sight before I'm mercilessly slaughtered."

"Cheer up," he said. "Maybe they'll only slaughter *me* while you'll be taken captive and dragged off to a life of miserable bondage as a free-range familiar to House Sammael. Sucked dry by any wizard who cares to sip. Or, if you're *really* lucky, maybe slimy Sergio himself will bond you for life!"

"Happy thoughts indeed!" she replied with considerable perkiness, and now he did chuckle.

"Love that optimistic outlook," he murmured. He didn't need to be quiet—the hunters were yipping as they galloped up the hill, creating an unsettling din—but his mouth was near the delicate shell of her ear as he focused his gaze through the dagger wheel toward the point where the hunters would appear. Despite the need to concentrate on making his invention work, he was tempted to kiss her there, just to see if she tasted as good as she smelled, like silvery cool rain, fresh and potent. "Steady."

"As a rock. Would love to know how this will work."

"Oh, me too."

"Not a rousing endorsement."

"What's life without some uncertainty?"

"Certain."

"Boring." Impossible that she amused him so, especially under such dire circumstances. The first hunter loped into view around the curve between the tall trees. It was a foul thing, standing out in horrific contrast to the spring sunshine dappling through the leaves. Probably a conglomeration of weasel and jackal—and dark arts knew what else had occurred to the House Ariel wizards to throw into the stew of that ill-advised incantation—it boasted a protruding snout and rows of long fangs suitable for rending and slavering and not much else.

Jadren had reason to know, as one of the things had rent and slavered all over him until Gabriel Phel rescued him, to Jadren's intense chagrin. The things also had claws on all four paws that impressively tore up the dirt road and they slunk-galloped at high speed.

"Jadren." Selly had tensed even more, her voice strained.

"Not yet."

More hunters followed, a boilingly ugly stamped of them. "They're coming," Selly said tightly.

"So I see." The vicious glee rose in him, amplified by Selly's luminously bright magic as he drew upon it. It was like being drunk without the downsides of dulled senses. Indeed, he felt sharper than he had in years, possibly decades.

The lead hunters raced toward them, only a few horse lengths away, more of the horde filling the road behind them. Selly trembled under his hand. She took a sharp breath, shrinking back enough to make contact with his chest. "Jadren."

That throaty semi-scream of his name shouldn't send a flare of desire through him, but it did—eliciting an immediate fantasy of burying himself inside her slim body while she gasped his name exactly that way. "Selly," he murmured, then indulged himself and kissed her ear with a flick of his tongue, just in case he died without a taste of her. Like rain after drought. "Now."

He activated the spell, the dagger wheel whirring to life, Selly bracing herself against the sudden momentum. Tossing a handful of arrow bits into the maelstrom, he pulled on her magic, fueling the barrage of missiles that flew into the tightly packed onslaught of hunters.

Like a fire doused by a bucket of water, the surge of loping hunters melted, turning into a slag of jutting bone fragments in a stew of rotting flesh. Selly let out an animal ululation of victory, turning back and forth to spray the still advancing hunters with the bits he tossed into the propulsion of the dagger wheel. The next wave melted, also, adding to the bog of rotting flesh on the once-pretty forest trail.

But nothing stopped the hunters. Whatever vile spell propelled them, it didn't allow for initiative on their part, or even justifiable caution. More hunters galloped toward them, clambering over and, in some places, wading through the disgusting remains of their comrades. Shelly shrieked with the fury of a true warrior, spraying the advancing hunters with excellent aim.

Until he ran out of ammunition.

"Tapped out," he told her, yanking the dagger wheel from her hands and thrusting the bow at her, along with her quiver of pitifully few arrows. "Cover me!" Seizing his machete, he raced bravely forward to slay the remaining hunters.

~ 2 ~

THE MAN WAS a blithering idiot. Selly stared after Jadren as he flung himself wildly through the rotting morass of creatures, swinging his blade with amateurish enthusiasm and stunning lack of skill. Her dumbfounded shock wasn't due only to Jadren's ill-considered charge. Though the others had told her of the hunters and warned her of their appearance and rapacious nature, nothing had prepared her for the reality. These things were not of nature. The wild cats of the western marshes were deadly predators, and the venomous snakes and biting insects there presented dangers she treated with appropriate caution, but none of them frightened her like these mishmash monsters that shouldn't exist.

And nothing had sent chilling fear straight to her bones like the hapless wizard currently attacking those monsters with a machete in one hand and a dagger in the other. *"Cover me,"* she echoed in dismay and disgust. She was no warrior and even she knew better how covering someone worked. The inexperienced sod was going to get himself killed and she wouldn't be sorry. She *would* be alone, however, and that prospect that chilled her with a rime of unreasonable terror. She could catch up with the others quickly enough, she consoled herself. She wouldn't be alone for long, as she'd been for far too much of her life, wandering those formless mists, not knowing if she was alive or dead, awake or asleep, sane or trapped in quivering madness.

"Get a grip on yourself," she said aloud, drawing an arrow from her quiver. Jadren had slain one hunter, but three more had jumped him, hampering his ability to swing either machete or dagger. Unfortunately, she didn't have a clear shot, what with him flailing about, trying to extract himself from the formidable teeth and claws of the hunters. She only needed to nick the things, though, not get a clean kill shot. During her time fending for herself in the marshes she'd gotten proficient at skewering the small rats cleanly enough to retrieve her arrow for her precious arsenal. If she could do that, she could at least graze a hunter.

Aiming, drawing, and nocking the arrow in one smooth movement, she loosed it—then cursed as it flew past her target by a hair. "Close," she muttered. "Now do better."

Taking a calming breath, but not holding it—that caused tension and tension ruined both aim and power—she ignored Jadren's scream of pain. Aim, draw, nock, release. *Boom!* The hunter raking furrows down the wizard's back melted in a pile of sludge. Jadren did his part, managing to get the edge of the machete into a hunter rather than the blunt side, melting it into a stew with ligaments unfortunately still intact enough to tangle around his arm. The third hunter currently trying to kill him snapped its unnaturally long jaws at Jadren's throat. Before she consciously planned it, Selly had let loose another arrow and put it right through the creature's eye.

Startled, Jadren glanced back at her, his grin flashing white amidst the auburn frame of his beard and gore-smattered visage. Another hunter rose up behind his back. Selly aimed, drew, nocked, and fired, enjoying the utter shock on Jadren's face as the arrow whistled past and embedded itself in the hunter's open maw. "If I was going to kill you, I'd do it up close," she shouted to him, gratified when his lips curled in a snarl.

No other hunters appeared around the bend, though Jadren waited and Selly remained poised with her last dozen arrows. Finally, he picked his way through the sludge, sparing her having to go to him, for which she was grateful—though she wouldn't admit it to *him*—as she didn't want to touch the oily remains, even with boots on. He grinned jauntily at her. "Rear guard accomplished! That wasn't so bad."

"If you say so," she replied sourly, so he wouldn't get the idea she found him even remotely charming. What had been up with him kissing her ear? And *licking* it... It should've been disgusting and distracting, not something that sent a shiver of heat through her body so intense it had driven out what should've been far more consuming concerns of death or capture.

"Oh, come on," he wheedled. "That was pretty much an epic deed. Now we can catch up with the others and brag."

"What I live for." Briefly she considered that she should search the dead-hunter stew for her arrows, as she had so few left, but... no. She simply didn't have the guts for it. So to speak. "Let's commence with the catching up," she said. "If we ride fast, we can meet them before they take the barge upriver."

"Easy as pie." He whistled a happy tune, leading the way toward where they'd left the horses.

"WHO DOESN'T KNOW how to tie up horses so they can't run off?" she demanded, trying to master her frustration as they tramped down the road.

"Why was it *my* job to secure the horses?" he demanded in return.

"Because you were the one to interrupt the saddling up to volunteer to play rear guard. You could have been securing the horses while everyone else was contributing weapons and supplies."

Jadren slid her an annoyed look. "I am a wizard, not a hostler."

"It's not possible to be both?"

"It's not necessary when one employs people to look after one's horses," he answered in an aggravated tone, made even more strained by the bags of supplies he'd shouldered. And him with numerous injuries, too, though they seemed to be less severe than she'd originally thought.

She hadn't been able to talk him out of leaving any of the stuff behind—but she had refused to help carry anything except her few weapons. She was accustomed to living off the land and valued being unencumbered, to having her hands free to shoot her bow. *Move fast and move often,* a small, feral voice whispered in the back of her mind. That was freedom. Running and fleeing, dodging, evading, always a hair ahead of the snapping madness threatening to hamstring her and drag her under.

And the madness was there. She'd thought she was doing better—and she had been, before the confrontation with the hunters—but now every shadow snagged the corner of her eye, seeming to slink and snap, making her start with alarm. The fear that hadn't paralyzed her during the fight with the hunters had arrived belatedly, like a drunk relative coming late to the party and ruining what should be a celebration with belching predictions of doom. Now matter how she tried to shut it up, it held court in the back of her mind, droning on with endlessly embroidered tales of what could have happened.

"If one lives in civilized Convocation society," Jadren continued in an arch tone, oblivious to her dark thoughts and still justifying how he'd neglected to secure their horses, apparently, "one uses magical conveyances for transportation rather than hay-chomping fart-beasts."

She could never decide if Jadren's carelessly cynical remarks amused or irritated her. The high house wizard was in some ways everything she'd assumed Convocation citizens would be like when she was a girl—and before she lost her mind—though she'd been admittedly ignorant, living in the distant wilds of Meresin on her parents' farm, hearing occasional tales of glittering and politely violent Convocation society. As with all tales, they'd represented only part of the picture.

"Nic grew up in civilized Convocation society and knows horses," Selly pointed out, very reasonably, she thought, given the insult to their faithful equine companions. Even their erstwhile steeds who'd abandoned them in a moment of panic could be forgiven. She'd certainly wanted to flee. Only determination to be useful to her house instead of a crazed burden had prevented her.

"I thought you've had about three sentences of conversation—sane conversation, that is—with your new sister-in-law." Jadren raised an auburn brow at her.

This was something else about Jadren that she both disliked and liked. He taunted her without remorse, and yet he was also the only person who directly referenced her recent madness. Everyone else tiptoed around her, giving her those bright, encouraging smiles reserved for newly recovered invalids who might relapse at any moment. They danced around admitting just how crazed she'd been. And how close she'd come to killing Gabriel.

Jadren didn't scruple about speaking the bald truth. It was accurate that she hadn't spoken with Nic much as a sane person. By the time Selly had emerged from the mists she'd wandered in confusion, Nic had already been abducted. She did remember, though, through the tattered and chill veils of madness, the story Nic had told Selly when Nic had first arrived at House Phel. An enchanted princess cursed so she couldn't explain to anyone about the evil spell she struggled to escape. Until her brother, the prince, broke the spell and they lived happily ever after.

The metaphor had somehow penetrated the morass of

confusion and layers of reality and dreams that had obscured her reason and touched a nerve of understanding. It had been a lifeline Selly had grabbed onto and still held with shredded mental fingernails of determined intent. When Gabriel had appeared in the pervasive mist she'd existed in, she'd known he was there to rescue her. And he'd done it because Nic had been the only person to know what was wrong with her.

Even without all Nic had done to help restore House Phel, and even if she hadn't made Gabriel happier than Selly could remember him being since the magic took him so hard and ferociously, she would love Nic for that.

She would die for Nic for that reason. And for Gabriel. Though she was wise enough not to say that aloud. People got uneasy when crazy people talked about dying.

"Gabriel talked about Nic with me," she explained. Not that Jadren deserved an explanation, but they did have a long walk ahead of them, unless the horses miraculously came trotting back. And ha to that. "He said Nic took care of Vale when Gabriel was incapacitated."

Jadren snorted. "Yes, well—there's an Elal for you. Sneaky, crafty, and always doing the unexpected."

"Knowing how to handle horses is sneaky?"

"You have no idea," he muttered darkly.

"So tell me."

He slid her a black look, both in mood and the color of his eyes. No telling what color he'd been born with, as working magic had turned his eyes as wizard-black as Gabriel's. With Jadren's auburn hair and beard, his skin the translucent paleness that went with that coloring, his eyes stood out a deep and depthless black that spoke of infernal magic and shiver-inducing power. "Tell you what?"

She shrugged blithely, a gesture that seemed to irritate him, so she made a note to add it to her repertoire for more frequent use. Turnabout was fair play. "I know very little about the Convocation. Tell me about House Elal and how all of them came to share the same characteristics."

He snorted at that. "You think you're being clever by pointing out that a high house comprised of thousands of people can't be reduced to a few common traits."

She didn't comment, diligently covering her surprise that a Convocation high house could have so many people. Were all the houses so large? There were only so many high houses and then lots of smaller ones. House Phel was comprised of maybe three dozen people. Not that she'd met all of them, few as they might be. Thousands was beyond what she could picture. She wanted to ask if they all literally lived in the same house—and, if so, how big were those houses?—but she shied from sounding *that* ignorant. For the most part, Jadren's opinion didn't matter to her, but apparently she had her lines she hesitated to cross.

"The truth of the matter," Jadren went on, fortunately needing no encouragement to wax chatty on this topic, "is that you have to understand how houses, especially the high houses, operate. The head of the house, large or small, is always invested in keeping control of their minions. This wizard will—"

"Is it always a wizard?" she interrupted.

That supercilious brow arched as he slid her an astonished

look. "Of course."

"But why?"

"Who else would head a house full of wizards?"

"Familiars?"

He laughed. "No, little familiar—no one in the Convocation is going to put a familiar in charge of anything except delivering magic to people who can actually make use of it. Even then they can't be in control of that, for obvious reasons, your eccentric sister-in-law notwithstanding."

Selly let that scathing assessment go without comment. What she didn't know about being a familiar could fill barrels. She hadn't even known that *she* was a familiar until she'd awakened from what Jadren so graciously referred to as crazyland to a serious sit-down conversation with Gabriel. Distraught as he was over Nic's abduction, he'd still taken the time to explain that—just like him—she'd experienced the same weird manifestation of magic skipping a few generations. Just as he'd suddenly manifested as a wizard at the late age of twenty-two, a bizarre aberration in their magicless family that hadn't produced a wizard in over a century, it turned out that she had magic also.

Only she couldn't use hers, because of this being a familiar thing. Where Gabriel had discovered his wizardry by suddenly and violently bringing rain, Selly hadn't even known about hers. Nobody had. Instead it had grown inside her like an infection with no outlet, until it poisoned her mind. Gabriel had explained that she'd be fine now that the stagnant magic had been expelled. That whole process remained unclear, largely because Gabriel had glossed over the details, but whatever had happened, her brother had ended up in the infirmary, unconscious and nearly dead, for a week. With him incapacitated, their enemies had pounced. House Sammael had abducted Nic, leading to their current situation.

So, while Gabriel had explained that regularly releasing her magic—which meant having wizards tap her to extract it— would keep her sane and healthy, and even though the whole concept made her feel uneasily like a keg of apple cider, she was resolved to offer her magic to any of the House Phel wizards who needed it. She'd already been too much of a liability, so whatever she could do to help, she would. More selfishly, she'd rather literally die than return to that soul-sapping mist of insanity that had already consumed too much of her life. Even if that meant, as it currently did, keeping company with the obnoxious El-Adrel wizard.

Because they still had a long walk ahead, and Selly was years behind in understanding much at all about her new life and role in the Convocation, she decided to press him more. "All right, if familiars are the lowest of the low and can't be trusted to do anything—"

"You're not the lowest of the low," he interrupted, scowling. "Familiars are highly valued by the Convocation, second only to wizards. Some familiars are considerably more valuable than wizards because of their powerful magic, compared to barely-there wizards who are lucky to be able to boil water without a fire."

Since boiling water *with* a fire was dead easy, Selly didn't find that to be a rousing endorsement of the value of magic. "So, who is the lowest of the low then?"

He snorted, adjusting the burden of their supplies. "Me, currently serving as pack mule. If the house of my birth could only see me now."

"I told you to leave that stuff behind."

Gazing steadfastly ahead, he walked on. "We already had this argument once. It would be ever so dreary to repeat it, so let's continue with this scintillating Q and A instead. Convocation rank goes as such: Wizards, ranked by a combination of magical potential and house status; Familiars, ranked by their wizard's status; then commoners, who have no magic, or none to speak of."

Like her parents and most everyone she'd known all her life. "Not having magic doesn't make you an idiot," she pointed out. "You can still make good business decisions. Why not have nonmagical types run the houses and free up wizards for…" She had very little idea of what wizards did when they weren't battling hunters or other wizards.

Fortunately Jadren didn't need her to finish her sentences under most circumstances. "Won't work. To control a wizard, you need a wizard."

"Why do you need to control wizards?"

"You have no idea," he answered, staring bleakly down the path.

She nearly bit out that this was why she was asking questions, but something about his taut expression stopped her. Jadren used that phrase a lot, and it occurred to her that his 'you have no idea' was communicating something else, something too awful, perhaps, to put into words. It gave her a pang of sympathy, though she indeed had no idea why the arrogant and privileged wizard deserved any pity. Still, it was nice to feel sorry for someone besides herself. "All right, so controlling minions leads to a house being a cultural monolith how?"

"Cute. The head of a high house sees their minions— wizards, familiars, commoners, even horsies—as extensions of themselves." He freed a hand to waggle his fingers. "Basically appendages of a single hand and mind. The more effective the head of the high house, the more consolidated in values, approach, and thinking are the members of the house." He slid her a glittering glance. "Nic is an Elal through and through. Her father, Lord Elal, is *very* effective."

"What about Lady El-Adrel?" Selly knew Jadren's mother was the head of House El-Adrel, and Gabriel had told her a bit about how the woman had brought Jadren to House Phel and essentially extorted them into hiring Jadren as a junior wizard, despite his lack of credentials and the clear implication he was there mainly to spy on them.

"Dear Maman takes 'effective' to an exponential level of control."

She waited, but this time he said nothing more. "How so?"

He slanted her a look. "I'm already exhausted, wounded, stinking like rotten stew, carrying bags like a servant, and traipsing through the middle of nowhere with a crazy girl. Let's not exacerbate my misery by talking about *her*."

Interesting. His bitter refusal only made her more curious. "My mother can be irritating." That was an understatement, as her mother had attempted every bit of emotional leverage in her considerable arsenal to prevent Selly from coming along to rescue Nic. If the others made it back to House Phel without Jadren and her, Daisy would likely explode from worry. "But I love her anyway," Selly finished.

"That's because your mother is capable of love and isn't a monster."

"Is Lady El-Adrel incapable of love?" What an astonishing concept. Selly didn't think she'd ever heard of a person who couldn't love. But then, the Convocation was a strange and foreign place. Even without the long and bitter history of House Phel's enemies having seen to the entire realm of Meresin being excommunicated from Convocation lands, along with all her people, Selly had known that they were better off. Monsters incapable of loving their children dimmed by comparison to the other horrors.

"I'm fascinated that you asked that first instead of whether she's a monster," Jadren answered in a dry tone. "Still, I have no intention of discussing her further."

"Because you're her spy?"

"What part of 'not discussing' did you fail to comprehend?"

"That's a question about you, not her."

Jadren slid her a glittering black look. "I think not even you are that naïve, so I'm calling you out on trying to be clever and failing. You saved my life back there, so I'm being nice, but you're playing with fire, little girl, by pushing me."

"I'm not a little girl," she retorted, stung. "I'm twenty-two."

"Oh, so very old as *that*?" he replied scathingly. "Besides, it doesn't count when you mentally and emotionally froze ten years ago. Your body may be a woman's, but the person inside is only twelve, if that. We're lucky you didn't insist on bringing your dollies along on this trip."

There were still dolls in her room, though Selly doubted Jadren could know that. He had to be guessing. Never mind that she hadn't remembered those dolls, not clearly, nor had she put them in her new room at the recently resurrected House Phel. She vaguely recalled her brother and parents trying to get her to sleep in that room they'd painstakingly put together for her in the dry core of the house. Fragments of distorted memory showed that she sometimes had slept there, though she'd been twenty by then, long past the age of dolls. Maybe everyone thought the same as Jadren, that she was mentally twelve years old, the age she'd been when she first started experiencing the spells that took her out of time and left her stranded on confusing shores.

Being inside, though, that had only made the feelings of oppression and madness worse. In the swamps and marshes of Meresin, she'd been able to simply exist. Not having to converse with anyone or deal with expectations had let her mind rest. In truth, she should be enjoying being out of doors, being quiet, and not trying to make conversation with Jadren. Normally she'd be more than happy to be silent.

However, the rapid events of the last few days had made it abundantly clear how much she didn't know. In some ways it wasn't wrong to call her mentally twelve years old, if that. She'd certainly stopped learning much about the world around then. If she didn't want to be relegated to being a child while the adults made choices for her, then she needed to stop hiding and start grappling. At least Jadren didn't try to protect her from the truth, so this enforced sojourn with him was an opportunity she shouldn't waste.

"You're not a fire wizard though," she informed him, since he didn't seem to be fond of questions.

"How is that apropos of anything?"

"You said I was playing with fire, but you don't have fire magic."

"First of all, that's an expression and not intended to be taken literally. Second, how would you even know what kind of magic I do and don't have, baby familiar?"

"I could feel it."

He stopped walking. Turning, he gave her such a long, icy stare of glittering obsidian that she had to dig her toes into the ground to keep from stepping back. It would be much easier going barefoot, but she was trying to be less wild. Shoes seemed to be an important sign of civilization to people.

"What," he drawled with cool sarcasm, "are you a walking oracle head now that you think you can assess my MP scores? Because I assure you, you cannot."

So much bitterness in him, along with anger that was only partially directed at her. She cocked her head at him, experiencing a sense of familiarity, even though that made no sense at all. "What's an oracle head?" she asked, taking the foreign references in order of his saying them.

He looked briefly incredulous, then shook his head with a huff of breath and resumed walking. "If I'm to serve as remedial schoolteacher on top of my other duties, I'm taking it up with Lord Phel. I should receive extra wages." He continued immediately, sparing her a response to that. "You know what an oracle head is—you saw it when Rat dragged you back from your feral, barefooted escapades in the swamps. The Convocation proctor was using it to evaluate Lord and Lady Phel's wizard–familiar bonding." At her puzzled frown, he freed a hand to wave it. "Looks like a decorated human head in a box."

"*That* thing?" she yelped in shock. She did remember it, but she'd been in the depths of madness then and she'd put that nightmarish image down to one of the worse phantasms of her deranged mind. "That was real?" she squeaked out.

"Real as you and me," Jadren answered, sliding her an assessing glance. "You're not going to lose your shit, are you? If you go scampering off to blither in the wilderness, I'm not equipped to stop you, and Lord Phel will have my head if I return without his baby sister."

"I'm fine," she bit out, stalking determinedly along. Never mind that every impulse in her screamed for her to do exactly as he insultingly implied she might. In the marshes, there was only nature. Nothing there was as horrible as that undead *thing* in the tabernacle.

"You're clearly not fine, poppet, but as that's actually a rational reaction to an oracle head, that works for me. Fits are acceptable, so long as you don't run off," he added with a meaningful head tilt.

They trudged along in silence while she wrestled with the bemusement that Jadren had been—if not exactly sympathetic to her reaction—at least understanding of it.

"I thought I imagined the... ah, oracle head," she admitted, feeling she needed to offer an explanation. "I don't expect you to understand or sympathize, but—"

He snorted. "You're learning, at least. Never expect sympathy from the Convocation, from House El-Adrel, or from me."

"In that order?" she questioned bitingly.

"Exactly." He waved a hand in *noblesse oblige*. "Continue."

Now she didn't want to, but she'd started down this road for a reason. She hadn't told Gabriel about this, not wanting him to worry. She certainly hadn't been able to tell her parents, who had hovered excessively as it was, and who didn't understand magic anyway. Probably she needed some kind of professional help, but she didn't know what it would be or even how to begin going about finding out. Perhaps this cynical and supercilious wizard, for all his faults, could at least offer some insight. "Whatever the stagnating magic did to me, it messed with my perceptions. There's a lot about the last ten years that..." She hesitated to say, but Jadren—rather uncharacteristically—didn't interrupt this time, only raised a brow at her. "Well, I'm not sure what was real and what wasn't."

He didn't respond for so long that she'd begun to bitterly regret the admission. Though maybe he was offering the courtesy of pretending he hadn't heard her embarrassing confession.

"There's not a lot of precedent for your situation," he said finally, and not altogether unkindly, to her surprise. "Familiars are too valuable to be let go to seed like you were. It was shockingly irresponsible, what they allowed to happen to you. So, while there are documented cases of familiars like you going nutso from magic stagnation, I suspect you'd be the subject of an entirely new textbook on the topic. That is," he continued cheerfully, "if your brother allowed the Convocation researchers to get their intellectual claws into you, which he won't—being the obstinate renegade he is—and for which I hope you'll have the wit to be appropriately grateful. You're a powerful familiar but they'd gleefully sacrifice your magic for the sake of experimental science, a life I can promise you would not enjoy."

"Are you speaking from experience?" she ventured, fully expecting a grim and unilluminating 'you have no idea' in response.

"Yes and no. It's a long story and not one I'm inclined to share, with anyone, ever. Suffice to say that I *do* understand." He was silent so long again that she glanced over to see if that was all he'd say. Since he was being unusually forthcoming, she didn't want to make the mistake of diverting him if he was composing some sort of salient remark. But no—his jaw was clenched tight, his wizard-black gaze focused on some distant point only he could see. "I know about having your magic twisted against you," he said in a much quieter tone, as if sharing a secret. "I understand what you mean about not being able to trust your memories and perceptions. To know that your own mind is the last thing you can count on to tell you the truth is… horrifying."

"Yes," she finally replied when he said nothing more. "I'm sorry," she added, feeling like she needed to acknowledge his obvious pain in some way, "for what you've suffered."

He laughed, no humor in it. "A sad and pitiful day for a scion of House El-Adrel when an untrained and half-insane baby familiar feels sorry for him. Save your pity, little girl.

Along with sympathy, there's no room for it in the Convocation. You'll need to get a lot harder and sharper if you're going to survive."

A day ago, even hours ago, she might've been hurt by his callous words. Now she felt as if she understood something about the enigmatic wizard that she hadn't before. "Thank you for the advice, Wizard El-Adrel," she said. "But I should clarify that I'm likely *more* than half insane."

Unexpectedly, he grinned, the smile making his usually cruel and brooding face boyishly handsome. "That's my girl."

~ 3 ~

"WHERE THE FUCK is this river anyway?" Jadren snarled, hours of agonizing trudging later. He'd never imagined his feet could hurt so much, closely followed by the rest of him. Recovering from injuries only worked if one didn't keep inflicting damage.

Selly raised her dark brows, amber gaze bland. "I imagine the Dubglass River is exactly where it normally is."

"Funny girl," he retorted. He had to give it to the skinny minx—she had spirit. Not many people, let alone mind-rotted and forlorn familiars, could stand up to him. She took his acerbic remarks and returned them with extra. He couldn't believe himself, that he'd spoken even that much to her about his bitter, twisted past. What he got for feeling sorry for the chit. She'd met him pity for pity and hadn't that stung? "I mean," he clarified in an exceedingly patient tone, "that we should've gotten to it by now. It's a big fucking river and we didn't ride all *that* long going the other direction before we got to the overlook across from House Sammael."

She shrugged, unconcerned. "Horses go much faster than people."

"I know that," he snapped, though he had to admit, if only

to himself, that he had no idea how to compare. Half a day's journey for horses came out to what for people? "If we don't get to the barge in a reasonable amount of time, they'll leave without us," he explained, still trying to exercise a modicum of patience. Surely even an inexperienced lass like Selly understood that much.

"You truly believed we'd catch up with the others in time?" she asked with considerable astonishment.

"Wasn't that the *plan*?" he bit out. "I heard you say that if we rode fast, we could meet them before they take the barge upriver."

"'Rode' being the operative word," she countered. "That was a possibility when we thought we still had horses. There was never any way we'd catch up with them in time on foot." She cast him a disparaging look. "Especially with you going so slowly."

"This stuff is heavy. And don't you dare reiterate that foolishness about how I should've left these supplies behind."

"Or what?" she demanded. "Will you incinerate me with that fire magic you don't have?"

This again? "Look, poppet. I—"

"Don't call me that. I am not your puppet."

He stopped. Upon consideration—and in resignation to the inevitable—he dropped the packs he'd been carrying so diligently to the point that every muscle and sinew in his body protested. They might as well take a rest break since catching the others at the barge was apparently out of the question. It would've been nice of Selly to mention that before—though probably he should've figured it out for himself. "Paah-pett," he said, facing her and drawing out the word very slowly, exaggerating the vowel sound. "Not puhh-pett. Paah-pett. It means a sweet and pretty little child."

"Oh." She shrugged her braid over her shoulder, which did nothing about the dark curls that had escaped to plaster themselves to her temples and the sides of her throat where sweat gleamed. Absurdly, he wanted to stroke those tendrils away for her, perhaps with his lips. She grinned, feline and canny. "Still not very accurate."

He blinked at her, scrabbling his thoughts back from their untoward direction.

"A sweet and pretty little child," she clarified, puzzled by his confusion, "doesn't describe me well."

"From the mouths of babes," he conceded, then sat heavily on the twisted root of a tree, leaning his back against it and reminding himself that Selly might appear to be a beautiful, sensual woman, but mentally she was truly a child. Dark arts, he was tired. Even though walking out the healing helped, it still drained him. He scrubbed his hands over his face, trying to make himself *think*. This was a shit situation and Phel really would have his head if something happened to Selly. "If you knew we'd never catch that barge, what did you figure our plan was?"

She crouched, picking up a stick and scratching at the dirt road. "Well, for a while I thought we might get lucky and come across the horses grazing down the road. Then, when that didn't happen, I figured…" She shrugged. "We'd walk."

"Walk," he echoed, his throbbing feet protesting the concept. "All the way across Meresin to House Phel."

"Well, and part of Sammael," she corrected. She looked very serious, an expression that sat naturally on her solemn face, suiting her haunted eyes and the downward turn of her mouth. A flicker in her cheek stood out, however, hinting at amusement. Jadren focused his eyes on that shadowy divot. Surely that wasn't a dimple? Because that would mean she was laughing at him.

"It will take days to walk all the way to House Phel," he pointed out.

Selly nodded, poked with her stick. "If we make it at all."

"Excuse me?"

"There are a lot of hazards between here and there," she explained, sounding as if she were discussing planning a party. "And those are of the natural variety. There also could be more hunters after us or other members of House Sammael chasing behind. They'll catch you and me before they reach Nic and Gabriel. I thought that's part of what it meant to be rear guard. You know—Nic and Gabriel don't have to be faster than their pursuers, just faster than we are."

"I thought it only meant for that one battle," Jadren griped, hating that she was right. He didn't really fancy sacrificing himself. It would ruin his image. Of course, it would also thwart his mother, which was a nice perk right there. "Phel will come looking for us, though—or send people to rescue us. Otherwise he'll be answering to my maman, which won't be pretty." That's all he needed: his maman to drag him back by the ear to the nightmare of life in House El-Adrel. "Plus, he cares about you."

She smiled, thin and mirthlessly. "That's assuming *they*

make it back safely, and that House Sammael doesn't succeed in destroying them."

"You're a regular ray of fucking sunshine, aren't you?" he growled.

"You don't strike me as the kind of person who engages in self-deception," she observed, watching him. "Would you prefer I kiss your pristine high-house ass and promise you all will turn up raspberries?"

"Roses," he said, after staring at her for a long moment of sheer consternation. "Everything turning up roses is the optimistic metaphor you're looking for there, you half-feral swamp creature. Raspberries is something else entirely."

"I like raspberries," she replied. "They're juicy and just the right balance between tart and sweet. They also grow in thick clusters, so when I was living in the wild, coming across laden raspberry bushes was one of the best things I could hope for."

"The charm of having very low expectations." It rankled at him that she'd celebrated something as trivial as finding wild fruit. If Selly had been born to a proper house, she'd have been dressed in Ophiel silk gowns and feted for her powerful magic. At least, she would've been until she manifested as familiar instead of wizard, at which point she'd likely have been slated for the Betrothal Trials. But even that life would have been better than what she'd suffered in this backwater realm.

Or would it? a sly voice whispered in the back of his mind. *You suffered enough that a few simple joys might have been precious to you, too.*

Maybe, he snapped at himself, *but I never had any to know, did I?*

"Since we're giving up on making the barge departure," he said loudly enough to drown out further comments from that insidious voice, "let's have something to eat and lighten these packs. I need to rest my feet anyway." He reached for his boot.

"Jadren." An intent expression darkened Selly's already solemn face. "Don't move."

"I'm not planning to. I'm going to take a good long rest. These boots were *not* made for walking," he noted grumpily.

"I mean it," her voice whipped out. "*Freeze.*"

He wasn't in the habit of taking orders, particularly not from familiars from lesser houses, but something made him obey. Perhaps it was the sharpness of her gaze, none of that bleary insanity in it. Only the focused intensity of a predator. The back of his neck prickled. "What?"

"Do you trust me?" she asked very softly, moving with slow smoothness to pull an arrow from her quiver and raise her bow.

He snorted with emphatic derision, long discipline allowing him to do so without moving. "Absolutely not."

A slight smile twitched her pressed lips. "Wise." Before he could retort, she'd drawn and released the bow. The arrow thudded into the tree behind him so close it grazed his cheek. A bright sting and a trickle of blood indicated it had more than grazed him. "Got it," Selly said in quiet satisfaction.

Arrested, both by her unexpected ferocity and sheer terror at whatever had prompted her to do such a thing, he stared at her, unwilling to twitch even to wipe the blood away. "Can I move now?"

Her gaze fixed on that point just past his cheek, then roved over the tree. After what felt like an excruciatingly long period of evaluation, she finally nodded. Good thing, too, as something both heavy and oddly sleek fell onto his shoulder, continuing to drape in boneless folds down his arm. He risked a look at it, then shrieked, rolling himself away from the thing. A loop of the shining coils clung to his arm and he shoved at it in atavistic revulsion, wanting only to get it off of him.

"What *is* that thing?" he demanded, his voice entirely too high-pitched still, but he was almost too panicked to care.

Selly raised one brow, entirely too calm. "Snake."

"I *know* it's a snake," he ground out, staring in horror at the yards of coils draped over the ground, an arrow pinning the head of the thing to the tree he'd been sitting against, blood trickling down the bark in a thick stream. Remembering, he swiped at his own cheek, the laceration—though it would heal quickly—in the exact spot where his mother had implanted one of her devices, far more painfully. His fingers came away bloody, the sight of it turning his stomach and evoking memories best left buried in the depths of the tortured past.

It was too late, however, to suppress all of them. He hurled himself at the shrubs bordering the road, vomiting up bitter bile.

The gut-deep wrenching held him prisoner for several more minutes, insisting with cruel thoroughness on emptying everything possible from an already vacant stomach. Finally, when it seemed as if he'd retch up his hated boots next, the spasms relented. Shaking with the viciousness of the attack and the humiliation of having to face Selly, he wiped his mouth with the back of his hand, remembering too late about the blood on it.

Just charming.

He was too rattled to muster a sardonic comment. Instead, not looking directly at his companion, he went to the packs to find a cloth to clean himself. Selly intercepted him, her scuffed boots intruding into his lowered gaze, replaced by the water flask and a towel. Muttering his thanks, he tipped his head back and emptied the flask over his face, embracing the cool wash of it to bring him back to the here and now, wetting his hair, too. The shock on his scalp helped. *It's in the past,* he told himself firmly. *Get a grip.* But those images burbled up, gleeful in their freedom, reveling in blood, pain, and screams not all his own.

Tipping the flask upright, he allowed Phel's embedded ever-replenishing water to refill the thing, then emptied it over his head again. It helped, but not enough. Desperate for distraction, he fastened his thoughts on the problem of the magical refilling being triggered by turning the flask upright repeatedly. No doubt that Phel was powerful in his water and moon magic, and innovative in blending the two to make the always-full flask, but the untutored wizard was clumsy in his execution in small ways like this one.

No blame to him, really, as Phel hadn't had the benefit of intensive tutoring in wizardry. Also, if Phel didn't have this failing, he wouldn't need Jadren. Well, not beyond satisfying the terms of extortion that Lady El-Adrel had used to leverage Jadren's placement at House Phel, without the usual documentation and providing of his MP scorecard. Jadren didn't have much of an applicable skill set with his fraught and shadowy wizardry, but he could perform simple enchantments like fixing this flask. What would be ideal was if the dropping water level triggered the refilling.

Fixing his thoughts on solving that problem helped to dispel the sickening memories and, after a third deluge, he felt slightly more in his right mind, the past firmly locked away in the depths where it belonged. Using the towel, he scrubbed his face and hair—carefully avoiding that particular spot near his eye orbit, just in case—then mopped at his water-soaked clothing. Belatedly, it occurred to him that his post-puking behavior likely looked just as bizarre as the sudden bout of sickness had to begin with. Too late to change it now, however.

Mustering his courage and covering the persistent concern that Selly would discover that his arrogance was a thin crust over a morass of debilitating weakness, he met her curious amber gaze with cool dismissal. He handed her the flask and damp towel, making sure to treat her like an underling, then ran his fingers through his hair to reorder it.

"Snakes or blood?" she asked.

"Excuse me?" he returned the question with cold hauteur that would shut down most reasonable people. Selly, however, was far from reasonable.

"Was it the snake or the sight of blood that made you ill? I know people can have irrational reactions to either thing. Although I suppose you could be afraid of both at the same time."

"I am not *afraid* of blood *or* snakes," he bit out, angry that she'd suggest such a thing.

"Then it's something else."

He set his teeth, swallowing bile. "You have no idea."

"Not unless you tell me about it," she conceded. "That's why I'm asking. I'm willing to listen."

"Well, I am not willing to discuss anything with a low-born, house-poor familiar. In the future, keep your puerile theories to yourself."

Selly didn't flush or stammer apologies as she should, given his scathing set-down. Instead, she cocked her head, studying him far too cannily. "Then this has to do with what you said before, about knowing what it's like not being able to trust your memories and perceptions. The thing that happened that you don't want pity for."

Which he still didn't want, still had no intention of discussing, and now deeply regretted mentioning. That's what he got for feeling even momentary sympathy for someone else. He'd learned long ago that opening even a sliver of access to his emotions allowed others too much opportunity to manipulate him. He was finally free—more or less, current losing-of-shit notwithstanding—so he'd be worse than a fool to subjugate himself again. "Keep your pity and your conversation, crazy girl." He aimed his words like a lash, to hurt her and shut her up.

She shrugged, unperturbed, then replaced the flask and towel in one of the packs. "I assume you're no longer in the mood to eat?"

"No." Just the thought had his sour gut threatening to revolt. "You should, though. You're still way too skinny. All knobs and twigs."

"I'm not hungry and my strength is good, thank you very

much." She shouldered the heavy pack, a stubborn set to her pointed chin, and held out the lighter one.

More pity. "I can carry the stupid packs," he told her. "I know you didn't want to bring them."

She stood there, pack dangling from her outstretched hand, expression bland. "Maybe I've realized having these supplies came in handy just now. Also, you're right—it will take us days to walk to House Phel, and that's if our enemies haven't destroyed it. In any scenario, we might need everything we have so I'll do my part in carrying the stuff."

Feeling as if he had been the one to receive justified chastisement, he yanked the pack from her and shouldered it. "Was the snake venomous?" he asked.

"Yes and no."

"Which is it—yes or no?"

"It has venom, yes, but the venom isn't lethal, which is what I assume you're wondering. Instead the venom paralyzes the snake's prey so it can leisurely consume it whole."

Oh. Delightful thought. "So the paralytic would've worn off eventually?"

She shook her head. "Sadly permanent. Your lungs would've stopped working after a while and then…" She slid him a grim smile. "I don't like to kill animals unnecessarily, but it was better that I did in this case."

Better for him, that was for sure. So, Selly had saved his life. What to make of that?

"WHY DO YOU always say that?" Selly asked after a while. "*You have no idea.*" She growled out the words in a voice he supposed was a passable imitation of himself. Also, a completely irreverent and impudent imitation.

"You know," he said, the burr of irritation in his voice ruining his attempt to keep it light and conversational, "if you were to treat me with this sort of attitude in Convocation Center, you'd be arrested and taken for retraining."

She made a show of looking around. Though they still hadn't reached the Dubglass River, which meant they were still in Sammael and had not yet crossed into Meresin, the sunlit forest had given way to a damper landscape, the trees casting deeper shade with bigger, waxy leaves. The ground squelched unpleasantly around his boots, which did nothing to ease his sore feet and overworked leg muscles. At this point he'd sell himself back to House El-Adrel for an elemental-powered carriage.

Not really. *Not at all.* Jadren shuddered at the thought. But it would be good not to have to continue this slog. Maybe he needed a less drastic metaphor.

"I may be a half-feral swamp creature," Selly said, "but even I can tell we're not in Convocation Center."

"The principle remains intact. It's unwise to antagonize a wizard."

Absurdly, she brightened. "Why, what would you do?"

He threw her flabbergasted look. Did nothing frighten the chit? *"This* is the first thing you ask?"

"I know so little about wizardry." She widened her eyes, miming the sweet puppy she absolutely wasn't. "Gabriel ripped the roof off the tower to free Nic. Can you do that?"

"No one should be able to do *that,"* he muttered. He still wasn't sure how Phel had accomplished that startling feat of long-distance magic. Who knew moon magic could be shaped into silver in the first place, much less shaped into sky hooks that could affect physical objects from across a valley? At least Phel was safe from Jadren reporting that feat to his maman, as she'd never believe it. No, Lady El-Adrel would immediately suspect Jadren of embellishing or, worse, outright lying, and would punish him accordingly. Of course, he wouldn't be reporting anything, ever again, if they perished out in the swamps of Meresin. An oddly cheering thought.

"Oh! Could you change me into a toad, or *worse?"* She bounced with all the gleeful horror of the child she wanted to leave behind.

"No," he answered forbiddingly. "That's only in stories."

"I saw Gabriel change Nic into a giant silver phoenix," Selly countered, "so that's obviously not just in stories."

"That's different."

"How?" she demanded, full of scorn.

He sighed with exasperation. "If you'd had a proper Convocation Academy education, you would know these things."

She snorted inelegantly. "If wishes were horsies, you wouldn't be sore-footed and tromping back to House Phel with me."

She had a point, though he wasn't at all sure how his life had gotten so fucked that he'd ended up explaining the basics of magic to a rogue familiar who shouldn't even exist. Oh wait—yes, he did. It was all due to his sadistic maman. "Fine, here is your *ad hoc* course on Wizard–Familiar Dynamics."

"Is that what they call it at Convocation Academy?"

"Yes."

"How do you know, if you didn't attend?"

He rolled his eyes to the uncaring sky as if it might rain patience. It did not. "Because I'm not ignorant."

"But if you didn't attend Convocation Academy, where did you learn this stuff?"

He wagged a finger at her. "Not relevant, poppet. No more peppering me with annoying questions if you want to learn. Less talking; more listening."

"One last thing?"

She sounded so meek and contrite that he let out a sigh and nodded. "One."

"I know you said poppet isn't puppet, but I still don't like you calling me that."

Not what he'd expected her to say. He also didn't expect to feel vaguely remorseful. "Fair enough." He waved it off along with the useless guilt. "Are all pet names off the table?" he added snidely. Not losing his touch at all.

"Since, I'm not a pet: yes."

Making a scoffing sound, he threw her a look. "Literal little thing, aren't you? Don't answer that. I suppose you want me to stick with Selly."

"Actually." She hesitated, uncharacteristically hesitant. "I'd prefer Seliah." When he raised a brow, having not expected that reply, she hurried on. "When I... I first started to lose track of time and myself, I was still a girl and everyone called me Selly and it was fine. It never occurred to me to mind it, in those days. And then—just recently, obviously—my mind cleared for the first time in a decade and I'd become a woman. But everyone still talks to me like I'm a child and they call me by my childhood nickname like nothing has changed when *everything* has changed! And I..." She ground to a ragged halt. "I know it's silly, and I'm obviously emotional about this and overreacting, but..." She waved her hand at him as if he'd said something biting. "Never mind."

"It's not silly." Better than anyone, he understood being treated forever like the child he'd long-since stopped being. Feeling like he should say something nice to her—not an urge he was accustomed to experiencing—he blurted, "Seliah is a lovely name."

Her smile was wobbly, but her lushly fringed amber eyes held a tentative light. "I think so, too," she replied quietly. Then she pressed her lips together, miming locking them with an invisible key she tossed over her shoulder, the amber lights dancing with mischief, belying the attentively scholarly expression she attempted to assume. It made her look girlish again and he was struck with an image of her as a restless and difficult student, gazing longingly out the schoolroom window at the outdoors she loved so much, ignoring whatever tutor they'd saddled her with.

The image made him want to laugh. At the same time, it drove him crazy how much she amused him. This imp in woman's clothing should not be able to get under his skin this way. He cleared his throat, focusing on the lesson to be imparted. "You are already familiar—if you'll pardon the expression—with the core principle of the wizard–familiar dynamic, which is that a familiar, by definition unable to express their own magic, yields up said magic to a wizard, who—also by definition—is able to wield it."

He glanced at her and she nodded encouragingly, though some of the light in her had dimmed. Understandable. "I don't make the rules," he added, though he didn't know why he bothered. "I'm just explaining them."

She grimaced, then gestured for him to continue, admirably keeping to the requirement that she not interrupt.

"A wizard can tap any familiar's magic, something you already know, having donated magic already to me, your brother, and to Alise on this benighted quest, but for there to be a permanent partnership, a wizard must bond a familiar. The bonding serves to expedite the power transfer and also prevents wizards from stealing familiars, as occurred in the bad old days. The bonding has a third benefit in that a wizard can trigger the transformation of their familiar into the familiar's alternate form. That is what you witnessed with Lord and Lady Phel; that silver phoenix is inexplicably and mind-bogglingly, if that's a word—Nic's alternate form."

He had Seliah's full and fascinated attention. Her lips, still pressed together, were now pursed and puffed, as if the questions caged behind her teeth fought to break free. He couldn't help laughing. "Fine, before you burst, ask your questions now."

Her breath whooshed out. "But Gabriel did bond Nic, and House Sammael stole her anyway—how is that possible?"

Jadren rubbed his forehead. Of course she picked the hardest question first.

~ 4 ~

JADREN LOOKED POSITIVELY pained by the question. Of course, he hadn't looked good since the snake incident—though Selly privately believed that it hadn't been the snake at all that had caused him to lose his shit, as he so pithily put it, but something to do with the cut on his cheek. It wasn't the sight of blood from the cut either, as the fight with the hunters had scored him in many places that bled.

No, it was something about that cut on his cheek. Or possibly almost losing his life, but he hadn't really put that together until later, so she was betting on the cut—though why that would bother him so deeply as to make him physically ill was a mystery. He'd gone a grayish-green she'd never have guessed a living person could take on, and for a moment, she'd been worried that the snake's venom had somehow gotten into his system. It had been a relief that he'd rallied on his own, because she'd been at an utter loss as to how to help him.

In truth, she didn't know what to do for him—and she was confused about why she wanted to help Jadren, if he would even let her. His prickly pride didn't allow much. She understood pride. Being broken inside made her feel like an injured creature in the wild, easy prey for the predators, and just miserable enough to occasionally fantasize about them ending it all. Jadren wasn't wounded like that. Nothing seemed to dent his determinedly careless shell. He had fortitude to carry him through whatever internal battle he fought. She rather envied him that. It would be nice to have some kind of purpose. That was the main reason she'd insisted on coming along on this mission. She'd had a bellyful of hanging out in the infirmary, obediently stuffing herself in order to "recover" while everyone tiptoed around the hard truth that she was broken to a degree that no amount of healing could rectify.

And now she was depressing herself. "How could House Sammael steal Nic if she and Gabriel were bonded and bonded familiars can't be stolen?" she prompted.

"You don't need to rephrase the question," Jadren replied, rolling his eyes. "I was thinking."

"That explains the burning smell."

"Ha ha. Conversation with you is like being ten years old again."

"At last you've found your mental equivalent," she retorted cheerfully.

"Keep it up and you won't get your answers."

"Apologies, professor."

He grunted noncommittally, squinting at a distant point, a line between his brows as he contemplated. "There are at least two complicating factors at play in this particular circumstance," Jadren said, then he tossed her a jaunty grin. "Though I reserve the right to add more as I think of them."

She nodded, reverting to keeping her mouth shut and her

attention on scanning for danger while he talked. They hadn't seen any of the Elal warrior spirits or spies, like they had on the journey in. That meant either she and Jadren couldn't detect them or they weren't there. It could be they were all focused on whatever was going on back at House Phel, but they didn't want to assume.

"The first and broader complication is that 'can't be stolen' is an over-generalization. Anyone can be taken captive, given sufficient guile or force. In the Convocation, however, the penalties for stealing another wizard's familiar are both inherent and external. Taking the latter first, the external penalties are severe: it's against Convocation law and breaking those laws results in such extreme consequences for the wizard—and possibly their entire house, which never works out well for the wizard, reference previous conversation about the heads of houses and their pathological need for ultimate control—that the prospect is usually a sufficient deterrent. By consequences, I mean exorbitant fines, primarily, though there might be other penalties."

He held up a hand, even though she'd made no move to interrupt. "There are several reasons the deterrent wasn't enough to stop Sergio Sammael—besides the fact that he's a fuckhead in general and a poor excuse for a wizard in particular—and I'll get to that. But first, we have to consider the inherent consequences of stealing a bonded familiar, which is that ultimately they become useless for the one thing that makes a familiar valuable."

"Their magic."

"Exactly." Jadren slid her a considering look. "As you are

the brand-new textbook entry in just how messed up it can get for a familiar whose magic goes south, you'll understand the logical trajectory here. A bonded familiar cannot be forced to give up their magic to any wizard but their own, which leads to, as we well know, an unpleasant level of insanity."

"There's a pleasant level of insanity?"

"Heh. Don't get me started. To continue with my point, the attenuation of the wizard–familiar bond exacerbates the problem for the familiar. Keep a bonded familiar separated from their wizard too long, especially if the familiar is loyal and refuses to cooperate by having their magic tapped, and you end up with a useless bag of flesh and bones. Makes the whole venture moot, and then solidly in the negative column when you factor in the external consequences."

Jadren sucked on his teeth, expression grave. "In this very specific situation, a number of factors led Sammael—we'll debate if Sergio was acting on his own or with the knowledge of the house, which changes things, as you've no doubt surmised, clever as you are—into thinking their gambit might work out to the profit side of the ledger." He ticked the points off on his long fingers. "House Phel is still on probationary status, so there's considerable question as to how vigorously the Convocation would pursue offenses against your house, especially given the multiple transgressions and irregularities of your rogue wizard of a brother." He ticked up a second finger. "Not mention the fact that Nic had the presumption to attempt to *escape* the Convocation. They really don't look kindly on familiars being rebellious in the slightest way, let alone something so egregious. That earns two points." Two more fingers shot up.

"Also, as our unloved in-house traitor Laryn reported to Sammael, the Convocation proctor herself questioned whether Nic was properly bonded, declaring it non-standard for all to hear." A fourth finger went up. "Finally—I think this is finally, anyway—Phel was incapacitated and thought likely to die from his attempt to clear out the incredible mess of garbage in *your* head, which Laryn also reported, which improved the odds of the Sammael gamble working. If Phel had died, any bond restraining or protecting Nic would've died with him. With her conveniently in-house, Sergio could've bonded her and the Convocation would have had to accept that as a *fait accompli*."

Jadren waved his five splayed fingers at her. "Even someone who isn't a shortsighted, overly ambitious sod with delusions of grandeur like Sergio Sammael might have thought the gambit was worth trying. It's entirely possible Sergio's father backed the plan, but stayed out of it in any observable way, for plausible deniability should Sergio fail."

"Should?" Selly echoed, her brain swimming from all the information. "He *did* fail. Nic is rescued and back with Gabriel."

Jadren shrugged philosophically, gazing into that middle distance as if none of it mattered to him. Maybe it didn't. "You, yourself, pointed out that we might trudge all the way to House Phel to find it sunk back into the swamps from whence it came, Phel and his minions all dead, remanded to the Convocation, or scattered to the wind." He flashed her an unpleasant smile. "Could be you're already the last surviving heir to the uncertain House Phel legacy."

Though she had considered the possibility that House Phel's enemies might destroy the house itself, it hadn't occurred to Selly that everyone could die. It was so... barbaric. "Do you really think they'd kill everyone?"

Apparently unaffected, Jadren shrugged cheerfully. "No, not everyone. Certainly not Nic, as she's the valuable playing piece here. Not only as the most powerful familiar in the Convocation, but as Lord Elal's precious first child. He may have publicly disowned her for her reprehensible disobedience, but that's a standard high-house tactic. Elal has to demonstrate that he doesn't support his daughter defying the Convocation. That doesn't change that she's his flesh and blood, and a young and healthy bearer of valuable magic-baby-making eggs. Any wizard who bonded Nic would have a hold on Elal, which is priceless."

"But everyone else would be killed," she persisted.

Grimacing, he tipped his head back and forth, weighing the possibilities, then finished in a sharp nod. "Most likely. It would be Sammael's safest bet to cover their tracks, especially if they can contrive to make it seem like they were simply defending themselves against a crazed attack. Given that ragtag collection of misfits and outcasts Phel has assembled, that story would be an easy sell."

"That makes you a misfit, too, you realize," she pointed out, struggling to control her anger at how easily he spoke of everyone she cared about dying.

"Oh, I realize that, popp—Seliah." He glanced over, all jaunty carelessness fled, his expression stark. "Believe me, I know exactly what I am. Though outcast is probably more accurate. Assessing the possibility of an outcome as likely does not mean that I like it. Savvy the difference?"

"Don't you care at all what happens to them?" she demanded instead of answering.

"Yes, I care," he answered somberly. "If I survive the gangrene that will inevitably set in once I walk my feet into rotten stumps only to find House Phel gone, it will be back to House El-Adrel for me. For the record: I do *not* like that prospect, however probable it may be."

"But you're a wizard," she pointed out. "Top of the ranking system. That gives you the freedom to go anywhere and be anything."

His black gaze snapped to hers in patent astonishment before he burst out laughing. He laughed so loudly, a flock of blackbirds exploded from a nearby tree, caroling in alarm. He laughed so long and hard that he clutched his belly, lurching in staggering steps to keep up with her increasingly furious stride. By the time he wound down, he had tears running down his cheeks and he was so out of breath he couldn't even gasp out the words of whatever he was trying to say as he pointed a finger at her, waggling it.

Finally, utterly fed up, she stopped, planting her feet in the dirt and her fists on her hips. "Fine. I'm ignorant. Is that what you find so fucking funny?"

Face red, Jadren wiped the tears away, then abruptly sobered, giving her a hard and slicingly black look. "You know nothing about me, little familiar. Don't ever presume to."

Taken aback by the abrupt change—or was it a change?

Now she wondered if the laughter had been an elaborate fake—she felt her face prickle with an embarrassed flush. "I apologize."

Without acknowledging that, he began walking again, ignoring her as if she'd never existed and he'd always walked alone. Through the numbness of being caught so awkwardly flat-footed, she began to nurture the glimmer of an idea. Perhaps that metaphor explained Jadren more than she realized at first. Jadren was a tightly wound ball of defensiveness, all spines and cutting remarks that ensured he continued to walk alone. Maybe he hadn't chosen that for himself to begin with, but he certainly chose it now—and she'd do well to remember it.

His stony silence didn't bother her, but some mischievous urge in her nevertheless prodded her to poke at him. Besides, he'd agreed to teach her and the trek may as well be put to good use. "May I ask a question?" she ventured.

"You just did." The retort was delivered without inflection or any other acknowledgment of her existence.

"To resume my *ad hoc* education," she clarified.

He released an exaggerated sigh of long suffering. "Fine. Can't be more mind-numbing than looking at endless rows of trees."

"So, a wizard can bond a familiar without the familiar's consent."

"That's a comment, not a question."

"I'm checking my understanding first."

"Such a diligent schoolgirl. Correct. 'Consent' isn't a concept generally applied to familiars. It's not necessary for a familiar to be enthusiastic about serving their wizard—though it's arguably easier for the wizard and more pleasant for the familiar if that's the case—they need only obey." He slid her a grimly amused glance at last. "The consequences for not playing nicely with wizards is all on the familiar, as you've learned. A lesson I doubt needs repeating."

She couldn't help shuddering at the thought of sinking into that morass of stagnant madness again. She wouldn't survive it a second time, she felt sure. "Why haven't you bonded me then?" she made herself ask.

She might've thought he hadn't heard the question, except his face took on a pinched, pained expression. "What makes you think I'd *want* to?" he finally asked.

Her turn to tick off points on her fingers, not that she took any petty pleasure in the turnabout. "I'm a powerful, unbonded familiar. You have no familiar. Wizards need familiars in order to be more powerful. You clearly would like to be more powerful. I may be the last surviving heir to the House Phel legacy, which may be uncertain, but is still better than nothing. If you bonded me, you would be my wizard, which means you could take over House Phel." She waggled her five fingers at him, maybe enjoying the triumph a little bit.

He snorted inelegantly. "More likely you'd come with me to House El-Adrel. Nobody wants to live in a swamp at the ass-end of nowhere."

"You do," she pointed out.

"No," he corrected carefully, sliding her one of those enigmatic looks. "I was instructed to do so. There's a difference. I had no choice in the matter."

She chewed that over, really wanting to ask more, certain he'd only slice her to ribbons for her temerity.

"Besides," he said, saving her further deliberation, "you're wrong on several points. I do not want to be more powerful— in fact, that's the last thing I want—and I do not need or want a familiar, either." Letting those black eyes rake her up and down, he produced a lascivious smile. "Your bonding-virginity is safe with me, little familiar. I'm not interested."

"Good," she snapped, absurdly stung, as she didn't *want* him to be interested. "Because I wouldn't have you."

"You would though," he pointed out implacably. "Maybe we need to revisit your understanding of consent. You'd have no choice in the matter. If I decided to make you mine, I could."

She contained a shiver of response at the way he said that. *Make you mine.* There was a throatiness to his voice, a suppressed longing. Probably for the concept of a familiar in general, though, not about her in particular. Whatever prevented him from having a familiar—his mother? Himself?— it bothered him more than he wanted her to know. "You wouldn't do that to me though."

He laughed. Not uproariously before, but sharp and bitter. "Don't make the mistake of thinking that I'm your friend or that I harbor some sort of scruples. If it came to that, I'd use you in any way that benefits me, and so would any wizard. Don't prance about in such doe-eyed innocence. All wizards will seek to use you to advance themselves without giving it any more thought than they give to the tender lamb that graces their dinner tables and tastes so delicious with fresh mint."

"Not all wizards."

"*All* wizards, little lamb."

"Alise isn't like that." She didn't think Gabriel was either, though he was a more tenuous example, after nearly going wild in his pursuit of Nic, laying waste to House Sammael to retrieve her.

Jadren rolled his eyes. "Baby Elal is exactly that: still an infant. She hasn't graduated from Convocation Academy. She shouldn't even be away from school now. The only reason she hasn't been spanked and sent back to learn to be a proper wizard yet is because Lord Phel has a soft heart and Lady Phel has a soft head."

"Alise is Nic's younger sister," Selly said, intrigued by Jadren's assessment. "Why is Nic soft-headed for letting Alise stay and become a House Phel minion?"

"Because," Jadren answered in an exaggerated drawl, "if they were thinking straight, House Phel would curry favor with House Elal by returning Alise to her designated slot. They're fools to pass up the money and favor they could receive. Instead they're risking inflaming relations with Elal even more with this sentimentality."

"Being loyal to a beloved family member hardly counts as being sentimental."

"Loyalty is an illusion created by those in power to convince those they hold in thrall that they don't shrug off their chains from their own inclination rather than because they can't."

"You're very cynical."

"You have no idea."

And there they were, back to his favorite conversation-ender. She was thinking up the next question to ask when he unexpectedly answered a previous one. "Not only am I not interested in acquiring a stick-insect of an untrained, feral marsh-cat of a familiar," he said musingly, "but I'm not that stupid. On the off-chance that Phel manages to defeat Sammael and consolidate his holdings, I'm not going to risk his righteous rage were I to take possession of his beloved disabled sister for the rest of her natural life."

"I am not disabled, you ass," she muttered.

He grinned cheerfully. "I can admit that I'm an ass. You shouldn't be ashamed to admit to a chronic disability that arose through no fault of your own."

She set her teeth refusing to rise to his bait. He was deliberately taunting her, trying to get a rise out of her, trying to... To distract her from whatever the real reason was that he didn't have a familiar. That he could never have one perhaps? "It's starting to get dark," she observed, deciding to let the topic simmer a while. Jadren was already brooding and, from what she'd observed of him so far, would continue to ferment until he couldn't prevent a revealing remark from popping out of his mouth.

"Nothing wrong with your eyes, at least," he replied with an approving smile.

"We're going to have to look for a place to camp," she pointed out, very reasonably.

"Camp?" he echoed, sounding appalled. He glanced at her with a narrowed gaze, clearly suspecting her of teasing him.

"As, in sleep outdoors, on the ground?"

She nodded somberly, resisting the urge to smile at his dismay. "We'll want to build a fire."

"I don't think 'want' is the operative term here."

"A fire will keep the snakes away," she explained with rounded eyes.

"Don't be cute," he snapped. "I told you I'm not terrified of snakes. You'll get no joy out of attempting that leverage on me."

"Other critters then," she told him, maybe a little disappointed that her needling hadn't worked that time. "Hunters."

He snorted. "You think I'm a fool and it's true I know next to nothing about camping in the wilderness, but even I can figure out that a nice bright fire with aromatic smoke wafting about will just serve to paint a target on our location. Too bad I'm no good at illusions or I could hang a big red arrow in the sky that says 'ripe captives for the taking here.'"

"Fire is good for cooking meat," she countered. "And brewing tea."

"You already know I'm not a fire mage. We have no fire elementals handy. What do you want from me?" he demanded, eyes flashing black with irritation.

"We don't need magic," she answered extra scornfully, so he wouldn't guess she'd seen through to his insecurity on the topic. "I can make a fire the old-fashioned way."

"Nothing is older than magic," he corrected. "You want a fire, knock yourself out, but if we want to sleep secure, we're sleeping behind wards"

"Wards?" Her turn to echo a word in surprise. She didn't

even know what that was.

"Yes. I may not be able to conjure fire to titillate your curiosity, but I can establish basic wards. I just need something with four walls, a ceiling, and a floor to structure them around."

"I think we're fresh out of those," she replied, looking around consideringly.

He muttered something under his breath about unsavory wildernesses and the crying need for inns. "Fine," he finally said to her, "I can build a shelter for us. I assume your half-feral, swamp-creature experiences will enable you to pick a likely location."

"You can build a shelter?" she cocked a dubious brow at his soft wizard's hands. They were pretty hands, elegant and fine, but they did not look like he'd spent much time swinging an axe.

"I'm not completely useless."

"I thought you only know how to make enchanted artifacts, assorted widgets, and do a few other tricks."

He laughed, shaking his head. "Do you memorize everything I say? I should be flattered, I suppose. You pick the spot, sweetling, and then you'll see."

"I don't mind sleeping on the ground." Under the sky, in the fresh air.

"I can't ward the ground. Besides, I mind. When you're on your wild escapades, you can sleep with the snakes if you prefer, but I have standards. Rapidly degrading and pitifully few standards, so I'm clinging to the dregs of what's left."

"Seems like an odd line to draw," she observed, "but I'll

play along." She began scanning for places to get off the road, somewhere with dry ground and well-screened in case anything came after them.

It was quite a while later that she heard Jadren quietly reply. "Sometimes keeping to your lines is the most one can do."

~ 5 ~

JADREN EYED THE small clearing Selly had picked out. Yes, it was off the road, reasonably concealed from anyone passing by, and—thankfully—not a bog, which satisfied her stated requirements. Nothing else made it look like a place he wanted to spend any time, however. Long ferny plant tendrils draped from the trees, waving in the evening air uncannily like spirits. He'd nearly jumped out of his skin, thinking Elal had sent some sentry spirits after them.

Of course, Selly had then reassured him they weren't snakes. She'd never let him live that down. One more reason to wish his maman would die in a lake of fire. As if he needed more reasons.

"Leave off with fussing with that campfire and come assist me," he instructed Selly. True to her word, she'd built and lit a small fire in the time that it had taken him to pace off the boundaries of the working he intended to perform. When Selly scowled at him, he held out a preemptory hand and snapped his fingers impatiently, well pleased when her amber eyes narrowed in anger. It was good for her to hate him. Then she'd spend less time trying to get into his head. Nobody needed to enter that vile, desolate landscape.

"I know nothing about building a shelter," she protested, but she stood and came over, eyeing the square outline he'd made with twigs. "Although even I know you'll need more wood than that."

"Familiars should be seen and not heard," he informed her.

"What?" she gasped, outraged. The chit had a lot to learn. Hopefully Lady Phel would spend some time polishing those rough edges. When he'd used the same line on Nic, she'd barely seemed to notice. But then, Elals were a cold-hearted lot, and he meant that in the nicest way.

"You don't need to flap your jaws to hand over that nummy magic," he explained with honeyed patience. "Less talking. More giving up the juice." He wiggled his fingers at her.

He thought she might be about to refuse, but she pressed her pretty lips into a thin line and slapped her hand into his with enough force to sting. That was his girl. Nothing daunted her spirited nature for long. "I can't wait to see this," she muttered.

"Oh, me too," he agreed cheerfully, then bent his attention to the twigs she'd sneered at.

"You mean you haven't done this before?"

With a sigh for the interruption to his concentration, he glared at her. "What, built a shelter in the middle of nowhere so I could hide with a half-feral familiar from rogue hunters because I somehow ended up as a junior wizard to a fallen house so imperiled that another high house attacked it? Why no, come to think of it. I haven't."

"Must you always be so sarcastic?" she gritted out.

He pretended to consider that. "Yes. Now be quiet or I'll

muzzle you."

"I'd like to see you try," she muttered, but she said nothing more.

Focusing again on the image he'd built in his mind, Jadren carefully constructed the shelter. It didn't need to be big, just large enough for Selly and him to sleep in without being too intimately crammed together. That was all he needed, to accidentally touch her long, lissome body during the night, fraying his already imperiled control around her. "It's just another artifact," he remined himself. "Basically a box. Don't get fancy."

"What was that?" Selly asked.

He turned a furious glower on her. "What part of 'be quiet' do you not understand?"

"I understand you don't *have* a muzzle," she answered sweetly, baring her teeth.

"I'll *make* one," he snapped, thumping his free hand against his chest, then pointing to the array of tool-elements he carried. "El-Adrel wizard, remember? We create enchanted artifacts. I can work up a muzzle that would stop you from speaking another word."

"Seems like all I'd have to do is keep talking while you try to conjure it up and you'll never get anywhere," she replied, adding a sly wink.

Oh, she did not just say that. The old frustration welled up in him, all the methods his maman had enlisted to break his concentration, all supposedly to train him to be the very best and all unbearable to recall. "Seliah," he said, setting his teeth and speaking through them, "if you want to wake up in the morning without a hunter's collar throttling you as they drag you off to Sammael, would you pretty please, with cinnamon sugar and candied cherries on top, be *silent?*"

She opened her mouth, then closed it abruptly, gesturing at him to proceed. *Finally.* Taking several deep breaths, he reached again for the meditative state he could achieve reasonably well. Then, bracing himself for the sharp, fresh flavor of her, he drew on Seliah's magic. It flowed into him with unimpeded force, unrefined, uncontrolled, like a mountain spring. It made his teeth ache with its potency—and he nearly fumbled his control in the face of the renewed vigor of it.

If drinking of Nic's magic had been like gulping an entire bottle of potent wine, Seliah's unfettered magic reminded him of being drowned in a lake of snowmelt while shards of silver pierced his limbs. Not that he'd ever experienced anything like that, but surely this was how it would feel. He also had frustratingly little experience working with such a powerful familiar. Now that she was getting better at not holding back, the magic flowed over him like an icy tidal wave. He grappled. Strained to shape and funnel it. Lost his hold.

Breaking his grip on her magic and on her hand, he gasped for breath as if he truly had been drowning. Dizzy with it, he bent and braced his hands on his knees, head swimming.

"Will you bite my head off if I ask if you're all right?" Seliah spoke very quietly, as if low volume would've made a difference, had he still been trying to concentrate.

"I'm fine," he bit out, making up in confidence what he lacked in believability. "Your magic is like standing under a waterfall and trying to take a sip by tipping back my head and opening my mouth."

"When we fought the hunters earlier, you said I was tense and trying to wring magic out of me was like sucking on a dried lemon rind."

Forcing himself upright, he gave her a weary look. "You *do* memorize everything I say. It would be touching if it weren't so bloody aggravating."

"I have a good memory," she replied stiffly, a high flush on her cheekbones visible even in the thickening dusk. "And I'm invested in learning this stuff, so I do pay attention to what you tell me in the hopes that it will be useful information."

"Well, there's your first mistake," he commented wryly. "I'm not known for being useful in any way, shape, or form."

"As you say." She was still stiff. Embarrassed? He could never quite predict which of her several distinct personalities would emerge at any given time.

"I apologize," he said on a sigh. "None of this is your fault. You're completely untrained. Worse than that, you know just enough to be dangerous. And I'm not experienced at working with familiars, so I'm not giving you good information."

"Oh." She unbent enough to offer a small smile. "I *am* trying to get better."

He recognized that in her, the wounded pride at not being good at something, even though she was diligently applying herself. "Yes, well, these things are complicated by the nature of magic—particularly yours, it appears—in that it's not a static thing. You're still generating magic at a crazy rate, so what you had earlier today is nothing compared to what's built up since.

Clearly you need to be tapped regularly."

Her lips twitched, lifting into a sensual half-smile that grabbed him by the groin. "Why does that sound dirty?" she purred, amber eyes lambent with a hint of silver moon magic.

Manfully, he cleared his throat and looked away from her. "You don't talk like a twenty-four year old virgin," he muttered, instructing himself to get a grip.

"Because I'm not. Are you actually blushing, Wizard El-Adrel?" she asked with a widening smile.

Curse his transparent complexion, he probably was. He'd been keeping his prurient thoughts off of the alluring Seliah by reminding himself that she was a child in a woman's body. How had she managed to have sex when she'd begun to lose her wits at adolescence? Then a terrible thought occurred to him, rage billowing in a blaze. "Who took advantage of you?" he demanded.

Seliah blinked, actually backing up a step at his forcefulness. "What? Nobody."

He wasn't buying that innocent act. Stabbing a finger in her face, he advanced on her. "You started losing your mind when you began budding breasts, so don't tell me you weren't abused. Either someone had you when you were little more than a child, unable to consent, or they had you when you were insane from magic stagnation, equally unable to consent. Now, tell me who it was."

She punched her fists to her hips, lifting her pointed chin, and refusing to back down further. She looked like a fey creature swathed in shadows, far too fragile for the cruelty of the world they lived in. His furious advance had brought him way too close to her. "What will you do—hunt them down and kill them for me?"

"If necessary," he snarled. "I may not be much of a wizard, but I can kill a commoner, which is who it had to be, as there wasn't anyone else *in* Meresin before the rest of us arrived." Then an even more horrible thought occurred to him. "Unless it was your brother."

"*What?*" she gasped, an expression of shocked horror contorting her face, too vivid to be a pretense. Something vicious and murderous in him relaxed slightly. Phel would be difficult to kill, but Jadren would've found a way. "Gabriel would never!" Seliah continued, unnecessarily.

He waved that off, putting distance between them. "I see by your reaction that's true."

"But how could you even think it? My own *brother!*"

Such an innocent. "Families do such things to each other."

She stilled. "Your family?"

His stomach turned uneasily. "The winters are long at House El-Adrel," he answered grimly, regretting the words the moment he spoke them. "But we're not discussing me. Who—"

"Jadren," she interrupted, "what happened to you?"

"More than your pretty head can tolerate," he snapped. "And we. Are. Not. Discussing. Me." He punctuated each word with ferocious certainty. "Are we clear?"

She nodded mutely, eyes wide.

"Better. Now tell me who defiled you so we can get back to work making a shelter before dawn makes it a moot point."

The stubbornness in the set of her jaw and the flash of her eyes gave him her answer before she opened her mouth. "I'll tell you mine when you tell me yours."

Infuriating minx. "You can't do anything about mine, little familiar," he replied with silky menace, "whereas I *will* punish whoever did that to you."

"What business is it of yours?" she retorted fiercely. "I never asked you to be my champion and I don't need it."

"You don't know what you need," he snapped back.

"Why?" she sneered. "Because I'm a familiar? A crazy girl? A half-feral swamp creature from a backwater house with no Convocation education?"

"Exactly." He congratulated himself for flummoxing her with his calm retort. "At least you're learning."

"I hate you," she muttered.

"As well you should, as I believe I explained earlier today. Look how much you're learning! Now go play with your fire while I make our shelter."

She gave him a long, disbelieving look. "I thought you needed my magic."

"Believe me, I have more than enough of that at the moment. All I require of you is silence. A tall order, I know, but I have faith you'll eventually learn to keep your mouth shut."

She gaped at him a moment longer, her lip curled in disgust. Then she stalked back to her fire, pointedly without saying a word, her tiny bottom twitching eloquently. With that too-penetrating gaze no longer on him, Jadren allowed himself to feel a short moment of relief and longing. He couldn't mire Seliah in his shitty life. And he was absolutely never speaking to her—or anyone, ever—about what had made him the half-man he was today. He'd just have to make sure she continued to loathe him. That way she'd forget her questions, or that she'd even cared to ask them.

It was better for both of them that way.

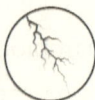

"I'm NOT GETTING in that coffin." Seliah said, not for the first time, and Jadren chewed his lips with frustration.

"It's *not* a coffin," he repeated.

"It *looks* like a coffin," she countered, "and I'm not getting in it."

She would if he knocked her over the head and dragged her inside. Seliah glared at him as if he'd said the thought aloud. To think he'd been proud of himself, making a decently comfortable, wardable shelter, out of wire and a few twigs. "You don't need to be able to stand up inside of it," he wheedled. "It's just so we can sleep safely."

"You sleep in it. I'll sleep outside."

"I can't ward you outside," he ground out. What sins had he committed that he was trapped in this eternal circle of argument with this creature? Oh, right: plenty.

"What is with your pathological need to protect me?" she demanded.

"My pathological need to keep my head attached to my neck," he fired back. "I'm not taking the risk that I'll be facing a hale and hearty Gabriel Phel and having to explain I let his baby sister die or get dragged off by hunters. I don't care if you're miserable or if you hate me, as long as you're alive and intact, I'm happy as a lark."

She snorted. "The image of you actually happy is the most impossible thing imaginable."

Fair. "Watch my face when I hand you over to your brother and walk away and you won't have to strain your imagination. Now get in the box."

"See? Even you call it a box."

"A box is not a coffin. Besides, they never bury two people in the same grave, right? Therefore it can't possibly be a coffin."

"Is that supposed to be a joke?"

Well, he'd tried. "Logic. Now stop being crazy girl and do the rational thing here. We're not exactly replete with alternatives. Quit being stubborn."

She glared unhappily, but lowered herself to her knees and eyed the interior of the shelter—fine, it *was* a box—like it held a ravenous tiger. Then she sat back on her heels and pressed a hand to her forehead, then wiped her cheeks. "Jadren," she said in a fragile, watery voice, "please don't make me go in there. I... can't."

She was crying. And he was a shit. That is, more of one than usual. Moving slowly, he knelt beside her, then ran a soothing hand down her braid. She was trembling, afraid all out of proportion to the situation. "What's wrong?"

"Closed-in spaces," she whispered. "There were times... I know you don't want to discuss these things, but they had to contain me, you know, so I wouldn't keep running away. Lock me in. I can't go in there. Even if I make myself, I won't be able to stand it. You'll see. I know you'll hate me for it, but I really just cannot—"

"Shh," he murmured, interrupting the rising flow of her hysteria, stroking her braid with firmer tugs so she'd feel it and be grounded again. He should've seen this coming, should've recognized the symptoms in her. Dark arts knew he had plenty of experience with fighting ghosts from the shattered past. "It all right," he soothed.

She shook her head, the sobs strengthening. "I'm sorry. I'm so sorry." Her frail shoulders shook, and she looked so small and alone that he had to do something.

"Don't be sorry." He patted her back awkwardly. "After all, I puked in the bushes. Some reactions aren't rational and can't ever be. I'm the one who's sorry that I didn't listen to what you were telling me. You don't have to get in the box."

"I don't?" She lifted her head, gazing at him with desperate hope, her eyes bright with tears in the firelight.

Unable to resist, he stroked away a curling tendril from her wet cheek, absurdly pleased to have put that light back in her eyes. It was especially ridiculous since he'd been the one to make her so miserable in the first place. "You don't," he confirmed, unable to restrain a sigh. This had been such an elegantly simple solution. "We'll think of something else."

"Thank you." She flung herself against him, embracing him with fierce tenacity, face buried against his neck, her chin digging rather sharply against his collarbone. For a slender, barely-there wraith, Seliah possessed a surprising amount of tensile strength. And she smelled of water in the moonlight, her tough, tense, thin little body vibrating with spiky silver magic, her breasts surprisingly—and distractingly—soft and full pressed against his chest. He couldn't help a tiny fantasy of how it would feel to be buried inside that intensity, to have that passionate body surging against his, embracing and engulfing.

It's never going to happen, he told himself firmly.

Are you sure? part of him whispered back slyly.

Yes. Ruthlessly banishing the image, he refused to touch her any more than he already had. Holding his hands out, even more awkward than ever, he kind of waved them around as he waited for the hug to end.

It didn't. Instead she held on, a buzzing bundle of intoxicating magic and tempting woman. Jadren tried patting her back, thinking maybe that would satisfy her enough to encourage her to go away, but she only purred, snuggling closer, like a cat who'd found the one cat-hater in the room and had no greater goal in life than encamping on his lap forever.

"Seliah." He squirmed in her fierce grip, which only resulted in her taking advantage of his movement to seal herself closer against him. He'd lost valuable ground in this battle and he didn't see how he could regain it. Especially with his own resolve to hold her off crumbling. "Sweetling, hey..."

An oily smear across his wizard senses shocked him out of his dithering. *Hunters.*

Fear galvanized him—although he was petty enough to relish the bit of vindication—and he seized Seliah and set her forcibly away from him. "Hunters!" he hissed, giving her a little shake.

To her credit, she snapped right out of whatever emotional

bog she'd fallen into, immediately hardening, eyes glinting in the meager light. Only her wet cheeks revealed the storm she'd suffered. "How close?" she whispered back.

He leaned in so his voice wouldn't carry, since it seemed safe to come near her again. "Close. My range for sensing them isn't that good. Maybe from here to the road? Approaching stealthily."

"Do they know we're here?" her voice, throaty still from her sobbing, thrummed in his ear, evoking an unfortunate sensory addition to the wayward fantasy that wouldn't quite let go.

"I think so," he murmured. "They're coming closer."

"Weapons are in your box," she pointed out.

Yes, where he'd so carefully stowed them in the futile hope that they'd be safely inside *with* them, warded against an attack of exactly this kind. Best laid plans. Also, he supposed there was no chance of getting Seliah to go in, even to fetch the weapons—not if he wanted her in fighting shape instead of a blubbering mess. "I'll get them. You..." What? Keep watch? This was ridiculous as she was the one most in danger. His life meant nothing to anyone—and arguably wasn't at risk anyway—but Seliah had a future. "Stay out of trouble," he finished weakly.

She grabbed his arm before he could move, fingers claw-like as they dug in. "I'll get them."

"They're at the back," he replied pointedly.

She took a deep breath, still gripping him way too hard. "It's my fault we're not in there and warded. I'll get them."

Then, to his utter astonishment, she kissed him. Full on the mouth and—trademark Seliah—far too hard. She was there and gone again like the wind. If the wind was hurricane force, had teeth, and fulminated longing in its wake. With no idea what *that* had been about, he whispered, "Slide me my machete first."

She didn't reply and he really hoped the confines of the box hadn't sent her into a catatonic state. Though... now would be the perfect opportunity to ward the thing with her inside. Or dive in after her and ward it behind him, forcing the issue. Oddly enough, however, the conscience he'd never before heard from until recently wouldn't let him. Annoyed with himself, with Seliah, with this entire benighted situation, he scanned the clearing with physical and wizard senses, checking for any sign of the advancing hunters.

He screamed when one leapt out of the shadows, raking him from shoulder to groin with its claws.

~ 6 ~

GABRIEL PHEL PACED the sloping, lushly grassy bank of the lake that graced the front of House Phel, and glared at the water. He valued the arcanium of course—and was infinitely glad that he and Nic had managed to reclaim both it and its magic by evicting her father, the conniving Lord Elal, from the private sanctity of the underwater dome—but he could wish his ancestors had put the arcanium atop a tower as seemed to be traditional for most of the Convocation.

It just figured that his family had to be contrary.

What he needed was something high, so he could see a long distance. Not something submerged in the watery depths of a lake. Frustrated, he kicked a rock into the placid water, the ripples sparkling prettily in the morning light as if nothing in the world was wrong.

"Has the lake offended you?" Nic asked, raising a brow as she approached him, her deep green skirts gathered in her hands as she picked her way through the waving grasses. As he'd hoped when he commissioned the gown, the color of the fabric brought out the rich emerald of her eyes, complimenting her dusky complexion, and the exquisite cut set off her voluptuous figure. "Or are you practicing skipping stones with your feet, perhaps?" she added with a teasing quirk of her full mouth.

He held out a hand to her, smiling ruefully. "I already know how to skip stones and hands work best for that—though that children's trick will do nothing to help me locate Selly and Jadren."

She slipped her warm hand into his, fire and sun-warmed roses filtering into him as her magic flowed with generosity as lush as her passionate nature. "They'll make it back here."

"They haven't yet," he reminded her, unnecessarily.

"They missed catching the barge upriver is all. That means they have to ride overland and that takes longer."

He knew that. It didn't ease his worries. Usually he appreciated her practicality, but at the moment he had no patience for it. Dropping her hand, he waved at the pastoral scene. "I can't simply sit here and do nothing."

"You're not simply sitting here," she pointed out. "You're pacing around the lake and frightening the minions."

"I thought it was my *job* to play arrogant Lord Phel and frighten the minions," he retorted, too worked up to be amused by her attempt at a joke.

"Yes and it is—except that they're already unsettled and afraid, having been nearly mass-murdered by House Sammael. Our people need you to be strong for them."

That she said "our people" instead of "your people" mollified him enough to attempt to rein in his annoyance, and worry. "Mom came at me this morning," he said on a sigh.

Nic winced in sympathy. "I can just imagine the state Daisy is in, worrying about Selly."

Gabriel nodded, releasing a sigh of part frustration and part resignation. "My parents both still see Selly as a child."

"Most parents never stop seeing their progeny as children, even when they've been adults for decades."

"True. Though we won't do that." He gave her a fond smile, because he did appreciate her making the effort to talk him out of his tree, and laid a hand over her still-flat belly where their child grew.

She gazed up at him, love warm in her gaze. "We probably *will* do that. It's a parent's job to drive their children crazy."

Children. He only hoped that would come to be, that this child would live to grow up in peace and prosperity, followed by siblings. It worried him, though, that the children he and Nic would make would undoubtedly have magic, which meant the Convocation would dig its claws into them and distort their lives into twisted versions of indentured servitude. He hadn't even been able to keep Selly safe—the sinking fear that something had happened to her ate away at him.

He sobered as he recalled his mother's half-hysterical tirade. "It's worse with Selly. Maybe it's the guilt. They feel responsible for not knowing the magic was eating Selly alive, that they could have helped her and didn't."

"Gabriel," Nic said softly, sorrow in her face. "They couldn't have known. *You* couldn't have known. Not everything is within your control."

They both knew they were no longer talking about Selly as she was then, but Selly now. "I shouldn't have let her come with us. She's only just emerged from the madness and she's still so frail, so…" *tenuous in her sanity.*

Though he didn't speak the words aloud, Nic followed his thoughts with ease. "I wouldn't let Selly hear you say that. She's an adult woman. Yes, she's been mentally ill, but none of us wants to be treated as if we're less than. She was perfectly sane when she volunteered to come with you and when she offered to stay behind to assist Jadren." She paused reflectively. "I think Jadren will actually be good for her."

"Are we talking about the same Jadren?" he asked incredulously. "The arrogant asshole planted in our house as a spy, likely as a tool in the conspiracy between El-Adrel and Elal to control or destroy House Phel."

Nic waited him out with a gimlet gaze. "Yes, as a matter of fact. Also the same Jadren who nearly died taking over draining Selly's magic after you collapsed from the effort. You were unconscious, so you didn't see, but he had no reason to endanger himself that way. He's also the same Jadren who accompanied you to rescue me. Those weren't the actions of an malicious tool. He may be an ass, but a good heart lurks under that hard shell."

"He was unkind to you," Gabriel reminded her, knowing that it had happened, even if Nic had refused to give details. "And he's harsh with Selly."

"Yes, which is why I think he might be good for her. Selly needs to find her foundation in herself again, to trust herself and her magic, to not be treated like she might fall apart at any moment."

He glared at her, furious and offended. That was *not* how he'd treated Selly. Besides, he knew his own sister, didn't he? "And you gleaned that about her from the all of, what, three minutes you spent with her between transforming back to human form and getting on Salve to ride away?"

Nic gave him a long look, fire sparking in her gaze. "You've been through a great deal, between worrying to death about me and now worrying about Selly, so I'm going to very gently remind you that I know a great deal more about being a familiar than you do, along with what it's like to feel helpless against your fate. So don't you take that tone with me, Gabriel Phel, or I will make you sorry."

His lips twitched despite himself. "If that was a gentle reminder, I'd hate to see the harsh one."

She sniffed, lifting her nose regally. "Keep that in mind." Then she relented and laid her palms on his chest, gazing up at him with concern. "Now, why don't you tell me what your stalking about the lake and scowling has to do with finding Selly? Maybe I can help problem-solve."

He laid his hands over hers, immensely grateful for her presence in his life, even when she was chiding him for his misguided ways. Perhaps more so for that. Since he'd become a fearsome wizard, few people dared to correct him in any way. "There isn't really a problem to solve. I was just fuming at my Phel ancestors for sinking the arcanium under the lake. Why can't it be atop a tower like other self-respecting Convocation houses?"

Eyes dancing with amusement, she dug her nails into his chest, very lightly, just enough to tease. "I suspect contrary behavior runs in the family."

"That was my thought, too."

"But why is this a problem? Under a lake or atop a tower,

an arcanium is an arcanium. Location is irrelevant. What matters is the power of the wizard using it and the ancestral magic embedded within. Your arcanium is the best I've heard of—even given the propensity of wizards to oversell their arcaniums and present them as bigger and better than any other wizard's," she added impishly.

"*Our* arcanium," he corrected, "and yes, I know it's a good one. It's only a problem is that if it were higher in the sky, I could use it to cast about with wizardry and try to locate Selly. And Jadren."

A line folded between her elegant brows. "I may regret asking this question, but why do you need to be up in the sky to do that?"

"It's how I reached you with my magic when you were trapped inside House Sammael," he explained. "From the overlook across the valley, I could see the tower and extend my magic to it. Jadren said there was no way I could affect anything magically from that distance, but I could, and I *did*." His finish was perhaps a bit more emphatic, and vindictive, than called for.

"Yes, my only love," she purred, petting him with soothing strokes. "You did what most wizards deem impossible because they lack both your power and your iconoclastic innovation with wizardry. Jadren was very wrong to doubt you."

He narrowed his eyes at her oh-so-bland expression and sweetly lilting tone. "You're making fun of me."

"Never," she promised, fluttering her lavish black lashes, then giggled. "Your face right now... All right, all right, I'm maybe teasing you a little. But I'm only needling you because you are so very powerful, and innovative with it, that you accomplished this incredible feat of magic to rescue me, then limit yourself with something as trivial as physical location."

"You're saying it doesn't matter where the arcanium is."

"I'm saying it doesn't matter where the arcanium is," she confirmed soberly, with the barest hint of humor. "You don't have to be able to physically *see*, Gabriel." She tapped his forehead between his brows. "Use your wizard senses. Those are not limited by your physical eyesight."

"But I want to use the amplification of the arcanium. My magic alone isn't enough to reach to where Selly is. I've tried."

"Oh?" she asked lightly, not fooling him for a moment as he'd learned to recognize that dangerous edge to her voice, even in a monosyllable. "When did you try this? Because I know *I* wasn't there."

"Last night," he admitted, telling himself he had nothing to feel bad about, "and again this morning. While you were sleeping."

"And *why*," she continued in a harder voice, "did you not ask for my assistance?"

"Because," he returned in the same tone, hopefully even harder, "you're still recovering from your ordeal. I have no intention of draining your magic even further, possibly endangering your health when I can—"

"When you can struggle to accomplish a critical task without me?" she demanded, yanking her hands away and fulminating with fiery annoyance. "I am not fragile, either, Wizard Phel! You retrieved your familiar from any enemy high house because you need me, not to—"

He seized her by the arms. "I rescued my *wife*," he snarled, "my lover, and the person in whom my heart resides entirely. I did not risk my family, friends, and myself because you're a valuable tool. And I have no intention of jeopardizing your health and recovery now, especially when I know I'm overthinking this and that you are confident Selly will make it home safely. How could I ask you to assist with that?"

"You ask because it's important to you, and what is important to you is important to me." She wiggled out of his grip and framed his face in her hands. "Not because I'm duty-bound as your familiar—though, let's be honest between ourselves, that duty is very important to *me*—but because I love you and there's nothing I wouldn't do for you."

"That's what frightens me."

"Always afraid I won't tell you no if I need to."

"Our bonding may be non-standard, but I'm very aware of how it, and your training by the Convocation incline you to… accommodate me, shall we say."

"Weasel wording worthy of the finest politician," she replied with a rueful smile, then she searched his face, lowering her hands to take his, squeezing them. "Is that why you're most worried about Selly—you fear that her familiar nature will make her subject to Jadren's commands, that he might even bond her?"

She saw through him all too well. "Am I wrong?" he asked, rather expecting her to reject the possibility out of hand, but she pursed her lips thoughtfully.

"You understand more about Convocation wizards than you once did," she allowed. "And normally I'd agree that this is a reasonable fear, even a foregone conclusion. Letting a powerful, unbonded familiar go roaming about with a wizard from an ambitious high house, one who has no familiar for no apparent good reason, is just asking for a hostile bonding." Her frown deepened. "Or there's always the chance that someone else could come across them and steal her. Sammael and Elal minions are swarming the region, and we certainly know that Sammael at least won't scruple about the ethics."

His hopes—never very high—sank at her frank assessment. "I never should have let her stay with him."

"It wasn't your choice," she pointed out calmly. "Besides, I—"

"I agreed," he interrupted. "It *was* my choice."

"Grudgingly, and only because you're so invested in everyone being equal. You can't rail about familiars not having the freedom that everyone else does on the one hand and then get all dictatorial about their decisions on the other."

He set his teeth. "It's not because she's a familiar. It's because this is Selly, and she isn't..." Trailing off as Nic's brows rose, he cursed himself for digging himself even deeper into a bog.

"There's just no good way to finish that sentence is there?" Nic asked after a beat, her tone oozing false sympathy. "Let me save you. What I was about to say is, while your thinking is sound, I think your instincts are off. I seriously doubt there's any danger of Jadren bonding Selly. In fact, I'm certain of it."

"Why?" It relieved him to hear that from her, especially as Nic knew so much more about the ruthlessness of the Convocation and its wizards.

She shook her head. "Logically, there's the fact that he hasn't bonded a familiar yet. There's something going on there. Also, less logically… my gut tells me so.

"That's what my gut says, too. I just worry I don't have a good reason to trust something so irrational. What if it's only indigestion?"

She chuckled in sympathy. "That cream sauce last night did seem a bit off. I'll speak with the kitchen staff. But what you're feeling is not irrational and it's not indigestion. Your wizardly intuition is real. Trust it."

He'd done that before, following his intuition in how to rescue Nic. "But there's your second point—the swarming minions of our enemies who wouldn't hesitate with Selly. My intuition, wizardly or otherwise, is prompting me to find our lost pair before anyone else does."

"Then let us proceed to the arcanium, wizard," she purred, a gleam in her eyes.

Giving her a disbelieving look, he cocked his head. "Questions of indigestion aside, I can't believe you're up for more sex after last night's epic recharging of the arcanium."

She lifted her chin, gazing nobly into the distance, hand over her heart. "My duty to house and wizard demands much of me, but I will soldier on!" Simpering mischievously at him, she dropped the pose. "In all seriousness, while sex magic is excellent for recharging the arcanium and for building power for major incantations, that shouldn't be necessary for this effort. It would be good for you to practice using the arcanium's focusing power without sex. I confess, I *am* a bit sore from all the wicked things you did to my helpless body last night."

Because she kept her knowing gaze trained on his face, he made sure not to wince, though he couldn't help the flush of combined heat and a tiny bit of shame. "I did go farther than ever before." He didn't pose it as a question, but he waited expectantly. This went both directions. If she wanted him to embrace his darker nature and follow his baser passions, then she had to be honest with him about whether he had gone too far.

"I loved every moment," she answered the unspoken question, a flush of her own gracing her high cheekbones. "And I'm fine. I visited Asa first thing this morning to be healed, so you don't need to feel guilty about having left any marks on me."

Now he did wince at the thought of the Refoel wizard-healer seeing the results of their long, impassioned, and violently erotic interlude. "Did Wizard Asa, er…"

Nic raised one raven-winged brow. "Comment? Express censure or voyeuristic curiosity?"

He blew out a breath, aware she was needling him and yet unable to quite get himself to a place where those possibilities didn't bother him. "Just tell me what he said."

"Very little, beyond the normal interchange between healer and patient." She rolled her eyes. "Gabriel, Asa is a Convocation wizard. A few love bites and bruises from chains between wizard and familiar are hardly going to shock him."

Not trusting his voice or words, Gabriel simply nodded. He didn't love the idea of Asa seeing the results of unleashing his dark nature on Nic's beautiful skin, but the alternatives were for Nic to not get healed or for them to stop doing it. Neither was truly an alternative, so he'd have to learn to handle it. "Good," he said, finally, in lieu of anything more articulate. "Let's go see about searching for Selly then. And Jadren."

Perhaps he imagined it, because he wanted to see it, but Nic gave him a look of quiet approval and understanding. She tucked a hand through his elbow, walking with him back toward the manse and their secret tunnel to the arcanium. "Asa also tended to Maman this morning. She's doing better, physically."

"I'm sorry I forgot to inquire." He'd been too caught up in his own concerns.

Nic smiled warmly, squeezing his arm. "You have a lot on your mind. Besides, Maman is in good hands. Alise is staying with her, reading and talking to her, and Asa looks in every so often."

"And her mind?"

Firming her chin, Nic gazed at the north wing of the manse where her maman was housed. "We don't know yet. Papa keeping her in her feline alternate form for so very long may have done permanent damage. Now that Alise has severed the wizard–familiar bond between them, we're hoping Maman will gradually recover herself. Only time will tell."

"I suppose that we could always ask Alise to sever any wizard–familiar bond again, if we're wrong and Jadren has bonded Selly—or if some scurrilous Sammael minion has." He left out the possibility that anyone from House Elal might have bonded Selly. Nic had enough to think about without worrying about further betrayal from the house of her birth.

Nic slid him a wary glance. "Perhaps."

Her non-committal reply didn't surprise him. The discovery that the wizard–familiar bond could be severed was potentially explosive. It would turn the rigid Convocation hierarchy upside down—if the news got out. For the time being, only a handful of them knew about the procedure and only Nic's teenaged wizard-sister could perform the feat. The Convocation had killed people and demolished Houses for far less. Nic, always wanting to err on the side of keeping their heads down, would likely argue that they shouldn't use the technique, at all, ever.

And, since that argument wouldn't lead them anywhere productive, he left it at that. Besides, first they had to *find* Selly, before they could think about anything more.

~ 7 ~

JADREN AWOKE TO a splitting headache and such debilitating wooziness that he refused to open his eyes, instead willing himself back to sleep. That was always the best way to recover from his darling maman's extreme methods for making him into something else: sleep as hard and as long as possible. The gambit also delayed additional experimentation, as she grew impatient if his strength gave out too soon.

Unless she decided to have him healed—a last resort for her, as having another wizard heal him wasn't the point—he could carve out maybe a day of rest before...

Before...

His thoughts snagged and stuttered to a halt. This was all wrong. That was all in the past. He'd gotten free of House El-Adrel and his maman's tender ministrations—as long as one used the word "free" loosely. Because his freedom had been conditionally granted, his parole a stint in House Phel where he was to—

"Shit!" he yelled, hurting his own head as he wrenched himself upright, looking wildly around for Seliah. No sign of her. It was full daylight. The little clearing was empty but for him, Seliah's fire a pile of cold ash. He'd been lying in a coagulated pool of his own blood—utterly delightful—and had most likely been left for dead. *Ha to that.* If only they knew how hard he was to kill. Dark arts knew, his mother had tested those boundaries plenty.

Being alive had a serious downside in that he *felt* like he'd rather be dead. His mouth tasted like the inside of a desiccated corpse—don't ask how he knew that—and the rest of him was practically a shriveled husk. Between blood loss—a lot of blood loss, judging by the dried blanket of the blackened stuff coating him—and lying unconscious in the heat of the day, he seriously needed water.

Maybe then his brain would kick into gear and he could face the fact that Seliah was gone. Taken by those fucking hunters, no doubt. Phel was going to eviscerate him. Although, he noticed as he tried to move, the hunters had come pretty close to doing that already.

First things first: hope that the hunters hadn't taken that water flask. Steeling himself against the pain, he crawled into the box he'd made. It was hotter than House Hagith inside there, the air practically unbreathable. Maybe it was a good thing Seliah had lost her shit and refused to sleep in there. They might've suffocated. Or roasted. Probably the suffocating would've come first, though, and wow he needed some water if he wanted orderly thoughts again.

To his immense relief, their supplies remained where he'd stuffed them, at the back of the box. Barely any light made it inside—yet another flaw in his not-so-brilliant plan—and he cut himself on some sharp-edged weapon as he rummaged around. Swearing, he settled for dragging everything out into the daylight, belatedly reminded of how much an abdominal laceration hurt when you tried to move anything at all. Crawling backwards was illuminatingly agonizing.

Back outside, he sprawled amid the recovered treasures, casting about for the flask. The silver shone in the sun like a beacon, and Jadren imagined a House Euterpe choir sending up a hymn of joy. All praise to Gabriel Phel and his water wizardry! Unstopping the flask, he drank it dry, upended it, and drank again, his mental praise quickly turning to familiar grumbles over the poor mechanism. He supposed it was a good sign that he retained enough El-Adrel spirit to be annoyed by shitty engineering, even half-dead and with his vulnerable companion taken captive.

"They won't kill her," he muttered to himself. "She's too valuable."

Keeping that barely reassuring information firmly in mind, his thirst temporarily quenched, he bathed the wound crossing his body from shoulder to groin. "Got you stem to stern, as it were, boyo," he muttered, his father's voice coming unexpectedly to mind. As bonded familiar to Lady El-Adrel, Jadren's father hadn't been able to interfere with any of her experiments on their son, but he'd done what he could, begging permission to tend Jadren, comforting him within the boundaries allowed him. Jadren had never understood how his father maintained such a jaunty outlook, but he admired it. And had gotten so he counterfeited the outward personality pretty well.

His wound nominally surface clean and seeming to be knitting fairly well—at least, he felt a reasonable level of confidence that his entrails wouldn't actually fall out if he moved too suddenly—he used his machete to slice a blanket into bandages to wrap around his middle. It was an uncomfortably hot solution, but… better than losing said entrails. "Fat lot of good you did me," he griped at the machete as he worked.

"A weapon is only as good as its wielder," the machete replied in Gabriel Phel's voice. Or maybe it was Han's, the familiar who'd been teaching him weapons work. Either way, that the machete was speaking to him at all was a bad sign. *"It's not my fault you just stood there and let that hunter slice you open."*

"Yeah, yeah, yeah," he replied, tossing it down. "Be that way." Not exactly a brilliant retort, but it was all he had. "At least I don't have to wait around for someone to wield me. Who's just sitting there now, huh?"

The machete didn't reply.

Moving laboriously, he sorted through the supplies. There was no doubt he'd have to go after Seliah. The other option was to make his way back to House Phel to face his liege lord's fury and disappointment. Never let it be known that the prospect of disappointing the guy was what bothered him most.

Jadren hadn't wanted to respect, much less like, Gabriel Phel. The provincial farm boy turned rogue wizard and Convocation iconoclast should've been a bumbling rube, easy to disdain. Jadren had fully expected to find that. It was unfair that the man turned out to be honorable, dazzlingly powerful, and foolishly kind enough to treat Jadren like a human being.

And Nic… Well, the reputation of House Elal spoke for

itself, plus all the gossip Jadren had heard about Lady Veronica Elal hadn't prepared him to meet anyone but a viper in an expensive gown. Not a familiar who shared her magic generously with him, out of loyalty to her new house, as obviously distasteful to her as it had been to open herself to him that way.

The ruminations got him through the painful processes of triaging necessities. Though he was healing, the process would be slow and draining. He was lucky he'd been topped off with Seliah's magic when he was mortally wounded or he might not be in even this good of shape. Still, he wouldn't be able to carry much, especially if he hoped to move fast enough to catch up with Seliah and her captors. Who was he kidding? They would take her back to House Sammael and they had a massive head start. He wasn't catching up with anyone. But he could get there as quickly as possible. Settling on the bare minimum of supplies, he stuffed everything else back in the box and used a precious bit of magic to ward it. There—at least the thing had come in useful in the end.

Seliah had been forced to leave her bow and quiver behind, so he carried that for her, since she'd want it for after he liberated her. The only other weapon he took was his machete, as they'd made up with each other in the interim. "I didn't mean it, buddy," he told it. "It's just that you can be pretty cutting sometimes, you know?" He laughed at his own joke, though the machete seemed unamused. He buckled it on anyway and set to trudging back in the direction Seliah and he had already come.

Maybe he had managed to die and his eternal punishment

was walking up and down the length of this forsaken road in the oppressive forests of Sammael. Seemed about right, given the nature of his many sins.

THE BRIGHT SUN rising behind Jadren to cast rosy light against craggy House Sammael only served to highlight what a grim monstrosity the place truly was. It stank of cruelty and despair, reminding him vividly of home. The El-Adrel ancestors, however, had at least made an attempt to hide the more phantasmagoric aspects of the house. In fact, House El-Adrel looked quite innocent and shiny from the outside, with its copper roofs and clockwork drawbridges. It was the ever-shifting landscape of an interior that revealed the diabolical nature of the house of his birth.

Typical of House Sammael that they had to plaster their monstrosity on the surface, the level of horror almost ostentatious. They took their branding as the punishers of the Convocation much too seriously. The house oozed malevolence, fang-like towers rising from a rugged defile. Who built an enormous manse on a peak with slopes so steep the structure looked liable to pitch into the abyss below at any moment? Oh, wait, he knew the answer to that one: the Sammaels. Crazed, every last one of them.

Of course, after walking the remainder of the previous day and all night, resting only when he found himself suddenly faceplanted in the road—and still delirious from fever, blood loss, and exhaustion—his own rationality was also in question. Even more so than usual. With a sigh, he glanced around at the undisturbed remains of the hunters he and Seliah had defeated. Wishing he could fly across that valley, which was at least blessedly empty now of a river of attacking hunters, he continued trudging down the road that led to the house.

Why yes, he did intend to walk up, knock on the front door, and introduce himself. Phel had been so suspicious of that suggestion, but Jadren stood by the approach as well within Convocation etiquette. Also, he couldn't simply pluck Seliah out of the tower with his ambiguous, unassisted wizardry. However, if he'd learned nothing else from his devious maman, Jadren could wage a polite war of negotiation.

He knocked on those doors a few hours later, having passed into the phase of exhaustion where his head felt like it floated an arm's length above his shoulders. It was a restful sensation, in truth, and a welcome counterpoint to his boulder-heavy feet, swollen inside the boots. A lightning bolt of searing agony connected his top and bottom, the skin and muscle of his lacerated midsection repeatedly tearing open and attempting to knit again. Just like old times.

He knocked again, using the gruesome iron knocker that was shaped like a coiled whip. Sure it was the House Sammael symbol, but arrogantly over the top of them to make visitors use the thing to request entry. Especially when the molded braids turned out to be sharp enough to sting. Just charming in every way, the Sammaels.

At last the door creaked open—literally creaked with a

squealing of hinges that had to be deliberately unoiled, more theatrics—and a large man filled the partial opening. With wizard-black eyes and an intimidating bulk, the guy must be a Sammael minion who did double duty as guard and gatekeeper. Probably possessed some kind of physical magic like crushing bones or paralyzing muscles. Jadren gave him a jaunty grin.

"Hi. Wizard Jadren El-Adrel. Is Lord Igino Sammael at home to visitors?" He was betting Sergio had made himself scarce. Besides, why not go directly to the top? It would be enlightening to discover if Igino Sammael was aware of his son's recent escapades.

The other wizard's lip curled and Jadren felt his lungs stiffen, making it harder for him to draw breath. "Don't you mean Jadren Phel of House *Fell*?" he sneered.

News traveled fast. Though Jadren had used the easy word-play joke himself, he had to admit it wasn't actually funny. "Still a junior wizard and minion, not unlike your fine self," he answered with an easy smile and nonchalant shrug, as if he didn't feel the other wizard squeezing his lungs. It wasn't like the guy could kill him. Just a bit of friendly torture on the doorstep. "Temporary assignment, while scion of House El-Adrel is forever," he added pointedly.

"I've never heard of you," the wizard noted with considerable scorn, looking Jadren up and down. Jadren could just imagine the picture he presented: jacket and shirt hanging open, blood-soaked bandages wrapping his torso, pants barely strung together by a few laces, Mr. Machete suspended from his belt, smirking.

"That should give you pause," Jadren noted. "What kind of wizard would lie about being the son of Lady El-Adrel?" He bared his teeth, allowing some of the pain and stupid anger to leak through. Oh, look, he'd become a half-feral swamp creature himself. Seliah would be amused. "Now: Lord Sammael. Tell him I'm here."

The other wizard grunted, looking thoughtful—and like thought wasn't his strong suit to begin with. "If you are lying, there will be consequences." The large wizard glowered, Jadren's heart clenching painfully, and not from natural causes.

"I'd expect nothing else from the House Sammael Garden of Punishing Pain," Jadren agreed, tossing off a salute that a more perceptive person would recognize as sarcasm.

The gatekeeper-wizard finally stepped back, opening the door wider. "You can wait in the parlor," he said, the dainty word incongruous in the guy's beefy mouth, "while I find out if Lord Sammael is in residence."

He turned to lead the way, and Jadren saw for the first time that a familiar accompanied the gatekeeper. The smaller man had been hidden by the bigger wizard's bulk and seemed to be attached by a device connected to a belt around the wizard's waist. A cuff embedded in the belt clamped the familiar's hand to the bouncer's bare skin, making it nearly impossible for the wizard to lose the contact he needed to access the familiar's magic. On top of that, the familiar wore a heavy collar with chains running to cuffs around his wrists that looked to be a permanent setup. The familiar kept his head bowed, not raising his eyes to Jadren's curious assessment, focused on moving smoothly with his wizard's steps. No doubt if he failed to keep up, he'd be dragged.

Jadren found it rather unsavory. He'd always heard House Sammael kept a stable of unbonded familiars for general use by the Sammael minions. It wasn't the usual practice among Convocation houses, but it wasn't beyond the pale either. Those heads of houses the most compulsive about control and paranoid about mutiny often chose to deprive their minions of a bonded familiar, using that as a sort of chokehold on those wizards' access to magic. If a wizard depended on being in their liege wizard's good graces to access magic beyond their own, then they weren't likely to stage any kind of rebellion— nor would they have the power to do it. It made sense, if one leaned toward the authoritarian dictator end of the spectrum. To be fair, most heads of houses did.

Still, this was a foul deal for Sammael familiars, even more so than the usual shitty life-plan the Convocation employed to keep familiars docile and in their place. Used by all, cared for by none, the House Sammael general-use familiars sometimes turned up at auction to be acquired by low-rent wizards so desperate for a familiar that they'd snap up even one broken-spirited and drained nearly to death. They'd eke out a few months of service—maybe a year or two—before the familiar collapsed entirely, well away from House Sammael and any blame. Though everyone knew where the fault truly lay.

Still it wasn't as if anyone would criticize a high house for the practice, and Jadren wasn't going to be the first, much as he suddenly wanted to. Maybe it was contemplating fierce, innocent, and brave-hearted Seliah being in these walls, but for the first time Jadren experienced a decidedly queasy sensation about how House Sammael treated its familiars. Even though he knew Seliah was far too powerful and politically valuable to be treated as an appendage, a tool attached to a belt, a fury rose in him that he barely contained. If he hadn't learned so well never to reveal what he truly felt, he might have blown his insouciant cover.

Instead, he whistled idly as the wizard and his miserable human caboose led him to a parlor done entirely in black on black. Really with this color scheme? Jadren liked black just fine, particularly in formal wear and lingerie on beautiful women, but this was too much. He was going to start referring to Sammael as House Over the Top. He made a show of examining the decidedly gory art hung on the (black) walls until the door closed behind them, leaving him there.

Just to verify his supposition and appease his natural curiosity, Jadren checked the door handle. Yup: locked. The heavy (black) drapes concealed no windows, only more of the flocked (black on black) wallpaper. He was tempted to sit on one of the (black) brocaded sofas, but was afraid the last of his energy would leak out, along with unmentionable fluids, into the (black) cushions and leave him passed out when Lord Sammael inevitably arrived.

For arrive he would. Sammael wouldn't be able to resist. There had been the slightest chance that Lord Igino Sammael had gone to House Phel, but smart money had been on him staying home while Sergio took all the risk. Sure enough, Igino seemed to be in residence, no matter how cagily the gatekeeper-wizard had attempted to frame the information. Otherwise they'd have shut the door in Jadren's face rather than sequestering him in the black-on-black parlor of doom.

Fortunately for his flagging strength, the door soon smoothly opened—the Iblis-made lock making no sound as it disengaged—and Igino Sammael strolled in. A tall, elegant man with short, golden blond hair, he wore a (black on black) lounging robe over (black) silk trousers. Jadren had to swallow the impudent suggestion that the man refrain from sitting on any of the furniture, lest he be lost in the camouflage.

With a lingering and considering glance, Igino sat in a (black) wing-backed armchair, propped his (black) slippered feet on a (black) ottoman, and relaxed. With his wizard-black eyes like pits in his pale face, Igino looked momentarily as if a blond wig and a white mask with empty eye holes had been propped on the back of the chair.

It put up the hairs on the back of Jadren's neck, and his shook his head to clear it. The fever delirium was not working in his favor.

"Jadren El-Adrel," Igino murmured. "I'm surprised your esteemed mother let you off the leash."

"Not all bonds are visible," Jadren replied easily. "You know Maman."

"Indeed I know Katica better than most," Igino replied with a knowing leer. He and Lady Katica El-Adrel had been occasional lovers, particularly when she had a yen for sharper-edged sex than Jadren's gentle father could offer. A familiar found it difficult to be rough with their wizard, even when requested. It went against the grain. Besides which, Lady El-Adrel had a restless appetite and varied tastes—though Jadren had never understood how his maman could bear the company of Igino Sammael. Of course, that went both ways, so perhaps they were made for each other. "You look somewhat worse for wear, Jaddy-boy," Igino observed with an arched brow. "Did you crawl here from House Phel?"

"Builds character," Jadren answered, neither confirming nor denying. No telling how much Igino knew about Sergio's shenanigans, but Alise had been confident of the presence of a powerful Elal wizard in or around House Sammael—though Jadren still had yet to detect any of Elal's nosy spy-spirits—and it was beyond unlikely for a wizard of Igino's skill and power to be in residence and unaware of a wizard of that magnitude. Thus, either Igino hadn't been here or he was in on the plot. It would be terribly interesting to discover which it was, though that wasn't Jadren's highest priority. "How are dear Sergio and Sabrina?" he asked idly. "I thought they might pop in for refreshments, too."

His pointed reminder that Lord Sammael had neglected basic Convocation courtesy by not offering Jadren food or drink—or maybe a towel—bounced right off. "Sabrina is off at Convocation Academy," Igino replied blandly. "Though I realize you're not familiar with the academy's schedule," he added with a thin smile, likely hoping the jab at Jadren's lack of formal education would cover his prevarication. Of course, Jadren only knew it for a lie because Sabrina had pursued Alise Elal and her duo of unbonded-familiar refugees from Convocation Academy to House Phel, and then had accompanied Sergio in the charade where they "arrested" Nic. Igino was definitely going for full deniability. Still, it was a step too far. Convocation Academy would absolutely have notified Lord

Sammael about Sabrina's truancy as soon as they were aware of her absence. Even Jadren knew that.

"How odd," Jadren said, stroking his beard thoughtfully, a gesture he quickly regretted as his fingers made contact with the blood-caked, dirt-encrusted hairs. How detestable to be so filthy in front of the fastidious Igino. That was no doubt a major reason Sammael hadn't offered Jadren basic hospitality, enjoying Jadren's discomfort. Therefore, Jadren couldn't show that it bothered him in any way. "Young Wizard Sabrina showed up at House Phel, oh, a week ago, in Sergio's company." Jadren pretended to think, then brushed it off. "They waved about some official Convocation paperwork in the name of House Sammael. I'm surprised you didn't know."

Ha, take that! Jadren crowed privately to himself as Igino's pale cheeks flushed slightly, black eyes glittering, so that he looked a bit more like a person than an armchair with a face. Now Sammael was caught between acknowledging that he didn't know everything going on in his house—anathema to someone as controlling as Igino—or admitting his culpability in Lady Phel being taken into custody and removed to House Sammael rather than to Convocation Center. Depending on what Sergio and Sabrina were up to, which had to include their being off at House Phel causing trouble, Lord Sammael would have some explaining to do.

In fact, Jadren was discovering he held more cards in his hand than he'd realized. Now to play them to best effect. Assessing whether Seliah was in House Sammael and then taking possession of her was the primary goal, but perhaps he could eke out a bonus. Always a good thing to have a few extra cards up his sleeve, in case he had to deal with his mother. Perish the thought, but it was good to be prepared.

Igino still hadn't settled on his strategy for extricating himself from the pinch between truth and lie. "Oh," he mused, tapping a white finger against the arm of the (black) chair. "Did Sabrina play hooky and accompany Sergio on the errand to arrest Lady Phel? How very naughty of her." He shrugged and evinced a weary sigh. "Teenagers. Always a trial."

"I can only imagine," Jadren said. "Though bad behavior isn't limited to teens, is it?" Sergio was considerably older than Jadren. "Rather impulsive of Sergio to bring Lady Veronica Phel to House Sammael rather than to Convocation Center."

Igino didn't visibly tense, but the air thickened. Like his son, Igino's magic manifested in causing excruciating pain. Jadren was counting on Lord Sammael being unwilling to antagonize his sometime lover and head of powerful House El-Adrel by attempting to kill her son, but he wouldn't be above a bit of torture. In fact, Jadren's wounds throbbed that much more—could be Sammael subtly prodding or simply his own increasing exhaustion. Either way, he didn't have time to dally.

"We thought it safer for Lady Veronica *Elal* here," Igino said, emphasizing Nic's birth house. Had Jadren been slightly less tired and more intemperate, he would've done a little jig at Sammael's admission of complicity. "We believed Lord Phel to be on the verge of death and the familiar improperly bonded. Given our longstanding and cherished alliance with House Elal, I thought to do my old friend, Piers Elal, the favor of keeping his daughter safe. Who knows what sort of rogue wizard might've taken it into his head to bond our sweet Nic for himself otherwise?" Igino's raised brow made it clear he suspected Jadren of being just that low and desperate.

"Oh, then Lady Phel is in residence?" Jadren practically cooed. "I couldn't possibly leave without giving my respects to my liege lady in that case. Maman would expect nothing less." He let his voice drop with the severity of the warning embedded in those final words. Sammael wasn't necessarily in Lady El-Adrel's confidence, but they were cut from the same cloth. He'd at least suspect the reasons Katica had gone to pains to plant her son in Phel's household—and that she wouldn't appreciate Sammael's interference with her carefully laid plans. Especially as it seemed that the outcome of the rescue and the return of the lord and lady to House Phel was still in question.

"You can reassure your lady mother that Veronica... *Phel* has returned to her house and wizard master." Igino gritted out the words, falling short of clawing at the armrests of his (black) chair, but not by much. "Or so I assume. She has quite vanished from her chambers here. Imagine my distress at returning home to discover the entire top of a tower missing and a guest along with it."

"You're not concerned?" Jadren asked, making a show of frowning. "It could be that a rogue wizard breached your defenses to unlawfully take possession of Lady Phel, just as you feared, and hoped to prevent."

Sammael nearly crawled out of his skin at the suggestion that a simple rogue wizard could perform such a feat. "I have it on authority that Lord Phel himself retrieved his property and worked an unusual spell to do so. Apparently he was operating under the misguided notion that his familiar was being held against her will. He understands nothing of Convocation ways." Igino sniffed, giving every appearance of looking offended. "If he'd simply requested an audience and asked politely, we would have naturally discussed the issue with him. There was no need for *violence*. So vulgar. So unnecessary."

"Guess Gabriel Phel wasn't as dead as rumor made out, eh?" Jadren winked conspiratorially. "The wizard is certainly an unpredictable element, rather fanatical about his property. Just imagine what he'd do if he felt compelled to return." He let the warning linger in the air. If Igino had captured Seliah, he had to be thinking about the possible consequences from Lord Phel. The hunters might have been acting on previous orders—or had simply been instructed to capture any wandering familiars, which was likely, as they weren't all that bright—and had taken Seliah prisoner through sheer bad luck. If Jadren played this right, he could position himself as helping Igino out of a bind. "Perhaps I can be of assistance?" he wondered blandly.

"Yesss." Igino drew out the word, regarding Jadren thoughtfully. "Katica was canny in her foresight, as usual, in placing you in that household. Tell me, how did she manage it?"

Jadren waggled a finger at him. This was going even better than he'd hoped. "Ah-ah-ah. That would be telling. I'm curious—*have* you heard from Sergio and Sabrina? Because if they've gone off to a certain house, perhaps believing the lord to be dead…" He shrugged fatalistically, watching Igino's pale mask of a face with keen attention.

Lord Sammael showed no emotion, flicking his fingers.

"Natural selection operates well in these scenarios. Any potential heir too stupid to survive is one I can eliminate from a very long list. I have many other children."

"Eminently logical," Jadren replied. "Gabriel Phel has none—and only one sister."

Igino tapped long fingers on the arm of his chair. "In light of the long and cherished alliance between House Sammael and House El-Adrel, perhaps we *would* benefit from a bit of information exchange and mutual aid," Igino offered at last. "Let me ring for refreshments, perhaps a grooming imp, as well? Along with a fresh suit of clothing. And, of course, I'd be delighted to loan the services of our in-house Refoel healer. I know El-Adrel is good for it. And you and I can talk further."

"Sounds fantastic," Jadren agreed, delighted with the bribe, at last plopping himself on one of the (black) sofas. Now that he had Sammael where Jadren wanted him, he wasn't above wiping his grimy hands on the upholstery, enjoying Igino's wince. That's what he got for taking so fucking long to offer basic hospitality. Now to walk the line between giving Sammael apparently useful information that Jadren's maman wouldn't mind being leaked and without harming House Phel at the same time.

Hopefully the delay wouldn't worsen Seliah's situation, especially if Jadren lost this particular gamble and she hadn't been brought here after all. A dangerous game. Good thing he excelled at this sort of thing.

The stakes for him were the highest they'd ever been.

~ 8 ~

I T WAS ALL her fault, Selly reminded herself yet again. If she hadn't been so weak-minded that she'd panicked at the prospect of getting in Jadren's box, then she wouldn't be wearing this iron collar, trapped in this dank and horrible cell, facing an even worse future.

And Jadren wouldn't be dead.

That was the worst part—and she might as well have his blood on her hands, as her actions had led directly to his death. She hadn't even fought adequately, hadn't even loosed an arrow before those hunters had her pinned. Then she'd seen Jadren cut down, his cleaved-open body limp and lifeless on the leaf litter, and she hadn't been able to help him. The hunters had bodily dragged her away, unmoved by her tears and raging, finally gagging her and binding her hands and feet, sadly reproaching her for being a recalcitrant familiar.

To think that being afraid of a stupid box had brought her to this. Probably there was a life lesson in there somewhere, but she had a hard time caring at this point. She was a captive in House Sammael, Jadren was dead because of her, and who knew what had happened at House Phel? They all might be dead, too. Even if they were alive, they'd assume she was somewhere in the Meresin or Sammael wilds with Jadren. When they never returned, eventually her family would have to face the most likely scenario: that she and Jadren had perished.

Half true, anyway.

Regardless, no one would be coming to dramatically rip off roofs and rescue *her*. She hadn't missed the significance of being dumped in a windowless cell clearly deep in the bowels of the mountain beneath House Sammael. They weren't running the risk of Gabriel being able to reach her as he had with Nic. Never mind that he had no bond to Selly's magic and couldn't perform the same long-distance trick, Sammael was clearly taking no chances.

She had yet to meet anyone from the Sammael family, which concerned her. So far only hunters, human guards, and lower-level wizards had dealt with her. She knew the wizards by their eyes, the buzz of their magic, and by the familiars so grotesquely tethered to them. One wizard had caught her aghast expression and grinned, turning so Selly could have a good, long look at the familiar chained to her. The middle-aged man with his hand cuffed against the woman's back had never looked up or even seemed to register anything outside himself.

The wizard had stroked a hand down Selly's bare arm. "Your magic smells delicious. What is that, water? It's sweet. Give me a taste," she suggested, "and I'll arrange for you to have special treatment."

"I'll pass," Selly bit out.

"See my friend here?" The wizard hooked a thumb at the

man behind her, who still gave no sign of sentience. "Could be you, pretty one. Keep making trouble and it will be." Fortunately, the woman left it at that, locking Selly into the pit alone.

Was that truly to be her fate? She couldn't bear the thought. It had also occurred to her, however, that she might be given a choice. The others had talked on the journey and before they left to rescue Nic, speculating as to Sergio Sammael's purpose. He needed a familiar and potential bride for when he took over House Sammael. And Selly recalled Jadren's taunting—in her grief over his death, she was actually nostalgic for his barbed comments—about her value as Gabriel's sister. She might not understand all the nuances of Convocation politics, but it seemed she'd be an inevitable second choice to be bride of Sammael.

If they offered her that, with the alternative being one of these tethered familiars, would she have the fortitude to refuse? Probably not. As she paced the small cell, trying to at least keep her muscles limber, she wished she could consult with Nic. Her new sister-in-law had faced a similar situation— at least so far as in being a familiar from a high house and having to accept her inevitable fate of being bonded to a wizard. Nic had employed a strategy of some sort. Yes, it had fallen apart because of Gabriel, but no one could predict the element of chaos her brother brought to everything. Still, Nic had spine and hadn't been about to resign herself to a life where she had no power. Selly needed to figure out a way to follow that example. She needed to get much smarter, fast.

So, when the female wizard who'd threatened her returned, Selly drew herself up in that regal pose she'd seen Nic use. "I protest this treatment and demand to see Lord Sammael," she declared. Dialogue from a novel she'd read long ago, but the best she could do.

The wizard regarded her with dry amusement. "Familiars demand nothing of their betters, pretty thing, but it so happens I'm to bring you to Lord Sammael, so you get your wish." She chuckled drily. "Though you should be more careful what you wish for. Turn around, wrists behind your back."

Much as Selly didn't want to comply, she did. Talking to Lord Sammael, however awful he might turn out to be, was better than rotting away in this cell. She even managed to contain the shudder of revulsion as the wizard clamped heavy manacle on her wrists, binding them together. The woman turned Selly around by the simple expedient of twisting her shoulders, then clipped a leash to the collar. Striding out of the cell, she pulled Selly along without paying further attention to her, and Selly found herself walking behind the wizard next to the tethered man, who shuffled along with practiced alacrity, still seeming unaware of his circumstances.

"Hi, I'm Seliah," she said to the man.

"Don't speak to it," the wizard said without particular bite. "It's unseemly, even for another familiar."

Selly didn't comment. The man hadn't seemed to hear either of them anyway. Perhaps waking him from whatever dream got him through this bizarre half-existence would be more cruel than anything else. She knew something about those mists and how, while their numbing fog could be maddening—further maddening, anyway—their shrouds also provided a level of comfort and protection.

They proceeded upward through twisting hallways and sporadic staircases, the décor growing grander as they went. The manse was clearly centuries old and bore witness to the generational wealth the Sammaels cultivated. Everything was meticulously maintained—markedly unlike House Phel with its graceful, homey decrepitude—and all in black. From the plush rugs to the brocaded wallpaper to the silken upholstery to the velvet window treatments to the polished wood, everything was in shades of black. Before this, Selly would've said black came in only one shade, and she'd have been woefully wrong. She'd also have said she liked black, but this overwhelming show of it felt oppressive and unnatural. She found herself longing for the vast and nuanced palette of nature even more than usual.

Finally they arrived at a salon not far from what appeared to be the great doors at the front of the house. Windows flanking the doors showed the road that wound up the crag, and beautiful blue skies beyond. The sight made tears spring to her eyes and her heart clench with longing. The jerk of the leash brought her back to the here and now, the wizard giving her an unpleasant smile. "This way," she instructed, yanking Selly away from the view.

Selly followed the wizard into the salon, braced to confront whoever might be inside. Then gasped in utter shock and a surprising stab of unadulterated joy. "Jadren!"

The El-Adrel wizard raised a supercilious auburn brow at her. "Hallo, little familiar. Didn't escape me so easily, did you?" He lounged elegantly on the black sofa, well-groomed and even clean-shaven, with no sign of the mortal injury that had felled him. He wore new clothes, all in black, that fit him as if tailored for him. They weren't the fighting leathers he'd worn on the quest, but looked more suited for a formal party. In point of fact, he held a glass of very dark red wine—apparently the Sammaels couldn't get black wine, or they surely would have—and raised it to his lips, sipping as if he didn't have a care in the world, as if she weren't filthy, hungry, and chained. Only his glittering gaze over the rim of the glass belied his pose, giving her a warning she couldn't quite interpret.

This was like one of those nightmares where she was supposed to act in a play but no one had told her what role she was to perform nor what her lines should be. She settled for saying nothing, only glowering at him in all-purpose simmering betrayal. Jadren's gaze slid off her again and returned to the other occupant of the room, a handsome older man with blond hair, wizard's eyes, and a regal air. "Really, Lord Igino Sammael," Jadren tutted. "You couldn't have at least hosed her down for me?"

The blond man, Lord Sammael, apparently, flicked his gaze over her. "I doubt it would help much. She's a scrawny, unattractive little thing. Leave us," he added, without looking at the wizard. She seemed to know who he meant, because she dropped the leash with a heavy clatter and an unpleasant tug on Selly's neck, then left, taking the tethered man with her.

"Stay a few days," Lord Sammael suggested, twirling his own glass of wine. "We can clean the familiar up for you, perhaps teach her a few things. I've been told she's quite rebellious. Another Phel rogue never properly trained. A disgrace to the Convocation and all we stand for," he mused with considerable distaste, as if the existence of House Phel was a personal insult to him.

Selly was watching Jadren—who appeared to be considering the possibility, the fucker. She glared daggers at him and he cocked his head, giving her a condescending smile. "She *is* awfully starved and mangy," he observed thoughtfully, then waved a negligent hand. "But, physical beauty is only icing with familiars. I agree that the real shame here is that this one was let go to seed. Hard to say if she can be recovered at all. Still, if you'd been to House Phel, you wouldn't be at all surprised. Backwater rubes, the lot of them." He swirled his wine and drank with an appreciative sound. "This is the first decent glass of wine I've had in ages."

"Then stay." Lord Sammael gestured to the remains of the feast, only crumbs remaining, laid before Jadren. "You deserve a bit of the finer life after what you've been through in the service of House El-Adrel and, by association, House Sammael."

Selly stiffened, shooting daggers at Jadren with her eyes. Or, at least, trying to. If she were a wizard like Gabriel, she'd hurl silver spikes at him. Was all of this an inevitable betrayal? Jadren had admitted to being an El-Adrel spy, but she'd thought... what? That he wasn't her enemy? Sammael was surely their enemy, and here Jadren sat in their house with their lord, happily feasting and talking about her like she was nothing. Less than nothing.

"I wish I *could* stay," Jadren said on a heavy sigh, setting down his wine and getting to his feet. He gave Selly a decidedly jaundiced look. "But duty calls. Maman wants the Phel familiar and you know how she is about waiting."

Lord Sammael smiled knowingly, sensually. It was not a nice smile. "Oh, I *know*. Making her wait for it is one of my favorite techniques to torment her. It's what keeps her coming back for more."

Jadren ignored the sexual implication. Or maybe Selly had imagined it. "So, now that you've returned my property to me, I must be on my way."

Sammael frowned slightly. "You'll explain the misunderstanding to your dear mother. The familiar is unbonded, so my hunters had no way of knowing she was yours."

"Nor of knowing who I was, attempting to kill me like that." Jadren tsked, then produced a genial smile that didn't fool Selly.

Lord Sammael sighed, acting wounded. "I did make it up to you. My hunters are simple creatures and cannot always be trusted to understand the complicated relationships between humans. Next time, be sure to identify yourself to them."

"Hopefully, there won't be a next time," Jadren replied, a hint of a lethal edge beneath the cheerful tone, "or even your *special* relationship with my maman won't spare you from her wrath."

Yuck. Selly hadn't imagined that sexual implication. Did she even want to know? No. No, she didn't.

"You know, Jaddy-boy…" Sammael tapped the arm of the chair with a black-manicured nail. "I believe you never did explain why you haven't bonded the chit already. Surely you've had the opportunity. Unless you lack the ability?"

Selly listened keenly for Jadren's answer. He hadn't mentioned the bonding requiring particular ability. Was this the reason he'd never had a bonded familiar?

Jadren only laughed, shaking his head. "You actually believe I'd bond a familiar without Maman checking her out first? Especially one in this condition." He looked Selly over, shaking his head in dismay.

"I always forget how obedient you lot are to her," Sammael answered with a tight-lipped smile.

Jadren shrugged as if entirely unbothered. "I don't forget. Speaking of which, I'll take my familiar now." He strolled over to Selly and sneered at the collar and leash. "You can keep your chains."

"Are you certain you don't want them? You seem to have difficulty hanging onto the creature."

Curling a lip, Jadren unclipped the leash, then spun her around, undoing the manacles. "House El-Adrel doesn't approve of such public displays. So gauche."

"Just private ones," Sammael quipped with a smirk.

Jadren hooked a finger in the collar and tugged. "The lock? I assume it's coded to you. Maman would be most displeased to find your branded restraints on El-Adrel property."

Lord Sammael's expression darkened and, to Selly's surprise, he actually seemed dismayed. "Overenthusiasm on the hunters' part," he explained, rising and tapping the iron collar with a finger. It released and Selly closed her eyes in relief, holding back from any further display that might reveal how very much she'd hated the thing.

"I have a solution," Sammael said, looking pleased. "I'll

have one of my carriages convey you to House El-Adrel. It's
the least I can do to ensure you and your prize travel safely to
your mother. That will make up for lost time."

No. No. No. Selly chanted the denial mentally, willing
Jadren to be her friend and turn down the offer. Or, she'd take
him being her enemy, as long as he refused the carriage. She
did *not* want to go to House El-Adrel. Jadren seemed to have
forgotten her existence, considering Sammael thoughtfully. "I
couldn't possibly impose," he finally said.

Sammael waved that away. "No imposition. It's the sec-
ond-best carriage as Sergio is off with the best on that errand
we discussed." He slid his gaze significantly to Selly and away
again. "Really, I insist."

Jadren shrugged and nodded. "Why not, then? I'd love a
ride."

"Excellent. Shall we have another glass of wine while I
have the familiar bathed?"

"Too late now." Jadren sighed heavily. "I'll just have to put
up with the stink."

Selly growled twisting away from him, but his gaze pinned
her with glittering warning. Wrapping insistent fingers around
her wrist, he held her close to his side. She hated him. She was
furious with him, so why did the sensation of his firm grip give
her a thrill of pleasure? It was a terrible time to be thinking of
it, but she couldn't help remembering how he'd held her on his
lap while she sobbed. How he'd seemed to understand why
she couldn't get in the box. How he'd been kind and comforting and hadn't thrust her away even when she impulsively
kissed him. Yes, she'd been half-crazed as he often accused her,

and yet he'd taken care of her.

Now he held her wrist tightly, but not enough to be painful. "No trouble, poppet, or we put the collar back on you." He raised a brow, waiting for her acquiescence.

She nodded, resolving to escape later.

"Have you Fascinated her then?" Sammael asked. "She's considerably more tame with you."

Jadren grinned. "How else do you think I wooed her away from Phel? That, and a few other enticements, if you know what I mean," he added suggestively.

Sammael laughed appreciatively. "The apple didn't fall far from the tree, I suppose." He gestured them out of the salon.

It seemed an interminable walk to the entrance, close as it was, Jadren and Sammael chatting and laughing like old friends. Jadren still held her wrist and she didn't fight him. She wouldn't, not until she was away from this house with its collars and chains and tethered, mindless puppets of familiars. They had to wait for the carriage to come around, at which point Jadren practically shoved her inside before embracing Sammael, thanking him for the hospitality.

She'd already tried the handle on the other side, considering leaping out and making a break for it. Surely scaling these steep rocks couldn't be worse than climbing trees. Before she made her move, however, Jadren snagged her wrist again, clamping on with a fierce look.

"Don't," he said, reaching over her to pull the door shut again, triggering some magical mechanism to lock it. The move pressed him against her, his freshly cleaned hair smelling of spices that should've been appealing, but that smelled more like House Sammael than Jadren's natural scent. Still, she nearly leaned into him for comfort, which made no sense at all.

Then he was gone again, turning to wave jovially to Lord Sammael as the carriage smoothly shot into motion. It surprised a squeak out of her and she grabbed wildly at the black leather seat with her free hand, unreasoning panic fluttering inside her. If not for the locked door and Jadren's restraining grip, she might've flung herself out of the carriage, uncaring of the steep drop on the other side.

"Elemental powered," Jadren informed her in world-weary tone. "You remember the rules, poppet. Speak only when spoken to." He gave her another of those meaningful looks she didn't know how to interpret. But he was also calling her 'poppet' again when he said he wouldn't, so there seemed to be some kind of code there.

"I thought you were dead," she said, defiant and also needing to know the truth. Besides, he'd spoken to her, hadn't he? Also besides, he wasn't the boss of her.

He arched a brow. "Clearly you were mistaken about my death."

"But I saw—"

"But," he interrupted sharply, "I'm willing to give you the benefit of the doubt, that you believed me incapacitated and otherwise wouldn't have abandoned me as you did. You're lucky our good friends at House Sammael were able to rescue you."

"Lucky!" she spat. "Do you have any idea what—"

He clapped a hand over her mouth, tightening his grip on her wrist even more when she fought him. "Hush, little familiar, or I'll gag you. I tire of your incautious prattle." His wizard-black eyes bored into hers, intense with that hidden meaning. Taking his hand off her mouth, he slid his fingers lightly over her jaw, gentleness in his touch now as he lightly gripped her chin and turned her head to make her look at a spot near the roof of the carriage. He flicked his gaze at it, then back, raising his brows.

She looked where he pointed her—not that she had much choice—and saw nothing of note. Still... her skin crawled a little when she gazed there too long, an odd sensation creeping up the back of her neck, much like the chill of fear she remembered from telling ghost stories around the campfire.

Then the magic inside her seemed to surge, to move of its own accord, like water stirring in a shimmer of moonlight. Selly didn't have much of a relationship with her magic. For most of her life, she hadn't known it was there—or, if she recognized its presence in herself, she hadn't known what it was. Magic felt like madness, the mists that had dragged her under and made the world an incomprehensible, ever-shifting landscape.

Now, at Jadren's silent insistence, she became aware that her magic was reacting to a presence. It was actually trying to inform her of something, and that feeling was real, not a figment of madness. The stunning revelation cut through the panicked need to flee, to demand answers from Jadren. For the first time, she understood that this curse of magic that she'd never asked for could serve a useful purpose. She relaxed in Jadren's grip, focusing on the oddness in the upper corner, then meeting his gaze and subtly nodding.

Relief softened the unrelenting black of his eyes, which she suddenly realized were very close, his mouth near enough for her to scent the wine on his breath, warm and fragrant against her lips. His fingers on her chin released, stroking the skin along the line of her jaw absently as he gazed at her, seeming to search her face. Was that concern in his expression? His fingertips trailed over her throat, caressing the bruised and abraded skin where the heavy collar had rested, soothing, offering... an apology? She shivered at the caress, warming to his touch, feeling herself melting and wanting more.

He inhaled, his touch against her skin seeming to drink her in, his expression taut. It seemed that he, too, had things he wasn't saying. She just didn't know and she had so many questions. If she could just ask—

Jadren seemed to read that impulse in her, shaking his head minutely, eyes hardening again in warning, the fingers on her throat briefly encircling and clasping. She pressed her lips together in resignation and his mouth quirked in an answering half-smile. He released her throat and tapped a finger against her lips. "There's a good poppet," he murmured. "Quiet and obedient, just as you should be."

The warning still in his gaze, he eased away from her, then held up the wrist he still held. Slowly he relaxed his grip until he loosely encircled her wrist with his fingers, a questioning lift to his brows. She made a face, but nodded, silently promising not to fling herself from the carriage. Patting her hand, he set it down. "Are you hungry, sweetling? There's food and drink for you, little familiar, so you may maintain your strength."

He popped open a polished wood cabinet set in the center

of the spacious carriage. The interior was as luxurious as House Sammael, and the cabinet expanded with a silky movement to display trays of cold and hot food, along with a bottle of wine set in a bin of crushed ice.

"Sparkling wine?" Jadren inquired, extracting the bottle and studying the label, then glancing at her. "No, I suppose it would be a bad idea to indulge." Another message there. He made her a plate, with generous portions, then handed it to her. "Have as much as you like, I already ate. By the way, your things are in that bag there."

Belatedly she noted the bag on the floor beside the cabinet, her bow and quiver protruding from one side. It made her feel absurdly teary that he'd brought her things, which meant he was on her side. Except the fact he'd been so cozy with Igino Sammael, and now Jadren was taking her to House El-Adrel.

She clutched the plate and staring at it. She was so hungry, and yet her stomach felt too tight to eat. All of this was so surreal. Had she lost her mind again? "I don't *want* to go to House El-Adrel," she whispered.

"Nobody ever said you were stupid," Jadren remarked, lying back and kicking out his long legs, crossing them at the ankles and folding his arms over his chest. "Eat. I'm going to get some sleep, since I got none at all, trudging all night to recover your petite ass. Do *not* disturb me. That's an order, poppet."

~ 9 ~

J ADREN SEETHED WITH the anxiety of inaction as he eyed the sentry spirit hovering in the upper corner of the carriage. Feigning sleep, he kept his lids cracked just enough to monitor the thing's movements. As exhausted as he was, he didn't dare fall asleep and let down his guard, lest Seliah take it in her head to do something foolish, like trying to escape him. He also wanted to be aware in case the spirit took action or—*please, please, please let it happen*—left to report to its wizard.

It would be futile to attempt to escape the carriage while it watched. They'd be recaptured immediately and Jadren would've lost all of his leverage. No, their best bet was to wait for it to go. Surely the thing wouldn't watch them all the way to House El-Adrel. Eventually—hopefully sooner, rather than later, so they'd be as far away from House El-Adrel as possible when it happened—it would go and he and Seliah would have a fighting chance of evading these particular coils of doom. He couldn't quite believe he was so very fucked that he'd been corralled into going to the house of his ill-conceived birth.

To think that he'd been practically begging for an ele-mental-powered carriage before this. Be careful what you wish for. *It would have been nice,* he thought to the receivers of wishes, whoever that might be, the capricious sods, *if the elemental-powered carriage you delivered hadn't been permanently set to take us only to the one place I least want to go.*

Just in case wishing actually worked, he kept himself awake by adding wishes for the sentry spirit to leave. So far as he knew, it couldn't report back to its wizard master from a distance. It clearly had been stationed in the carriage to monitor them—he was supremely lucky Seliah possessed the wit to heed his silent warnings not to reveal too much in front of it—so now he fastened his hopes on the necessity of it eventually departing to report back. Otherwise they'd soon be on the doorstep of House El-Adrel. At which point, things would only get worse for both of them—and he wasn't sure how much more Seliah could take.

I don't want to go to House El-Adrel, Seliah had whispered in that broken, quiet voice, and he'd been hard-pressed to keep his supercilious, faithful-scion-of-House-El-Adrel attitude. He'd had to feign sleep to stop himself from touching her again, her magic still so deliciously buoyant despite all the hunters and House Sammael had done to her. Seeing her collared and chained, bruised, scratched, and beaten had about pushed him over the edge. Worst of all had been the darkening of those pretty amber eyes at seeing that he'd been drinking wine with Igino Sammael while she'd suffered.

She'd believed him dead—and had been grieved by it. More than being afraid for herself, she'd actually been bothered by his apparent death and that first flash of joy when she'd gasped his name humbled him beyond belief. The guilt was nearly more that he could bear, too.

Especially when she'd caught up to the situation, looking so deeply wounded by his apparent betrayal that he'd nearly given up the game right there. Fierce and determined Seliah might be, but she was far too innocent to grasp the malevolent nuances of the layers of plotting that consumed him. He wanted nothing more than to explain everything to her and regain some of scanty trust they'd built.

Trust he'd had no business indulging in the first place. He didn't have friends and, even if he did, Seliah couldn't ever be one of them. It had been irresponsible of him to be anything but awful to her, something he needed to remedy immediately.

It would be far better for her to hate and distrust him, just in case they did end up in the bowels of his birth house—now or later. She'd play her role more convincingly if she believed he'd betrayed her and that the part he'd be forced to act with his darling maman was his real self. In addition, having Seliah loathe him would help him keep track of *which* self he was supposed to be. He'd lost his compass somewhere in the happy company of the House Phel idealists. No wonder spies in stories were always portrayed as being so enigmatic and mercurial. After a point, it became confusing who he was double-crossing.

In fact, he wasn't at all sure whose side he was on.

No, wait, of course he knew the answer to that: he was on the side of Team Jadren. Dark arts knew no one else was. He'd figured that out a long time ago and he'd better not lose sight of that singular truth. Seliah was a survivor. If he could help her without jeopardizing himself, he would. Otherwise, she'd do better believing him to be the enemy, just in case he had to be that to save his own hide. Yes, better she remain ignorant and never have any idea how he felt about her.

And how do you feel about her? An insidious internal voice asked.

I feel sorry for her, he replied to himself, satisfied with that answer. *She's an innocent kid caught up in a crap deal she has no frame of reference to understand.*

You didn't think of her as a child when she kissed you, or when she trembled against you just now, the voice pointed out.

She's terrified and justifiably so. Of course she's quaking with fear and stress.

You and I know that's not why she trembled.

You and I are the same person, he bit out. Just great—he was taking arguing with himself to an entirely new level. This was like being back in his maman's experimental chambers, feeling his mind and personality splinter into fragments. Wonderful.

You like her, the voice said.

I like protecting a valuable resource and thus my own skin, he retorted.

You love her, the voice sing-songed, now sounding exactly like his next oldest sibling, Ozana, back when her cruelty consisted only of childhood taunting. *You want to kiss her and marry her.*

"Shut up!" he snarled, clapping a hand to his forehead as he did, belatedly aware that he'd spoken aloud. And that—fuck him—he'd apparently fallen asleep. Careless and negligent. Fortunately, or not, depending on how you sliced it, the sentry spirit remained in place. They weren't free of it, but he hadn't lost any valuable escape time by missing its departure either.

"Are you all right?" Seliah asked tentatively, gazing at him owlishly, laying a light hand on his forearm.

"Did I say you could speak?" he snapped back.

"You *did* speak first," she pointed out, sounding an awful lot like his dream voice before Ozana took over with her infantile teasing.

"Now I'm speaking last. Be quiet so I can sleep."

She moved, curling up her legs on the seat and scooting over to lean her head against his shoulder. He held himself rigid, hoping she'd get the hint. Her magic infused him through the connection, minty and fresh, green leaves and high mountain lakes, moonlight on snowfall. He wanted to roll around in her magic like a cat in catnip. He shrugged his shoulder, trying to pop her off of him, but she was back in persistent feline mode, cuddling closer and working her head into the crook of his shoulder and neck. It couldn't possibly be comfortable for her—it certainly wasn't for him—but she stayed there, making soft, snuggly sounds he found perversely erotic, fantasies blooming in his mind of other things he could do to make her moan like that.

He was definitely losing his mind.

In fact, he nearly lost control entirely when her lips brushed his ear, the sensation lightninging straight to his groin. "You can sleep," her voice wisped into his ear, very nearly soundless. "I can watch it and wake you if anything changes."

"Get off me," he growled. "You're filthy and you stink."

Undaunted, she wrapped her arms around his waist, managing to slide the insidious things around his rigidly held posture, then pressed a kiss to the hollow beneath his ear, sending another bolt of lightning through his body. "I mean it," she whispered. "You walked all night to rescue me."

Rescue? Uh oh. This wasn't good if she'd settled on that for his motivation.

"Sleep while I keep watch," she continued, lips against his skin. "Let me do that for you, Jadren."

The sound of his name spoken by her throaty, bedchamber voice galvanized him. Steeling himself, he unfolded and seized her by the waist. Picking her up bodily—she weighed no more than a starving kitten—he deposited her on the opposite seat, taking note of how she immediately scooted to the corner farthest from the sentry spirit. He hadn't been sure if she could see it, untrained as she was. Familiars couldn't wield magic, of course, but many of them, particularly the more powerful ones, could passively sense the presence of magic. Whichever wizard had parked this spirit with them, however—Jadren's coin was on Lord Elal himself—was powerful and deft enough to erase extraneous magical signatures. But Seliah knew it was there all right, though whether she knew *what* to watch for was something else entirely. And he couldn't teach her the fine points, not without betraying to their spy that he wasn't simply using Seliah Phel, as per his maman's instructions.

"Sit," he instructed Seliah in his most condescending tone, pointing at her. "Stay."

Her amber eyes flashed with ire. That was better. He plopped himself back onto the opposite seat, glaring at her disdainfully. "I realize you may be Fascinated by me—who could blame you?—but cuddling up to me won't get you anywhere. Quite the opposite, in fact. You've been spoilt and coddled all your life. It's time you learn your place."

"My *place?*" she echoed, managing to look both waifish and powerfully angry at the same time, as only she could.

Dark arts take him—that combination of sweet naivety and gritty spine undid him every time. "Yes. Your. Place." He spaced out the words, making it clear he suspected her of being too stupid to fully understand. "You are uneducated in anything that matters, from a backwater swamp so ignorant that no one had the wit to recognize you as a potent familiar for over a *decade*, jeopardizing your sanity and your very life. You're lucky I was able to save you from your degenerate state."

"*Gabriel* saved me," she retorted, offended on her brother's behalf where she wouldn't be for an insult to herself.

He waved that off. "Oh, Phel took the brunt of the initial backlash, sure. More the fool he for doing so, as it very nearly killed him. But remember that *I* am the one who bled off the rest of your foul, stagnant magic. You should be showing *me* your gratitude." He made a show of yawning—which was a mistake, as his jaw nearly cracked as his body took over, begging for sleep. "You're welcome," he added, as nastily as he could manage.

"I *am* grateful," she replied softly. "Thank you."

"Don't bother about it. I had my reasons."

"Then why did you bring it up?"

"The question you should be asking is why I saved you."

She didn't fire the question back at him immediately, unlike her usual quick witted self. Instead, she considered, assembling the clues in her mind, amber eyes darkening as the puzzle pieces formed an image for her. "That's what you were planted in House Phel to do: abduct me."

Tossing off a jaunty salute, he grinned at her growing consternation. He didn't love doing this, but he was glad to see her growing angrier—she'd need her anger—and he couldn't help but be pleased at the success of his manipulation. That was a key to acting the part: find the emotion in yourself and turn it to the purpose at hand. The grim pleasure he felt at his own cleverness could be rechanneled into creating the appearance of satisfaction at his trap having worked.

"Not *you*, in particular, poppet. You were a delightful surprise, as House Phel had been surprisingly effective at keeping your existence a secret. Naughty them." Now he was working to feed the sentry spirit, and thus its wizard guide, selected information also. "We'd rather thought Nic would be up for grabs, given Phel's enormous lapse in losing track of her and then his embarrassing lack of education, much like yours, which it seemed had prevented him from bonding her correctly. Imagine my raptures at discovering your existence! The only thing more enticing than an unbonded familiar is an unbonded familiar who is unknown to the Convocation and so ignorant as to be a blank slate, so malleable and moldable."

"What are you saying?" Her voice had dropped to a bare whisper, her face pinched, gray under the golden tone.

He tutted at her. "Perhaps you *are* an idiot. Don't pretend you can't put one and one together and make two—or is that math too advanced for whatever they teach in your one-room-schoolhouses?"

"How about you just tell me what two signifies," she replied flatly.

He was getting to her. She still wanted to believe he was her friend, but she was wavering. He'd successfully sown enough of the tiny black seeds of doubt to poison the camaraderie he'd carelessly allowed to fester between them. Now he need only water those seeds and encourage the choking vines to grow. This was what he wanted and what she needed. He shouldn't feel this cloying sense of... surely not loss.

Shoring up his resolve, he infused his attitude with sneering pride. "House El-Adrel hoped for Nic—and I must say I'm a bit disappointed, as her magic is as intoxicating as anything I've ever tasted. Dark arts but that woman is delicious—but that's water under the bridge, so to speak." He made a show of chortling at his own joke. "Phel successfully retrieved her and they clearly *are* duly bonded, plus he's not dead, so..." He shrugged, smirking at her. "You're the consolation prize."

"You *were* trying to betray Gabriel by encouraging him to ride up to House Sammael."

He had to think back, quickly evaluate his best option for a reply, and produced a rueful grin. "Everything would have gone much more smoothly if he'd just played along. We'd have had you, Nic, plus Sabrina's much-sought unbonded boy-toy of a familiar Han, and Phel could've been easily dispatched." He shrugged, making a sad face. "Alas for best-laid plans. But it's come out well, at least for me. Not so much for you."

"What about Alise?" she asked, watching him cannily.

He had no easy answer for that one, so he waved off that

consideration. "Baby Elal is hardly consequential. No doubt she'd have been sent back to school to learn to be a proper wizard."

A shadow passed over him, shivering through his wizard senses like a cloud passing over the struggling sun on a bitter winter day. *Fuck.*

"What?" Seliah demanded. "Why do you look ill all of a sudden?"

How he was so transparent to her, he really didn't know. Waggling his brows at her, he attempted to transmute the plunging sense of dread into anticipation. "We've crossed into El-Adrel lands. Almost home, poppet!" His voice sounded strained to himself.

"You can feel it?"

"Any proper wizard should recognize their own house's territory," he replied with enough condescension to drown out his increasing panic. "In the case of El-Adrel, there are artifacts buried in the soil at our perimeter that alert our guardian wizards of anyone crossing the border. It's simple for me to sense when they're triggered." And he was babbling—why tell her all this? "Elal has something similar, only they use spirits to guard their border, naturally. Meresin is unusual in that your lands are as open to trespass as..." He grinned salaciously. "Well, as an unbonded familiar."

She didn't bite on that bait. "Then why could we cross into Sammael unnoticed?"

Seliah might be ignorant, but never forget how sharply she observed and how quickly she learned. A blank slate indeed. He hated to think what his maman would do to that fresh, unadulterated mind and magic. Eyeing the sentry spirit, he weighed his options. They could make a run for it, but with that thing on their tails—not to mention on foot, with neither of them in peak condition—they likely wouldn't get far before the El-Adrel guardian wizards captured them, and then he'd have tipped his hand and lost any good will his maman might bear him for bringing her this prize. *Maybe* they could make it, with Seliah's knowledge of the backwoods, but he'd be a liability to her. He was healed, but exhausted and horribly ill-equipped for wilderness survival.

On her own, however... If only he could engineer a way for her to escape him and soon. Thing was, if she escaped and the guardians caught her—very nearly an inevitability, even with her agile and canny ways—they would be unkind to her at best. At worst... Well, it didn't bear considering. The prospect of being unable to protect her galled him on a deep level. It wasn't as if he'd be able to do much to protect her from his maman, but he'd have slightly more control than if she ran and was captured.

He shouldn't *care* this much.

It was driving him insane that he did.

"Jadren?" she asked softly.

"What?" he snapped back, earnestly wishing he'd never crossed paths with this wretched waif of a gamine who should never have appealed to him as much as she did. She was a liability and he should shed himself of her.

"Why could we cross into Sammael unnoticed if the high houses protect their borders so stringently?" she persisted.

"*This* is the question at the foremost of your feeble mind?"

he asked in astonishment.

She shrugged a little. "Better than the other things I could be thinking about."

"Arrogance," he answered shortly. "Sammael fears no one."

"Must be nice," she commented in a small voice.

Nice indeed.

~ 10 ~

S ELLY WOULD'VE BEEN terrified at the prospect of being
taken to House El-Adrel under any circumstances, but
seeing Jadren sweating bullets truly rammed home the severity
of the situation.

Oh, he wasn't literally sweating. Not Jadren. His pale complexion was smooth and unflushed, his wizard-black eyes
glittering with the uncaring sheen of a natural predator, and he
sprawled in languid indolence over the carriage seat he'd
claimed entirely for himself after evicting her. With his
characteristic insouciance and fine clothing clinging to his lean,
elegant body, he looked every bit the arrogant lordling of a
high house.

But he was bone-deep afraid. She couldn't have explained
to anyone how she knew that. She felt it somehow in the
charge of his magic, the restlessly surging coil of it. In the way
his gaze lingered on her, assessing. In the mercurial shift of his
moods as he tried to convince her that he wasn't her friend.

And should she need convincing of that bald fact? He'd
been obviously chummy with Lord Sammael. Jadren himself
cheerfully admitted to being an El-Adrel spy, something that
was common knowledge at House Phel. Lady El-Adrel had

used literal extortion to force Gabriel to take on Jadren. On top of all of that, he was very often not a nice person.

And yet... She couldn't get over the conviction that Jadren cared much more than he wanted anyone to know. That he cared about *her*.

Staking one's life on an intuition seemed as foolish as Jadren regularly accused her of being. He was eyeing the sentry spirit again, that inscrutable expression on his face that seemed both pissed and despairing. Though maybe she was reading too much into him, seeing what she wanted to see. He'd no doubt tell her exactly that. If she attempted to escape the carriage now, would he stop her?

Moving slowly as pond water, she slid a hand closer to the door handle. She didn't look at him. That was a trick when hunting or evading the stalking marsh cats. Animals sense the attentive gaze of others. The best way to evade their attention, to achieve a kind of invisibility, is to look away. She was already positioned, huddled against the wall, as that sentry spirit made her skin crawl. So, she gazed out the window, her hand drifting like a leaf, settling on the handle. Gently tested.

Locked.

Without even a sigh—because it hadn't truly been a possibility, right?—she let her hand drift away again, running fingertips along the glassed-in window's edge, as if in idle thought. Feeling Jadren's gaze on her, she looked his way, meeting those hard black eyes. He shook his head minutely, warning and ... a hint of apology? She opened her mouth to ask, but the cadence of the carriage's wheels changed just then, going from paving stones to a surface so smooth they made almost no sound. Jadren shook his head, looking disgusted.

"What is it?" she asked.

"We're there," he answered. "Pull yourself together."

With a sigh like a soughing breeze, the sentry spirit evaporated at that moment. Jadren flicked a supremely frustrated glare at the place it had been. "Figures," he muttered.

"Quick," Selly said, pouncing on the opportunity to talk while they were unobserved, "tell me what's really going on."

He gazed at her, varied emotions shifting through his magic, though his handsome face remained stonily composed. Something in his demeanor altered, subtle, but there, and he opened his mouth, leaning forward. A thump on the side of the carriage startled her and stopped him. The carriage came to a halt. She nearly screamed her frustration.

"What's really going on?" he echoed with raised brows and a smug smile. "What's *really* going on," he said, raising his voice in ruthless mimicry of her breathless question, "is that you are the newest guest of honor at House El-Adrel. I don't want to sound like an overwrought villain in one of the novels, but look on and despair, for your fate awaits you here and it won't be a pleasant one. The sooner you realize that and resign yourself, the better off you'll be."

Catching and holding her gaze, he seemed to be communicating something else, his depthless black eyes a well of meaning, but she didn't know what. The door opened, a strange creature that looked like a man but didn't seem to be actually alive standing there. Jadren leapt out casually and surveyed something out of sight, his shoulders sagging ever so slightly. Then he held out a demanding hand to her, snapping his fingers when she hesitated. "Don't make me have the automaton drag you out, poppet. It's so unseemly."

She put her hand in his, taking scant comfort from the way his fingers curled warmly around hers. This was the same person who'd understood why she panicked over crawling into a box, who'd held her while she cried, even if he had been awkward about it later. She gave him a tremulous smile, hoping for something encouraging in return, but it had the opposite effect. He hardened, sharpened, face growing cold and mean as he tightened his grip and yanked her out of the carriage. "When I say move, you *move*, familiar." If not for his grip on her, she would have fallen, but he showed no remorse, looking away from her. "Oh, hallo, Maman. How charming of you to take the time from your busy schedule to greet us personally."

Selly, regaining her footing from her abrupt exit from the carriage, felt her jaw sag in astonishment as she tried to take in the house looming above and around her. If you could even call the edifice by a word as puny and unprepossessing as "house." She'd thought House Sammael was huge and menacing. This place was leagues beyond that in size. It also had little in the way of symmetrical architecture. Wings, towers, arcades, and other unidentifiable protuberances piled one atop the other, some of them moving on great cogwheels. It was made of or covered in metal for the most part—shades of copper, bronze, silver, gold, and platinum almost blinding in the sunlight—and exuded a power that made the hairs on the back of her neck stand up.

Impulsively, without thought, purely on animal instinct,

she tried to run. Only Jadren's grip vising on her hand stopped her. "Maman, may I present Lady Seliah Phel," he droned courteously, as if she weren't writhing like a captured animal in his grasp. He sounded almost bored, but some aspect of his tone reaching her through her panic. He drew her closer, shifting his grip to her wrist, still firm, fingers lightly on her pulse. His metallic, mechanical magic seemed to tap along her frantically firing nerves, grounding like a lightning rod. She stopped tugging at his hand, wheeling back to search his stranger's face. Wizard-black eyes narrowing in that same implicit warning, he nodded toward the woman standing before them, watching Selly with cruel-edged amusement. Jadren's mother. Lady El-Adrel.

She was tall, wearing elegant ivory pants and a slim gold top with a jacket that matched the pants draping nearly to her gold high heels. Lightning bolts threaded through the ivory silk in a gold so pale it was nearly white, subtly flashing as she moved. With the same long nose as Jadren, she looked down it with wizard-black eyes, her long, straight and glossy hair raven-dark, threaded with platinum that evoked streaks of lightning in a night sky. She exuded power, malevolence, and a cold indifference in equal measures. No wonder Jadren hated her.

"*Lady?*" Jadren's mother echoed, raising a thin, platinum-threaded black brow. "Surely that's an inappropriate term for such a feral creature. Is it even housebroken?"

Jadren laughed as if he found that punishing joke truly funny. Somehow, among all the times he'd called her feral, it hadn't struck her as being so cruelly directed. "The familiar is filthy, true, and not at all sane. Allowed to go fallow for most of her life. That's a long story there, but suffice to say that the ignorant bumpkins of Meresin had no idea what she was."

Lady El-Adrel considered Jadren, looking not at all impressed. They stood in an inner courtyard, open to the sky, the high walls topped by gold wire with lethally sharp spines studding it. It coiled, snakelike, constantly rotating as if driven by some clockwork mechanism. She couldn't have run far, Selly realized, enclosed as they were—and she couldn't have made it over that wall without being lacerated to the point of death. Jadren had done her a favor by preventing her attempt at flight. Or he'd simply stopped her from running to save them the trouble of recapturing her.

She wished she knew what to believe.

Behind Lady El-Adrel, blindingly smooth platinum doors stood closed, with no knockers or handles in evidence. Two of the non-human guards flanked the doors, the eye-holes in their metal faces empty as they stood unmoving as metal sculptures or a propped-up empty suit of armor. The lady herself seemed to pose with languid and predatory grace between them, like a lion in human form, guarding the gates to her domicile. She'd yet to offer Jadren any gesture of affection—or even to welcome him inside, as if waiting to be persuaded that her son was worthy of being granted entry. "I believe my instructions to you were to bring me Veronica Elal, not some..." She trailed off, looking Selly up and down, lip-curling. "Not some insane Phel by-blow."

"Maman," Jadren said in an affectionately chiding tone, "Veronica Elal is duly bonded to Lord Phel. I witnessed it myself."

She transferred her raking gaze to him. "I heard he was dead."

Jadren snorted. "From Igino? Yeah, no. We just came from there, obviously." He gestured to the Sammael carriage. "Young-and-dumb Sergio made his bid to capture the Elal familiar, too. Phel rescued her and now both Sergio and Sabrina Sammael are missing, presumed dead. At least by me, knowing what I know of Phel."

"Mmm." Lady El-Adrel made a moue along with her fake sound of sympathy. "I should send Igino a note of condolence."

"He didn't seem all that broken up," Jadren confided.

"He does have many potential heirs, much as I do, so I'm sure this development only simplifies matters for him." She smiled with a lethal baring of teeth. "A form of natural selection that eliminates heirs too stupid to survive."

"Funny, that's what he said."

Selly, feeling indeed like an incidental side-note to the conversation between wizards, flinched internally at the cold assessment. It seemed targeted at Jadren, though he showed no sign of being bothered.

"Suffice to say, darling Maman," Jadren continued, "Lady Veronica Phel is beyond anyone's reach now. What I've brought you is just as good, if not better. Valuable. Igino wanted her, but I convinced him of your prior claim."

"Did you." Lady El-Adrel looked more excruciatingly bored than ever, though her black eyes gleamed with some inscrutable emotion as she transferred her piercing gaze to Selly. "I remain unimpressed."

"Give her a feel. She's potent. Better, she's unbonded and untutored. A blank slate," Jadren added coaxingly. "You know how you love that."

She flicked him a glance. "Impertinent child. Don't presume to know what I like." But she glided forward, reminding Selly of a marsh snake with its venomous and stealthy attacks. She only realized she'd tried to run again when Jadren's grip tightened on her further, something that didn't seem possible, that hand already numb from having the circulation cut off. Selly wasn't short by any measure, but Lady El-Adrel seemed to loom over her as she cupped Selly's face in her hands.

The woman's magic arrowed straight into Selly, swift and piercing like an iron nail driven through her forehead, painful and horribly invasive. This wasn't a gentle draw like the other wizards who'd tapped her magic. This *hurt*. And, though she fought the draining tide, she was helpless to resist, less able to flee with this wizard's magic locked onto hers than she could from Jadren's grip. That Jadren held her prisoner for this violation, that he'd encouraged his mother to do this, that he stood there watching impassively, no expression on that cold face she'd once thought handsome, finally convinced her of what she hadn't wanted to believe: Jadren was her enemy. And he'd betrayed her most foully.

"Mmm." Lady El-Adrel finally released her on that lilting purr, flicking her index finger over the corners of her mouth, as if to catch the last drops of something tasty. "Deliciously fresh, indeed." This time, when she glanced over at her son, her expression had warmed considerably. "Perhaps I underestimated you. This is Phel magic?"

"Water and moonlight," Jadren confirmed.

"Unexpectedly potent," his mother mused. "It never seemed likely to me that anyone could do anything with those nebulous magics."

"You would be surprised," Jadren replied drily. "Gabriel Phel's control of water is astonishingly effective. He can actually brew storms and bend rainfall."

Selly glared daggers into the side of Jadren's head for this additional betrayal. He ignored her completely, except for that unbreakable grip on her wrist.

"I don't recall that information from the missives you sent." Lady El-Adrel aimed her considering gaze at her son, brows raised in sardonic expectation.

Jadren shrugged as if none of it mattered to him. Probably it didn't. Probably nothing mattered to Jadren but his own precious hide. Selly had been a fool and worse to imagine otherwise. "I'd hardly be an effective spy if I'm sending sensitive information about Wizard Phel via Ratsiel courier, would I? I knew I'd be seeing you in person soon and could report then. Besides, the information pales compared to the prize I've brought you."

Lady El-Adrel sniffed unhappily. "She's still not what I hoped for. Veronica Elal's magic is said to be intoxicating, it's so potent. If only you'd been able to apply for her in the Betrothal Trials."

"That wasn't my fault, was it?" Jadren shot back, a danger-ous edge to the question. "I think we know whose fault that was."

His mother gave him an icy stare. "Careful."

"Besides," Jadren continued jauntily, as if that one-word warning hadn't been hair-raising, "I tasted the Elal familiar's magic and it was tasty, but nothing life-altering." He waggled Selly's arm. "*This* is something special."

"Completely untrained," Lady El-Adrel noted dubiously.

"Exactly. Ripe for molding."

"I suppose you think you're going to bond this one as *your* familiar."

"I wouldn't presume. Besides," Jadren added, looking her up and down, much as his mother had, "she's not much to look at. Awfully scrawny. No manners to speak of."

"Yes, well..." If anything, Lady El-Adrel seemed pleased by his assessment. "Your father wasn't a jewel either, to begin with. They can be cleaned up and taught. The advantage of a blank slate, you know."

Jadren smiled, but it was brittle and didn't reach his eyes. "Yes, I know."

She offered her cheek. "How about a kiss for your maman?"

A strange shadow crossed Jadren's face, a tremor of vicious rage in the magic tapping through the grip on Selly's wrist, and for a moment she half-expected him to launch himself at the woman and throttle her. She could see it, as if a shadow self had separated from Jadren's body and performed the deed before her eyes. But no—that had been some trick of her mind, no doubt brought on by her own emotional extremity—Jadren only leaned in, brushing a cool kiss over his mother's cheek.

She smiled, a parody of maternal affection, and patted his arm. Magic surged from her, mechanical and metallic like

Jadren's, but exponentially more powerful. Selly flinched from the force of it, but Jadren held her immobile, casting her a curious black glance. The doors to the manse opened gracefully and soundlessly, as if on well-oiled and invisible hinges. But it was magic, Selly realized. That's why no knockers, handles, or locks. What could be more secure than doors that opened only via the lady's magic?

By the sour feel of Jadren, he thought the same, and Lady El-Adrel reveled in her superior position. "Come in, wayward son of mine, and bring your new toy with you. Though you'll have to hand it over. We can't have it soiling the carpets." Answering a silent summons, a cadre of servant types—thankfully all apparently human—popped out of some side hall, surrounding Selly and separating her from Jadren. She gave him one last look, pouring appeal into her manner, begging him mentally not to leave her, but he looked away. "The usual treatment for a new familiar," Lady El-Adrel instructed the servants breezily, "and do your best to clean it up."

The servants took custody of her as Jadren strolled off with his mother, chatting amiably and never giving Selly another glance. The silent group of servants gently but firmly herded her down a set of twisting hallways. At least they didn't have the horrors of Sammael house with its tethered familiars, but there were no windows anywhere that Selly could see. Then, as she watched, a nearby staircase appeared to fold itself up, then shot upward and into the room it had led to, the ceiling smoothing behind it as if it had never been. Shouting dimly echoed from above, but none of the people around her even paused.

The lack of the ability to even *see* outside, much less search for a way out of this place that changed shape before her eyes, sent Selly into a crushingly dark mood. The mists of insanity crept along the edges of her vision, even though Lady El-Adrel had taken so much of her magic that Selly felt lightheaded. The mists at least were familiar, even comforting, and the temptation to give over to swirling depths was almost more than she could bear.

But that would be the coward's way out. Giving in would be letting Jadren, in all his duplicitous treachery, win. She hadn't had a choice before, not knowing what was wrong with her, no one able to help, slowly succumbing to the madness of stagnant magic she didn't understand. Now she was armed with knowledge, so to give in and give up would be making a conscious choice to be sick and helpless again. She would not do it.

To her surprise, her escort took her to a set of rooms, rather than a cell. There were three—a sitting room, bedchamber, and bathing chamber. Still no windows, and the walls appeared to be metal, but they were otherwise pleasant. And they held still, at least for the time being, which she appreciated. She was hustled into the bathing chamber, the group of servants silently and efficiently stripping her of her clothing. She'd long since been divested of her weapons. Though Jadren had them all in their bag, he'd never given them back to her. With a stab of sorrow, Selly saw one servant bundle up her clothes and carry them off. Yes, they'd been filthy and torn, but they'd been *hers*.

Now she had nothing but herself. A good reminder.

The servants produced several bottles, little spirits leaping out as they were uncorked. Selly yelped as the creatures attacked her, which made the servants giggle at her expense. Realizing these must be the grooming imps the others had mentioned, but that she'd never had an opportunity to try for herself, Selly forced herself to stand still, finding the sensation unsettling but not wholly unpleasant. They certainly cleaned her well, leaving her skin feeling soft and dewy.

As the imps worked, the servants talked among themselves, ignoring Selly as they spoke about her. They discussed her too-thin frame and long, tangled hair, arguing about various gown choices and makeup options. Pretending to be meekly steered, taking advantage of their complacency regarding her, Selly surreptitiously searched the chamber for escape routes and potential weapons. Were there really no windows? Maybe they just got covered over, like that staircase going into the ceiling. She'd gotten excellent over the years at squirming out of all kinds of traps. Even Rat had finally had to resort to a snare to bring her in to be healed. She spared a wincing bit of regret for the wily tracker who'd nearly killed himself chasing her. She owed him a big bottle of that whiskey he liked. If she ever got home.

This place, however, was of another ilk, built by people invested in keeping their denizens in and their enemies out. She could explore more, once they left her alone—*if* they left her alone—but the metal walls were bare of hangings that might cover any openings and the single door might be her only way out. Out of these rooms, but how to escape a place that shifted and changed by the moment, with doors only one person could open?

She needed weapons. She could break the bottles into shards, though that cut could go both ways. Or the mirrors. Catching sight of her naked—admittedly scrawny—self in one reflection, she doggedly looked away again. No wonder Jadren had been so scathing in his assessment. Not that she cared what he thought of her. He was unequivocally her enemy and she hated him. All of that holding her and offering her comfort, teaching her what she needed to know, it had all been a pretense. Lulling her into trusting him.

Well, two could play that game. So, she docilely allowed the servants to groom her, obediently sitting for them to sic their bottled imps on her tangled hair, which was actually a relief to have cleaned and tamed into a streaming fall of curls down her back. Another imp tickled her face as it applied cosmetics, Selly feeling like a little girl playing at dress-up. A game that quickly changed as they helped her shimmy into black lace underthings, the chemise plumping and lifting her breasts with extraordinary results.

Then they dressed her in a slip of a gown unlike anything she'd worn in her life. With a start, she realized it was a woman's gown, daringly low cut over her hefted and displayed bosom, the shimmering amber silk cut so the fabric clung to what meager curves she possessed. When the servants wedged her feet into the strappy high heels that matched the gown, and like the ones Lady El-Adrel wore, they then helped her to her feet, steadying her as she tottered on the unfamiliar things. They turned her to the mirror, saying words of happy praise that flowed over her without meaning.

She hardly recognized the woman in the mirror now, the dislocation jarring. Gone was the scrawny, filthy waif, replaced by a woman who looked almost elegant. Her face even possessed a kind of ephemeral beauty, the gown exactly matching her eyes and making them glow, surrounded by lashes newly thickened and lengthened, her mouth a sultry bronze. Despite her brave words to Jadren, she'd never thought of herself as much of a sexual being. Those adolescent experimental fumblings had been full of enthusiasm but little sensuality.

Seeing herself thus transformed, here and in this place, left her more unsettled than if she'd been thrust into a cell. What was the agenda here? She knew it couldn't be kindness, so she supposed it must be part of her role in House El-Adrel. In Sammael, the familiars had been treated as faceless tools, mere appendages. In this place... well, apparently she was to be ornamental as much as a provider of magic. *Physical beauty is icing with familiars.*

Thoughtfully fingering the perfume bottle she'd palmed, she mused over the possibilities. No one expected an ornament to attack. And she'd rather die taking down Lady El-Adrel— and her faithful scum of a son—than become their pet familiar.

She went compliantly enough with the servants who escorted her back out to the sitting area, finding her balance on the heels and smoothing her gait as she did. Selly stopped in surprise, however, at the sight of the auburn-haired man relaxing in one of the armchairs.

For a short moment, during which a storm of emotions battered her—hope, despair, fury, love, rage, hate—she thought it was Jadren come to see her. A painful, idealistic part of her actually thought he'd come to rescue her.

But no.

It wasn't Jadren at all, but an older version of him. So alike that they could be brothers. He waved a hello, a fluttering of fingers, and smiled with apparent sincerity. "Hello. Seliah, is it? I'm Fyrdo. Jadren's father."

She didn't know why that revelation shocked her. Of course Jadren had a father and she could see now that this man had glints of silver in his hair and beard, and his eyes were a spicy brown, not wizard-black. Had Jadren's eyes been that color once? The man—Fyrdo—was also a familiar, she realized with another start of recognition, along with surprise that she knew that so readily. Apparently her sense of magic was improving.

Fyrdo continued to smile warmly, gesturing to the chair beside him as the servants streamed out again. They seemed to trigger the door mechanism in some way, but Selly couldn't quite see, blocked as it was by their bodies.

"I can see why Jadren likes you," Fyrdo commented. "You're a very beautiful young woman. A potent familiar, too. Wine?"

He leaned forward to pour wine into two fragile glass goblets tinted pale gold like the wine. "An Elal white, in celebration of spring," he said, lifting both glasses and extending one to her. "Please. Sit, and be comfortable."

Warily, she perched on the edge of the chair, not drinking from the glass, not at all sure how to process this next phase of her captivity. Surreptitiously, she tucked the purloined perfume bottle into the wedge between cushions.

"You can speak now," he prompted with an understanding smile. "No wizards about. Just us familiars."

Chagrined that she'd already become accustomed to being seen and not heard—though it was restful to take refuge in silence when she didn't know her lines—it took a moment to find her voice. "Jadren doesn't like me," she said. "He hates me."

Fyrdo tilted his head in a maybe yes, maybe no gesture. "Rarely are things as they appear," he replied cryptically. "But Jadren did ask me to look in on you, and he's never asked me anything like that before, or been interested in a familiar, so your assumptions might require some revisiting. How are you holding up?" he asked, before she could respond to that extraordinary remark.

"I don't know," she answered honestly. Why was she sitting here, pretending to have a civil conversation when she should be running as fast as she could? She was the half-feral swamp creature Jadren had named her, not a lady of falsely polite Convocation society.

"It's a big change for you, I'm sure," Fyrdo said, sounding sincerely sympathetic. "I come from something of a backwater, rural house also, and I recall my first days here vividly. A word to the wise: don't go about unescorted. The house has ideas of its own and the unwary can become trapped if a wing shifts while you're inside. You can drink the wine. It's not poisoned and it's best cold." He tapped the carafe. "A lovely spell embedded in the bottle keeps the wine chilled, but it quickly warms once poured."

Not quite able to keep up with the apparently friendly chatter, still processing what he could mean by the house shifting and having its own ideas—even though that explained the staircase—she sipped the wine. The other option was to refuse to eat or drink anything while in the house of her enemy, like a heroine from some epic tale, and she highly doubted that would be practical. She wanted to die destroying her enemies, not fainting from starvation and dehydration. Or survive to go home. Just the thought of being able to return to House Phel gave her a pang of longing.

"Delicious, yes?" Fyrdo asked with an encouraging nod at her wine glass.

In truth, she'd barely noticed how it tasted. "Will I have the opportunity to go about, escorted or otherwise?" she asked.

He looked charmingly puzzled. "Of course! You're not a prisoner here."

She set her glass down. "Then I'd like to go home to House Phel immediately."

"Ah." Taking a sip from his own glass, he considered her. "There is a bit of a gap between not being a prisoner and being allowed to leave altogether. Katica wants you here. Lady El-Adrel," he clarified to her puzzled frown. "Her word is law. Besides, familiars don't run around without a wizard to protect them, you know. To do so would simply invite trouble. We wouldn't want you to be harmed by nefarious interests. You're too important to Jadren."

"As a hostage."

"As a familiar," he corrected. "I have to hand it to my

son—he may have found the one familiar Lady El-Adrel will let him bond. Cleverly played, I must say."

"You're Lady El-Adrel's familiar?" she asked, realizing she should've put that together already. He certainly spoke of his wife in an oddly formal way. "Her husband, that is. Lord El-Adrel."

"No, no, no." He looked amused, chuckling softly. "Lady El-Adrel heads the house alone. I am her familiar, yes, but not her husband. Not all wizards wed their familiars. It depends on the house custom, to a large extent, and the wizards. They are a law unto themselves, as I'm sure you're discovering." He slanted her a conspiratorial grin that she didn't know how to respond to. Though Gabriel certainly did things his own way, expressing disdain for Convocation law, so she nodded.

"I am, however, the father of all of Lady El-Adrel's children," he added, with pride that seemed oddly misplaced to Selly. "We're an excellent match procreationally, as well as magically. I impregnated Lady El-Adrel—though she was not yet head of the house at that time—the first week she bedded me."

His tone was so boasting, his eyes so bright with the expectation of congratulations, that she murmured something to that effect, not really understanding at all.

"That's an advantage for you," he said with compassion, "that Jadren discovered you as he did. You won't have to undergo the Betrothal Trials. For us guys, it's not so bad, but for the females, being sequestered to guarantee parentage can be difficult. You're truly lucky, Seliah. I hope you'll come to see that. Jadren will be a wonderful wizard for you."

Selly decided against arguing, still sorting through all the clues and partial information, he'd dumped in her lap. "Is that why you're here," she finally asked, "to convince me to bond Jadren?"

"Oh, honey." He reached over and patted her hand sympathetically. "You *are* an innocent. No. That's not why I'm here because you don't need to be convinced. If Katica decides Jadren will bond you, he will. But don't fret—it's painless. I'm here because Jadren thought you might need a friend and us familiars have to stick together." He brightened. "If Jadren decides to marry you, maybe you can call me 'Dad.' I would like that," he added wistfully.

Over my dead body, she vowed to herself. *Or, perhaps, over Lady El-Adrel's.*

~ II ~

"GABRIEL," NIC SAID, trying to restrain her impatience and only partially succeeding, even to her own ears, "you are overthinking. This should be easy for you."

From his cross-legged position seated under the luminescent lens of the moon window that topped the uppermost curve of the arcanium dome, Gabriel cracked open one wizard-black eye and glared at her balefully. "Just because I have the boost of your magic, plus the arcanium doesn't mean I have the power to reach as far as wherever Selly and Jadren have ended up."

"You reached across the valley to House Sammael to affect a physical object. This requires less punch."

"But I could see what I was—"

"No!" She paused in her pacing to stomp her foot. "Stop thinking in terms of your body. Use your wizard senses to look. And this is about finesse. You're good at the heavy-lifting stuff—probably better than any wizard in existence—now you need to get good at refining, narrowing, using less magic and more control."

He dropped his face into his hands, scrubbing his fingers over his scalp. "Maybe we have to face that I'm that I'm too old to learn finesse. I never thought I'd regret not attending Convocation Academy, but maybe if I'd learned these lessons when I was younger…"

"Gabriel." She dropped to her knees in front of him, easing his grip from his hair and combing her fingers through the sole black streak in the moon-silver white. That lock at his left temple matched the wizard-black eyes that gazed at her soulfully. "My only love," she added more softly, "you are perfectly capable of learning this. Very few wizards, if any, have the problem of too much power. No one at the academy would've been capable of teaching you this anyway."

He grimaced wryly, leaning into her caress, taking her other hand in both of his. "Except for you."

She wrinkled her nose. "I am no doubt a terrible teacher. We both know I lack sufficient patience. Besides, I never learned the advanced wizardry stuff, so I can only help so much."

"Maybe it's time to call in Alise. Your sister can send spirits looking for them."

"Alise doesn't have the power for that, full stop."

"She would if we let her use the arcanium."

Nic was already shaking her head. "No, no, and no. Never let another wizard use your arcanium."

"Your father got in here and it didn't cause any lasting damage."

"First, we don't know that. The arcanium still isn't quite the same and you don't know what an additional personality will do. Second, Alise will refuse. She's not confident in her skills yet and has a lot of growing to do. Quit ducking the problem and apply yourself. I *know* you can do this."

Leaning in, he kissed her, the brush of his sensual lips sending a dark flutter through her. It didn't help that they were in the arcanium, the silver bed with its alluring chains so nearby. They didn't need sex magic, however. Quite the opposite. So she pulled away, releasing him and scooting back. "Again," she prompted briskly. "Connect to the moon, or whatever it feels like to you, and look through its eyes."

"The moon doesn't *have* eyes," he grumbled.

"Then pick the metaphor that works for you."

With a sigh, he complied, closing his eyes again. Along their intertwined bond, Nic followed the silver-bright thread of his moon magic as he reached for its source. "Finer, thinner," she murmured, pleased when he complied. "Good. It's stable, precise, resilient."

He connected to the moon, the radiant source of magic like a vast sea of argent brilliance. Nearly overwhelming. "Steady," she coaxed. "Skim the surface. You don't need all that power." But, oh, what he could do if he did find a way to use that source without turning himself into solid silver or something equally disastrous. She kept that notion to herself, in reserve for the future. "Let the moon find them."

"Like riding a horse, in a way," he said, almost to himself.

"Yes, just like riding Vale, responsive to your guiding hand. Faithful to you, eager to take you where you need to be."

With pride and vindicated delight, she felt him indeed ride that wave of moonlight, some of his water sense giving him the balance and control. She couldn't follow all the way, couldn't sense what he did, but she felt the moment he found what he sought, and his explosive reaction. The bolt of terror and incandescent rage shattered his control, flinging him back to his body with an impact that made her wince in sympathy. She caught him by the shoulders, bracing him with her magic while he reeled in reaction. Though she'd naturally never experienced this herself, she'd witnessed plenty of her wizard classmates losing the reins on their magic and fainting from the crushing backlash. Their professors hadn't even needed to chide those unlucky sorts—the pain was punishment enough.

Fortunately, she and Gabriel had built up enough trust between them. Their reciprocal bond, stronger and more braided than ever, allowed her magic to flow into him with bolstering effect and little to no effort on his part. He recovered, steadied, raised his hands to grip her forearms with fierce intensity, eyes flying open. They were starkly black in his whitened face. Though she desperately wanted to know what he'd discovered, she also knew prompting him before he'd settled enough into his body to find his voice would only stress him more. So, she waited, letting her love and magic flow into him, relieved when a semblance of humanity returned to his being.

"Brilliantly done, my heart," she murmured. "Take all the time you need."

"There is no time," he croaked, as if he hadn't spoken in a hundred years instead of less than an hour. "They're in House Sammael."

Well, shit. She offered a crooked smile. "Well, then. I suppose this calls for a strategy session."

NIC INSISTED THAT Asa check Gabriel, just in case, and over Gabriel's protests that he didn't have time for healing and that he was just fine, thank you. Among his many strengths, Asa brought a no-nonsense refusal to listen to the blandishments of his liege wizard. In every other way, the Refoel healer deferred to Lord Phel, but within the infirmary, Asa ruled with absolute authority.

"Nice case of magic backlash," Asa noted, his tone as cool as his healing magic. "Lady Phel was right to have me treat you. This kind of thing creates a shock to the system that will only worsen if not immediately addressed."

"I don't have *time* for this," Gabriel growled irritably, though he subsided when Nic raised a brow at him in reminder that he'd promised her.

"Alise is here," she said, as her little sister walked into the bright and airy infirmary, "along with Han and Iliana," she noted, as the pair followed Alise. "So we can discuss strategy without further delay."

"And I'm done," Asa said, removing his fingers from Gabriel's temples and stepping away. "You should feel better now, Lord Phel."

"That would require admitting I didn't feel good before," Gabriel said drily, then caught Nic's hand and kissed her fingertips. "I do feel better now. Thank you, my heart."

"Why the summons?" Alise asked. She looked weary, running a hand over her sleekly styled short hair, her wizard-black eyes dull, her dusky skin drawn.

"How's Maman?" Nic asked, squeezing Gabriel's hand lightly, hoping he'd take the hint and give Alise a moment to vent her worries.

Alise shook her head. "The same. The bond with Papa is definitely severed, I can feel that much, but she just lies there and stares at the ceiling with those feline eyes…" Her voice wobbled a bit on the words.

"The eyes are healthy, as is the rest of Lady Elal," Asa put in. "There's nothing physically wrong with her."

"There's also nothing right with her," Alise snapped.

Nic went to her baby sister and put an arm around her. They weren't close—at least, they hadn't been in recent years since Nic lost her dream of becoming head of House Elal when she manifested as only a familiar, while Alise turned out to be the wizard she wasn't—but they had found a new affection with recent events. Especially with their mother, who'd they'd rescued from their father's cruelty, and yet could not seem to fully extract from the aftereffects of being kept in her alternate form for too long.

It was Nic's fault, as her papa had forced her maman into feline form in retaliation for helping Nic, but Alise had never spoken a word of accusation. They both felt terrible and there seemed to be nothing they could do.

"Time will tell, Wizard Alise," Asa said with compassion.

"Yes, I know." Alise straightened, shrugging off Nic's embrace, but not unkindly. Wanting to stand on her own, something Nic understood. "There's something you should know, Wizard Asa, which is that Laryn isn't doing well either."

He stilled. "The severing of the bond?"

"That could be. She's listless, wan. I can't tell if it's depression or something more. I assume you haven't been to see her?"

He shook his head. "I didn't see any need to. Besides, it's…"

"Difficult," Gabriel finished for him, gripping the healer's shoulder. "No one blames you for that."

"Nevertheless, it's my duty to see to her health, both as her former wizard and as House Phel healer. I'll go examine her after this."

Alise nodded, turned to Gabriel. "So, Lord Phel, is this about Jadren and Selly?"

"Yes," Gabriel replied, scooting off the examination table. "The news isn't good. I've been able to determine that they're in House Sammael."

Iliana murmured in dismay and Han took his lover's pale, freckled hand in comfort. "Prisoners, I assume?" Han asked with a concerned frown.

"I don't know," Gabriel answered. "I wasn't able to determine specifics. Only that they're both inside the manse."

"Still, that's impressive magic, finding out that much," Alise noted. "I'd love to learn that trick someday."

"If I can figure out how to teach you, I will," Gabriel promised with a warm smile. Though Nic couldn't say she felt zero envy that Gabriel and her little sister shared wizardry—a club she could never belong to—that green-eyed monster had lost considerable bite with recent events. Alise had given up her birthright as the heir-apparent to House Elal to stay at House Phel and help them build a new, more equitable society. Or die doing it, more likely. She'd also risked her life to save Nic and had been spending all of her time and energy nursing their maman. At this point, there wasn't anything Nic begrudged her wizard sister.

Also, though she knew their maman's lack of progress in recovering weighed heavily on Alise, Nic worried about her sister's dark mood. Alise was too much alone, sitting with their maman—and, clearly, checking on Laryn, too—doing her work about the manse, installing the desperately needed elementals for basic comfort and setting cleaning gremlins to work on the seemingly endless task of getting the once-sunken and still-decrepit place to a habitable standard. They had a long ways to go before the manse would be presentation-ready for the expectations of a Convocation high house, but Alise was all work and no play.

Of course, none of them had time to play.

"We have to rescue them, of course," Alise said firmly, with a grave determination far beyond her tender years. Recent events had aged her, too. The young wizard should be at Convocation Academy, enjoying her classes, the tournaments and holidays, being with other wizards her age, not scheming against high houses.

"I hate to say it," Gabriel said slowly, looking to Nic, probably to see if she'd immediately disagree, "but it's entirely possible that Jadren is not there against his will."

"You think he betrayed Selly into Sammael's hands," Alise said flatly.

"I don't think anything," Gabriel said, his gaze still on Nic, "but the possibility should be acknowledged and accounted for."

Nic let out a heavy sigh. "I agree. Though I still don't think Jadren would stoop that low."

Gabriel stared at her with some consternation. "I thought you were the cynical one."

"I am," she protested, not at all sure why she was the one defending Jadren, of all people. "Or, I was. You've no doubt corrupted me. But, I'm arguing this point with full acknowledgment that Jadren is capable of cheerfully committing all sorts of nefarious acts. I just don't see him turning Selly over to Sammael."

"Not when he's in love with her," Alise agreed.

Everyone but Nic turned on Alise with varying degrees of astonishment to outrage.

"What?" Gabriel demanded of Alise, then turned a blackly betrayed look on Nic. "This is why you're defending him. Why didn't you tell me sooner? If that rotten, treacherous scoundrel has laid a fingertip on Selly, I'll—"

"I didn't tell you because I don't know anything of the kind," she fired back. "This is Alise's theory. Although," she admitted, sliding a look at her sister, "I don't disagree."

Gabriel fulminated with glimmers of silvery rage. "I can't believe you're all so sanguine about this possibility. Jadren is preying on someone who is not in her right mind."

Before Nic could say anything, Alise rounded on Gabriel with rare lack of deference. "Selly is my friend and I take offense to that on her behalf. Yes, she's struggled with sanity because of the magic stagnation—no one debates that—but she's whip-smart and no one's fool."

"She's a fool if she thinks herself in love with Jadren, as you say," Gabriel countered.

"With all due respect, Lord Phel, that's *not* what I said," Alise retorted crisply. "I said Jadren is in love with Selly. If she's noticed, I'll be surprised. I don't think even *he* knows it."

Gabriel raked a hand through his hair, looking to Nic in frustration. "Can you translate this for me?"

Relenting, she went to him and took his hand, then combed her fingers through the hair he'd disordered. "We're simply speculating, but Alise noticed what I did—that Jadren showed an unusual regard for Selly. He stepped in to help recover her mind when he didn't have to. In fact, it would've been more in character for—"

"Or more in line with his assumed persona," Alise inserted, and Nic nodded.

"That, too. For him to stay out of it entirely and protect himself."

"Jadren was different around Selly," Iliana agreed. "I absolutely support this theory. Besides, it would be terribly romantic."

Han, Asa, and Gabriel all exchanged uncomprehending looks. Then Gabriel shook his head, shedding himself of the entire conversation. "What's important is that I must recover Selly from House Sammael as soon as possible, and we can't know where Jadren stands in this. I'm leaving immediately."

That pronouncement elicited a storm of response, everyone speaking at once, protesting and volunteering to go—

again except for Nic, who simply folded her arms and glared
coolly at her wizard. He cut everyone off with a chop of his
hand, then raised a brow at her. "I rescued you. I can rescue
Selly."

"It won't work twice." She shook her head when he
opened his mouth to argue. "It *won't*. They underestimated
you before, but they're not fools. They'll know Selly is your
sister and they'll be prepared for a long-distance attack this
time. Also, keep firmly in mind that you killed Sergio Sammael. Though you were well within your rights so far as
Convocation law will see it, House Sammael will want
vengeance. That's a matter of strength as much as affection for
a lost heir. Not to mention that you sent my father back to
House Elal half-blinded and mysteriously severed from his
familiar. They are allies in this conspiracy of theirs, so if Lord
Sammael doesn't know all of this yet, he will soon. Including
the fact that you are holding his daughter hostage. That's a fair
amount of hostility to overcome."

"*I* am not holding Sabrina hostage," he corrected, though
mildly, chastened by the reminder of their precarious political
situation. "*You* wanted to keep her here, to teach her the error
of her ways."

All eyes fell on Nic, glimmering with a range of interest
and doubt. Iliana wrapped her arms around herself as if
suddenly cold, glancing to Han and reassuring herself he was
still with her and not stolen away by Sabrina. All right, yes, it
had been an unorthodox decision on Nic's part, an impulsive
move, and likely the wrong one. But Sabrina was even
younger than Alise and sending her back to the house of her

birth would only cement her character forever as set on selfish deeds and furthering House Sammael's reign of terror. Nor had Nic been able to stomach seeing Sabrina executed along with her brother. Maybe it was Nic's pregnancy making her tender-hearted; maybe it was Gabriel's influence, but Nic no longer saw things the same way. Nothing was as black and white as it had once been.

"It may not have been my intent," Nic admitted, "keeping Sabrina as a hostage, but unless and until she voluntarily decides to stay with House Phel—"

Han, Iliana, and Alise—Sabrina's former classmates and victims/nemeses—all snorted at that.

"—then a hostage she is, which was my doing," Nic continued, undaunted. "And I concede that keeping her here may not have been the wisest idea."

Gabriel nodded crisply. "Then we'll offer to trade hostages: Sabrina for Selly."

"And then do what to balance Sergio's death?" Nic kept her argument coolly logical. "Will you offer your own heir in exchange for Lord Sammael's?" Though she knew he'd never do such a thing, Nic couldn't help setting a protective hand over her womb.

Gabriel's eyes flashed with silver. "How could you think it?"

"I don't," she answered with considerable exasperation, "but I can guarantee Igino Sammael will. There's also the question of Jadren. He is still your minion, a part of your household. If he is being held against his will, it's incumbent on you to ransom him also. Anything else would violate your contract with him and House El-Adrel."

"Lady Phel is correct," Asa said, the quiet healer speaking for the first time in quite a while, still subdued over the news about Laryn. "The Sammaels are controlling and vindictive at best. Igino is also canny. This is an opportunity for him and he'll want to play it to best advantage."

"I would ask if he wouldn't be concerned about his daughter, but I assume that's a foolish question," Gabriel said grimly.

"You're learning," Nic replied, not without sympathy. "He'll regard Sabrina as a valuable asset and a critical playing piece in this game; you will have to adopt the same attitude about Selly."

Gabriel held out his hands, studying them bleakly. "I just want to get her back." He lifted his stark gaze to Nic's. "What would I tell my parents?"

They were all quiet a moment, absorbing the impacts of humanity colliding with the ruthless wall of Convocation politics.

"Maybe we should discuss this with Sabrina," Alise suggested. "What?" She raised her brows at whatever she saw in Nic's face. "You're the one taking on Lord Phel's idealistic ways, wanting to rehabilitate our erstwhile classmate. Let's find out what blondie thinks about the Sammael situation."

"It's not a bad idea," Iliana ventured. "I'd be willing to go with you."

"You would?" Han asked with considerable surprise.

Iliana shrugged, her sweet, pale-skinned and freckled face somber. "It's not like she can hurt me."

"She does still have her wizardry and innate power," Asa

cautioned.

"Then she can't hurt me without consequence," Iliana revised, nodding at the healer. "I want to do this. It would be good for me to confront her."

"I'll go, too," Nic said, then flashed her sister a smile. "And Wizard Alise will protect us."

"Am I to simply cool my heels?" Gabriel asked grumpily enough that Nic slid her arms around him, letting magic infuse him with soothing wine-red love to counter his silvery spikiness.

"There's a great deal of correspondence awaiting your attention," she said gently, giving him a stern look when he began to protest. "Some of it may contain important missives from Convocation Center, Sammael, or Elal. We need to be prepared to answer any challenges or summons. You also have a number of applicants with potential moon magic awaiting your assessment."

"Plus we could use more moon-magic weapons, Lord Phel," Han put in. "We left the bulk of what we had with Selly and Jadren. If we get attacked by hunters, we'll need a lot more than what we have."

"And there's the ever-replenishing flask prototypes Jadren worked on for you to test," Nic reminded him.

"Why do I have to do everything myself?" Gabriel bit out in bad temper. "I thought this is why you wanted us to acquire minions. Instead there's more distractions than ever."

"Minions need direction," Nic said soothingly. "I'm simply pointing out that you have things to do to put your house in order, tasks that are not 'cooling your heels.' You do that. Let us do this. It won't take long."

"Fine," he grumbled, but his magic smoothed slightly and he embraced her in turn, laying his cheek against the top of her head. "I'd prefer the information about Jadren and Selly's whereabouts doesn't leave this room," he told everyone and they acknowledged it as an order.

That was only wise.

ONE OF THE new wizard minions stood guard outside of Sabrina's room. They had yet to arrive at an agreement with House Iblis to procure their enchanted locks. House Phel might have resolved the bad feelings engendered by Gabriel essentially stealing their familiar, Narlis—though he saw it as rescuing the elderly woman—by paying way too much for her, but it would take considerably more negotiating to repair relations enough for trade. Nic hadn't had the mental energy to think about that, much less the time. So, they were making do with their two prisoners by having apprentice wizards establish and monitor wards on the doors.

"Lady Phel," the dark-skinned young wizard said with a respectful nod.

"How has Wizard Sabrina been?" Nic asked.

"Subdued," the woman answered. At Nic's gesture, she released the wards on the door, standing to the side as Alise sent a sentry spirit in first, just in case Sabrina proved hostile.

Alise nodded to Nic, then followed her into the room, Iliana trailing behind. It was a pretty room, not large, but with the graceful, airy feel of all of House Phel. The glassed-in window admitted the watery sunlight that followed the recent rain, and the high floor gave an excellent view of the back lawn and the river beyond. Somewhere in the distance lay Sammael lands, and Nic wondered if whoever had decided on this room as Sabrina's prison had thought of that as a torment, for Sabrina to be able to look that direction, but be unable to go home.

Sabrina gave no indication she'd noticed the view. She lay on her bed, still in the gown she'd worn to House Phel, which was now stained with her brother's blood, her once sleek blond bob in disarray, her golden skin pale with fatigue, deep shadows under her eyes. She cracked those eyes open, giving a glint of dull wizard-black, then closed them again wearily. "Come to crow over my downfall? Let me shortcut this session and tell you whatever you want to hear. I've lost. You've won. My brother is dead. I'm in your power, so just wreak whatever revenge you have in mind. I won't stop you." She turned her head listlessly to the blank wall.

Iliana paused, hovering by the door. With her gentle nature, her warm brown eyes held pity now. Alise flicked a cynical glance at Nic, making sure neither Iliana nor Sabrina saw it. Yes, they were in agreement there.

"Sit up and pay your respects to Lady Phel," Alise directed in a crisp, remorseless tone. "Or has a Sammael fallen so far she forgets basic Convocation courtesy?"

"Or you'll do *what* to me?" Sabrina asked sullenly. But she sat up, raked fingers through her greasy hair, and inclined her head to Nic. "Lady Phel, I am at your service. Clearly," she added in a drier voice.

"Haven't you been provided with a water elemental or grooming imp?" Nic asked, taking in Sabrina's much-changed appearance with a frown. Even when Nic had been a prisoner at House Sammael in that horrible windowless tower, they'd provided her with the ability to keep herself groomed, and in clean clothes, even if Sergio had questionably lewd taste in what he'd provided for her to wear.

Beside her, Alise stiffened in outrage, but before she could defend herself, Sabrina gestured at a pile of things on a nearby dresser. "I have. I just don't care," she said dully. "In all honesty," she said, meeting Nic's gaze, "I don't understand why you haven't killed me yet. Why bother with grooming if I'm just going to die?"

Was this broken appearance subterfuge? Nic wouldn't put it past the wily Sammael teenager, but somehow she believed otherwise. "We have no plans to execute you," Nic answered, "because we don't do things that way in House Phel."

Sabrina snorted, evincing more spirit at that. "All Convocation houses do things that way, Lady Phel. After all, your wizard master killed Sergio quickly enough."

True. "A clean death, no torture, which was more than Sergio deserved after what he did to me. In your case, it's not clear how much guilt you bear."

Sabrina's eyes flicked cagily to Iliana. The soft-hearted familiar still hovered near the door, not out of fear, Nic thought, but because she couldn't bear to see anyone in pain, even the wizard who'd have cheerfully tormented her. "I haven't been interrogated," Sabrina said, "so I assume you already know everything about my plan to bond Han as my familiar and bring Iliana into House Sammael to ensure his good behavior."

"Reprehensible and loathsome plans," Nic agreed, "but not against Convocation law."

Sabrina nearly smiled, a wry twist of her mouth that should be pretty, if it weren't pressed in the bitterness of defeat and grief. "Trust an Elal to split those hairs."

"If anything," Nic continued, "it's Han, Iliana, and my own sister who are on the wrong side of Convocation law in this instance, for evading a duly executed contract on the part of the familiars and for stealing them, on the part of Alise."

Alise showed no reaction—perhaps the jibe about Elals had merit—but Iliana gasped, moving slightly in Nic's peripheral vision. Nic glanced at her, raising a brow. Either Iliana trusted her or she didn't. The redhead subsided, but fidgeted with one long braid.

Sabrina regarded Nic with cynicism. "Am I to believe you'll turn over my familiars to me, arrest your sister, and send me on my merry way?"

Nic laughed. "Of course not. There's Convocation law and then there's how things are done between high houses."

"House Phel is not a high house."

"Not yet," Nic agreed airily, "but we will be. And, as you point out, I'm an Elal by birth and breeding, which means that I'm going to offer you a bargain. I suggest you listen carefully."

~ 12 ~

FYRDO CHATTED AMIABLY as he escorted Selly to dinner on his arm—a necessary assistance as she still wasn't entirely proficient at walking on the high heels. When she'd rebelled and made to take them off, saying she'd prefer to go barefoot, he'd stopped her with a gentle hand and a grave expression. "Lady El-Adrel would be unhappy with you and I promise you would regret it. I know you feel you don't care about angering her at this juncture, but I am sincere in telling you that you are far better off not annoying her over something so inconsequential."

He was absolutely correct that she didn't care, but there was also something so grimly serious underlying his quiet words that she conceded. Thus, she hung onto his arm like a lady in an historical novel, concentrating on her balance as he pointed out features of House El-Adrel, along with copious warnings of the parts to avoid at all costs. "The testing labs are down that way," he said, pointing to a tunnel of bright aluminum concentric circles that appeared to be expanding and contracting as she looked. "You really don't want to go there."

She believed him. Just the term seemed ominous, making

her skin crawl with foreboding. They reached the immense dining hall, the ceiling soaring with what looked like gravity-defying arches to her. Needle-thin spires of copper held up a roof that appeared to be made of glass, a sunset sky showing above in shades of violet streaked with the peaches of spring clouds, making her long with a physical ache to be outside.

A clockwork mechanism whirled with stately grace, apparently suspended from nothing in the center of the dome, spheres moving in orbits around each other. She couldn't imagine its purpose, but it seemed to be something more than beautiful.

Several long tables filled the room, people standing by their chairs and chattering at such a volume that their conversation bounced off the hard ceiling with a dull roar. Selly had attended a few formal dinners at House Phel—subdued ones with Gabriel unconscious, and then him convalescing and Nic absent—so she knew it was Convocation custom to assemble the house junior wizards, students, and other minions for dinner, and she'd thought herself prepared via that prior experience. This boisterous crowd and resulting din, however, sent flutters of panic surging through her. Without thought, operating on animal instinct, she yanked her arm from Fyrdo's—he didn't have Jadren's experience, too startled to stop her—and bolted blindly for the door.

Her slick heels skidded on the polished metal floor, and she teetered precariously, but she managed to catch her balance, pushing past shocked faces. Until strong hands caught her by the arms, holding her still in an implacable grip as she flailed wildly. Fiery auburn hair trimmed neat as his beard, wizard-black eyes intent on hers. Jadren.

"Seliah," he said with quiet deliberation. "Stop. *Think*." He said nothing more, holding onto her, holding her gaze, firm expectation in his eyes.

Stop. Think.

That's right—she couldn't run. She didn't know the way out. Even if she did, the way out changed constantly, the doors opened only to one wizard, and then there was the wire topping the walls. She was a prisoner in House El-Adrel, no matter how they dressed it up. "I hate it here," she whispered, finally ceasing her struggles. She'd meant to spit the words at Jadren, the traitor, her abductor, but they came out like a plea. "I want to leave this place."

He squeezed her arms, steadied her, then let go. "You may be crazy, but no one ever said you were stupid," he muttered quietly before stepping back. His black gaze traveled over her, an odd expression on his face. "I'm sure you hate the shoes, but there's no doubt you are gorgeous cleaned up. You look truly lovely, Seliah."

The fervency in his quiet voice had her flushing from the unexpected compliment, off balance and searching for a response, she wondered how she could be flattered and hate him at the same time.

His lips twisted in that ironic half smile and he cleared his throat. "Now," he continued in a patronizing tone, "try to be pretty on the inside, too, and don't upset Maman. For all our sakes."

Crooking his elbow in an invitation to take his arm, Jadren indicated the high table at the far end of the room. It perched on a dais, sitting under an enormous banner suspended from the ceiling, which glowed white, diagonally bifurcated by a lightning bolt worked in metals of all shades. Centered beneath it, as if she were one of her automatons brought to life by the glittering zig-zag of enchantment, Lady El-Adrel watched them with stone-black eyes in her cold face, her slow-burning, calculating gaze crawling over Selly's skin.

Lady El-Adrel would be unhappy with you and I promise you would regret the results.

And there was Jadren, his gaze on her with similarly cool assessment and challenge, so like his father in build and coloring, with his mother's eyes and manner. How much was he his mother's creation? She had no way of knowing, but Jadren had quelled her ill-advised panic, and he stared her down now. So, she took his arm, slipping her hand through the crook of his elbow, aware of how his manner relaxed infinitesimally, though his muscles remained tense. It was in his magic, she realized, that the prickling insistence had subsided. Some wizards, she'd heard the others mention in passing, had the ability to compel others. Had Jadren been using that on her?

She didn't think so, but she had no reason for that belief. He walked with a measured pace, not chatting as his father had, but acting as if they had all the time in the world, which allowed her the dignity of moving with more grace— something she sorely needed after her impetuous flight. Not that she imagined Jadren was doing it out of consideration for her. All right, she *did* imagine that because, despite all evidence to the contrary, she couldn't seem to stop thinking of him as, if not her friend, at least her ally.

"Remember, poppet," he said as they reached the stairs to the dais, "familiars should be seen and not heard. Eat, drink, keep your mouth shut otherwise."

She bristled and he smiled coolly, as if pleased to have annoyed her. He led her to a chair beside his mother—not a seating arrangement that boded well for eating anything, hungry as she was. The food she'd gobbled in the carriage had been ages ago and the wine she'd drunk with Fyrdo on an empty stomach burbled with swimming discomfort.

The essence of gallantry, Jadren held the chair for her and helped her ease the heavy metal thing closer to the table. Again her imagination confused her, because the brush of his fingers over her shoulder felt like a caress, affectionate and encouraging. But when he took the chair beside her, his expression remained sardonically amused at her expense and he turned his back immediately, exchanging wry observations with a wizard on his other side, ignoring her thoroughly. Lady El-Adrel did likewise, so Selly perched like a forgotten novel between two uncaring bookends.

At least the food wasn't metal. Determined to eat, she helped herself to a basket of bread, slathering butter and jam on a flaky popover that seemed to melt in her mouth, making her nearly groan in delight. The food blessedly helped settle her stomach. She prepared another to savor more slowly and dug into the pile of greens before her—surprisingly tasty and fresh, though seasoned with unfamiliar spices and oils—and studied the room.

The familiars were easy to pick out as the people who weren't talking, steadily eating with quiet attitudes that weren't exactly head-down and meek, but that allowed attention to slide away from them. She spotted some wizards eating in taciturn silence, their black eyes discernible even from a distance, their proud demeanor proclaiming their status in other ways.

There were other people, too, ones who were neither wizards nor familiars, some eating and some serving. All in all, hundreds of people filled the tables and streamed in and out of doorways. Maybe even a thousand or more. Certainly more people than she'd ever seen in one place in her life. She'd take a marsh crowded with blood-sucking insects over this and she found herself gazing up at the darkening sky showing through the glass above the endlessly orbiting spheres. Pillars and balconies ringed the room below that. She could climb up there easily enough, but would there be a way to exit to the outside?

At House Phel, when she'd been still recuperating physically and confined to the infirmary, she'd gotten in the habit of haunting the seat under the big bay windows. The glass wizard, Sage, and her familiar, Quinn, had glassed in the arches, and wizards Wolfgang and Dahlia had collaborated to make her a cozy nest of pads and pillows, so Selly could gaze out at the lawn sloping to the river. Moths and flies got trapped inside sometimes, hurling their bodies with mindless persistence against the glass, incapable of comprehending why they couldn't get through.

One of the infirmary workers, a magicless boy from one of the outlying farms, had the job of swatting the bugs. Selly would find the crushed, withered shells of the ones that fell through the cracks in the pillows, sorry for their little lives lost. She began trying to herd others outside, to spare them that sad fate, but there were always more.

She'd be like that, perhaps, if she tried the climb: trapped against the curving glass dome, flailing to escape and unable to understand why she couldn't. The image made her shudder, but would that be worse than this meekly accepting the threat of Lady El-Adrel's displeasure? Better to die trying than like a spineless, witless insect.

Jadren's hand settled on her leg under the table and, in her startlement, she flinched from the touch. His fingers tightened and she glanced at him. He lolled indolently in his own big chair, wine goblet in the other hand, which he waved as he told some story to the other wizard. He showed zero sign of being aware of her existence, much less that his hand rested so intimately on her thigh. Now that she'd frozen under his warning grip—though she didn't know how he could have such an instant effect on her, nor how he'd known what she was thinking—his fingers relaxed and he petted her, smoothing over the silk draping thinly over her skin. Lulling her to accept her captivity. Threatening her with being crushed, if she didn't. A husk crumbling away in the crevices of this house.

"Eat," Jadren ordered quietly without looking at her.

She realized she'd been simply staring at her plate, now empty of the greens. He set a small bowl on top of it, filled with ripely red raspberries on a bed of cream. Her gaze flew to his intent one. "Raspberries?"

"You like them," he reminded her. "Your favorite. Enjoy what you can, while you can. That's my best advice."

Bemused that he'd remembered her chance remark, she ate the raspberries, which were indeed delicious, bright with sunshine, a perfect balance of sweet and tart, the cream providing a lush background flavor.

Still hungry, when a servant replaced the empty bowl of berries with another course, Selly dug into that, the airy pastry encasing a succulent fish. A rich sauce poured out when she cut through the crust, and she ate with enthusiasm, quite sure she'd never tasted anything so delicious in her entire life. She was mopping up the last of the sauce with yet another popover, when Lady El-Adrel shifted in her chair, turning her full attention on Selly.

"So, little Phel familiar, how much training *do* you have?" she asked, sending Selly rigid with alarm. Jadren's hand which had never ceased its soothing slide while she ate, gradually tightened. More warnings without context or useful advice. "Answer me," the wizard woman prompted. "Though your silent obedience does you credit."

On the other side of Lady El-Adrel, Fyrdo leaned forward just enough to be in view, giving Selly an encouraging smile. The easygoing expression on the face so like and unlike Jadren's harder one still disconcerted her.

"All I know about being a familiar, I learned from Jadren, Lady El-Adrel," Selly said, choosing her words carefully. It was mostly true.

"How enterprising of my apathetic son."

Jadren turned at that. "My ears are burning," he said in a jaunty tone, acting as if he hadn't been listening to every word before that. Still elegantly relaxed, he held up his goblet to a server to be refilled. In the same movement, he released his grip on Selly's thigh—leaving a cooling spot that felt oddly bereft of his touch, though she was also relieved to be rid of it, yet another quandary—and draped his arm over the back of her chair, idly toying with one of her curls.

"Seliah knows nothing, Maman," he answered for her, shaking his head with a weary sigh. "It would be sad and shameful to witness if the vast lacunae in her education didn't offer us such a stirring opportunity."

"I asked the familiar, not you," Lady El-Adrel returned, cold black gaze going to Jadren's possessive arm around Selly. "And I take exception to your use of the word 'us.' Don't think you'll be laying claim to her. I have other wizards in need of a powerful familiar. Wizards more useful and loyal than you."

"I only went away because you sent me, Maman," Jadren replied, just shy of wheedling. "Pretending to be junior to a wannabe like Lord Phel was a test of my loyalty to House El-Adrel that I'll hazard none of my cohort could have passed."

"Yes, well..." Lady El-Adrel sniffed, gaze crawling over Selly with uncomfortable intensity. "I selected you for the job because you make an ideal minion. No other child of mine could have been so convincingly impotent and submissive."

Because Jadren leaned so near, his chest nearly brushing Selly's arm, the heat of him palpable on her bare skin, she felt his reaction, the frustrated hurt and murderous rage, the clean-oiled sense of his magic ticking in slow ratchets to ever greater tension. Under the table, she set her hand on his thigh, squeezing hard enough to make his breath catch.

All right, yes, it was partly payback. To her surprise, however—after his initial shocked reaction—Jadren's ticking magic relented slightly, his lean thigh muscle flexing under her hand, and he tugged on the curl he'd been fondling, then transferred the caress to her bare collarbone. It shouldn't have sent warm shivers through her, but it did, and she became excruciatingly aware of how close to the heat of his groin her hand lay, of the clean, spicy scent of him, and his warm breath wafting over her ear and cheek as he leaned around her to converse with his mother, holding Selly in the circle of his arm, as if to protect her. Though she knew better than to think that was his motivation.

"Underestimate me some more, Maman," he breathed, so quietly only the three of them could possibly have heard.

"Careful, boy-o," Lady El-Adrel hissed just as quietly. "I may start suspecting you're not sincere in your protestations of loyalty."

"And after I brought you such a lovely gift, too," he purred.

"You mean, a gift for *you*," she replied in the same tone. "You clearly want this familiar. Careless of you to tip your hand. I should give her to one of your siblings, just to teach you your place."

Selly felt Jadren's shrug as he eased her against him, splaying his fingers over the base of her throat to draw her back against him, pinning her there. "I saw her first."

"Are you a child to claim possession over a treat simply to keep it from the others?"

"You promised me." His tone still low, but now with a dangerous burr. "We had an agreement."

"Pah." She flicked her fingers. "You did as you were told. If you have an ounce of sense, you'll still do as you're told."

Jadren's fingers caressed Selly's throat, feather-light but arranged so they could become a chokehold in an instant. She felt like a tender piece of meat caught between two marsh cats and knew one thing: whoever won, nothing ever turned out well for the meal. "Or what?" he taunted.

"Are you *challenging* me?" Her brows rose in patent astonishment, as if such a thing were impossible, especially from Jadren. She also looked more interested than she had at any point during the brief window Selly had known the wizard.

"What answer will get me what I want?" Jadren inquired in turn.

"You know what *I* want." Playacting dispensed with, she'd gone lethally serious.

"Done," Jadren said promptly, and she cracked a disbelieving smile.

"Not so fast. We'd have to agree to terms," she cautioned. "And forgive me if I don't quite swallow your easy capitulation after all these years."

"You and I both know there's nothing easy about this capitulation," he shot back. "I simply waited for a reward worth the cost."

"This?" His mother's gaze raked Selly, disdain evident. "You'd do far better with an educated and well-trained familiar. You're not wizard enough to handle a recalcitrant rogue."

Jadren shrugged against her. "I like this one. I will enjoy Phel's fury, which is what he deserves after the way he treated me."

"Your appetite and ambition exceed your ability, yet again."

"Which is it—am I too ambitious or not enough?"

"You're a humbug who overestimates his abilities and allows his ego to delude him. You know perfectly well the greatest part of your magic is not within your conscious control, regardless of all my attempts to teach you better. You'll lose control of this familiar, mark my words."

"That will be my problem."

Lady El-Adrel snorted disdainfully. "And when the Convocation takes me to task because you ruined a valuable familiar, or because the reins slipped your grip, causing trouble?"

"That's the beauty of Lady Seliah here," he pointed out cheerfully, fingertips resting on the pulse point in her throat. "She barely exists. No MP scorecard. It's not like House Phel is going to lodge a complaint about losing a familiar they negligently failed to register with Convocation Center in the first place. She's perfect for me, when you think about it. Both of us shadow citizens."

"Hmm. There's a certain logic there, if twisted. First things first, let's assess exactly what we're working with here. I have your promise that you'll cooperate, and ensure the familiar's cooperation, yes?"

"Yes," Jadren agreed, his magic tamping down so Selly barely sensed it anymore. She didn't know what was coming, but it wasn't going to be good.

"I look forward to this demonstration." Lady El-Adrel stood, everyone in the vast hall immediately following suit, the scraping of chairs creating a thunder of noise.

Jadren hopped to his feet, dragged Selly's chair back, too, and pulled her up. She glared at him and yanked at the grip he fastened on her arm. He smiled, a baring of teeth that gave her chills, and only tightened his hold. "Behave," he warned in a low voice.

"I'm not going to try to run away," she hissed under cover of the noise.

"You're not going to succeed, anyway," he muttered back cryptically. "Now hush."

She opened her mouth to tell him what she thought of his orders and he laid a finger over her lips. "You've been doing so well, poppet. Don't ruin it now."

Lady El-Adrel waved a hand at the assembly and they resumed movement, either sitting again to finish eating or wandering out, conversations once again filling the previous silence. Her meticulously painted lips curved as she observed the exchange between Jadren and Selly. "It will take more than that to make her truly obedient," she noted.

"Yes, well." Jadren tapped Selly's lips, wizard-black eyes glittering. "In due time, eh, sweetling? I know how to tame a wild girl." He smirked at her incensed expression. "After all, Maman, you've always said that a spirited nature goes hand in hand with powerful magic."

"Yes—and I also say that spirit must be broken to harness," she observed coolly, "as I have no doubt you recall very well."

Jadren didn't physically flinch, but his magic quailed, a tremor running through it and, for some odd reason, Selly thought of the aftermath of the snake attack and how ill he'd been. *I am not afraid of blood or snakes. Keep your pity and your conversation, crazy girl.* Once again, she wondered what it was that had scared and scarred him so deeply that a minor wound years later had been enough to cause that kind of physical reaction. She also knew with panicked certainty that she was about to find out.

Lady El-Adrel led the way, her arm looped through Fyrdo's, while Selly followed behind on Jadren's arm. The primary difference was that Jadren rested his far hand on top of hers, where it lay on his forearm, his fingers lightly encircling her wrist in a tacit reminder of her captivity.

"I told you," she said through her teeth, "I'm not going to run. I'm aware that there is no viable escape route."

He chuckled as if she'd said something amusing, nodding at a black-eyed wizard who'd stepped out of their path and bowed first to Lady El-Adrel, then to Jadren. Once they'd passed out of earshot, he hissed back at her, "And you and I are both aware that your, shall we say, 'impulses' to flee are not always logical or well-considered ones."

He had her there. It was just like him, too, to bring up the way the panic overtook her, overriding her good sense.

"Not that I blame you," he continued on a dark mutter, glaring balefully at his mother's slim back. "But running won't save you."

"What will?" she asked in all honesty. For the first time since before House Sammael, the Jadren beside her seemed like the one she'd known in the forest. Was this the real him— or another deception?

"Nothing," he answered bleakly. "Endure and survive is the only advice I can give you."

The rich food in her stomach curdled. "You're frightening me."

"Good," he grunted. "You should be afraid. Focus on your breathing," he added in a quiet voice. "Breathe from the belly. In through the nose, out through the mouth. Count five on inhale, ten on exhale. It will calm you and the calmer you can remain, the better."

That advice was dramatically unhelpful.

"If I can aid you, I will. But I won't be able to," he added, almost as an afterthought. "Best to treat me like an enemy."

"You *are* my enemy."

"There you go. Trust no one but yourself."

"If that's what you believe, that explains a great deal about your behavior."

He only nodded complacently. "At last she understands."

THEY WENT DOWN the corridor that Fyrdo had explicitly advised her to avoid. The testing labs. She didn't want to know what that meant. She was going to find out.

To her chagrin, she found herself trying to tug away from Jadren, more than once, only the tightening circle of his fingers on her wrist keeping her from breaking away. He didn't chide her again, only continued forward with grim determination, not letting her go. In the concentric confines of the pulsating tunnel, he said nothing more to her and Selly understood why.

Everything Lady El-Adrel said to Fyrdo was clearly audible, as were his deferential replies.

It was all so surreal, so unlike any reality Selly had known, that she wondered again if she might be still insane. Perhaps none of this had occurred and she still lay in the infirmary, strapped to a bed and raving, dreaming up this endless scenario of bad to worse. "Jadren," she whispered, "I don't think I can do this."

His fingers on her wrist relaxed minutely, stroking the sensitive skin over her pulse point. "We have to," he murmured back. "Therefore we will."

At last they entered the testing labs, which appeared to be a series of rooms, all in metal—of course—but lacking the decorations and whimsy of the rest of the manse. The rooms were all square and sterile, sporting long workbenches, overhanging hoods, and cabinets full of various kinds of equipment. Glass-enclosed spaces lined entire walls. Some of the enclosures appeared to be occupied, shadowy figures moving silently within, but Selly couldn't quite see inside to pick out details.

Jadren squeezed her wrist, not hard, but deliberately. "Don't look," he advised under his breath. "You'll regret it."

"What's that, Jadren-dear?" his mother asked brightly, glancing over her shoulder with a sharp smile. "Remembering your tenure here, I imagine. Now, which room was yours? I'm happy to take a moment if you'd like to revisit it. A bit of a nostalgic homecoming for you."

Jadren had lived in one of those cages? She glanced at him, stabbed with unexpected concern. He shook his head minutely. With a sigh she allowed him to steer her away from the row of enclosures. He was probably right that she didn't want to know.

People populated the rooms they passed through, mainly wizards wearing white jackets with familiars silently assisting them. At the sight of Lady El-Adrel, they immediately paused in their work, turning to bow and offer greetings. Some she acknowledged; most she did not. In the wake of their passage, activity resumed, with much clattering and chugging of various mechanical parts. At last they turned into a smallish room, occupied primarily by a chair canted back in the center of the room. Straps dangled from it, terrifying tools arranged on an attached tray.

Jadren gripped her wrist before she'd even thought to run. Meeting her gaze and holding it, those black eyes glimmered with a message. This one she read with no trouble. There would be no escaping this.

Not unless... She surreptitiously studied the tray of sharp instruments as Lady El-Adrel donned a white coat over her outfit. Yes. Selly needed only bide her time to seize her slim opportunity.

"The newest version of my magical-potential quantifier," Lady El-Adrel announced with considerable pride. "The MPQ is state of the art. Far better than the one you assisted with, Jadren."

By the sour feel of him, Jadren hadn't been a willing assistant.

"I know. I know," Lady El-Adrel continued airily, stroking a proprietary hand over a thing at the top that looked like a helmet. "Familiar Phel, you're wondering how I justify trespassing on House Hanneil's license to have the oracles used exclusively for MP testing."

Selly hadn't been wondering that at all. The Convocation obsession with trademarking of particular magics and devices still made no sense to her.

Lady El-Adrel gave her a sly look. "Not that you'll be reporting this to anyone, even if you had contacts in the Convocation, but this is perfectly legal. It uses no psychic magic at all. Instead the mechanism—solidly within El-Adrel purview—employs gauges designed to detect magic through its physical effect on the smallest energies in the world around us. You'll find it's far more accurate than the Hanneil method. Much more scientific than those archaic mummified heads. So gauche. You've never been tested at all?"

"No, Lady El-Adrel," Selly answered humbly. She needed the woman to underestimate her, to remain close to that tray. Jadren gave Selly a considering look, not fooled at all. Hopefully he wouldn't guess what she planned.

"Excellent. I do have an oracle head, as an experimental control." Lady El-Adrel patted the seat of the chair. "Upsy daisy."

Jadren held onto her a moment too long—afraid for her or afraid of what she might do?—but released her wrist as she moved obediently to the chair of horrors. Selly pretended to hesitation, slowly hitching herself onto the seat, and Lady El-Adrel impatiently pulled at her arm, ready to secure it with the strap closest to her. Quick as a snake, Selly twisted the grip, seizing the woman's hand in return, snapping up a sharp implement from the tray, and yanking Jadren's mother down at the same time that Selly stabbed upward, slicing for the wizard's throat.

She drew blood—and a shocked shriek—viciously pleased with her success.

Then needle-thin darts flew at her, burrowing into Selly's flesh with hot spurts of agony. Time seemed to slow, each instant delineated with the light of desperation. It felt impossible to persevere under that assault, but this was an all or nothing moment. She wouldn't get a second chance. She hung onto Lady El-Adrel's thrashing arm with the tenacity of a marsh leech, knowing that she needed to stay close if she wanted to kill the wizard. She twisted the implement, desperate to widen the wound, but her muscles responded sluggishly. More missiles flew at her.

"Fyrdo!" the woman shouted, throwing out her other arm, and he leapt to assist, holding out a hand as he crossed the small space. Selly knew what that meant. In a moment, Lady El-Adrel would have the full power-boost of her bonded familiar. The darts still flew, making squeaking noises as they screwed themselves into her exposed skin and even through the thin material of her gown. Blood made Selly's grip on the sharp tool slip. Lady El-Adrel turned her head. Fyrdo closed the distance, all moving with excruciating slowness.

Jadren moved also, colliding with his father and sending the older man flying into the wall. He seized Selly, wrenching her away from his mother, and Selly screamed in inarticulate fury, turning the implement on him. He fought her with grim determination, wizard-black eyes blazing like a lightning-stabbed night sky. She sliced at him with all the wildness in her, catching him across the hand as he reached to take the blade from her. He howled in pain, but followed her slashing strike to grab her by the fist clenched around the haft. "Stop!" he shouted in her face, pushing her up against the wall, pinning the hand with the weapon above her head.

"I'll kill you!" she screamed, thrashing. "I'll kill you all, even if I die trying!"

~ 13 ~

*H*OW DID THINGS *go so sideways so fast?*

Because Seliah is involved, Jadren answered himself grimly. She was like an unstable enchantment: as likely to turn on its wizard as what it was pointed at. He should've known she'd blow rather endure even the minor trial of his mother's testing. Not that he blamed Seliah for panicking, but he'd rather hoped this delaying tactic would buy him more time to formulate a plan to get them out of there.

Now his mother was bleeding from a gash to her throat while her missiles screwed their way into Seliah's flesh. Unless his mother called them off, the vicious little attackers would tunnel all the way to Seliah's vital organs, inevitably killing her. And with Seliah so obviously frenzied, completely out of control, there was no way his mother would relent. Not now.

Things had been going reasonably well, too. He should've known Seliah would lose her shit at the sight of the labs. It didn't help that his own mental state had frayed under the onslaught of memories he'd buried for good reason. In another moment, his mother would connect with her familiar and then she'd—

"Move aside, Jadren," his mother ordered. Magic blazed

past and through him, and Seliah convulsed, screaming as the darts accelerated, changing course to target those vital organs as his mother's augmented power took hold and directed them.

Moving aside was the last thing he was going to do. Instead he flattened himself over Seliah, pinning her to contain her thrashing—fuck, but that little blade had laid open his hand—and shield as much of her as possible. "I've got her!" he snarled at his mother. "Pull back."

"Not a chance," she snarled, sending her mechanical darts drilling into Jadren's back, too.

"No, Katica!" Fyrdo yelled. "Don't hurt our boy!"

"Give me your hand, familiar," the wizard woman demanded, harsh and astonished that Jadren's father had apparently wrenched himself away.

The darts slowed their spinning, and Jadren took advantage of his mother's distraction to slam Seliah's hand hard against the wall. He hated that it hurt her, but there was no reasoning with her in this state, even if he'd had time. Her nerveless hand dropped the implement, even as she howled in aggrieved betrayal. He felt as if he'd punched himself in the heart.

"Not until you promise not to hurt Jadren," his father pleaded, followed by the sound of scuffling.

Jadren focused on Seliah. Holding on, trying to still her thrashing, he spoke into her ear, telling her to calm, that he had her, that it would be all right, to trust him—and her teeth sank into his ear, tearing a chunk out.

"You *dare* defy me?" Lady El-Adrel growled, the anger in her voice making Jadren shake inside with old terrors. "I'll make you regret this, Fyrdo."

"Not defiance, no," his father insisted. "Never that, my lady, my love, my wizard—only caution! Think of all you've invested in Jadren. To lose him forever over an accident—"

"An *accident*? That feral creature tried to kill me!"

"She's crazed. We knew that. Out of her mind from magic stagnation. But look! Jadren has her under control now. He can contain her, as he promised."

That was overstating things by quite a bit, but Jadren attempted to look as if he had Seliah contained, never mind the hot blood running down his neck from his ear. In truth, she'd lost some of her fight, collapsing into broken-hearted sobbing, reminding him brutally of how she'd been before they'd healed her. "I trusted you," she whimpered, breaking his heart.

Hopefully she hadn't totally reverted, hadn't lost the tenuous grip on sanity she'd achieved with such determination. Even if she had, Jadren would take responsibility for her. He owed her that much. Turning to look at his parents—keeping the copiously bleeding, throbbing ear carefully to the wall—he grinned over his shoulder. "Did we say spirited, or what?"

His mother looked so flat-footed, so completely incredulous that, under any other circumstances, he'd have relished the triumph. It was nearly impossible to take the formidable and jaded Lady El-Adrel by surprise. "You're crazed," she pronounced in a faint tone. "As out of your mind as she is."

"A perfect pairing," he replied, making it sound like he agreed and it was a good thing. At this point he'd do anything to save Seliah from being bonded to one of his siblings. Seliah was safe from being bonded to him. His mother would never allow that; it would give him far too much power, perhaps the ability to slip her hold forever. She was only stringing Jadren along to get what she wanted. And he was playing the delay game. Appear to cooperate just long enough to get them out of there.

A tactic that had totally failed because he'd fucked up with Seliah, trying to make her believe he'd betrayed her and was her enemy. With anyone else, the strategy would have worked. With Seliah, however, he hadn't factored in her traumatic past, the ferocious instinct to fight and flee that overrode all rationality, and the bare fact that she trusted very few people and he'd somehow become one of them. *I trusted you,* her broken whisper reverberated in his mind. He couldn't repair what he'd destroyed, but he could save her life—and her future as a familiar—no matter the cost to himself.

"You can't possibly still want this creature after this... *display,*" his mother hissed.

"On the contrary, I want her more than ever. Who else will have a familiar who'd take a blade to a high-house wizard to defend me?"

"Defend you?" his mother repeated, scoffing. "You don't expect me to believe *that* crock of shit?"

"Oh yes," Jadren answered with confidence. "Just as you were readying Seliah for the testing chair, she saw..." What in the dark arts could she have seen?

"She saw Jadren stumble," his father put in, a save from a truly unexpected corner. "He tripped on the corner of the cabinet there, but Seliah only saw him start to fall."

Lady El-Adrel leveled a hard stare at him. "Are you lying to me, familiar?"

"Never, my wizard," he averred, raising a hand to touch the wound on her throat. "You're bleeding, love. Let me call a healer for you."

She brushed him off, but put her own fingers to the copiously bleeding tear. The blade had been small and hadn't penetrated as deeply as Seliah had no doubt intended. Still, it had made a long slice, barely missing the artery, and Lady El-Adrel looked at the bright blood on her fingers with considerable disgust. "I should kill that creature for this. The Convocation would never tolerate such disobedience."

"We knew this going in," Jadren reminded her, supporting the weakened, weeping Seliah more than pinning her now. "Seliah hasn't been molded by Convocation training and she's… impulsive. It's something to take advantage of, not destroy."

"*Impulsive?*" his mother echoed, then barked out a laugh. "I *should* let you bond this crazed familiar, just to watch you tear each other apart."

"Challenge accepted," he replied with a jaunty grin. "Thank you, Maman."

"I wasn't serious."

"I am." Deadly serious.

"She'd be a liability to House El-Adrel. You both would be."

"Then we'll go away. Send us back to House Phel. The perfect sabotage." Dared he hope it would be that easy?

Lady El-Adrel narrowed her black eyes. Curse it—she knew him too well and he'd laid it on far too thick. Then she astonished him. "I'll accommodate you in this request, son of mine. You may bond the familiar, and may you have joy of the little monster." She paused, but he couldn't even summon the proper gratitude, his mind racing to assimilate this new move of hers. Surely she'd renege. "*But,*" she added coolly, "I'll want to exploit this valuable research opportunity. You'll agree to stay—and cooperate with whatever I ask—until I decide otherwise."

She'd backed him neatly into a corner. Until she decided otherwise could be a very long time. "If I refuse?"

She smiled in triumph, knowing she had him. At last his dear maman had found the leverage on him she'd sought. "Refuse and I give her to Ozana. Decide now."

He shrugged as if it didn't matter to him, though internally he cursed himself. If he wasn't so rattled being in this place again, he'd have handled this whole thing better. "You have a bargain—but only if Seliah lives to be bonded. Let's summon that healer, shall we?" he suggested casually, making sure to sound like a request that she pass a carafe of wine, not showing his fear for the internal bleeding that might be killing Seliah even as he held her in his arms.

"Testing first," his mother decreed. "If she dies I at least want to extract some data from her first. Put her in the chair. She appears to be compliant now."

Jadren knew better than to argue—or to point out that a healer would ensure Seliah lived to provide that data. His mother was simply being cruel at this point, exacting her vengeance. Lady El-Adrel enjoyed cultivating her image as a rational scientist, but that was more a convenient façade for her sadistic nature. Many of her "experiments" were excuses to inflict suffering in the name of the pursuit of knowledge.

Jadren had learned that lesson very early on, also. His father knew it, too, coming to help Jadren carry Seliah gently to the chair, surreptitiously giving him a rueful smile that his wizard couldn't see. His father had clearly taken to Seliah, as Jadren had thought he might and hoped he would, and now worked subtly to protect her as he'd once done his best to protect Jadren. Well, as he still tried to do. Without his father's intervention at the height of his mother's fury and outrage, it was hard to say what could have happened.

Working quickly, Jadren buckled Seliah into the chair, steeling his heart against her hopeless sobbing, keenly aware of how she loathed being strapped down. Worst of all, even in the midst of whatever phantasmagoria consumed her mind, she was lucid enough to recognize him, to fasten a betrayed glare on him. "I hope Gabriel skins you alive before he pulls out your entrails," she whispered as he strapped the helmet onto her head.

"Keep that spirit alive, poppet," he replied, kissing her nose now that she couldn't bite him again, "and perhaps you'll live to witness the moment. Something to look forward to."

THE TESTING DIDN'T take long, though it felt like it lasted forever. His mother relented on being healed—mostly because the in-house Refoel healer arrived on her own, the wizards in the nearby labs having heard the screaming. Lady El-Adrel also, to Jadren's immense relief, agreed to have Seliah healed also, albeit still strapped to the chair, if only because blood loss was affecting the test results.

Watching the bronze darts unscrew their way back out of Seliah's willowy body, barely swathed in her ragged gown, rent and soaked in blood, had nearly made him faint. Only iron will kept him on his feet. That and his mother's clinically curious gaze. "Still can't bear the sight of blood?" she asked with interest.

"No one likes blood," he answered through gritted teeth.

"No, but it's more for you, isn't it?" she countered thoughtfully, keenly seeking the precise weapon to skewer him with. "It's the pain. You promised to cooperate," she reminded him.

"Seliah isn't bonded to me yet," he retorted.

"Soon you'll tell me what I need to know," his mother replied cheerfully. "It's foolish to play at resistance now."

He simply grunted in non-answer. There weren't many secrets he could keep from his maternal tormenter, but he'd be even more dammed than he already was once she knew how to exploit that particular crack in his psyche. If she discovered that, she could use it to lever open the last bastion of his resistance.

He certainly wasn't going to reveal before he was forced to, that this time his fear was all for Seliah, that he cared about her more than as a potential power source and political tool. He pretended to only clinical interest in her healing, resisting the urge to apologize to Seliah for each knitting wound, to kiss the tender new skin and whisper promises he couldn't possibly keep.

Pretending not to care was made infinitely easier by the way Seliah glared at him, her furious amber gaze burning with promises of retribution over the brass plate his mother had enchanted over Seliah's mouth to quiet her cursing. Jadren hadn't forgotten that Seliah had sincerely tried to kill him, as well as his mother, and he reminded himself he'd wanted it this way. Seliah *should* treat him as an enemy. After all, look what he'd gotten her into.

"Shall I heal Wizard Jadren also?" the Refoel healer asked Lady El-Adrel deferentially.

"No, he's fine." She raised a brow at Jadren, daring him to protest. He met her gaze evenly, showing no reaction. "You may go," she said, dismissing the healer.

Once the Refoel wizard departed, his mother eyed him. "I'm interested to assess any changes in your healing abilities during your tenure away. Fyrdo, take notes on Jadren's current condition."

While his father measured and recorded the extent of Jadren's injuries, the machine ran through its enchanted program, spewing out—at last—a scorecard on Calliope cardstock, with the rows and columns the Convocation used for their MP scorecards, plus a few extra. Jadren had numerous iterations of his own card beginning in earliest childhood, showing fluctuations in his magical potential as he grew older, and as a result of his mother's attempts to train his magics in particular directions. She'd compared it to espalier, a technique she also employed in the ornamental gardens in the various courtyards of House El-Adrel—with considerably more success. The unruly, shadowy magic in Jadren evaded all attempts at being similarly directed. And Jadren aimed to keep it that way.

Lady El-Adrel frowned at the scorecard. "Water magic, I understand, though I don't like that it's 'too high to be measured.' But this other part that's unidentified... anything should be quantifiable." She cast a speculative look at the testing machine, clearly considering some adjustments.

"Which part don't you understand?" he drawled to divert her.

As he'd hoped, his mother speared him with an annoyed look. "It's not that I don't *understand*," she defended herself with prickly pride. "The machine is inadequate. Look at this." She thrust the card at him, the spectral intensity distribution showing the spikes in the spectrum of magical elements. Tapping a jeweled nail against a spike at the far end, she scowled. "It's positioned like reverse fire, but it's distinct from water and occupies an unidentified part of the spectrum."

"Moon magic," he replied, thrusting the card back to her. He'd already memorized it and it wouldn't do to show too much interest in the data. No sense prevaricating on the moon magic, either. It wasn't that much of a betrayal of Phel, and anything to free Selly of that vile chair so she could rest was worth it. Gabriel would agree. "No one's been testing for moon magic since House Phel fell," he continued to his mother's raised brow, "but they have it in their family and that's what it is."

She tapped the card thoughtfully against her palm. "What

could a wizard possibly do with moon magic? It sounds utterly useless. Water… there's the ever-full flask you brought me. If we do establish a product line with House Phel—if they manage to keep from being destroyed by all the Convocation enemies they're making—that could be quite lucrative. But moon magic…" Her eyes narrowed and he mentally cursed. He'd been hoping she'd forget, but that had been a long shot. "The weapons. The dagger from the barge and the ones you brought along—is that how he's doing it? Somehow employing moon magic to enchant weapons, for whatever purpose?"

Leaning against the wall, arms folded nonchalantly, Jadren pressed his slashed palm into his elbow, using the pain to keep himself sharp as he planned his careful path through this dangerous conversation. His mother was no fool, but she didn't have all the information, and Jadren had no intention of betraying Phel to the extent of telling her just how lethally Gabriel's moon magic could be employed. "I helped enchant the weapons as you instructed and—"

"I told you to create a profitable product," she interrupted. "Not make pretty silver swords and arrows."

He allowed himself to look irritated and chastened. Far better that she not know the special properties of those weapons. However, if he managed to escape this place with Seliah, they'd better take the weapons with them, or arrange for the things to be destroyed. He had a few friends still here in House El-Adrel, though more were inexplicably missing and he didn't dare ask after them.

"As you note, the moon magic isn't useful for much," he lied smoothly, "but it does have an affinity for silver. In his bumbling, Phel managed to infuse magic into the silver weapons, which are otherwise too soft to be useful." Seliah squirmed in the straps binding her to the chair, making irate noises behind the brass plate that gagged her, shooting knives from her eyes. He smiled at her patronizingly. "Our little filly dislikes any slur against her brother. It's true, however, that the water magic is where the potential profit lies."

His mother's eyes gleamed with acquisitive interest, well diverted, indeed. "If I allow you to bond this familiar, do you think you can make water-related artifacts using her water magic?"

"What about House Phel?" he asked in return.

She waved that off. "They're being handled."

Jadren wondered if that were true, but far be it from him to correct her misinformation. The truth would make it to them sooner or later—probably sooner—of whether the idealistic lord and lady of House Phel had survived Sammael's attack. Stroking his beard, he pretended to ponder. "House Elal could put up a fuss over the products that cross over with their water elementals."

"I can handle Piers Elal." She dismissed that also with a slight smile.

"I noticed the automatons are powered by Elal-programmed spirits," he said, tossing out a bit more bait.

"Oh, did you finally notice that?" Lady El-Adrel looked him up and down. "I'd decided you lacked the sensitivity for it. Perhaps your travels have sharpened you."

Seliah was sagging in the chair, fighting exhaustion, each renewal of her struggles making it clear she was losing strength. The Refoel healer had taken care of her wounds, yes, but that wouldn't restore her vitality. Nothing replaced the restorative effects of rest and sleep, especially for Seliah, who'd already been in less than robust health.

"I'd love to hear more about your plans," he said to his mother. "And I have information for you—sensitive information I didn't dare entrust to Ratsiel courier—that I'd love to relay in return, in private."

"You have to tell me anyway," she countered. "Remember our bargain."

"I haven't forgotten," he returned mildly. "Just as I haven't forgotten our bargain doesn't go into full effect until the familiar is bonded to me. I just thought you might care to hear some of it this evening. I suspect there will be interesting news making the rounds tomorrow and that you'd prefer to be prepared."

"Tell me now," she demanded, rounding on him, her experiments forgotten.

"Here?" he asked, making a show of looking about.

"We have no secrets from our familiars."

"I was thinking more of yon minions." He tipped his head at the warren of labs beyond the closed door. "Remember that spy who used a listening device to discover and leak sensitive information on a new product line?"

Lady El-Adrel fumed in remembered fury. It had been a minor leak—and the wizard made into a cringeworthy example—but her paranoia came second only to her pride. Jadren was counting on that to propel them into the privacy of her meeting chambers, which she zealously warded.

"Fine. Fyrdo, have the familiar housed in one of the enclosures here in the labs. I want her readily available for further testing."

Jadren fought not to react, especially as his mother watched him keenly, clearly anticipating his negative reaction. "Unless you object?" she inquired silkily.

"It's your call," he managed to reply tonelessly. He wasn't fooling her, but he'd never convince his mother that those enclosures didn't evoke terrible memories for him. There had been a time that he agreed to anything she wanted, just to escape them. No, he'd understood Seliah's aversion to small spaces quite well, even if the box hadn't affected him the same way.

"I'm concerned about the psychic impact on the familiar, however," he made himself say. He nodded to Seliah, who'd finally, blissfully, passed out. "This is all new to her, and she's unaccustomed to enclosed spaces. Recall that House Phel is an actual house with windows and doors and pitifully little security. Waking in one of the specimen enclosures will be upsetting to her."

His mother shrugged. "Suffering builds character, as you experienced for yourself."

"I thought you'd concluded that all my suffering had led to a decided lack of character," he couldn't help saying, the old bitterness welling up. There'd been a time when he'd believed her song and dance that she was sincerely attempting to improve him, both his character and his magic. He was no longer that fool. "Regardless, I want the familiar placed in my old rooms. Put her in my bed and I'll work on taming her to your satisfaction."

She narrowed her gaze on him, assessing with glittering intelligence. "I begin to suspect you care about this familiar."

Uh oh. "I do care," he agreed blithely, and without any hesitation that might alert her. "She represents what might be my sole opportunity to gain a familiar of my own."

"You once said you didn't care to bond a familiar, that you didn't *want* the power, but with this one you suddenly care very much."

He laughed, making it sound careless. "That was before I saw the opportunity before me, the chance to be lord of a high house."

"You will never be head of House El-Adrel," she snapped. "Your inability to harness your native magic for external use means you'll never be more than a minion. You know that."

He did know that and, for the first time, the knowledge bothered him not in the least. His mother had never intended for him to be her heir. She'd guaranteed that by homeschooling him and keeping him from a Convocation Academy education, all under the guise of addressing his unfortunate condition. All the better to keep him under her thumb. "Not House El-Adrel," he corrected lightly. "House Phel. With her as my familiar, my willing and ardent lover, I can take over House Phel."

~ 14 ~

SELIAH AWOKE SLOWLY, struggling up from the miasma of such a deep sleep that she was thoroughly disoriented in the dark room. She was in a bed. That meant she was inside, not in the marshes. But she wasn't the infirmary either. That had happened several times, that she'd awakened in the infirmary—sometimes strapped to the bed—with no idea how she'd come to be there. At those times, the soft night air wafting in from the marshes had reassured her.

There was none of that here, only the scent of sterile air, the tinge of metal, a far off ticking like a thousand clocks, and...

Magic coiling against her skin like a copper spring.

Jadren was here, in the bed beside her, lying so still in sleep that she hadn't registered his presence at first. Even if she listened intently, she could barely make out his breathing. Why were they sharing a bed? Surely he hadn't... She ran her hands over her body, finding she wore the underthings the servants had dressed her in, but not the gown. That's right—the dress had been rent by those agonizing darts Lady El-Adrel sent into her. She remembered the healer treating her, and that nightmare of a testing chair that Jadren had forced her into.

She wouldn't think about that now.

Slipping her fingers between her legs, she found no soreness, no evidence of moisture not of her own body. Jadren hadn't raped her while she was unconscious then.

Did you really *think he'd stoop to that?* A voice in the back of her mind asked.

Apparently we haven't yet plumbed the depths of what he'll stoop to, she reminded herself.

There is that, her other self agreed glumly.

Regardless, she wasn't staying in this bed mostly naked with him. Moving stealthily, she slipped out from under the covers, easing her bare feet onto a plush carpet. Her eyes were adjusted to the dark, so she began to make out the outlines of the furniture, the boundaries of the room. Not the room she'd been taken to earlier that day. No sign of a robe or clothing, either.

Well, she might be nearly naked, but that didn't render her defenseless. Probably Jadren wouldn't have left a weapon where she could reach it, but he'd also been foolhardy enough to fall asleep with her free to kill him at first opportunity.

She would teach the treacherous bastard to underestimate her. Following the shine of silver, hoping to locate something sharp enough to finish what she'd started, she found, to her great astonishment, an orderly collection of their weapons. The moonsilver tips of her few remaining arrows were still attached to their shafts, arrayed on a table beside her bow. Jadren's machete lay there, too, along with the other swords and daggers the rest of the group had given to them. He hadn't even kept one to hide under his pillow, so far as she could tell.

Arrogant and overconfident, that was Jadren to the core.

She was good at moving silently, having learned that skill the hard way, stalking marsh rats and avoiding the marsh cats stalking *her*. Even though the bow had been unstrung while not in use, the string had been neatly coiled beside the bow. She fixed it in place, then slid an arrow from the table—she'd only need one—all while keeping an eye and ear on Jadren's slumbering form.

Padding silently over the thick rug, she came around to his side of the bed. He lay on his back, the covers pushed down to his waist, arms splayed, bare chest gleaming pale in the shadows, a clear target. All the better to put an arrow through his heart.

He still slept deeply, that lean chest barely rising and falling, and Selly steeled herself to see it through. She could see well enough to aim. In fact, that there wasn't more light worked in her favor, as she might be distracted by the sight of his skin, of his narrow waist, the shadows indicating enticing musculature. Surely she was cursed that she felt lust for a man she hated. She would kill him cleanly, no suffering, which was more than he deserved. Then she'd arm herself and wait to be found. With any luck, she'd get another chance at his monstrous mother, too.

She drew the bow.

"Good choice on the bow," Jadren said quietly, not moving, not even opening his eyes, so far as she could see in the dimness. "It's much easier," he continued, sounding not at all alarmed, "to kill from a distance. Blades are so... intimate."

"Don't move," she warned him, calming her suddenly

racing heart. She should have loosed the arrow already. Hearing his voice, knowing he was awake... Doing this necessary thing had just gotten much more difficult, curse the man.

"Or what?" Now he sounded sardonically amused, levering himself up on his elbows. "You'll kill me? Seems like that's your plan, no matter what."

"You strapped me to that chair," she snarled in a burst of betrayed fury. "You stopped me from killing that monster of a woman and let them—" She broke off, unable to continue. Her hands were shaking, her palms coated with cold sweat, threatening her grip on the bow. She shouldn't have hesitated this long.

Jadren heaved a sigh, sounding ever so put upon, then reached over to touch a lamp on table beside the bed. It glowed with low warmth, magically radiant.

"I said, *don't move!*" she repeated, hearing the desperation in her own voice.

Sitting up fully, Jadren scooted back against the headboard, which was covered in some dark color that framed his moonlight pale body. He adjusted the blankets over his lap, then held out his hands. "Think of it this way," he said conversationally, "the light can only improve your aim. And it's already improved *my* experience considerably." His eyes caught the warm light as they traveled up and down her body with leisurely sensuality. "If I have to die, being killed in my own bed by a beautiful, long-legged woman in scanty, lacy, black lingerie is definitely the way to go. I'd been wondering what you had on under that nothing of a gown. I'm most gratified to report the reality exceeds the fantasy."

She'd forgotten what she wasn't wearing—and had planned for him to be dead already—and was annoyed with herself for blushing at his frankly sexual perusal. Not that she believed him. He'd called her a stick-insect, scrawny, and not much to look at, words a person didn't forget. Yes, he'd also flattered her, but Jadren said whatever was convenient in the moment and she'd do well to remember that.

"I couldn't find anything to put on."

"Yeah, that's a problem. You're kind of a menace where clothing is concerned. You could ring for someone to bring you a robe?"

"Nice try, but I won't fall for that."

"Doesn't bother me. Like I said, the view is excellent from where I'm sitting."

"Look all you want," she scoffed. "I'm sure you did already, since you obviously put me to bed this way." *His* bed, he'd said. This was his bedroom. She didn't know how to take that.

His gaze skimmed back up to her face. "Not me. The servants took care of you while I conferred with my bitch of a mother. I only came to bed a bit ago, unfortunately. What is with you and your refusal to let me get a decent night's sleep?"

"Conferring with her about what?" she demanded.

He flicked the question away. "This and that."

"House Phel secrets you spied out."

"Of course."

That he admitted his betrayal so easily, without even a pretense at guilt, restored her anger. She leveled the arrow at his heart, no doubt a black and twisted thing beneath that muscled chest dusted with red-gold hair. "I'll kill you for that."

"The way you're trembling, the arrow will go wild," he said, as if offering advice.

"I'm not trembling," she argued, ridiculously, as her shadow leapt wildly, looking like it danced along the wall where the lamp cast it. "Besides, I can hardly miss at this distance."

"You could miss the killing strike, though," he pointed out, very reasonably for a man about to die. "If I'm only wounded, that will be upsetting for us both."

"For *you*," she spat.

"Have you ever killed anyone before?" he asked, raising an auburn brow. "Killed someone human, not an animal or melting one of those hunters," he clarified before she could answer. "Someone you know. A person you've spoken with and looked in the eye, perhaps even kissed. It's not easy."

"Have you?" she challenged. A lot of this shaking was muscle fatigue. It had been foolish to draw before she was ready to loose the arrow. It should be one smooth movement: draw and loose. Not this standing here forever, having a conversation of all things.

"Yes," he answered gravely. "I know what I'm talking about when I say it isn't easy."

"You're a liar." She wished she didn't sound so plaintive.

"I am that," he agreed, far too easily.

"You lied to me, betrayed my trust," she persisted, not at all sure what she was trying to prove.

"Can't deny any of that." His voice was light, teasing even, but his wizard-black gaze was somber. Holding hers.

"You're not even sorry," she marveled.

He released another sigh, looking down at his hands. "I *am* sorry," he said in a quiet voice. "More than you can ever know, about so many things."

"Well, I don't feel sorry for you," she informed him, hating that she felt even a twinge of sympathy for him. Those horrible laboratories. Those glass-walled cages. The hints dropped in conversation about his being an experiment of his mother's. Probably those were just more lies spun to manipulate her into seeing him as some kind of fellow captive.

"What is your plan for after you've killed me?" Jadren asked, sounding curious and more his usual capricious self. "Do you even *have* a plan?"

"What do you care?"

He shrugged, gaze drifting over her body again. "As stimulating as the view is, I grow rather bored with waiting for the arrow to strike, as it were. I figured we might as well chat if you're just going to stand there keeping me from sleeping. Unless you've changed your mind?"

"I have not. Once you're dead I'll wait for your body to be discovered and then I'll kill your mother.

He raised a dubious brow. "You envision her rushing to my bedside, distraught and careless in her grief, wailing over my corpse?"

That was uncannily close to the scene Selly had indeed pictured.

He read that in her face, shaking his head sadly, then propped his hands behind his head, elbows wide, displaying his excellent chest. "It will never work."

"How many times do I have to tell you not to move?"

He glanced at his chest. "I'm presenting you with a clear target. You'll need all the help you can get, the way your arm is tiring."

The fatigue was getting to her, curse him for seeing so much. "I should have killed you while you were still asleep."

"You should have," he said agreeably, with a twitch of a smile, "though I wasn't asleep. I woke up the moment you did. Old habit."

"And you just laid there, pretending to sleep?" she asked incredulously.

He shrugged a little, smile curving wider. "I wanted to see what you would do."

"How can you be so unconcerned that you're about to die?" she demanded, utterly bewildered by his mercurial shifts in mood.

His smile faded, lips twisting ruefully. "Seliah… you were never going to kill me. It's not in you."

"I could have killed your mother—I nearly did."

"You made a brilliant show of it," he agreed, "but you didn't even come close."

"Because you stopped me."

"I stopped you because she was going to kill *you* otherwise. Wizards are not so easy to kill as that, particularly not ones powerful enough to head a high house. You never had a chance. Believe me: others have tried and the results of their failure provided many a great cautionary tale."

"So I'm supposed to believe you acted to protect me."

He settled himself more snugly into the pillows. "I don't

really care what you believe. Either fire that arrow off or don't, but I desperately need to sleep." His eyes closing, he made a cozy murmuring sound, as if finding the bed delightfully comfortable.

That was the final straw. She loosed the arrow.

And it flew wild, embedding itself in his shoulder. "Fuck me!" Jadren roared, eyes flying open and magic charging through the air around her like lightning striking ground. He jerked his chin down at the arrow pinning him to the head-board, blood dribbling bright down the pale skin of his arm and chest. "You shot me!"

"I told you I would." She sounded—and felt—wobbly.

"I didn't think you'd actually *do* it," he snarled, tentatively tugging at the arrow and turning even whiter. "Fuck that hurts. Did you have to hit my dominant arm? Get over here and pull it out."

"Maybe I'll get another arrow and finish you off," she said defiantly, instead. "Or a dagger to cut your throat now that you're incapacitated."

"Whatever you're going to do, then stop dithering like an idiot and do it. Finish me off, if you're so determined to."

She wasn't at all determined, not anymore. The sight of her arrow in his shoulder had her feeling stricken, and guilty—and also consumed with the urge to help him. But that was the trick, the lure. Reinforcing her determination, she strode to the table to get another arrow. He was right—killing him from a distance would be much easier than having to look in his face as she cut his throat. She reached for the arrow—this would be over soon—and her hand hit an invisible wall.

"What?" she gasped in surprise.

"I lied," Jadren said in a strained and weary tone. "I've got the weapons warded now. You won't be able to touch them." When she snapped her head around to glare at him, he smiled weakly. "I told you: wizards aren't so easy to kill."

"Then I'll just sit here and wait for you to bleed out." She plopped herself in a chair, crossing her arms, then uncrossing them when Jadren's pain-bright gaze lingered on the way her already pushed-up breasts bulged as a result.

"You could spread your legs a little," he suggested. "Give a dying man a last view of paradise."

The suggestion flustered her far more than it should. "Why are you being flirtatious all of a sudden, especially when you're in pain?"

He considered the question thoughtfully, canting his head and looking her up and down. "I have experience dealing with pain—distraction works nicely—also, you're the one prancing around wearing nothing but lingerie deliberately designed to be sexy."

"Except you don't find me attractive."

Casting his eyes up, he seemed to be searching his memory. "I'm certain I never said that."

"You said I'm scrawny."

"You are. You need to eat more." A frown crossed his face, quickly replaced by a salacious smile. "Since you plan to ensure I don't see the dawn, you could take the rest off and let me make the final judgment call. I'm betting I'm going to fall out on the side of thinking you exceptionally attractive."

She nearly spluttered at his audacity. "That will *not* happen."

"It's the perfect scenario," he pointed out. "I'm pinned to this headboard and can't ravish you. Unless you want to come over here and see what I can accomplish with one hand." He gestured to his lap with his uninjured hand. "And a prehensile penis."

"There is no such thing!" she retorted, hoping the dim light hid her furious blush—at the image and at her embarrassment that he'd gotten her to respond to something so ridiculous. "Do you take *nothing* seriously?"

He grinned crookedly. "No. I'm rather shocked you're just figuring that out."

Studying him intently, she detected the shadow behind the insouciant attitude. "You're lying," she decided. "You take many things seriously, possibly everything."

His grin dimmed at the edges, the pain showing in the brackets around his mouth as his gaze left her to drift aimlessly about the room. "Maybe it's a circular spectrum, with taking everything seriously at one end and nothing seriously at the other—and somewhere between is the fine line where they meet. That's the line you'll find me dancing along, a place of shadows and nothingness."

"I don't understand you."

"It's a bit of a complex metaphor," he allowed, grimacing.

"I understand the metaphor," she bit out. "I just don't understand how you can be…" She gestured in a circle to encompass all of him. "How you are."

"No worries there. You're far from alone in that. Half the time I don't understand myself. If you're not going to pull out this arrow you so carelessly lodged in me, would you at least bring me some brandy? There's good stuff on the credenza over there."

"No. I'm not coming near you until I'm sure you're dead."

"Ah. That. Hmm."

"What? Are you finally realizing the severity of your situation?"

He breathed a laugh. "Seliah, darling, I admire your dedication to the goal, however misguided, but take note of the bleeding. I don't think waiting for me to bleed out is going to end the way you intend."

"If you're suggesting I'll regret killing you, I'll do my soul-searching after you're dead." She did focus on the arrow in his shoulder, however, and the wound that had indeed stopped bleeding. "You're saying I didn't wound you enough for you to bleed out."

He shook his head, then nodded, then sighed. "It's a bit complicated. It's also a secret. I could tell you, but... well, you know."

She wrestled the disconcerting relief at knowing he wouldn't die. It made no sense, as she'd been determined to punish him for his betrayal, and she hated him still, with consuming passion.

"Let's negotiate. What would it take to convince you to pull this arrow out?" Jadren finally asked.

"I want nothing from you," she spat.

"I can get you out of House El-Adrel," he offered.

"Lies. You're the one who stopped me from escaping when I had the chance."

"Incorrect. You never had the chance. I stopped you from

throwing your life away. I always intended to get you out of here." He met and held her gaze. "That's truth."

Stupidly, she wanted to believe him. "Then why were you so awful to me?" She really hated that her voice sounded so small, so pitiable.

He closed his eyes, looking pained, and not from the wound this time, she thought. "I thought it would be easier on you, being here, dealing with this metal-clad shit show of hideous proportions, if you hated me and saw me as your enemy."

"You couldn't just tell me the truth?" she demanded, not at all sure how to feel.

"Which truth?" he demanded in turn, black eyes opening, his gaze drilling into her. "You don't understand me, by your own admission; you have no reason to trust me, to believe anything I tell you."

"And I still don't!" she snapped.

"Exactly!" he fired back.

She had no response to that, had in fact lost track of the argument.

"So," he continued in a tone of weary exasperation, "would you, pretty please with cherries on top, pull out this fucking arrow so I don't heal pinned to this bed for the servants to find us in the morning? I can promise things won't go well in that scenario. Maman would be aggravated and we really don't want that."

"I'm getting tired of everyone warning me not to annoy Lady El-Adrel," she grumbled.

"Do you doubt the validity of the advice?" he asked with a

raised brow.

He had a point. She edged closer to the bed, staying out of his reach in case it was a trick, and peered at the arrow wound. Jadren obligingly tapped the bedside lamp to increase the light from the fire elemental contained within. "It *is* healing," she breathed. "I can almost see the tissues knitting together."

"Now you know my secret," he said with grave intensity, "which makes you the fourth person in all the world. Me, Maman, my father, and now you."

She would have accused him of lying yet again, but she couldn't deny the evidence. "You *were* dead," she realized. "After the hunter attack. I knew you couldn't have survived that wound."

He shrugged as much as the arrow allowed. "And yet, I did survive. I woke up later feeling like I'd *rather* have died, but I've never been given a choice in the matter. No matter how much I'd prefer not to live through some of what I've experienced, I still seem to. Every time." He sounded so grim, so resigned at that last that she felt that unwelcome twinge of sympathy again.

"So you let me believe I was crazy rather than admit the truth to me."

"In front of Lord Sammael? Absolutely."

"Then afterward."

"In front of Elal's spirit spy? Absolutely." He held her gaze, no apology in it.

"What about now?"

"What *about* now?" he countered, though not at all playfully.

"You knew I couldn't kill you!" No wonder he hadn't been afraid, feigning sleep to see what she would do. "You'd have let me shoot you through the heart or slit your throat and believe I'd murdered you."

He cocked his head. "Would you have been sorry to think you'd succeeded?"

"No." *Yes*. She didn't know.

"You could say I was simply accommodating your goals. Satisfying your thirst for vengeance and so forth. After all, you're totally justified in being pissed at me, in hating me."

"So you'd just let me kill you."

"Well, let you go through the motions anyway." He grinned. "I actually believed you'd relent."

"You made me angry," she admitted, "acting like you didn't care either way."

"Remind me not to make you angry," he returned softly, grin fading to a half smile.

"Though now I know why you don't care, either way. Can you really not die?"

No smile at all now, those grim shadows returning to his face. "Apparently not. My charming maman certainly gave it her level best. Though she was leery of going to extreme methods like decapitation, removing my heart, complete immolation, or full dismemberment. She didn't want to risk losing her prize subject entirely."

"She experimented on you." Selly had gathered that earlier, but so much had been going on—including overwhelming fear for her own skin—that she hadn't quite thought it all through.

"Can we not discuss that?" Jadren replied lightly, though

his pale skin had turned greenish. "Preferably never, but at least, not while my shoulder is healing around this arrow. The longer you take to pull it out, the more it will hurt when you do."

"You assume I will."

"I think we've reached an impasse, so yes."

She eyed it, not looking forward to this. "Maybe I should call the Refoel healer."

"Seliah." He said her name so seriously she met his intent gaze, wizard-black eyes fringed with copper lashes. "My mother is already concerned about your unstable nature and my inability to control you. If she discovers you tried to kill me—and I doubt we'll be able to pass this off as kinky games— then she *will* take steps to break your will. Once she has you biddable, she'll have you bonded to one of my siblings. I hope you'll believe that I'm absolutely sincere in warning you that none of them are anyone you want to give your life and magic to."

Her mouth was dry. "You bargained with her to have me bonded to you."

Letting out a long breath, he let his head fall back. "I don't see any other path out of this situation for you. The only way you'll leave this house alive is bonded to a wizard. The choice lies entirely in who it is."

"You said we could escape."

"After you're bonded, yes. Until then, there's no chance. You'll be watched too closely. Once you're bonded, they won't worry about it, since you can't voluntarily leave your wizard."

"You could've let me escape before we got here."

"You'd rather have been bonded to a Sammael wizard?" he asked incredulously. "You saw what they do there."

She repressed a shudder of remembered horror. "I could have survived in the wilds between here and there. You know I can."

He was shaking his head. "Not with that fucking Elal spirit watching. I ran every scenario I could come up with on that long carriage ride and the only thing I could come up with is to use what leverage I have on my mother to bond you as my familiar and get you out of here again. Once you're safely back at House Phel, I'll go away and leave you alone forever. They can tap your magic to keep you healthy. I never wanted a familiar anyway."

"So you say," she scoffed.

"Believe me or not, Seliah," he replied wearily, letting his eyes drift shut. "I don't blame you for doubting me. But I'm being as honest as I know how. This is your best bet to get home with the tattered remnants of what's left of your sanity intact."

Absurdly, it reassured her to have him poke at her again. "Why can't you die?"

He opened one eye. "You're asking a question my mother has spent my lifetime attempting to answer."

"Tell me what she's found out."

"Fine. I will, *if* you pull out the arrow so I can begin healing again."

"All right." She supposed it was the least she could do. Edging her hip onto the side of the bed, she reached for the arrow shaft.

"Excuse me," Jadren said, glaring at her. "What do you think you're doing?"

"Pulling the arrow out," she snapped. "Obviously."

"Not without cutting the head off. Remember how the arrow head flares at the base? You're not going to be able to pull it back through, not without ripping a new hole. You're a scrappy little thing but I doubt you're that strong and I know I don't want to endure that. You're going to have to break or cut the shaft, then pull me forward off of it."

Oh. She felt a little ill just contemplating it. "Let me get a blade then and try cutting it. Take the ward down?"

"Done."

~ 15 ~

JADREN, FOR ONCE living up to his word, did indeed savor the view as Seliah glided over to the table where he'd laid out their weapons. She possessed a natural grace, made more evident by the lack of restrictive and unfamiliar clothing. Though the black lingerie she wore was far from natural, Seliah looked more in her element wearing so little. More animal, less fettered. Her hair hung long and tangled down her back, coming to a point that formed an arrow above her tiny, perfect ass.

Like he needed his attention called to it. Especially when she—dark arts take him—bent over the table, showing the golden moon undersides of her tidy bottom. He really shouldn't be ogling her this way, but the brandy he'd consumed to get through the interrogation with his mother on top of the salient side-effects of the self-healing, then seeing Seliah dressed like one of his adolescent wet dreams, well… It would take a stronger man than he to look away.

Besides the fact that you couldn't control your reaction to her before she shot you, his mocking inner voice pointed out. He had no retort for that. The sight of her poised to shoot him, all tall, slender menace in black sex gear had done more to immobilize him than all her threats.

Able to reach the blades again, Seliah selected several and came back toward him. Her breasts were fuller than he'd imagined, golden and rounded, rising above the lacy contraption with mouthwatering smoothness. Her dark nipples thrust tautly through the lace. He was a lost man. "Grab that brandy for me, too, would you?"

She frowned, glancing at the bottle. "Do you really need to drink more?"

He pretended to consider. "Yes."

He thought she'd refuse, but she went back for the bottle and a glass, even pouring him a couple of fingers and handing it to him. Drinking it down, he savored the liquid fire that burned at the edges of the pain, along with the exceptionally smooth finish. So much better than the rotgut at House Phel. Not that any amount of good brandy made him prefer the waking nightmare that was his birth-house. He'd drink bad liquor all day in exchange for being in the land of idealistic fools who at least didn't breakfast on infants.

"If you can't die, why'd you bother warding the blades from me before?" she asked, sitting on the edge of the bed. Her scent, all spring water and full moon magic, laced with the floral fragrance the servants had used to wash the blood off of her, enveloped him like a net of silken threads. He focused on the pain of the wound, of all things, to distract him from her.

And how very much he wanted to touch her, to place his lips just *there*, in that sweet hollow between her perfect breasts.

"Jadren?"

Right. She'd asked a question. "Getting wounded still

hurts—case in point—and blood loss is no picnic. Besides, if you'd cut my throat, there'd have been blood everywhere and while a few smears and spatters can be explained away as rough sex, not the equivalent of a stuck pig."

That worked, making her blush and focus on the arrow shaft, which was what he needed her focusing on. His mother had gone through a run of experiments testing whether he'd heal around objects of different compositions—including her cherished goal of permanently implanting various enchanted artifacts intended to "enhance" him—and the results hadn't been pretty. They'd also been agonizing. His body simply continued to attempt to heal around the intrusions, which meant never fully healing. The upside had been that his predilection had foiled his criminally insane mother's grand plans to turn him into a living version of one of her automatons.

"I told you, I'm not a virgin," Seliah muttered.

He had to pull his scattered thoughts together. No luck. "What?"

"Blood," she said, meeting his gaze boldly, "from sex. Isn't that what you mean?"

Oh, my lovely innocent. He couldn't help grinning at her, utterly charmed by her artlessness, which said something, that she could be a ray of pure light in this morass of depraved corruption. So much so that he decided against correcting her misapprehension. "Right, that's what I meant. I forgot we discussed it."

She wasn't fooled. She was also close enough to kiss, which couldn't happen. "No, you didn't. What did you mean then?"

"Arrow." He raised his brows significantly. "Embedded in my shoulder. Really hurts."

"You don't act like it hurts."

"You have no idea."

"Ah, there's the Jadren I know." She said it drily, then continued in a more serious vein. "This serrated blade should work best, but if I try to saw through the shaft from the front, it's going to pull on you, which will hurt even more."

"It has to come out. I can handle the pain." He swallowed more brandy and let his head fall back, mostly so he wouldn't be overcome by her nearness.

"Well, I'm thinking that if I pull you forward on it some now, it will loosen the wound and create a gap behind you. Then I can hold the front, saw through the piece between your shoulder and the headboard, then yank the rest out."

"Fine." He doubted it would go that smoothly, but whatever would convince her to get it done already.

"All right." She plucked the glass from his hand and set it on the bedside table.

"My brandy…"

"Hush. Be a good boy and you can have it after."

"Tyrant."

"At least I'm not your murderer." She laid her hands on his bare shoulders, her skin hot against his. His head swam. Hmm. He might have lost more blood than he'd realized. That fucking moon-magic arrowhead might've torn a chunk out of his back on the way out. Charming. "Ready?"

"I was ready half an hour ago."

"Tsk," she chided. "So grumpy."

"You tried to *kill* me," he snarled. "What do you exp—Argh!" He broke off on a guttural scream as she suddenly yanked him forward. The tissues tenaciously holding onto the arrow shaft tore. Fresh, hot blood ran down his back. Shooting sparkles obscured his vision and he found himself clinging to Seliah, forehead pressed to her shoulder and hands gripping her slim waist, battling nausea and old memories. "Fuck me," he gasped.

"Are you going to puke?" she asked. "You're awfully clammy."

"Probably," he admitted.

She reached for a decorative bowl and thrust it into his lap. "Another reason you should've gone lightly on the brandy."

"I didn't know you planned to shoot me."

"*After* I shot you!"

"Ah well," he muttered. "Tastes better than most stuff coming back up anyway."

"Trust you to know that." She crawled over him and onto the bed, bracing her hand against where the arrow entered his shoulder, and looking behind him, blade in hand. "*Oh, Jadren...*" she gasped. "There is so much blood. I don't—"

"Replaceable," he gritted out. "Quit dithering and do it."

"Don't scold me when I have a knife in my hand and you at my mercy."

"Going to plant it in my back? Oh, wait, you already did, metaphorically."

"We can argue about who betrayed who later."

"Can't tell you how much I look forward to that." Though he'd loaded his reply with sarcasm, he discovered a glimmer of real anticipation. Arguing with Seliah was always stimulating—if aggravating—and setting that as an aspiration made perverse sense. It would mean they'd survived to see daylight.

"I'm sawing now."

"Goodie."

"Lean on me if you need to."

"That bony shoulder? I—" Bloodred-black agony crashed over him as she increased pressure on the wound, the pain coming in waves as she sawed. He groaned, clenching his teeth, pressing his face into the sweet nook between her throat and shoulder, willing himself not to puke. Why couldn't his weird magical gift have given him imperviousness to pain? Dark arts, he hated pain. He'd had enough to last several lifetimes.

"Almost there," she breathed, sounding as ill as he felt. "Good thing the shaft is only wood and not silver. There!"

The pressure released and she yanked hard on the shaft, pulling it out the front—along with more gobbets of flesh and a bright spray of blood. And a thin, shrill gurgle from himself.

"It's all right," Seliah told him soothingly. "It's done now. Just lie down. Lie still. Look—you didn't even puke!"

"Hooray for me." He wasn't sure if he said that aloud, feeling like putty in her hands as she coaxed him to lie on his good side, hissing in bruised pain as she wadded up the bed coverings to press them against the bleeding wounds front and back.

"I should've had towels ready," she said under her breath. "No way this will look like kinky anything."

"I don't know," he said, bemused by the enticing stretch of

her bare inner thigh in close proximity to his face. She was kneeling up to reach both sides of him at once, giving an excellent view of the hollow between her thigh and pelvis, the lacy lingerie showing glimpses of her mound covered in hair as black and shiny as on her head. Because his good hand was right there, he stroked it down the outside of her thigh, then pressed a kiss to the satiny skin on the inside.

She yelped in surprise. She also shivered under his hand in tantalizing responsiveness. "Jadren!"

"Yes, dear?" He asked innocently, inhaling the scent of warm woman and moonlight. Would her sex taste like moonlight? Whatever moonlight might taste like. He nuzzled higher up her thigh, using his leverage on her leg to bring her closer.

"How can you be rutting at me when you're nearly dead from blood loss?" she demanded.

Still too far for him to taste, so he licked her thigh instead. Oh, yes, she liked that, heating to a keen vibration. "*Nearly dead* being the key phrase," he purred. She was so succulent he just had to nibble, a teensy bite.

She jumped like she was snakebit. "You're unbelievable. I should have done a better job of killing you."

"The odds were stacked against you," he said comfortingly. "You can be pleased that you came much closer to succeeding than most. Lower yourself a bit, darling, and sit on my face. I promise you'll like it."

Muttering something he couldn't make out, she clambered over him, putting herself behind his back. He started to reach for her, to pull her back, but weakness and dull agony greeted the attempted movement. "How much of my back is still stuck to the headboard?" he wondered.

"Most of it," she shot back. "Are you sure you'll survive without help? I really think I should call a healer and screw the consequences."

"Regretting your murderous vengeance already? It was the love bite, I'll bet. No woman can resist that."

"Something tells me you'll regret all this in the morning."

"Your attempt to murder me? I regret it already."

"In the end it was an accident," she argued. "I really think I should call for the Refoel healer."

"Don't."

"There's so much blood and… other things."

"I'll live to drive you into a killing rage another day," he promised. "Don't call anyone. Just let me sleep."

"Are you…"

He lost the rest of her words to blessedly numbing unconsciousness.

AND WOKE WITH a mother of a headache. Which, considering the nature of his own mother, was saying something. His mouth was dry, his body ached all over, and his skull throbbed like earth elementals were digging at it from the inside. People didn't realize how much blood loss feels like a hangover. Torture and binge-drinking: two sides of the same coin. It all came down to dehydration.

"Water," he croaked, before remembering he was likely alone. Before remembering next that he was probably with Seliah. Cracking open one eye, he searched the murk of the unlit room to spot Seliah huddled in a big armchair, wearing his shirt and fast asleep. Some nurse she was.

With a groan he also recalled all the salacious comments he'd made during the night. Oh, and biting her. And inviting her to sit on his face. What a fucking mess, only without actual fucking to make it worthwhile. Needing the fortification, he reached for the brandy carafe on the bedside table.

"You'd do better with water than more liquor," Seliah said, her eyes open now and owlish in her piquant face, watching him warily.

Swishing the brandy in his mouth to remove the foul taste of near-death, he spat it into the empty glass. Dark blood turned the liquid nearly black. Part of the healing process, though even his maman wasn't sure why. It was mostly old blood, it turns out. "Except you didn't leave me a handy carafe of water, did you?" he returned, feeling surly. Pushing himself up out of the bed, he pulled on the trousers he'd dropped there before he staggered to his feet.

"Should you be up?"

"I might not be able to die," he answered, feeling oddly freer that she knew about his nature, dangerous as that would be for both of them going forward, "but near-death feels like shit. I need water."

"There isn't—"

Holding up a hand to stop her, he used his wizardry to

trigger the fire elementals in the lamps to brightness and went to the empty water pitcher. Setting it under the tap on the wall, he woke the water elemental. Before the pitcher was full, he tipped it up and drank deeply, allowing the excess to dribble over his face.

"I didn't know how to do that," Seliah said quietly.

He grunted, filled a glass from the tap, and took it to her, still holding his partially full pitcher. "House Elal water elemental tied to House Hagith plumbing. Nothing but the best for El-Adrel." He drank more water. "Anyone can trigger it. Remind me to show you the trick."

Refilling the pitcher, he wandered back to the bed, studying the bit of shaft still sticking out of the headboard, the arrowhead so deeply buried there was no sign of it. His dried blood soaked the material, dull black now, along with bits and pieces of shriveled gunk that used to be part of him.

"I *am* sorry," Seliah said in a small voice, from right behind him. He glanced at her, swathed in his black shirt, legs bare and hair tousled. She looked like she'd crawled out of bed with him, only after far more enjoyable activities than the near impalement. Ridiculously, he wanted nothing more than to gather her up into his arms and kiss her senseless, then make real use of that bed. After he'd dealt with the gore, naturally.

Also naturally: that could not happen.

"No worries, poppet," he drawled, making it extra sardonic. "We both know you don't exactly have a stable temperament. Take a crazy girl to bed and..." He gestured to the gruesome mess. "Well, one gets what one gets."

He'd expected fire to light her plaintive amber gaze, but

she flinched, pale beneath her dusky skin. Miserable and guilty. "I think we *do* have to face that I'm unstable," she said in a fragile voice. "I've been sitting here all night, watching you sleep, smelling the blood, and I don't know what I was thinking. I nearly killed you, Jadren."

"In point of fact, you didn't," he said lightly, oddly compelled to relieve her guilt and misery. He began stripping the blood-stained sheets from the bed. "You couldn't and can't."

"I didn't know that," she argued. "In the moment, all I wanted was to kill you and damn the consequences."

"You're a determined little monkey," he agreed, adding his pillow to the pile on the floor. "You have a knack for following through on whatever idea takes you. I've always admired that about you, inconvenient as it's proved to be at times."

"*Inconvenient?*" she echoed on an astonished breath. "You call me trying to kill you *inconvenient?*"

He patted his bare chest. Streaked with dried blood and other unmentionable fluids, yes, but perfectly intact once again. "A minor detour. In fact, given your murderous impulses, I'm likely the perfect wizard for you. If I piss you off and you decide to hack pieces off of me, at least with me they'll grow back." The headboard cushion had to go, too. Finding the serrated blade Seliah had used, he pried out the arrowhead, handing the silver instrument of destruction to her. Then he wrestled off the headboard and added it to the pile.

"What are you doing?" Seliah asked, turning the flashing silver arrowhead thoughtfully in her hand.

"Disposing of the evidence. Anything else with blood or other bits of past-me on it?"

"This." She set the arrowhead aside and retrieved a bundle, blushing as she handed it to him. He unfolded the stiffened bunch of lace and ribbon. It was the black lingerie she'd been wearing. "When I pulled the arrow out," she explained defensively, "your blood sprayed everywhere. After you passed out, I wiped it off of me as best I could, but..." She raked a hand through her tousled hair, fingers stopping short as they hit snarls caked with dried blood.

Now that he was able to focus better, he could see the smears on her skin. It also aroused him to an immediate and alarming degree to know that she was entirely naked under his shirt, that he need only slide a hand up her long thigh to find her hot, unprotected sex. The scent, taste, and sensation of touching her the night before rushed back, increasing the already nearly unbearable need. So, he firmly turned his back on her, adding the unlucky lingerie to the pile. "I'll introduce you to the grooming beasties once this is dealt with. What did you use to wipe off with?"

Wordlessly, she handed him a cloth. With resignation, he recognized it as a favorite old scarf, and philosophically tossed it on the pile, too. Then he dumped the mattress atop it all, leaving the bedstand bare. Freeing a fire elemental from its lamp, he gave it instructions, then set it loose. Seliah drew up beside him, watching silently as the elemental gleefully reduced the pile to ash. It was clearly another expensive Elal-brand elemental, well-trained and responsive to a wizard's touch, carefully and thoroughly burning only what he'd asked to be burnt. After it finished, he freed an earth elemental from the bathing chamber and set it to devouring the ash.

238

"That's amazing to see," Seliah breathed.

"Elal magic. There's a reason your buddy Nic's family is so rich and powerful."

"Won't someone wonder about the missing bed and stuff?"

"Nope." He tapped the wall, hoping the house would co-operate for once. "I need a replacement headboard, bed, and linens, please." For a long moment, nothing happened, and Seliah raised a sardonic brow. Then the wall shimmered. The previous bedstand shifted, morphing into a new four-poster bed, the linens spinning into place over a newly produced mattress. Carvings spun and settled, showing a pattern of arrowheads all along the posts. "Very funny," he muttered at it.

"That's incredible." Seliah couldn't quite believe this sort of magic was possible.

"That's why *my* family is so rich and powerful," he informed her. "Come in here." He went into the bathing chamber, taking stock of himself in the high grade House Byssan mirror as he washed up, surveying the damage as he had so many times over the years. He'd grown up in these rooms—when he wasn't confined to his cozy cage in the labs—and had confronted the evidence of his mother's experiments on his body many times. This wasn't so bad. Even when he checked out his back, triggering the enchantment that had the mirror show him his back side, it seemed to be healing nicely. Ridged pink skin still showed divots where that moon-magic arrowhead had torn the chunk out of his shoulder blade. No wonder the cursed thing had hurt so much. Experimentally, he lifted his arm, finding the range of motion still limited. Ah well, a few more hours should fix that.

Seliah stood in the doorway, watching him, clearly hesitating to enter.

"Come on in," he told her. "It's a bathing room, not a torture chamber."

"One never knows in this place," she retorted, bristling.

"Heh. That's my girl." He did admire her spirit and tenacity. She'd need both before they escaped the doom-ridden house of his birth. "Water elemental, for cleaning." He pointed to the bottle. "Strip off, trigger it like this. It's been preset to know what to do. "Fire elemental to dry off. Same mechanism." He pointed to each bottle in turn. "Grooming imp, to fix your hair. Makeup imp, for obvious purposes."

"I don't need makeup."

"You do, because you'll be attending our bonding ceremony today, which will include pomp, ceremony, and witnesses, so you'll want to look your best."

She gazed at him in open-mouthed horror. "Today?" she squeaked.

He hardened himself against the stab of sympathy. "Yes, it has to be today. Maman capitulated last night and it's best to get it done before she changes her mind."

"Is that why I was in your bed last night?" she asked, expression growing tight. "These are your rooms, you said so."

"The one has nothing to do with the other," he answered, suppressing a surge of aggravation he didn't understand. She didn't need to make it sound so horrifying. "Wizards don't necessarily fuck their familiars," he added, being deliberately crude and congratulating himself for shocking her when her cheeks darkened with color. Never mind that he'd implied as much to his mother to get Seliah somewhere other than a lab enclosure. "Even if they do, they don't necessarily share a bed or bedchamber."

"Gabriel and Nic do." She lifted her chin defiantly, amber eyes bright with answering annoyance. She looked impossibly adorable in his too-big shirt, delicate and wild. He wanted to see her naked. He walked out of the bathing chamber.

"Your idealistic, foolish iconoclast of a brother is the exception to the rule," he said over his shoulder. "Toss my shirt out, would you? I need to summon servants to bring us clothes and food, and I can't have questions."

"About being bare-chested with me?" she asked, pulling the door mostly shut, then holding out the shirt from a slim hand thrust through the crack.

"About new scar tissue healing from a mortal wound," he corrected. "Secret, remember? Which, by the way, don't tell anyone. Seriously."

She peeked through the crack, only one amber eye and a slim, bare shoulder showing through. "I won't. Your secret is safe with me." Her smile flashed before she disappeared again.

She was entirely naked beyond that door. All he wanted to do was go back in there and wash her himself, to tend to her, to make her smile with dreamy pleasure, to relieve her fears and worries. Except she *should* be worried and afraid. Even though he was saving her from a greater evil, he was still evil, however lesser. He was losing his mind.

"Jadren?" she called through the still-cracked door.

"What?" He bit out the question, making it short and impatient. "Don't just stand around, yakking. I can't get cleaned up until you finish, unless you want me to come in there."

She was quiet a moment, making him wonder what he'd do if she called his bluff. "Why did you flirt with me so much last night?" she finally asked.

Rolling his eyes to the ceiling—usually decorated with dancing cog wheels and lightning bolts, noting that the house had added arrowheads to the design—he scraped the bottom of his corrupt soul for patience. *Flirting,* she called it. She claimed not to be a virgin, but her innocence oozed out in her very word choices. *She's mentally and emotionally a child,* he reminded himself for the umpteenth time, banishing the image of her sweet womanly sex poised above him, fragrant and emanating tantalizing heat. "I was drunk," he answered, "and something about being wounded makes me randy. If I was a dog, I'd have humped your leg. It's not personal."

His maman had taken advantage of that, he recalled with bleak horror, fighting off another onslaught of things best left forgotten. Those women she'd put in the holding cells with him... He wouldn't think about it. Going to the brandy, he chugged straight from the carafe, then triggered the Ratsiel bell to call the servants, triggering several times to convey his urgency. As if they could save him.

As if anyone could.

~ 16 ~

SELLY TOOK HER time playing with the hair and makeup imps. No reason not to, not until Jadren came through with clothing for her. Until then, she was trapped by her nudity in a "bathing chamber" that included no towels to wrap up in. Since there was no tub or other water in evidence, she supposed towels were unnecessary.

All hygiene was handled by elementals. Such a strange world Jadren came from. Nic, too, for that matter, though Jadren's upbringing had a horrific tenor that put it beyond the pale. She'd learned so much about him since they'd arrived, understood so much more about his mercurial nature, how he could be so kind, so tender one moment, then sardonically cruel and mocking the next.

Thinking about him helped her not think about what would happen to her that day. Bonded to Jadren. That was forever, unless one of them died, no matter his claims of leaving her alone once they got back to House Phel. *If* they got back to House Phel. Though… perhaps he would come through. If nothing else, Jadren did keep his word—once you sorted through the lies and deflections—and she believed him when he said he'd never wanted a familiar. He didn't even seem to want a lover. Another way he ran hot and cold, raking her with that avidly sensual gaze one moment, turning his back in calculated indifference the next.

But he did want her, she was sure of that. He'd claimed it was being drunk and the magic…well, she had no idea how magic worked, so that could be true, also. *If I was a dog, I'd have humped your leg. It's not personal.* It might not be personal, but he'd touched her with those erotic kisses and caresses, nibbling at her skin like he wanted to devour her.

She'd never experienced anything like it. And she wanted more of it. Having him touch her that way had been the lone bright spot of this entire ordeal. That was fine if it wasn't her personally, if it was that she was convenient and magically tasty to him, or whatever, but she wanted him to want her. She'd always been good at getting what she wanted. If she had to give up her independence and will to Jadren to survive this, then she wanted a piece of Jadren in return. That was only fair.

Examining her naked body critically in the mirror as the hair imp buzzed around her doing its thing, she could acknowledge its many flaws. She *was* too skinny, her belly concave, her hipbones jutting out sharply. But her breasts were pretty—Jadren's black eyes had been glued to them—and he liked her long legs, commenting on them.

Her face was striking enough. She'd always liked that about herself. And the makeup imp turned out to have a setting to repair skin damage, she discovered, upon reading the instructions. Though her skin had begun to clear up with the tapping of all that stagnant magic, scars from the terrible acne had remained. Wizard Asa had done some healing of it, and now the grooming imp did even more to restore a smooth glowing complexion. The makeup covered the rest. When the imp was done, her hair hung in lustrous, glossy dark waves. She would even call herself beautiful, if only in the dubious quiet of her own mind.

It wasn't much, given her dire situation, but it was something. Jadren was right: she did want to look her best today. For herself and for him. When she was a girl, she'd dreamed about her wedding day, as many of her friends did. Of course, back then she'd imagined a simple, country wedding. In the spring-blossoming orchards, perhaps, and she'd wear a lovely gown and carry a bouquet her father picked for her. Today wouldn't be anything like that—probably the polar opposite—but this might be as close as she'd ever get. She didn't think familiars married anyone but their wizard masters.

And she was secretly happy that it would be Jadren. Even if he was only doing this to save her from a worse fate, that still meant something. He cared about her enough to make that sacrifice, no matter how he tried to divert her attention from that with his sarcasm. If she had to be bonded to him, which she'd begun to accept as an inevitability, then she wanted all of him. She'd have Jadren as a lover, if only once. He owed her that much. Meeting her own gaze in the mirror, she nodded at herself. She didn't have a lot of sexual experience, but Jadren shouldn't be difficult to seduce. Especially now that she knew how to get to him.

"Seliah," Jadren called through the door, then cracked it wider and thrust an arm inside, waggling a silky robe at her. "Clothing has arrived. Try not to destroy the robe before you can get dressed in what they brought."

Suppressing a snicker at his dry humor, she snatched the robe and put it on. Swiftly belting it, she flung the door open. "Your turn," she sang out, gesturing grandly at the bathing chamber.

Jadren eyed her warily. "Why are you so perky all of a sudden?"

Because I'm going to have really good sex later today, she thought, giving him a sly smile. "Feels good to be clean," she said aloud.

He grunted, looking her up and down, expression carefully neutral. "You certainly look less like a murder victim. Oh, wait—that's me."

"*Nearly dead* is the key phrase," she reminded him, tossing his earlier words back in his face.

"Assault victim, then," he grumbled, stalking into the bathing chamber, but not before she caught the glimmer of laughter in his wizard-black eyes. Not many people would so easily forgive a murder attempt. Jadren was simply that sort— probably because he'd done just as bad or worse. "Get dressed," he ordered. "And eat something. Not necessarily in that order, but no dawdling. Ceremony is in an hour."

With that he slammed the door shut. Someone was certainly in a mood. Food was laid out in the adjoining sitting room, showing signs of Jadren having had at it. She wasn't really hungry, her stomach tight with nerves, but she made herself eat, knowing Jadren would badger her about it if she didn't. Seeing a bowl of fresh raspberries among the offerings, she smiled, deeply touched by knowing Jadren had thought of her. His actions revealed far more than his insults.

He emerged not long after, fully dressed and looking like his usual sharply groomed self—except for the lurking, haunted shadows in his face. He wore tailored black clothing, from his glossy, knee-high boots to the high-collared black jacket buckled over a silk shirt. The points of the collar stood up, giving him a dashing, dangerous look, and the coat boasted epaulettes with glittering lightning bolts forking over the repeating House El-Adrel crest.

"You look nice," she offered.

"Nothing but the best for our bonding day," he replied with dry sarcasm, his acute black gaze going to her half-empty plate. "Eat more than that."

"I already ate all of this," she protested, indicating the space with her utensil. "You don't want me puking all over your mother during the ceremony, do you?"

His mouth twitched into a wry, half-smile. "The image carries a certain appeal." His gaze softened, roving over her, and he lifted a hand as if to touch her hair before he dropped it. "It's a pity about your hair—it's really beautiful long."

That gave her pause. "What will happen to my hair?"

"You don't know?"

"Of course not," she answered his surprise with considerable impatience. "I have no idea what this ceremony entails."

"Right." He shrugged. "I suppose you'll find out soon enough."

"Or you could tell me."

"And ruin the surprise?" He lifted a brow in false astonishment.

She pressed a hand to her curdling stomach, shoving her plate away. "Please don't tease me about this. I don't think I can take it, I'm so nervous."

"I apologize." He grabbed a chair and sat beside her, looking solemn and uncharacteristically compassionate. "I'm nervous, too," he admitted, "and I've never witnessed a bonding ceremony, so I only know what I've been told. I'm not sure where Maman plans to hold it. I obviously don't have an arcanium and she obviously won't let us anywhere near hers—which is just as well because I don't want to think about what a thoroughly magical room in an already rogue magical house would be like." He shook his head and considered. "She might make it public, just to see if I'll fail to manifest enough power to do it properly."

"Is that a problem?"

He narrowed his eyes. "Worried about me having performance issues already, darling?"

"It happens to everyone," she reassured him.

"Funny girl. No, I should have plenty of magic, thanks to your boost, to do the job, even with an audience."

"Is it…" She hesitated to ask, bracing for his mockery. "Is it sexual?"

His auburn brows flew up in true astonishment. "No! Well," he amended, "not overtly, but it is… intimate, is the word, I suppose."

"Thus the audience," she commented drily.

"Exactly. That's Maman for you." He paused. "You do have to be naked."

Um, what? Her stomach tightened into a fist. "We have to

be *naked?*"

"Not me—just the familiar," he said, rueful gaze on her. "It's tradition—symbolizes that the familiar comes to the wizard with nothing, that the wizard, or the wizard's house, will provide for them forever after."

"In point of fact, pretty much everything I have now is from you."

"Extenuating and temporary circumstances."

She thought about it. "I don't want to belong to House El-Adrel."

"No, you don't. Which is why, as soon as Maman is satisfied you're properly bonded to me, and as soon as I've satisfied her current curiosities, we're getting out of this place. Phel will make sure El-Adrel can't ever lay claim to you." He smirked slightly. "He has a penchant for stealing familiars from other houses, after all."

She hated everything about this. "Just tell me the rest."

"The short of it is that we'll enter a power circle, I'll set wards, you'll kneel—"

"I won't kneel," she interrupted.

"You have to."

"I won't do it."

"Seliah." He breathed her name on a sigh, then turned her entire chair to face him, scooting closer so their knees bumped. Raising his hands slowly, as if making sure not to startle her, he threaded his fingers into her hair, combing it back from her face. "It will be only for a moment, but it's a ritual that must be conducted in particular ways. If you don't comply, I'll have to force you, to the point of wrapping you in chains. Maman's chains are particularly evil. I'm begging you not to put us both through that. It won't mean anything."

She should shake him off, but his touch soothed her. "If it doesn't mean anything, then why do I have to do it?"

"It won't mean anything to *us*," he corrected. "This is how it goes: the naked familiar kneels, you vow to be mine, I'll bundle your lovely hair like so." His hands slid through her long locks to gather it together at the base of her neck. "I'll cut it off with a blade, and the binding will be complete."

Her mouth was dry, from nerves or his proximity, she wasn't sure. "That's why you're sorry about my hair." Remembering, she added, "That's why Gabriel cut his hair. Mother said it was some odd custom of Nic's family, but it was from the bonding ceremony."

He nodded, hands still in her hair. "Being them, they did it both ways. Traditionally, only the familiar's hair is cut."

"Good thing," she remarked, "as you have nothing much to cut off."

He didn't laugh, still regarding her somberly. "Can you do it? It won't be easy, I know."

"Do I have a choice?" She'd meant to sound arch, or even resigned, instead the words came out like a plea.

He shook his head slowly, regret lining his face. "If you don't go willingly, you'll be stripped and chained and the end result will be the same, except that Maman might decide I can't control you well enough and choose another wizard to bond you to. Your best chance lies with gritting through this—I'll make it quick—and getting out again."

Definitely not the wedding day she'd dreamed of. "Fine,"

she agreed quietly. "But I want you to promise me, on whatever you hold sacred, that I can trust you in this. That this is how it has to be."

"I promise," he averred in a resonant voice, "that you can trust me in this, if in nothing else, that this is how it has to be."

"All right." She took a deep breath.

"I am sorry, though," he said quietly. "For all of this. If I could've spared you any of it, I would have."

"I believe you." And she did.

Lips quirking, he studied her face intently. "Despite the lies and betrayal?"

"I know now you were trying to protect me, in your perverse way."

"My perverse way. That about sums up my entire life." His tone was wry, but his expression still oddly intent, a hint of vulnerability in it. "I didn't want this for you, Seliah. This from you."

"What *did* you want?" She breathed the question, the moment fraught and humming with anticipation. This was a Jadren she hadn't seen before.

"I don't know. I..." He trailed off, hands tightening in her hair, his magic taut between them. He wasn't tapping her magic, but hers flowed eagerly toward him regardless. "Who knew I'd turn out to have romantic ideals after all this time?" He seemed to be asking the question of himself. "The Phel virus, infecting us all."

He moved closer, lips a whisper away. Then his mouth closed on hers, hot, brandy-scented, gently feeding on her lips with tender nips that evoked the sharper bite on her thigh.

Both the immediate caress and the memory flooded her with startling heat, and she moaned, leaning into the kiss and opening her mouth to his.

In another moment he was gone, nearly leaping away from her, standing an arm's length away and wiping his mouth with the back of his shaking hand. "I apologize," he informed her with stiff formality, even adding a half bow from the waist.

"Jadren?" She had no idea what to make of this sudden shift. "There's nothing to apologize for. I liked the kiss."

He huffed out a laugh, a despairing sound in it, then his expression hardened, eyes going flat-black. "You asked what I wanted for you? I wanted someone better than me. Unfortunately, you're stuck with me, so let me apologize in advance for that, too."

"Well, as you say, if I have to be stuck with any wizard, it might as well be you," she offered with a smile. "I'm not sorry it's you."

He stared at her, stricken, then opened his mouth. She'd never know what he'd been about to say because the intricately wheeled timepiece on the wall, one that reminded her of those orbiting globes in the dome of the feast hall, chimed the hour. "And now you're out of time. Get dressed."

"Why bother if I'm going to be naked?"

"You really want to be paraded naked through the halls for everyone in the house to see?"

"Good point," she muttered.

"Fix your hair, too—it's all messed up now."

Standing, she strolled toward him, catching a glimpse of wild emotion in his gaze before he hid it from her. "I'm not afraid of you," she told him.

"Maybe you should be." He held himself with stiff wariness, stepping back when she lifted a hand to touch him. "Don't."

Because he seemed like the fragile one now, she dropped her hand again. "It will be all right." Quite the turnaround, that she should be offering him comfort—particularly after she'd tried to kill him not hours ago.

He was thinking it, too, she could tell, dry amusement flickering behind the impassive mask he'd assumed. "You are a very strange woman, Seliah."

"I don't understood you, either."

That got a chuckle, if a humorless one. "Oh, poppet, you have no idea."

Perhaps not, but she would, she'd make sure of it.

A DOZEN GUARDS in formal House El-Adrel uniforms arrived to escort them. She wore only a simple gown—no lingerie this time—also black, a match of Jadren's outfit with the El-Adrel lightning bolts zig-zagging down the sleeves and down to the trailing hem. Long slits up the sides revealed her legs to the thigh as she walked. Straps tied at the shoulders, the front dipping low, revealing what little cleavage she boasted, and even lower in back, with the gown open to the waist, as if showcasing the long fall of hair she'd be losing. She didn't mind that part as much as Jadren seemed to. Hair was hair and it would grow back. That was the least permanent piece of what she faced.

Would she be able to make herself kneel?

Better than being forced to kneel, part of her acerbically noted.

Or is it? she retorted.

None of her inner voices had an answer to that. Jadren walked by her side, hand resting on her lower back, hot against her skin bared by the gown. Every now and then his fingers lightly caught the trailing ends of one curl or another. He wore that icy mask, revealing nothing, but his magic squeaked against her, buzzing with agitation.

"Are the guards to stop me from bolting," she asked under her breath, "or you?"

He glanced over at her, a hint of a smile softening his harshly blank expression. "Both."

And then they entered a round atrium. Another glass window domed the top of the room, allowing in spring sunlight so much brighter than the glow shed by the fire elementals in their lamps that she squinted from the change. So wrong that natural sunlight already made her flinch. "Why are there only skylights and no windows in the walls?" she whispered to Jadren.

His soft fingertips scratched lightly along the valley of her spine. "The house moves. Seeing the landscape outside disorients the inhabitants. No more questions. Seen, not heard."

She clamped her lips closed, not out of obedience so much as being mindful of his warning. Lady El-Adrel stood on the far side of the circular room, presiding over it all with coolly regal poise, her glittering black gaze resting with expectation on Selly. Around her, fanning out like the wings of a great bird, wizards in black robes with shining lightning bolts stood in rows. They filled the half circle of that side of the room, then slid in behind Selly and Jadren as the pair of them entered, the guards remaining outside as they closed the doors. The circle of wizards filled in, silent and smooth, putting Selly in mind of the sliding doors on the oiled rails of the laboratory.

There were no other familiars in the room, not even Jadren's father, and the encircling wall of black eyes focused on her made her feel small and easily devoured. As if sensing her unease, Jadren flattened his hand on the small of her back, urging her forward, tacitly reminding her there would be no escape. Not yet, not for either of them.

He stopped at the center of room and Selly, unable to face all those blackly predatory gazes, cast her eyes down. The floor had been tiled in concentric circles, all in glittering metallic shades that reflected the light overhead. They formed patterns of zigs and zags, like the omnipresent lightning bolts of El-Adrel. The dizzying pattern seemed almost to move, the various levels of circles gliding in reverse or tandem, the effect disconcerting. Then, as she watched, one circle did move— spinning and then flipping its tiles in a cascading ripple, turning over a new side with silver arrowheads on them. Jadren eyed it, snorting humorlessly, and she wondered if the house could possibly have chosen that image and color on purpose. But why?

She and Jadren halted on the center circle, a burnished

platinum mirror that reflected the sun overhead, just now moving into the circular center window above. Blinding. And yet better than facing all those wizards looking like carrion crows waiting to devour her still-twitching corpse.

"So, son of mine," Lady El-Adrel crooned in a smooth voice. "Do you still wish to bond this familiar?"

"I do, Maman," Jadren replied firmly, lightly caressing Selly's back under her hair.

"Her fertility has not been established," she replied doubtfully, "nor your compatibility in producing magically gifted progeny for the further glory of House El-Adrel."

"True, but I have proven my own fertility countless times, with more contributions to that glory than even I know," he said in tightly restrained voice.

Selly looked up at that, taking in Jadren's coldly still profile. Did that mean what she thought it meant? Jadren had sired children, many he didn't know about. That seemed bizarre, if not impossible, and yet—Jadren pinched the skin on her back, not painfully, but enough to remind her to be silent. She jerked her attention back to Lady El-Adrel who was observing her with cold interest. "You will, of course, give me first dibs on any children you produce between you."

Selly gasped. "What?" she burst out. "Never! I—"

"You'll be given an option," Jadren interrupted, wrapping fingers around her hair and yanking sharply. "I'll see to it, Maman."

She nodded, gaze still on Selly. "*If* you're able to control this one."

"I can," he replied with easy assurance, turning his attention to Selly. He continued to wind her hair around his hand, inexorably reeling her head back so that she arched in response. Bracketing her throat with his other hand, he caressed her skin, setting his thumb and fingertips on her pulse points. A reminder of his promise and hers.

She hoped she wasn't wrong to trust him.

"Kneel for me, familiar," he ordered softly, an answering tremor from him as she trembled. His magic tick-tocked against hers, steady, even soothing. *If you don't comply, I'll have to force you, to the point of wrapping you in chains. Maman's chains are particularly evil. I'm begging you not to put us both through that.*

She thought her knees might not obey, but they flexed, lowering her slightly, and Jadren subtly adjusted his grip to support her as sank. Jadren held her gaze, face still controlled to show little of his internal thoughts, but eyes gave a window into a softer place. In another person she'd call it compassion. She wasn't sure Jadren was capable of the empathy required to feel real compassion, but he did seem to understand her better than almost anyone else. At least, he anticipated when her control would break, when she wouldn't be able to withstand a moment more.

Lady El-Adrel snorted softly. "Is this the same feral creature? I can hardly credit it."

Jadren still held Selly's hair wrapped around his fist, but he released her throat, caressing her cheek lightly, holding her gaze with steadying calm. "You're doing well," he said so quietly only she could hear. "Ignore them. This is only us."

His magic spoked out, forming a wheel, then a column, his wards shimmering into invisible place. With quick fingers, he flicked touched the straps on each of her shoulders, the silky-thin fabric falling away to pool around her kneeling form, cool air and sunlight touching her naked body. He'd done it out of order, she realized, waiting until she knelt to remove the robe, putting her slightly less on display.

Jadren also looked only into her eyes. His magic coiled around her, metallic and resilient, like a spring, the sense of cogs and wheels clicking around and around. "Repeat after me," he told her, as serious and intent as she'd ever seen him. "Take my power with the severing of my hair, wizard."

"Take my power with the severing of my hair, wizard," she repeated in a whisper, but that was apparently loud enough because he nodded encouragingly.

"So that I may be bound to you while you live."

"So that I may be..." She faltered, not able to say it. *While he lived.* Did his self-healing gift make him immortal? That would mean he'd live forever. Wildly she wondered if she was making the biggest mistake of her entire existence, one she might rue every moment of every day hereafter. Here she knelt, abasing herself, naked and at the mercy of her enemy, willingly handing him the keys to her very soul. Gazing up into those black eyes, full of remorseless determination, she reviewed what she knew of this man. A self-admitted liar, spy, cheat, and manipulator. This whole thing could be an elaborate ruse to trap her and she wouldn't know.

Was she being fatally stupid? She wavered, unable to speak those final words that would seal her fate.

Jadren's hand tightened in her hair, tipping her head back, face full of warning, adamant, a hint again of that wild emotion. There was no way out of this. "So that I may be bound to you while you live," he repeated insistently, something in his manner, his magic, reminding her that he'd be bound to her, too. For better or worse, their fates would be tied together.

"So that I may be bound to you while you live," she said, flinging the challenge back at him, meeting his magic with hers, sealing the connection that would bind him to her as surely as he meant to bind her.

Something flickered in his wizard-black eyes, an acknowledgment, maybe a glint of approval. Challenge accepted. He moved swiftly, slipping a blade she hadn't seen him draw beneath the rope of her hair and slicing up in one clean stroke. His magic pierced her, a penetration almost sexual, an incantation clicking into place and sending ripples of reaction through her.

With the releasing of her hair, Jadren no longer held her in place—but his gaze still did. Standing over her, blade in one hand, the long tail of her hair in the other, he stared down at her with a fierce expression, his magic hooked deeply into the very core of her being.

Then he tucked her severed hair through his belt, sheathed the blade, and crouched, drawing the robe back up and fastening it over her shoulders. She was so shaken that she'd forgotten her nakedness. Jadren slipped a hand behind her neck, the grip steadying. "Are you all right?" he asked softly, seeming as if he might actually care.

"I... don't know," she answered faintly.

"Just a bit more. You're almost there. Remember: mouth

shut, eyes open. Follow my lead." He stood, drawing her to her feet and dropping the wards, keeping a loose grip on her wrist as he drew her against his side. "Lady El-Adrel," he said, adding a formal bow, "may I present Seliah El-Adrel, the newest familiar of your House."

Seliah El-Adrel. Something deep inside wrenched apart, bleeding tears and laughter. Nothing would ever be the same again. It had been her wedding day after all.

~ 17 ~

JADREN FACED HIS mother, braced and wary for her next move, aware of Seliah swaying on her feet beside him. She'd been dazed by the bonding, her amber eyes huge in her drawn face, pupils bare pinpricks, her emotional and mental state uncertain. He'd had no idea if the newly embedded enchantment that enacted the bonding from the familiar's side would work. The in-house Haniel wizard had put Seliah unconscious while she was in the testing chair, installing the bonding spell and placing the geas on Jadren that would prevent him from speaking about it.

It just figured that when he really wanted to explain something secret to Seliah, he literally couldn't. He kept a light grip on her, less than because he feared she might bolt, than to be ready to catch her should she faint.

"I'll be the judge of whether the familiar is truly bonded to *my* house," Lady El-Adrel said, summoning that same Hanneil wizard from the crowd of observers with a flick of her fingers. The older man stepped forward, carrying the tabernacle containing the oracle head that was the tool of his trade. Jadren's maman might like using her homemade testing equipment to satisfy her own curiosity, but when it came to official House business, she always employed Convocation methods. She was a stickler for documentation when it suited her purposes. Jadren had studied wizards she'd assembled for this little ceremony—and public show of her munificence in granting her black-sheep son a powerful familiar, even if said familiar was of dubious provenance—and noted that they were all loyal to her. No one would be reporting Seliah's questionable status back to Convocation Center, but there would be a record of her bonding to House El-Adrel, should a legal challenge arise.

The Hanneil wizard flicked open the tabernacle doors, the mummified head within opening its lifeless eyes. This specimen was less decorated than most, but the sight of one was always a shock. Essentially a bodiless head ensconced in their protective tabernacles, the oracle heads weren't exactly alive, but they weren't dead either. No one knew what proprietary magic House Hanneil employed to animate the heads—rumored to be those of former wizards—but the oracles were never wrong, and therefore much in demand. They were the last word in all Convocation legal wrangles.

"Drop your wards, if you will, Wizard Jadren," the Hanneil wizard requested with polite formality.

Chagrined that he'd forgotten his wards were still in place—no doubt out of a subconscious desire to protect them both—Jadren did so, feeling as naked as Seliah had been. He didn't know what he'd do if the oracle head delivered a negative verdict. If he had Gabriel Phel's power, he'd use that to blast their way out of this elaborate trap. But he'd tried that before, failed dramatically, and suffered consequences that still gave him nightmares.

Having awakened the oracle head, the Hanneil wizard made a show of asking the formal question, and the powerful thread of the thing's psychic magic lashed out and sank its claws into Seliah and him with irresistible might. It didn't hurt so much as it felt simply wrong. Seliah whimpered and Jadren slid his hand down her wrist to interlace his fingers with hers.

Hold on, sweetheart, he thought at her—she wouldn't be able to hear his thoughts, but the new bond between them might allow her to sense his intention—*just a bit longer and then we can be alone.*

And then what? the snarling, sardonic part of him wondered.

He didn't know. He'd heard stories, of course, of wizards celebrating the bonding of their new familiar by immediately using them in some complex incantation that had escaped their abilities before that day. Often it involved sex magic, or pain, or both, none of which he intended to subject Seliah to, ever. In fact, he didn't intend to employ Seliah's magic for anything beyond the expedient. He had no intention of becoming his mother, which meant confining himself to making smallish artifacts and keeping his own wretched skin intact.

Seliah tugged at his hand, her self-control slipping as the wild urge to flee palpably surged within her. He'd always empathized with her that way, sharing a profound understanding of feeling trapped and vulnerable to the predator's tooth that lashed at the inside of your skin. As with facing many predators, however, running didn't work. It only excited them and incited them to give chase. As wrong as it felt in the moment, freezing, hunkering, down, pretending to be innocuous—the magical equivalent of a possum playing dead—that was the surest way to surviving.

Then, if the predator attacked anyway, there was still the option to run.

The oracle withdrew its psychic tentacles and Seliah relaxed slightly, no longer quite so tensed to fling herself at the nearest escape route.

"Yes," the oracle said, a terse answer to the question of whether he'd properly bonded Seliah. Relief washed through him with the intensity of a Meresin downpour. His mother frowned in disappointment, naturally, but her brow quickly cleared—for show and because she no doubt realized the opportunities now open to her.

"Welcome to House El-Adrel, Familiar Seliah," she intoned with a patently fake smile, one that brightened with malicious glee when she turned it on Jadren, her gaze going to their joined hands. "We'll retire to the laboratories now."

"No," Jadren replied, keeping his tone easy though his gut curdled with unease.

"Excuse me?" His mother's brows and tone arched alarmingly. "I believe we made an agreement."

"Do you truly want to discuss this here?" he inquired silkily, gesturing at their audience.

Her brows lowered, drawing together, and she flicked her fingers at their avid witnesses. "Leave us."

They did, with the alacrity of minions well-versed in avoiding the ire of their liege wizard. In a moment, it was only the three of them in the room. Seliah had calmed, her magic settling into the reflective brightness of moonlight on still water, curiously soothing to him, even though he wasn't drawing on her magic. She glanced at him, caginess in her amber gaze before she lowered it, lush black lashes like lace against her golden skin.

"You promised me," Lady El-Adrel hissed at him. "Are you reneging on our deal because you believe you have the power now, having gotten what you wanted? Because I warn you, there will be consequences."

"No, Maman," he answered, keeping his jaw relaxed and the edge out of his tone. "I'm requesting a bit of decorum. It's rather unseemly to insist that your son submit to your experiments on his bonding day. What of observing the traditional celebrations?"

She considered, and—for a fleeting moment that would have filled him with glee, had he been a happier, more optimistic person—she wavered. He caught it the moment she saw through his ploy, expression icing into her true face, the one she wore while indulging her most primal interests. "Ah," she breathed. "I see. You're not afraid for yourself, but for *her*. You've never cared in the least for traditions or celebrations or really anything that matters to advance this house. This is why you could never be my heir, Jadren: you're simply not... enough." Her glittering black gaze slid to Seliah, who tensed warily, her skin palpably chilling, her magic going silver sharp.

He could use that, all that brilliant, potent magic now at his disposal. There was a slim chance he could take his mother by surprise, since his father wasn't present to amplify her magic. Possibly, just possibly, he could incapacitate her long enough for them to get away.

But he wouldn't be able to kill her, not with her resistance to death that he'd inherited from her, along with her cruelty, madness, and inability to empathize with anyone.

"Try it," she invited silkily, seeing it in him, both of them knowing the other obscenely well, with all those far-too-intimate sessions over years upon years of torturous experiments. With a sense of crushing defeat, he realized the profound mistake he'd committed. Seliah was right. He should have gotten them out of the carriage and taken the risk in the wilds with the spirits and the hunters.

He'd failed. Worst of all, he'd failed more than himself this time. Despite all his promises, he'd failed Seliah. Perhaps his mother was right about him and always had been.

His mother read the defeat in him, cold lips curving in satisfaction. "I knew you didn't have it in you."

"Leave Seliah out of it," he begged. "I'll double my commitment."

Lady El-Adrel raised a brow. "Such devotion. I swear I never thought I'd see you care about anything this much. I do believe this emotional investment could lead to the breakthrough I've sought." The brow lowered. "I already have your full cooperation until I decide I've exhausted all avenues. You can't double that. The familiar will provide the magic to sustain your recoveries, so I expect exhausting my ingenuity will take a very, very long time. Come along now like a good boy."

She glided away and he turned to follow, utterly defeated. Seliah's hand vised on his and, reluctantly, he met her demanding amber gaze. "The laboratories?" she hissed, alarm in every icy, moonlit line of her.

He shook himself free of her grip. It wasn't as if he was going to access her magic, familiar or not, and he obviously couldn't provide comfort or reassurance. "There's no way around it," he told her dully. "The only path is through at this point. Endure and survive."

"That's it?" she whispered harshly, trotting beside him in his victorious mother's wake.

"That's all there is."

"I never thought you'd accept defeat so easily."

Seliah's assessment, so like his mother's, burned like salt carelessly caught in the lip of a wound that couldn't be closed. He set his teeth. "Which only goes to prove you don't know me at all, poppet."

"You promised this was the way to survive, the only way. Was that a lie?"

He stopped. Faced her. She looked ravishingly gorgeous, her hair curling wildly without the weight, the light black silk gown clinging to her slender shoulders, revealing those delicate winged collarbones that enticed him to run his tongue along those lines and sensitive hollows. The silk flowed over her breasts—surprisingly full even without being trussed up and given her underfed condition—and snagged on her hard nipples alluringly. He'd been careful not to look at her nakedness, since it hadn't been her own wish to be thus revealed, but his mind had eagerly assembled a complete image from the fragments gathered by his peripheral vision, and the sight of her slim, perfect body, like a tawny flame in the midday sunlight, haunted him. She would forever star in his sexual fantasies.

At least he'd have that. Dark arts knew he could never have her, not that way.

Her gaze accused him now and he had no sufficient reply. "It was and is the only way to survive. Take comfort in the reality that you have no choice."

"Comfort?" she echoed incredulously. "You can't be serious."

"Deadly serious," he answered bleakly. "There's a restfulness in surrendering to the inevitable. Fighting takes a lot out of you. Give in and eventually it will be over."

She gazed at him for a long moment. "You're right. You're not at all who I thought you were."

And so, he mused, despondently facing the realization of his worst expectations, *I'll lose this, too, the regard of the only person I've met whose good opinion mattered to me.* With the possible exception of Gabriel Phel. And didn't that just figure? The Phel family had a knack for this sort of thing. He produced a thin smile. "Then I'll take my own comfort in the knowledge that I *did* warn you. Not my fault you didn't listen, poppet."

Her amber eyes firing, she opened her mouth to retort, but his mother—ironically enough—saved him from whatever justifiably scathing assessment of his courage and character Seliah had been about to level on him. "*Now,* Jadren!" his mother commanded. "Don't make me use the chains."

Involuntarily, he shuddered, breaking into a cold sweat as his stomach turned threateningly. Seliah's frown softened. "Is that what you—"

"Seen. Not heard," he gritted out, unable to withstand a moment more. Seizing her by the wrist, he bodily dragged her to a torment that would no doubt scar her for life on every level. All his fault, his failure. He couldn't save her from what would come, but he could spare her the chains.

"YOU WANT TO let Sabrina Sammael just go home, on her own?" Gabriel demanded incredulously, wrestling his rising ire. Nic stood before his desk, meeting his gaze calmly, her emerald eyes assessing his mood, her magic twining around his with calming tendrils. He didn't want to be calmed, however. Though the tedium of dealing with the tasks of being Lord Phel had settled his temper—exactly as Nic had predicted, which he wasn't sure if he found reassuring or aggravating— the prospect of setting free the vicious teenage witch who'd gleefully caused so much pain to so many had him seething anew.

Nic folded her hands demurely, regarding him with regal poise. With the way she'd laced her fingers together, he could see that she'd decorated her nails again, wearing them long with glittering blue and silver gems, much as the first night he met her, only now she wore House Phel colors. No doubt if he looked closely, there would be tiny silver moons there. She also wore another of her new gowns, a more formal one, perfectly fitted as only Ophiel magic could produce, and also in their house colors. Her hair and makeup had been touched-up, too, crisply perfect.

She'd dressed up to meet with Sabrina, he realized, presenting herself as the glossy image of Lady Phel. "Correct me if I'm mistaken," she answered with cool patience, "but I rather believed ensuring Selly's safety is more important than either revenge or rehabilitation concerning Sabrina Sammael. You wanted to expedite the rescue and this is the fastest method I could come up with."

"You're right," he conceded on a sigh, raking fingers through his hair, then scooting his chair back and patting his thigh. "Come here, my heart. Don't stand there like a supplicant applying to Lord Phel for some favor or decision."

She smiled with warm affection, happily taking him up on the invitation and settling her ripe bottom on his lap, winding her hands behind his neck. "A *lot* of correspondence, I take it?" she asked with gentle sympathy.

"You called it," he replied grimly.

Hesitating, she glanced at the missives scattered over the desk. "Anything from House Elal?"

"Not yet."

"They're being too quiet," she commented. "I don't like it."

"I understand. I don't like sitting here dithering with business when I could be going after Selly."

"Doing business isn't dithering. You're consolidating wealth and power which will do more to benefit Selly in the long run than recklessly haring off to antagonize House Sammael further."

"They antagonized me first," he growled.

"A legitimate point, but please believe me that all-out war with Sammael is truly the last thing we can afford, if only on a purely practical basis. It would be terribly expensive."

"Sometimes your practicality can be an annoying hindrance to my fantasies of vengeance." He burned to fight, to take action, to chop his enemies into pieces so tiny he could use them to fertilize the fields of Phel.

Nic smiled sympathetically, not at all bothered. "Good thing you love me anyway."

With a sigh, he kissed her. "I do love you anyway."

She urged him into a deeper kiss, lavishing him with her lush mouth and a generous flow of rose-red, wine-rich magic. He'd love to sink into that offering, perhaps to turn her to straddle his lap so he could lose himself in her body, love, and infinite comfort—but that wouldn't save Selly. Withdrawing from the kiss, he leaned his forehead against hers. "I apologize for my snarling. Tell me your plan."

"We create a debt with House Sammael by voluntarily returning Sabrina," Nic answered promptly. "Preparations are underway for her to depart within the hour, unless you say no."

"I trust you," he replied simply, "and it's a relief to be taking action, if only by proxy." In truth the coiled, seething need to fight relaxed in him somewhat. Nic knew the Convocation and if she thought this was the way to extract Selly intact from House Sammael, then it was. "But do explain," he added, curious now what her wily brain had concocted. "Your last take was that a hostage-exchange wouldn't be enough."

"That's why the voluntary aspect. In return for her freedom, Sabrina has promised to represent Sergio's death as self-defense on your part. The duel will be repainted as a much narrower victory than it was," she added with an apologetic wrinkle of her nose, "with Sergio nearly defeating you and you lashing out with a desperation move, using a sword, that took him by surprise as no self-respecting wizard would stoop to a non-magical attack. I know it's a blow to your pride, but…"

"But my pride can take the hit, for Selly's sake," he finished for her.

"I figured as much. Sabrina will also be able to spin her involvement in Sergio's scheme however it best suits her needs and her father's mood. She'll assess Jadren's status, and Selly's. She promises to do her best to see them both sent home to House Phel and will communicate with us if she needs help."

It could work, he supposed. But… "How do you know Sabrina will keep her word?"

"Hanneil magic," she answered promptly, grinning at his confusion. "You didn't tell me you accepted a Hanneil wizard minion during my unplanned absence."

He frowned at her capricious description of her abduction and those agonizing days he'd spent recuperating and longing for her, not knowing if she was dead or alive. In truth, he hardly recalled much about those days, slogging through the work of House Phel without the one person who'd come to make it all worthwhile. He'd interviewed a number of applicants with dogged determination, knowing they'd need the numbers should it come to that expensive war with House Sammael, accepting pretty much anyone who would sign their non-disclosure agreement and contract, figuring he could always fire them later.

"Wizard Ziv," Nic filled in with quiet amusement. "They are quite a powerful wizard and deft with their magic."

He remembered Wizard Ziv, a soft-spoken, austere personality, who informed him they identified as gender neutral and asexual, mentioning that first in case Gabriel found that objectionable. He'd replied that it mattered to him not at all, though he privately wondered if other houses had objected and thus sent Wizard Ziv to House Phel. "That's something they can do?"

Nic nodded, toying with the short hairs at the nape of his neck, a caress both soothing and arousing. "Recall the geas that prevents Convocation Academy-trained wizards from mentioning the enchantment embedded in familiars that allows the bonding to occur."

Not trusting his voice, he nodded curtly. That bit of underhanded nastiness was far from the worst trick the Convocation played on familiars, but it rankled nevertheless.

"It turns out that it's a fairly simple magic, along the lines of basic warding, particularly as Sabrina agreed to having the geas implanted. It reinforces her internal resolve. Han was able to provide the power for Ziv. The pair of them worked quite well together, in fact," she added with a lift of one brow.

He didn't like the sound of that. "Are you suggesting what I think you're suggesting? Because you already know my answer."

"Surely you'll accept that not all wizard–familiar bondings are negative, abusive relationships."

He had to say something. "You won't like this, but we should discuss the possibility of having Alise sever our—"

Nic pressed her fingers over his mouth. "You're right, I don't like it. Don't even suggest it."

"I want you to know the option is out there," he persisted.

"I know and I don't want it." She glared at him fiercely, then softened, wriggling winsomely on his lap, brushing his groin with her shapely thigh. "You're not getting rid of me so easily, wizard."

"You're trying to distract me," he admonished severely, because it was absolutely working. And sheer relief filled him that she didn't want to be severed from him. That possessive wizard instinct in him she always wanted him to listen to had nearly gone mad at the thought. A good caution for how other wizards would react.

"I just want my wizard to be happy," she purred sensually, then stopped teasing him, sobering. "The fact remains that the best way to protect our unbonded familiars—Han, Iliana, and Selly, too—is to see them safely bonded. You have the power and discretion to choose good wizards for them. I'm not suggesting that you take the choice away from Han, but it could be an ideal partnering. Wizard Ziv is not interested in a sexual relationship with their familiar, so that would allow Han to be faithful to Iliana, which is their ideal. There are far worse solutions."

"I'll think about it," he allowed grudgingly. "I suppose if the bonding becomes a problem, we could always have Alise sever the bond again."

"*If* we want it known that we've discovered this massively

powerful weapon that promises to destroy the supremacy of wizards in the Convocation, which means they'll crush House Phel and exterminate anyone with the knowledge of it before allowing that to happen."

"Unless too many people know for them to kill everyone. We need to disseminate this knowledge widely," he argued. "How can you not be in favor of this? It would mean freedom for all familiars, the ability to govern their own lives. No more second-class citizenship."

"Don't lecture me," she replied tartly. "I *am* in favor of it. I'm just more in favor of keeping *your* foolish head attached to your body!" She yanked on his hair for emphasis, eyes glittering green ferocity, his personal marsh cat unsheathing her claws. "You're more important to me than all of them."

"Than all the world?" he teased, drawing her to snuggle against him, tipping her head so her silky curls fit under his chin and wrapping his arms around her. What had he done to deserve such unconditional devotion? Nothing. Sometimes it terrified him how much he didn't deserve Nic.

"Yes," she answered firmly. "I'm selfish that way. You made me bond you, too, and I'm not giving you up, not for anything."

"What if Sammael has bonded Selly to a wizard?" he asked softly, giving voice to one of his fears for his fragile, naïve sister. "What if it's Jadren—or someone worse?"

He felt more than heard her sigh. "Let's not borrow trouble. The priority is getting Selly home safe. We can make decisions once we know more."

"If Jadren bonded her, I'm going to kill him." Gabriel felt

better for putting that out there. He'd enjoy taking apart the duplicitous El-Adrel spy, joint by joint, starting with his fingertips.

"Again, let's cross that bridge when we come to it. Sabrina is to send terms for us to retrieve them both. We'll know by evening and perhaps have them here by morning."

"Good," he grunted, mollified by that much. "I want this episode over with so we can move on with other issues."

"Like destroying the Convocation?" she asked, lifting her head and meeting his gaze with amusement and a bit of rebuke.

"Yes." He kissed her, harder than before, showing her his determination. "You'd condemn the world for me; I'll remake the world for you. No other familiar should ever feel they have to give up their friends, family, homeland, and lives simply to avoid a terrifying fate."

She laughed softly, stroking his cheek, a glisten of emotion in her glowing eyes. "You're not so scary, wizard."

"No?" With a mock growl, he lifted her, turning her to straddle his lap and hiking up her full skirts in the same motion. Manifesting a silver blade from moon magic, he sliced away her panties and cupped her hot sex, making her gasp in shock and instant arousal. Thrusting his fingers inside her sleek passage, he held her in place with a hand at her back, so she arched over it, taken by the convulsion of pleasure. The movement forced her full breasts to swell over the low neckline of her gown and he buried his face in her bosom, inhaling the scent of roses, then licking a long line between her breasts up to her mouth, capturing her lips in a savage kiss, driving her ruthlessly higher with his fingers.

"Gabriel," she panted, clutching his shoulders. "Let me—"

"No," he informed her. No question this time. "Let *me*."

It was a long time before she had any breath to argue.

~ 18 ~

SELLY PACED THE small enclosure, waiting for Jadren to wake. Through the sole glass wall, she could see the wizard-scientists and engineers moving about their work, ignoring her as if she were just another piece of lab equipment.

Which was probably more accurate than she wanted to think about. Though it was better by far than thinking about the harrowing last few hours. Jadren had taken the brunt of it, willingly complying with everything his mother demanded of him, not even drumming up enough spirit to argue with her. He'd behaved like one of those automatons, woodenly obeying, seeming unaware of Selly's presence except to draw on her magic to attempt to heal himself around the various attachments his monster of a mother wanted to implant.

And, every time, when he'd accessed their bond and her magic flowed into him, she felt his agony through the connection. That and a despair so profound she didn't know how he bore it. Perhaps he couldn't bear it and had broken entirely. He certainly seemed to lack any vestige of his usual spirited and sardonic nature. Except for a panicked moment when his mother had brought out the promised chains in order to hold him still for a precision implantation around his eye that upset him so much he couldn't help twitching. Then he'd been like the half-feral creature he named her, screaming like a wild thing as the hooks penetrated his skin and dug into his flesh, curved like the fangs of that snake.

No wonder he'd puked at the memory that had evoked. Selly didn't know how Jadren was even a functional person if he'd spent his life this way. Maybe he wasn't. That would explain a great deal.

He'd finally lost consciousness and nothing his mother had tried had revived him at that point. Selly had been frankly relieved to be tossed with him into the test-subject enclosure. At least inside of it, no one could torment him further, or her by proxy. She didn't understand her feelings for Jadren—it would help if they stayed one way for more than a few hours at a time—but watching him suffer had hollowed her out far beyond the magic he'd drained from her.

Pacing back to Jadren, she crouched to check on him. Though the guards had dumped him in a heap on the floor, Selly had rearranged his splayed and bloodied limbs into the most comfortable position possible, which wasn't saying much, given the hard and sterile space. If she'd hadn't seen him heal from the arrow wound, she'd be panicking herself, certain that he couldn't recover. As it was, his body and inherent magic was working on its own. She'd tried feeding him some of her magic, even though everyone had told her it never worked that way.

Sure enough, it didn't. But he seemed to be recovering anyway, if slowly. They'd been provided with a pitcher of water and some cloths, which she'd used to clean up the worst of the blood. Reserving one of the cloths and keeping it clean, she soaked it in some water and wrung drops into his open mouth, trying to get some into him. As she watched, a coil of copper wire extruded itself from his swollen and bruised eye orbit, uncannily like a worm emerging from its burrow, then fell to the floor with a ping. She shuddered in sympathy, plucking up the thing and flinging it to the far corner with all the other bits and metal pieces his mother had implanted and that his body was rejecting.

"Such a touching display of devoted care." Lady El-Adrel's cool voice broke the silence in the room, making Selly jump. She hadn't been able to hear anything through the thick glass, but the monster herself now stood on the other side, watching them with clinical interest, Jadren's father standing behind her and just to the side. His gaze was fixed on his son, expression impassive, but concern straining his posture. Fyrdo had been present for the extended experimental session, also, assisting his wizard with singular focus. Something else Selly couldn't understand.

"Is that why Jadren wanted you so badly, because he knew you already loved him? Is there Fascination at work, perhaps?" Lady El-Adrel mused, her voice coming clearly though no other background noise did, so some enchanted mechanism must allow her words to penetrate the cage.

Selly didn't bother to reply. She had no answers anyway, except that caring for a companion who'd been brutalized was simply the human thing to do and that wasn't something a person of Lady El-Adrel's corrupted heart could understand. *Incapable of love.*

"It's always better when a familiar loves their wizard," the woman continued, "isn't that so, Fyrdo?" She looked over her shoulder at him, turning enough to caress his cheek with elegant fingers.

"Always, my love," he agreed fervently, sounding for all the world as if he meant every word, his eyes all for her. But when she turned back to Selly with a smug smile, his gaze went directly to Jadren, all semblance of affection gone, strident worry bracketing his handsome mouth.

"It's good that you love him. He won't be able to resist bedding you, though apparently he has so far." Lady El-Adrel shook her head, regarding her son with what on anyone else would look like a fond smile. "Stubborn fool. But he's always been so desperate for affection and he's clearly attached to you, plus you're in his power now which is the greatest aphrodisiac for any wizard. I'm inclined to keep you two boxed in here together until his self-restraint fails."

"But...why?" Selly asked, unable to imagine what this woman wanted or how she could know about their intimacy or lack thereof.

"To demonstrate that I control every aspect of his life and body," Lady El-Adrel answered coolly. "Jadren has a distressing tendency to think he'll be able to escape me someday. I imagine that somewhere, in the rotten depths of his worm-ridden heart, he thinks you'll be the key to his freedom. But he's mistaken. You are yet another chain by which I bind him."

"How could you?" Selly demanded, her own restraint collapsing. "How could you torture your own child like this?"

Her smile never dimmed. "Science requires it, little familiar. I answer to the demands of a higher calling. Besides, he'll recover. He always does. Surely you know that about him by now?" She lifted a brow. "You can't be that dense. If you are…" She shrugged philosophically. "Well, you'll understand Jadren's little secret soon. It's up to *you* to make sure that he's ready for another session in the morning."

"Another?" Selly echoed, almost unable to fathom it.

"Yes. We all have to keep working until I'm satisfied that I've pursued all variables." She pursed her lips in irritation as she gazed at the pile of extruded gadgets. "There must be a way to solve the rejection problem. I've arranged to have food delivered. I suggest you both eat and sleep well. You'll need your strength. Come along, Fyrdo." She glided away and, with a last, longing look at his son, Fyrdo followed.

"Is it gone?" Jadren whispered through cracked lips, his voice hoarse and broken from his unending screams.

Relief surged through her, along with fury. The typical mix of opposing emotions he elicited in her. She thumped him— gently—on an uninjured spot on his arm, not wanting to hurt him more, but needing to relieve the urge to touch him. "You were faking unconsciousness, leaving me to verbally fence with your monster of a mother!"

He produced a weak grin. "You were doing so well." Grimacing, he worked his jaw, then spat out another metal piece. She threw it to join the others.

"What is she trying to do to you?"

"Make me a better man?" he ventured. "No wonder she's finding it an impossible task. Help me sit up."

"I don't think you should," she replied dubiously, nevertheless supporting him as he struggled to a sitting position.

"All the blood has pooled to my back," he said on a pained grunt. "If I were a corpse, you'd see all kinds of nasty corruption of the flesh. In an ostensibly still-living man, it hurts like you shot a dozen arrows into my back. Now to stand." He took a deep breath, tipping back his head to look at the ceiling as if he might will himself closer.

"I really think you should stay still."

"Being upright and moving accelerates the healing. Trust me." He grimaced. "And, ah—I could use your help again."

"Do those words burn in your mouth?" she muttered, looping his arm over her shoulder and pushing up with her legs, glad they were strong enough to lever them both upright.

"Yes, burns my throat like that pitiful excuse for brandy your brother serves." He gritted out the sarcastic reply, trying to sound like his usual uncaring self, but his breath came in pained gasps and he leaned heavily on her as they limped across the small enclosure.

"You need more of my magic." That emptiness in him called to her, tugging insistently, ravenous and needy.

"I'm fine."

"Even your mother said—"

"Now you're listening to *her?*"

"And I can feel it through the bond. It's like a great sucking hole inside you."

"Wow, thanks for that uplifting metaphor."

She took heart at his meanness. It actually seemed to invigorate him, his movements slightly less labored. "In the marshes, there's this particularly treacherous sort of unstable boggy ground," she told him. "It looks like a thick mat of vegetation that should hold your weight easily, but if you step on it, it gives way in this big slidey motion."

"You're quite the poet with these colorfully creative words and metaphors."

"It's so slidey," she continued undaunted, in fact encouraged by his poking at her, "that there's no purchase, no way to prevent yourself from going down. One wrong step and, before you even realize you've fucked up, you're in over your head with no ability to climb out."

"I perceive that we've reached the extended analogy phase of our story." They completed two more passes back and forth across the room. "Don't stop there. I assume that you, our plucky heroine, suffered such a plunge and survived to tell the tale, as you're currently here attempting to teach me a moral lesson."

"I thought I was done for," she agreed. "My lungs were bursting, heart hammering, vision going black. I wanted to breathe so badly even though I knew I'd only inhale mud and water and it would just kill me faster. Even knowing that, it took everything in me not to give in."

He grunted at that. Could be from pain, but she took it as a sound of sympathetic solidarity. Because she still wanted to think the best of him, despite everything.

"Then I hit bottom," she said, before he could prod her again. "My feet touched solid ground and I pushed up up up with all my strength. Luckily I broke the surface near some tectona tree roots and was able to pull myself out."

They made three more labored circuits of the room.

Though it might be her imagination, and a dollop of wishful thinking, he seemed to be moving better, though his face still looked terrible. "Well," Jadren finally said, "if the point of your morality tale is to instruct me to find power and ultimate escape from peril after hitting rock-bottom, then I suppose I'm poised to break surface. Any moment now," he added darkly.

"It's just a true story," she said quietly. "No great message to it."

"Ah yes," he breathed. "All spurred by your observation that I'm akin to your sucking bog of doom. Have your own feet touched bottom yet, poppet?"

She had thought she'd already hit the lowest point, but somehow she still continued to fall. Like she'd simply hit a false bottom and broken through it, helplessly plummeting to some doom even worse than both of them dying, if Jadren even could. It seemed he'd be forever denied that ultimate escape, just as his mother predicted. "Just take some of my magic already," she answered instead, and with considerable exasperation.

"I don't *need* you," he bit out, sounding more like he was trying to convince himself. "I've been through this innumerable times before, all without your nubile assistance, tasty though you might be."

Nubile? Tasty? Uh oh. He'd reached *that* stage of the healing process, apparently. Sure enough, at the next turn, he nuzzled her temple, turning his face more fully into the side of hers and inhaling deeply. "Mmm," he purred. "Now, wanting you is something else. You smell like moonlight on still water."

Absurd pleasure fluttered through her. *We are in a glass*

cage, she reminded herself. No doubt someone was observing them, taking notes on their behavior. She should put distance between them, not melt into him. "What does that even smell like?" she retorted with extra tartness to counterbalance the will-sapping desire to yield.

"*You* smell like that." His lips whispered over her ear, then found the hollow beneath, sucking lightly on the skin to draw it tightly into his mouth where he licked the taut flesh, then released it with a nip of his teeth that sent a lightning bolt of need straight to her groin. "And you taste like snowmelt from a glacier, pure and invigorating."

"When have you ever licked a glacier?" And what was wrong with her that she couldn't seem to find it in her to shove him away?

He laughed, warmly, and licked her neck. She repressed a shudder. The man was infuriatingly seductive. If she wasn't insane again, he'd drive her there. "The glacier came to me," he purred, making it sound ridiculously sexual. "A beverage featured at a fire and ice banquet to celebrate my beloved maman's natal day. No expense was spared. But let's not talk about her."

With surprising agility and sudden strength, he pinned her to the wall instead of making the next pivot. One moment he had an arm around her shoulders, leaning heavily on her, the next she had her back to the wall, his hand behind her neck, the other stroking down the thin black silk gown she still barely wore. At least she'd managed to keep that intact. Not that it felt like much protection with Jadren's caress burning over her ribs and waist, sliding intimately over her hip and, finding the slit in the skirt, down her naked thigh. She groaned as she managed to duck his kiss, his mouth catching the corner of her lips. Apparently unbothered, he took advantage of her exposed throat, gliding kisses along the astonishingly sensitive hollows there.

"Jadren..." she choked out, but managed nothing more as his hand closed over her breast and she lost all breath. The shock of his thumb grazing her nipple was like nothing she'd ever felt before. Nothing like the clumsily sweet fumblings of her teenage lover. He circled the areola through the flimsy silk, scraping his thumbnail over the tiny, sensitive bumps as her nipple pebbled. He knew exactly what it did to her, too, his lips curving knowingly against her jaw, kissing along the line of it as she tipped her head against the wall. She made some sort of strangled, incoherent sound she didn't recognize from herself.

"Seliah," he purred against her skin. "Seliah. Seliah." Chanting her name, he pressed kisses between. "Seliah, my beauty. Let me pleasure you. I will be so much better than whatever lovers you scrounged out of that swamp. I know what I'm doing." Proving his point, he pinched her nipple lightly between thumb and forefinger, just hard enough for a fleeting stab of pain that made her gasp, followed by a moan at the ensuing erotic release. He chuckled, another sensual stimulation as he found the hollow at the base of her throat. "It's driving me mad to know you're mine now. I have to have you. All of you. Say yes. You'll know when you feel me deep inside you, my magic in yours and yours in mine. Let me, Seliah."

She was clinging to him, fingers digging into his leanly

muscled shoulders, not to push him away, but to draw him closer. Trying to muster her wits and rally the very good reasons to say no that had been present in her mind only moments before, she opened her mouth, hoping the words would find their way.

Instead, Jadren found his way in, his lips closing over hers with consuming passion. This wasn't the awkward kiss she'd pressed on him and regretted almost immediately. This wasn't him tensing, making it clear he wanted nothing more than for her to go away. This was him drawing her in, inhaling her, holding her in place with that burning hand gripping the back of her neck with erotic intensity as he plundered her mouth—and her magic.

Despite his earlier refusal, he drank of her magic now, pulling with deep, demandingly visceral tugs that touched intimate places inside her. She groaned and he swallowed that, too, his magic roaring through hers as he pressed her to the wall, hard chest crushing her breasts and teasing her nipples so her head swam with dizzying darkness. She yielded to that demand, too, seemingly unable to summon any inkling of rational resistance, her body heating, slickening, softening into submission.

His hand slid hot up her naked thigh, cupping her bare bottom, and he murmured into her mouth about needing, wanting, possessing, urging her to spread her legs…

Reality roared back. "No," she managed, finding it in her to push that hand away, to lever him off of her. "Jadren, we can't. Not here. They're watching."

"That's all right," he assured her, drawing her seductively

close, his lips finding hers again, nibbling, nudging, enticing her back, fingers trailing up her inner thigh. "They always do."

Wait, what? Discovering renewed resolve, she pushed him away firmly, managing to duck out from the sensual cage of his knowing embrace.

"What does that mean?" she demanded, putting her back to the far wall and thrusting out a hand to stop him as he pursued her. "Stay back, Jadren. I mean it."

He halted, offering open palms, though his gaze drilled into her with obsidian fire. He simmered with magic now, bruised and swollen face healing almost before her eyes, the power of it making him more compelling than ever. He crooked his finger at her, beckoning. An instinctive, newly yielding part of her leapt to respond, and she squelched it with ruthless desperation. "It doesn't matter," Jadren coaxed. "Come here."

"No." Everything in her screamed *yes.* "And it does matter. Tell me."

"Then I'll come there." Easing closer, he stalked her with sinuous grace.

"I swear, Jadren, if you come any closer, I *will* fight you and I will *never* forgive you."

Some semblance of sanity returned to his eyes, replaced by wary resignation. "It's pointless. You can't resist the bonding for long. Even now your instincts are screaming that you belong to me, aren't they?" His lips curved in satisfaction at her shock that he knew that. "You are mine, Seliah, like it or not. More, you *want* to be, in every way."

She did want that, did want his hands on her again, even as

her rational mind—never all that reliable since the madness anyway—quietly whispered of future regrets. "Just tell me this what you meant, that they always watch. I deserve the truth. I need the truth, Jadren," she added, holding his gaze and silently beseeching the part of him that had been her friend. If that had been real.

"You have no idea." He glanced around the enclosure, seeming to register the glass window and people moving beyond. "You really don't want to know," he added on a sigh, sliding her a rueful grimace.

"I not only want to know, I think I *should* know. What do you mean always? Am I not the first woman who's been confined in here with—" The ugly truth dawned on her. "That's what your mother meant about your fertility being confirmed. They've put other women in here with you, waiting for the healing frenzy to send you into raping them."

"I never raped anyone," he bit out. "They were all willing. In fact, they were downright eager to have my wizard babies."

"Or familiar babies." The correction didn't matter, but she was struggling to wrap her mind around this revelation.

He shrugged, as if that didn't matter. "A roll of the dice for everyone."

"How many?"

"How many babies? I have no idea. No one keeps me apprised of the results of those particular experiments. Well, really any of them. I'm not exactly in charge here, in case you haven't noticed."

"How many female familiars did they breed you to?" Selly ground out, struggling to comprehend the monstrous enormity of the bog she'd fallen into. *False bottom.*

"They weren't all familiars," he corrected, a curious dullness coming over him. "Wizards, too. They were all happy enough to be pleasured. You will be, too. If nothing else, I've learned to do that much. Dozens," he offered, and it took her a moment to realize he was finally answering her question. "Could be a hundred or more. They blur together and I wasn't exactly in my right mind much of the time." Lifting fingertips to his temples, he massaged them. "Trying to remember is painful. What I think is real isn't always."

"Oh, Jadren..." She wanted to comfort him. She didn't dare go near him. "Don't think about it. I'm sorry I asked."

He scrubbed his hands over his face, then dropped them, staring at them for a long, fraught moment. His gaze traveled their sterile prison, lingering briefly on the pile of parts extruded from his body, then returned to meet her eyes, expression taut, a disturbing edge to it. "Seliah." He sighed her name, drawing out the syllables. "Who are you, really?"

She hadn't expected that. "You know who I am. You met me at House Phel. We've traveled together."

He snorted. "It's quite the flimsy cover story, don't you think? In what world would I have been at House Phel, if it even exists? House Phel perished from the rolls ages ago. And why would this Lord Phel let me *travel* with his sister, an unbonded familiar?"

"I..." This was bad. He didn't seem to be playing a game with her. "Don't you remember?"

"I *remember* plenty." He placed odd emphasis on the word, casting it into doubt. "But I can't trust those memories. It could be that I never left this place, that everything I think I remember about the time out in the world was a delusion. Perhaps this is some new trick of Maman's to entice me to do what she wants." He grinned crookedly. "It's working, too. I like you better than all the others. Where did she find you?"

He cornered her easily, especially as some wild and willing part of her didn't truly want to evade him. Had they been alone, she'd have yielded utterly at that point. Laying one splayed hand over her collarbones, he lightly clasped her throat, the way he seemed to like to do when certain dark moods were upon him. His wizard-black gaze drilled into her. "I can feel the bond between us." His magic caressed hers, like an intimate stroke on the inside of her skin. "I think you really *are* my bonded familiar." His other hand unerringly found the slit in her gown, caressing her naked thigh. "I have an image of you branded into my brain. You, naked, kneeling at my feet. Mine. That's real isn't it?"

His fingers found the nest of curls at the juncture of her thighs. Though she squirmed, he held her in place with that commanding hand at her throat and the power of his gaze. She clamped her thighs firmly together, but he slipped a finger into the gap, the slickness there making it absurdly easy for him. They both groaned, the stark pleasure reverberating through them physically and magically. "Seliah," he murmured, finding the swollen peak of her helpless arousal, "you've been lying to me."

"I haven't," she gasped.

"You have," he asserted, circling that peak with an insistent fingertip, sending ripples of enervating pleasure coursing through her. "You're so wet, swollen, hot with need. You want me. You want this."

"I don't." The denial came out ragged, his clever fingers strumming a desire unlike any she'd ever experienced. There was truth to it—she did want him. Wanted, craved him. She gazed into his compelling face, his black eyes so intense on hers. It would be easy to give in, to drown in him, to give herself over, to hand him those final keys to her heart. And they'd both be lost forever.

Realizing she'd been clinging to his shoulders, she lifted her hands to his face, framing it. "Jadren." She spoke his name with all the quiet ferocity she could muster. Trying to reach him at the bottom of whatever bog of insanity he was drowning in. She understood what that was like—and she had new insight into why Jadren had always seemed to understand that about her. He knew what the suffocating depths of magic-induced insanity felt like. He'd been there. He'd also risked his life to drag her out. She could do no less. "Jadren," she repeated, losing his name on a gasp, her eyes nearly rolling back in her head as his finger found the portal to her most intimate self and pressed up inside her. Somewhere along the way she'd forgotten her resistance and opened her thighs to him.

"Seliah," he answered on an ardent growl, adding a second finger and curling it inside her. "I'm going to devour you whole."

"Jadren," she gritted through her teeth, saying his name for the third time. "You said I could trust you. You *promised* me."

Those words penetrated his frenzy, his determined assault of her senses relenting ever so slightly. Pressing her advantage, she sliced her fingernail along his cheek, just hard enough to be painful on the laceration and healing bruises, marking the previous line where his cheek had been scored and healed. Reminding him of the scar beneath the new ones. "This was real," she told him. "Your mother would never have thought of the snake."

Sanity glimmered in his eyes, the fingers curling inside her faltering, his hand cupping her mound stilling, holding her almost gently. "The snake," he echoed, a shudder rippling through him.

"Yes." Encouraged, she eased a hand between their bodies, creating a separation both disappointing and a necessary respite. Grasping his wrist, she eased his hand away from her, her now empty passage mourning the loss. "Remember the snake." She focused on that decidedly non-erotic image also. "And the box. Remember how I wept?"

His expression softened further, his clasp on her throat relenting. "You were so afraid."

"You understood my fear of being trapped, being captive, because of this place. We're both in a cage now and you promised to save me from that. I'm afraid, Jadren. You *have* to get me out of here. Please."

His mind cleared further, a dawning expression of horror creeping across his face. "Dark arts," he breathed. "Seliah, what have I done to you?"

"Nothing," she assured him, but he backed away, fully releasing her and taking in her dishevelment. Lifting the hand he'd been caressing her with, he stared at it, how it was slick with her arousal. He might as well have been holding that snake, the way his face contorted in revulsion. Wiping his hand on his torn clothing—in a gesture of abject disgust that would have offended her if she hadn't understood the reason behind it—he raised his wizard-black eyes to hers. The depth of emotion in them staggered her and she reached out a hand to him, to do what, she didn't know, but he stepped back in alarm.

"Don't," he warned her sharply. "I'm not completely in control."

Dropping her hand slowly, she nodded. "It's all right, Jadren. Everything is all right now."

He barked out a bitter laugh. "Oh, poppet, you are so very, very wrong."

~ 19 ~

GABRIEL STARED AT her, apparently frozen in place by Nic's news. "What do you mean, they're no longer at House Sammael?"

Nic had tried to choose her moment wisely. Giving Gabriel the bad news was never going to be easy, but there was also timeliness to consider. He'd have been beyond angry if she'd delayed telling him. Also, he was going to lose his shit regardless. So she'd chosen their bedroom as a place where they could be alone—no incidental casualties if he lost control of his magic—where he felt safe, and where she could employ whatever means necessary to calm him. This would not be the sort of explosion she could redirect into rough sex, however. It would take all her wiles to keep him from charging off into the night.

Now she wasn't sure about the wisdom of being alone with him. Gabriel stood too still, wizard-black eyes glittering dangerously, his body rigid with freezing fury, magic spiking silver against her skin. Even though she knew Gabriel would never hurt her, she had to take a breath. Nothing like being in a locked room with an enraged wizard. "Sabrina sent the courier, as promised. Selly—and Jadren—are no longer at

House Sammael. She was captured by hunters and taken there. Jadren followed after. They were both gone by the following morning."

Though Gabriel didn't move, shadows stirred around him, nearly like amorphous wings unfurling. The dark side of the moon showing its face. "The following morning," he repeated in that eerily whispery calm.

"Yes." She inclined her head, acknowledging the blame, the guilt. She'd asked him to wait and now this.

"And yet they haven't made their way here," Gabriel continued, sounding almost musing. If not for the silver-bright tension in the room, a person might think he was taking this calmly. Outside in the formerly clear night, rain began to patter against the window.

Here we go, Nic thought to herself. *The deluge begins.*

"Tell me the rest," Gabriel commanded, wizard-black eyes drilling into her. Her knees weakened, wanting to commence kneeling. "There's worse news. I can see it in you."

Taking another breath, she found it didn't help. She really wanted to kneel and beg for his forbearance. "They went to House El-Adrel," she said in a rush, then knotted her fingers together in dread.

Gabriel regarded her almost curiously. "El-Adrel."

She nodded.

"I'm going to disembowel Jadren," Gabriel said thoughtfully. "Unless I can think of another way to kill him that's slower and more painful."

"We don't know that—"

He held up a hand to stop her, the gesture so definitively

commanding that she immediately ceased speaking. "Tell me everything Sabrina said. In order."

"I can do one better," she replied, relieved not to have to speak the words. Moving warily closer to him, she held out the missive Sabrina Sammael had sent via courier.

Gabriel raised a brow at her skittish behavior, but didn't comment, taking the folded paper from her outstretched hand. As he read the report, she observed him closely, assembling her arguments. He must have read it several times, because the minutes dragged on, excruciatingly slow. Finally he raised his gaze to hers, and lifted one dark brow. "He took her in a Sammael carriage to House El-Adrel. I'm not at all clear why you're defending him."

"We don't know the extenuating circumstances," she began.

"*What* extenuating circumstances?" he thundered, the words cracking like lightning, echoed by the atmospheric versions outside.

"Mind your magic," she cautioned him, fully aware that her words were blown away in the growing gale of his rage.

"He has her!" Gabriel shouted. "That treacherous, manipulative bastard abducted my innocent baby sister and took her to House El-Adrel. They'll tear her to pieces. How can you stand there and ask me to mind my magic and consider extenuating circumstances?"

Following instinct—or unable to withstand her familiar nature and need to humble herself before his displeasure—Nic dropped to her knees and pressed her forehead to his boots. "I apologize," she said, not sure if he'd hear, so repeating. "I'm sorry, Gabriel. More sorry than you know."

For a long moment the only sound was the rain flinging itself viciously against the glass windows. Then Gabriel crouched, taking her by the shoulders, levering her up. "Don't do that, Nic." He thumbed away her tears. "Why are you crying? This isn't your fault."

"It feels like my fault," she confessed. "I urged you to wait, to use Sabrina, to negotiate with House Sammael."

"Now we'll just negotiate with House El-Adrel," he said with grim intensity.

"But you can't!" she burst out, regretting it instantly as the storm clouds lowered his brows and darkened his visage. Gamely she plunged on. "Remember what Lady El-Adrel has on you: proof that you created an illegal magical artifact, transgressing on their trademark. The Convocation will revoke your house status without a trial, the evidence is that conclusive."

His grip tightened on her arms. "I am beyond tired of being threatened with having the House Phel status revoked. At every turn I'm expected to give up another piece of what matters to me most, simply to please your bloody Convocation. And you expect me to sacrifice Selly too? The price is too high, Nic." He shook her slightly, eyes wild. "It's too cursed high."

"They won't harm her," Nic said, willing him to listen. "She's too valuable. The worst that will happen is they'll bond her to a wizard and—"

"The worst!" he shouted. "That *is* the worst. How can you say that's no harm to her? I can't believe that you—"

"You bonded me," she cut in fiercely, "and it was the best thing that ever happened to me." She forged on in the face of his astonished silence. Wriggling out of his slacking grip, she threaded her fingers through his silver hair, tracing the single, thick lock of black that was all that remained of who he'd been before the wizardry took him. "Gabriel, you changed my life. Everything is different now because of you and I've begun to believe you can change the world—but not if you give up the game before it's won."

"This isn't a game," he insisted, but remained still in her hands, not pulling away. "This is Selly's life, her autonomy, everything that matters."

"If you attack House El-Adrel, we're lost," she replied. "All of us. With their weapons of war, they would crush us in an outright conflict and we'd have no support from any other houses or the Convocation because we'd be the aggressor. It's incredibly likely that Lady El-Adrel staged this entire plan in order to draw you into that exact scenario. She plays a very long game and this is almost certainly a trap. If you take her bait, you'll lose more than Selly."

He was silent a long time, searching her face. "I can't abandon my sister. I can't do nothing about this."

"I'm not suggesting that," she replied on a rush of relief. She'd placed good odds on Gabriel storming out immediately upon hearing this news, ignoring all consequences. At least he was listening.

"If not hostage negotiation and not war, then what?" he asked grudgingly, not at all pleased.

"It's our turn to lodge a complaint with the Convocation

regarding a stolen familiar." She hurried on, encouraged that he hadn't argued immediately. "We make a case that Selly was awaiting testing—we'd offer a judicious mix of truth and lies there—as we'd brought her home and back to health. She was unbonded, yes, but only due to extenuating cir—other reasons," she corrected hastily when his magic spiked at the tepid phrase. "The Convocation proctor can verify that much."

"Even though I evicted that proctor in a rage?" he asked drily.

"Even so." She risked a smile. "Your behavior was consistent with that of a mercurial wizard and lord of a house. She angered you and you expelled her from your house, but you were still complying with her instructions to recover Selly and arrange for testing. It's not the fault of House Phel that a representative of House El-Adrel unlawfully stole her first. There's a great deal of legal precedent on our side here. If they have bonded her to one of their wizards, then they'll owe us a *fortune*. Plus concessions."

"I won't be paid off," he snarled, breaking away from her and rising to pace in his renewed fury. The downpour increased and Nic cast a wary eye at the ceiling, hoping the roof—not in superb condition to begin with—would withstand the impact. "I'm not going to *sell* my own sister to enrich myself!"

Pushing to her feet, Nic took her time brushing the wrinkles from her skirts, even though the Ophiel gown didn't need it. Giving Gabriel a considering look as he paused in his pacing, breathing hard and practically frothing at the mouth, she raised a brow. "Anything else to add?"

"It's my line in the dirt, Nic," he answered blackly. "I may have agreed to a precarious slide down a slippery slope under your political tutelage, but I won't go there. Not even for you."

She nodded, keeping a placid expression despite the pang of insult that he'd think that of her for a moment. "What about for Selly?" she asked pointedly. "For your parents who've lost their daughter? If you refuse this approach, Selly stands a very good chance of remaining in House El-Adrel forever. On the other—"

"I don't understand how you can treat this like another business negotiation," he growled, flexing his fingers, wizard-black eyes flickering with silver.

"*On the other hand,*" she said, raising her voice and letting her own temper show, "if you exploit this rare advantage, you stand to regain Selly, add to our accounts—which I don't think I need to remind you sorely need it—elevate the status of House Phel among our peers, and shame House El-Adrel. To put a cherry on top of it, we have the ability to break any bonding they've subjected Selly to. You won't get a cleaner win than this, Gabriel."

He turned his back on her, staring out into the drenched night through the glass doors that led to the balcony. Rain pelted the roof. Silver condensed in the air of their bedroom, pinging musically to the wooden floor, the sound somehow evocative of grief. She went to him and slid her arms around his waist. Leaning her cheek between his rigid shoulder blades, she wafted her magic into him, giving him back the love and understanding he'd always shown her.

"Why do you have to be always right?" he finally said.

A smile trembled over her lips. "It's a compulsion. If I'm not right all the time, my sense of self crumbles clean away."

He didn't laugh, but a tremor of amusement flickered through his magic, the rain abating somewhat. Turning in her embrace, he wrapped his big arms around her, muscles humming with tension. "I don't like it," he sighed, "but I'll do it. As long as the priority is getting Selly back in the best shape possible."

"Of course." She tipped her head back, gazing up at him. "How could you think for a moment my priorities would be any different?"

He slid his hands up and down her back. "Maybe it's my compulsion to be always wrong."

She breathed a laugh. "Hardly that. These are difficult times. I'm afraid, too."

"You never seem afraid."

"Not true. You knew I needed to be held after you rescued me from that tower. It's just my turn to hold you."

He kissed her, a lingering, intimate caress of deep emotion. "I suppose we make a good team that way."

"In *every* way," she averred. "But Gabriel?"

"Yes, my heart?"

"Reel the magic back now, please. We're going to need it more than we need rain or silver dust on the floor."

With a chagrined curse, he did.

JADREN HAD NEVER been all that fond of himself—that simply wasn't in the cards for him—but it was a revelation to discover these new depths of self-loathing. An all-time record.

Have we hit bottom yet? He wondered wryly to himself.

If we haven't, I really hate to see what the real bottom is like, that other voice answered.

Certifiably insane. So much so that he'd attacked Seliah, all but raping her.

All but? The sardonic inner voice echoed. *Just because you didn't actually get your cock inside her doesn't make it any less of a rape.*

Shut up, he told himself.

Yeah, like that will work. I'm inside your head, you idiot.

He clutched his hands to said head, digging in his fingers as if he could pry his skull open. Even if he could, he'd probably just heal from it. His mother had gone to new lengths in her experiments this time, carried away in a frenzy of delight that he could draw on Seliah's magic to bolster his healing. Some pieces still rattled around inside him, slowly migrating through his flesh, and if he'd had a blade handy he might've taken it to himself to cut them out already.

Fortunately, Seliah had fallen into an exhausted sleep, so wasn't awake to question his behavior. She'd been far too forgiving, seeming to think he hadn't been in his right mind. When he'd refused to discuss that—or the fact that he remembered every detail, including the intensely erotic clasp of her tight sheath on his fingers, which must mean he'd been perfectly sane—she'd finally stopped trying to get him to talk to her. The labs were dark, everyone gone.

Just him and his self-recriminations. He'd fucked everything up.

Not exactly a brilliantly executed plan, asshole, his inner voice agreed.

This time, he couldn't argue.

Something clinked on the glass and he jerked up his head, narrowing his eyes to make out a shadow moving in the darkness beyond, black on black. The clink came again, tapping softly: three pulses. The child in him nearly wept at the old code his father had used to communicate without words. A squeeze of the hand. A tap on his shoulder behind his back where no one could see. I love you.

He tapped it back. One, two, three. I love you. And didn't even hate himself too much that tears leapt to his eyes. His father had come to see him. Fyrdo couldn't *do* anything—he was as powerless as Jadren, perhaps more so because his love for his wizard chained him more thoroughly than any threats—but it meant a great deal that his father had risked even this much. Would Fyrdo be able to help Seliah escape? There was a slim chance. Though—he kicked himself—Seliah couldn't leave without him now. She'd suffer too much from the bond attenuation before she managed to get to Gabriel. With her still tenuous mental stability, the risk wouldn't be worth it. Of course, if she stayed with him, she might end up dead.

Death or insanity? his inner voice mused. *Always so difficult to choose.*

Another click and, to his heart-thudding shock, the cage door opened.

His father stood in the doorway. "Come with me, both of you," he said. "Hurry."

~ 20 ~

JADREN WASTED NO time waking Seliah. One positive about her traumatic experiences fleeing from whatever ghosts and shadows her madness had generated was that she woke fully alert, silently, and ready to run. All he had to do was whisper in her ear that they were escaping and she slipped her hand into his, following with a perfect trust that shamed him.

She's not trusting you, his inner voice commented acidly. *She trusts Fyrdo.* Which was fair. He only hoped his father knew what he was doing. Jadren couldn't imagine what could have prompted his father to take this unprecedented action. He only knew he was beyond grateful for the rescue, particularly for Seliah's sake. She trailed close behind him, fingers interlaced with his, moving with him with a grace and synchrony that was new.

He followed his father's dark form, staying close behind. Hopefully Fyrdo knew the location of all the embedded information reporting devices. He carried no light, but moved with deliberate care through the darkened labs. To Jadren's great interest, Fyrdo didn't go in the direction of the aluminum bridge that was, so far as Jadren knew, the only entrance and exit to the labs, one with extensive traps and triggers that only authorized wizards knew how to manipulate. Instead, they moved through a labyrinthine series of rooms, the path so twisting Jadren quickly lost whatever orientation he'd had. How his father had discovered this route, Jadren had no idea. And that wasn't even taking into consideration how the house tended to get ideas of its own on how it wanted to be laid out. Too many enchantments layered into the bones of the house by careless or crazed—or both—El-Adrel wizards had given the structure a kind of intelligence that bordered on sentience.

Fyrdo stopped abruptly enough that Jadren nearly plowed into him, though the more agile and sensitive Seliah avoided repeating the error. The apparently blank wall before Fyrdo emitted a sudden crack of intense light, blinding after the near-complete darkness.

"Through here," Fyrdo hissed.

Jadren and Seliah went through into the very narrow hall-way. She had her head ducked, eyes shaded with her free hand. Smarter than he was, with his eyes watering at the sudden change, but he wanted to *see* his father, who still stood in the doorway, an expression of wrenching sorrow and love on his face. He handed Jadren a heavy bag that clinked. "Supplies and some of your things," Fyrdo explained. "What I could find in your rooms, anyway. Follow this hall to the catacombs."

"The *catacombs*?" Jadren echoed. House El-Adrel entombed their dead in the subterranean reaches of the manse. It was not a place anyone went on purpose.

His father nodded. "It's the only way. There's a tunnel that will take you under the wall."

"How are we to find this tunnel?" Seliah asked.

Fyrdo tipped his head at Jadren. "The house will help. It's always liked him. You'll find it. Follow it to the end beyond the walls. It's up to you to get away from there." He shrugged helplessly a bitter turn to the gesture. "I'm sorry I can't help more than this."

"I'm surprised you helped at all," Jadren said hoarsely, and Seliah gave him a sharp look.

But his father only grimaced. "I know." His gaze went to Seliah. "He's not wrong to be surprised. All these years I could have helped and didn't."

"But could you have?" Jadren persisted. "I always knew that wasn't an option for you."

"We'll never know, will we?" His father smiled sadly. "At least I did this."

"Thank you." Jadren wished the words said more, unable to shake the dread that he might never see his father again. "I love you," he added impulsively, the first time in his life that he'd ever said the words aloud.

Fyrdo pulled him into a fierce embrace, patting his back. One. Two. Three. "I know," he said, then released him and hugged Seliah. "Take good care of my boy," he told her.

Seliah nodded, tears brightening her amber eyes. "I will. Thank you—for this and for all your kindness."

"We're out of time," Fyrdo told them, then fixed Jadren with a significant stare. "I don't think I have to warn you of the dangers or urge you to hurry."

"But how did you—" Jadren began.

His father cut him off with a hard shake of his head. "Goodbye. Don't come back this way."

On those oddly ominous words, he stepped back and sealed the door, leaving them in the bright and narrow hallway. A light pattern of arrowheads flickered along the floor, white on white.

"As if we'd *want* to go back to those horrible labs," Seliah commented.

"We should get moving," Jadren told her, setting a swift pace down the hall, not taking her hand again. No need for it now. The floor sloped downward noticeably, making acceleration easier, adding credence to the tale that it led into or through the catacombs. "How fast can you go?"

"How fast can *you?*" she countered. "You're the one still recovering."

"Good as new," he said in the jauntiest tone he could muster, breaking into a jog. She kept pace with him, the hallway so narrow that they barely fit side by side, her bare arm brushing his occasionally. He ignored those brief sparks of contact, even though each one sent showers of silver moonlight and surges of magic like bracing sea spray into him. "And that's not what my father meant," he continued. "No matter what happens now, we're on a one-way trajectory. There's no retreat. Could be we're still sinking through the bog to that bottom." He slid her a glance to see if she understood.

"Right." She gave him an opaque look. "Tigers in the tunnels ahead. No guarantees. But I'm glad to be taking the chance regardless. I'd rather die escaping than as a captive in that place."

"Can't argue with that reasoning." The hallway continued in a perfectly straight line, which worried him greatly. Nothing in this house was as it seemed, but straight lines weren't in its repertoire unless it was messing with you.

"Shouldn't we get out the weapons, to be ready?" she asked.

He shook his head. "Not those kinds of tigers. Weapons won't be any help and it would only slow us down to dig them out."

"But—"

"Later." He bit that out harshly enough to silence her.

As if that ever worked. "We should talk about what happened," Seliah said after a few moments, her voice even and not breathless at all. Unlike himself, who was already panting—and also fighting the unpleasant grinding sensation in one lung.

"There's nothing to talk about." He coughed into his fist, then surreptitiously checked his hand. Yep: blood. Wonderful.

"Jadren, I don't hold any of this against you," she persisted. "I won't pretend to understand everything that happened here, but I believe that all you said and did was in an effort to protect me. We're tied together now, bonded, which means we're partners, for better or worse."

"Not *partners*, poppet," he sneered in a deliberately insulting tone. "You're my possession now. In the eyes of Convocation law you're—" A sudden, involuntary cough convulsed him, wrenching enough that he stumbled, then bent over as a wave of dizziness hit him, bracing himself with hands on knees. An incriminating spray of bright red blood scattered across the floor.

"You're still too wounded," Seliah fretted. "I knew it."

"Doesn't matter." He wiped the blood and spittle from his mouth with the back of his hand. "There's no going back." He'd meant to shoot her a harsh grin, but when he met her eyes, so lambent and lovely, filled with concern and other emotions he really hoped were a product of crisis and not anything more, he felt the smile fade away. Stepping around the blood, he broke into a slightly less brisk jog than before. "No going back and no stopping. We have maybe one chance here, if that."

"At least take some magic." She wrapped her fingers around his wrist, cool silvery water beckoning him to drink. And drain her dry.

He shook her off. "Look alive. We're at the end." And at the bottom, by the feel of it. Ahead of them, a dark archway loomed, lined with ancient-looking stones. A dank flow of air wafted from it, musty with old death and ghosts of the newly dead. "Ready for this?"

"Catacombs, huh?" she asked, raking her unruly curls out of her face as they slowed on approach. "I think I'm not afraid of dead people. It's the living ones in this house that have proved dangerous."

Including himself, he presumed. "Eminently logical." Taking a breath for fortitude—a mistake as something ground painfully against a rib—he led the way into the graveyard of House El-Adrel.

THE CATACOMBS WERE quiet, dimly lit by embedded fire elementals, and oddly peaceful. Seliah had the right of it that they had more to fear from the living. Unfortunately, the catacombs were also labyrinthine, with innumerable alcoves and blind alleys. Though they both tried to keep up the pace, they lost time getting repeatedly lost and having to retrace their steps.

"Are you sure there's a way out of here?" Seliah asked as they backtracked for the umpteenth time.

He slid her a sardonic look. "No. Although there's usually a way in, else they couldn't entomb the dead in the first place. It's a special skill set and we keep a cadre of wizards whose sole responsibility is opening passages to various aspects of the house that require access."

"This is a very strange place."

He breathed a laugh. "You have no—."

"At this juncture," she interrupted, "you have to admit, I *do* have an idea."

She had a point. And she actually knew more about him than anyone outside the cruel embrace of his immediate family did. He stood at a crossroads of equally likely looking stone corridors, their destinations hidden beyond the curving walls of the passageways. He had no idea how to navigate this maze.

"Are you all right?" she asked, peering at him in the gloom. "You don't look good."

"You say the nicest things." Picking one corridor at random, he started jogging down it. "We have to keep moving. Time is ticking."

"I think we've been down this one before."

"No, we haven't"

"I recognize it—look there's the effigy of Elizabetah El-Adrel in her niche."

"How do you know who it is?" He sure didn't.

"Her name is etched on the plinth there." Seliah was right. He remembered the scarlet-clad statue now.

"Fuck me," he muttered, spinning on his heel to reverse direction, then colliding with Seliah. She caught him around the waist.

"Take some magic," she urged.

"No time. Whatever my father did to delay them discovering our escape, it will run out soon."

"Breathe," she advised. "*Think*. Like you're always telling me to do. Fyrdo said the house likes you and will show you the tunnel we need."

"The house doesn't *like* anyone," he assured her.

"Your father had a reason to believe it does, that it will show you the tunnel. Maybe you just need to show it you like and trust it."

He raised a brow. "I *don't* trust the house." Behind Seliah, the formerly blank face on the effigy of Elizabetah El-Adrel sharpened, pretty features contorting into an astonished and offended grimace. He nearly made a rude gesture at it. "Because the house is not trustworthy. It doesn't like for people to leave," he added, speaking directly to the stone statue. It stuck its tongue out at him. And people wondered why he was the way he was.

Seliah glanced over her shoulder at the effigy, which was back to its blank, dusty state. Turning back to him, she lifted her hands to his face, stroking his beard. "I understand why you don't trust anyone, Jadren. Given what you come from, it would be a miracle if you did. But we need the house to show you the way out."

He resisted the sweetwater tide of her magic offering itself through the thin barrier of skin-to-skin contact. "Why don't *you* ask it? You're part of House El-Adrel now."

"Fine." She stepped away from him. "I will." Turning in a slow circle, she offered her hands in palm-up supplication. "House, I am the newest member of your family and don't know you well yet, but we need your aid. Your scion, Jadren, has suffered here and must leave. I must go with him, to care for him. But if you let us go now, I promise we'll return."

Jadren grabbed her arm. "What are you saying?" he hissed.

She jerked her arm from his grip. "Houses need to be lived in and loved. Of course it wants people to stay. Failing that, it will want us to come back. I'll make sure we do," she promised.

"This is a terrible idea that will only lead to trouble," Jadren predicted darkly.

Seliah threw him an impatient glance. "Worse trouble than we're already in? No," she answered for him. "Do we have a deal?" she asked the air.

The effigy of Elizabetah smirked at him. And a door appeared in the pedestal beneath her.

It was a small door—child-sized in height—the frame embedded with silver triangles that looked like stylized arrowheads, all pointing inward from the edges, as if he needed additional clues. "There you go," he said to Seliah, indicating the miniscule portal. "Ask, and you shall receive, more or less. In this case: much less."

"Why is the door so small?" Seliah asked.

"The house likes to amuse itself at our expense."

She laughed. When he only tossed her a grim stare, she sobered. "Seriously?"

He bent to examine the door. Tried the handle. It was, of course, locked. And not with an Iblis lock, either, but with an archaic brass mechanism. *Must there always be a test?* Above him, the effigy giggled. "You have no idea."

"I can't decide if I hate it when you say that or if I'm becoming perversely fond of it."

He decided there was no good answer to that. "I need to make a key, which means I need your magic." With a pleased smile, she held out her hand. "Put it on my shoulder," he instructed. He wasn't touching her more than necessary, ever again.

She huffed out an impatient sigh, but complied. Bracing himself, he drew on her magic, trying to pretend it wasn't addictively delicious, that he didn't need it desperately. The enchanting moonlit water of her hit him hard, however. That instinctive healing aspect of himself, seemingly forever beyond his conscious control, as his mother loved to remind him, sucked it up greedily. He hadn't realized how much pain he'd been in until it eased. Even his next indrawn breath didn't rattle as badly. "That's enough. Let go."

"Jadren." She said his name with gentle patience he didn't deserve. "You need more. I may be a rank amateur, but even I can feel that."

"Incorrect, poppet," he replied, knocking her hand off his shoulder with brusque purpose. "You've been precipitously launched into the pro leagues, which also means you should do as you're told. Now be silent and let me work."

"Funny. It's almost like we've had this conversation before."

"Yes—leads me to wonder how many times I'll have to repeat myself to get the lesson through your thick skull." He almost felt her roll her eyes, but she said nothing more. He selected a slim, short rod of metal from one of his jacket pockets, glad he'd transferred the tools to his formal clothes, just in case. Setting a finger on the lock under the brass doorknob, he focused his magic on the metal shank in his hand, willing the enchantment into it. Feeling the spell take hold, he pushed the pin into the slot, held his breath, and turned it. The lock clicked and the door sprang open, the house sending a wave of approval into him. The bitch.

Unfortunately, the inward-swinging door revealed a knee-high passage. They'd have to crawl—just like that box Seliah hadn't been able to handle. Of course. "Good news and bad news," he told her.

"No luck unlocking it?"

"It's unlocked. That's the good news. The bad news is you're going to hate what's on the other side."

"More catacombs? I told you, the dead bodies don't bother

me."

If only. He turned around, facing her worried frown. How she could be so enticingly lovely, even so disheveled and under such dire circumstances, he'd never understand. A tangle of curls hung around her face, tempting him to comb them back. The flimsy black gown draped low over her bosom, revealing far too much, reminding him of the satiny weight of her breast in his palm, the way her nipple had pebbled eagerly for him. Determinedly, he averted his eyes and met her serious ones. "It's dark and closed in," he told her gently. "We'll have to crawl."

Closing her eyes briefly, she dipped her chin in acknowledgement. "I understand." Opening her eyes again, she stared him down. "I can do it."

"That's my girl." Risking the touch, he chucked her on the chin, hoping it would feel like elder to child. It didn't. "Lead or follow?"

"I'll lead. That way you can make sure I keep going."

In wry agreement, he set the bag of supplies inside the doorway. "Push this ahead of you. It will give warning in case there's a drop or obstacles you don't see in time."

She blanched a little at that. "Is that likely?"

"The house likes to test people, remember? Apparently it's your turn. So, yes, it's not going to be a clear shot. Just remember that, although the house isn't necessarily on our side, it's also not against us."

She blinked, assimilating that. "I begin to understand why you're so messed up, growing up in this place."

Absurdly, he nearly smiled. He'd never expected that anyone would ever know so much about him, certainly not via direct experience. "I would say you have no idea, but—as you pointed out—you clearly do."

"At last, I've transcended the phrase of doom." She pushed past him, lithe and silky, then—without pause—knelt and crawled inside, firmly pushing the bag ahead of her. "I'm keeping my eyes closed," she called back to him in a muffled voice. "Maybe if I don't see it, I won't be so bothered.

Oh, yeah, that always works, his sardonic inner voice commented.

Jadren didn't reply. He was too busy hoping Seliah could keep going. Locking the little door after himself—he really didn't need anything sneaking up behind them—he pocketed the key and made the contorted turn to follow after Seliah. Good thing the tunnel was dark. If he'd had to fight the temptation of having Seliah's delectable rear in his face, he probably wouldn't succeed. As it was, he decided to focus on whatever still rattled around in his lung, however less painfully now. Maybe with the boost of Seliah's magic in him he could direct some of the healing to that spot.

Concentrating on that got him through the seemingly interminable crawl, and the increasing worry about what he'd do if Seliah lost her shit. She'd been slowing incrementally, her breath growing audibly pitched with anxiety, each shove of the bag before her preceded by a more pronounced hesitation. If they were lucky, they'd reach the end—or reach something—before she lost her nerve entirely. But, who was he kidding? The house wouldn't let it be that easy for her, Seliah's resolve notwithstanding.

Sure enough, on the heels of that thought, the walls of the tunnel groaned, the wood creaking as it shifted. Seliah froze. "Have to keep moving," he reminded her, going for steady and calm as a first stage of motivation.

"I'm sure it's my imagination, but for a moment I thought the walls were closing in," she replied in a breathless voice.

He'd been hoping she wouldn't notice. "Just your imagination," he reassured her. As if annoyed by the lie, the walls creaked again, contracting enough to brush his shoulders. Seliah squeaked in alarm. "It's just a test," he told her calmly. "The house won't kill us. It just wants to play with us a little."

"So, nobody ever finds bodies in the walls or caught in some ghoulish trap?"

"Never," he lied. There were always those who failed the house's tests. The House El-Adrel denizens maintained a lively running debate on what those failures had in common, along with a betting pool on who would be next to disappear—and whether they'd be heard from again. The walls creaked, tightening more.

"I think you're lying to me."

"We have to keep going," he repeated. "If we stop here, we will be trapped. If you can find it in yourself to forge ahead, we just might survive. We've come so far already."

She began crying softly. "I'm sorry, Jadren. I just... I don't think I can."

She'd made it so far, too. He considered his options. Cajole? Bully? Physically drag her? He was at a loss, completely unequal to the challenge. Nothing new there, but...

Then it occurred to him that the house was actually testing

him with this trick, not Seliah. "Yeah, fuck you, too, you bitch," he muttered to himself.

Seliah began sobbing. "I'm sorry. I'm so sorry."

"Not you," he said, a bit too harshly, beyond aggravated with himself.

"I *am* sorry though," Seliah got out. "*Shit!* After the box and the hunters, I promised myself that I wouldn't do this again."

"It's not something you can control," he told her. "You feel what you feel. Let me help you."

"Ho-how?"

"Lie down flat, on your side."

"What??"

"Just do what I say for once in your life." He felt around, found her ankle, tugged gently on it to straighten her leg. "Lie down on your side, arms stretched over your head."

Trembling and weeping, she complied, and he scooted up beside her, wriggling his way on his side, pulling himself along with one outstretched hand, using the other to hold down her gown so it wouldn't ride up. All he needed was her naked crotch pressed to his groin.

Finally he made it up to her face, folding his outstretched arm under her head to make a pillow, holding her and caressing her long body in soothing strokes with the other. "Seliah," he crooned, making a lullaby of her name, brushing his lips over her wet face to kiss away her tears. "It's all right. I'm here with you. We're together."

"You h-hate me," she sobbed. "I don't blame you."

"I don't hate you at all." *Exactly the opposite.*

"It's all my fault that you got trapped here. If it weren't for me, you'd never be in this position. And now we'll end up as corpses in the walls of this place. Or I will."

"Oh, Seliah," he replied on a soft laugh, touching her face with his fingers and picking away the tendrils of her hair plastered to her cheeks and temples. Even in the dark, she *felt* beautiful, with her delicate, tensile strength and skin soft as moonbeams. "First of all, we're getting out of this. I have no desire to be a corpse in the walls haunting the house of my birth. Second, my returning here has always been inevitable. What was special, dramatically unusual, and sacred to me is that I got out at all. Being in House Phel, knowing you, even tromping around with you in that fucking forest and fighting off hunters and spirits with you have been the best days of my life."

"Then you've had a pretty shitty life," she sniffled.

"You have no idea," he replied, gratified to hear her laugh. Sliding a hand behind her neck, he kissed away more tears, tasting their salt and the sweetness of her skin. Her magic shimmered over his lips, seductive, addictive. Seeking more, he brushed his lips over hers, even softer, parting to offer him her heat. Though he knew he shouldn't be doing this, had firmly resolved not to again, he held her head cupped in his hand and feasted on the kiss. If he was going back on his decision, he could at least give her everything he'd failed to offer her before.

So, he made it infinitely gentle, sweetly caressing, sensually evocative. Loving, even. At least, to as much as his shriveled heart allowed.

She moaned and softened against him, her long body curving into his in yielding supplication. Unable to help himself, he wedged his thigh between hers, brutally aware of the wet heat of her mound grinding against him. She fed on the kiss eagerly, moving with ardent undulations that undid him. Much more, and he'd climax in his pants like an adolescent. Well, if they did die, they'd be happy corpses in the walls. Maybe the house needed a change of pace for her collection.

With a chuckle of shifting wood, the house relented, finally appeased. The walls receded, giving them space—though he and Seliah clung to each other as tightly as before—and fresh air blew down from ahead of them. Light filtered into the passage from somewhere. Could it be they'd reached the outside and it was dawn already?

"Seliah," he said into her increasingly passionate kisses, trying to back out, but she followed him eagerly, seemingly unaware that she could only be running her hands over him with such abandon because the space had expanded enough to allow that freedom. "It worked. We're free. And much as I'd love to continue this, we have to escape. We must go now."

His words finally penetrated and she pulled back, gazing at him in wide-eyed wonder, her lush black lashes spiky from her tears. "Do you mean it?"

"Yes. We have to get out of this house as soon as possible. We'll be discovered soon."

"Not that. Do you mean you'd love to continue this?"

Ouch. There was a tight corner he'd backed himself into. "Yes." *That's not totally a lie,* he thought fiercely at the house, just in case she tried to punish him again. He *would* love to continue this. He just wasn't going to.

Seliah narrowed her eyes in suspicion, long, willowy limbs wrapping around him with their deceptive strength. "Promise."

"I promise," he said, thinking fast, "that as soon as you're safe, I'll take you to bed and fuck you senseless."

The crudity didn't make her miss a beat. She smiled with radiant happiness. "Good. I'll hold you to that."

He didn't feel all that guilty for the deception. And apparently the house bought it, too. It was in Seliah's best interests, after all, to save her from him and what he'd inevitably do to her. By the time she realized that her being safe meant him being far, far away from her, it would be too late. She didn't really want him in her bed anyway—that desire was born of the bonding and would fade with his absence. In some ways, he was being noble here, sacrificing himself for her happiness.

Yeah, keep telling yourself that. Apparently his snide inner voice wasn't in complete accord, but Jadren didn't care.

Seliah was on the move again, crawling eagerly toward the growing light, quickly outpacing him. The walls and ceiling hadn't expanded enough for them to stand more than half-bent over, so crawling was still more efficient. Whatever had been rolling around in his lung had now wedged painfully between two ribs, so he labored to keep up with Seliah, back to her usual agile vigor now that she scented freedom, and the outdoors. Unfortunately, hanging back and having to watch where he was going put her adorable behind squarely in his line of vision. The gown obviously wasn't meant for crawling, either, the long slits in the skirt giving him tantalizing flashes of the backs of her lean thighs.

Who knew the backs of a woman's thighs could be sexy? They shouldn't be, particularly under these conditions, but he couldn't help catching glimpses of golden skin and firm muscle, his gaze obsessively following them to where they disappeared under the black silk clinging to her compact rear, his fevered brain supplying an image of the enticing crevice there, the satiny, heated folds he'd touched but hadn't seen. He ached for her, *wanting* in a way he'd never before wanted, his magic reaching for her.

You've had as much as you're going to, he told himself firmly. *You've done enough damage.*

This time, no inner voice responded.

"Jadren?" Seliah whispered loudly, half-turned around to see him—which gave him a full view of her naked breasts hanging ripely inside the gaping bodice of the gown. Groaning, he closed his eyes. "You're still not well," Seliah said worriedly. "Let me help you."

"You can help by moving your tiny ass," he bit out, hoping to be sufficiently scathing, an effect completely undermined by his strained breath. Yeah, and it had zero effect, Seliah seeming completely unbothered. In fact, she looked more worried than ever.

"You're too wounded to do a good job of being mean," she said, confirming it. "How can we get out of here if you can't even move?"

"Do we have a choice?" He pointed. "Go. Go on now. Get!"

"Still not a puppet." She crawled back to him, breasts swaying like mesmerizing pendulums. "Yes, we have a choice. Take my magic, wizard." Kneeling up, she clamped her hands on his shoulders on the bare skin inside his shirt. Her touch seared him and he reached for her wrists to tear her away. "Don't," she told him sharply. "You're my best chance of getting out of here, Jadren. Please. I need you."

Her amber eyes gleamed with her concern, black curls waving wildly around her fine-boned face as her lovely lips shaped the words. *I need you.* If only she meant it for real. Some broken, lonely part of him longed for it to be so. The desiccated, jaded rest of him knew better.

Still, he closed his eyes and inhaled her magic through his skin, the moon-bright pure flood of it pouring into the aching black hole that was his body attempting to heal at blazing rates of speed. The thing lodged in his ribs broke free, making him gasp as it fractured the nearby ribs on its way out and then tore through his flesh. It fell, hot and sticky with blood, inside his shirt.

While he shuddered, letting his body heal in the wake of that brutal eviction, Seliah fished out the thing, firmly gripping his shoulder still with her other hand. Digging out the brass device, she turned it in the light from the end of the tunnel, examining it. Perhaps she'd done that with all the pieces his body had extruded while he was unconscious, before she tossed them into her makeshift midden pile in the corner of the cell.

"Keep that one," he told her, having a pretty good idea of what it was, the way it scintillated with his mother's magic.

Her gaze met his. "Why?"

He managed a smirk. "A memento for you. You can thread it on a chain around your neck and think of me." He'd meant to be sarcastic, but the moment became oddly fraught, emotionally intense. *One last kiss,* he told himself, and impulsively closed the distance between them, kissing her with sweet longing. Then breaking the contact, lips and magic both, firmly and forever. "Crawl, poppet," he instructed. "I'm fine now and we're not out of here yet."

Wrapping her fingers around the device, she nodded and crawled back to their bag of supplies, slipping the brass instrument inside. He followed, making himself move with a semblance of vigor. They'd still have to trek across the wilderness and somehow evade pursuit.

He could sleep when Selly was home safe.

~ 21 ~

NIC WAS GETTING better at thinking like herself while in silver phoenix form. The strangely globular vision still disoriented her, but only if she thought about it too much. Fortunately, her wings were tiring enough that she could only think about staying in the air. It had been difficult enough to talk Gabriel into riding her to House El-Adrel for the negotiations. She wasn't going to give him any reason to feel bad about the decision.

The one good aspect of Gabriel being out of his mind with impatience to get to Selly was that he'd capitulated to the idea of putting her in alternate form and flying to El-Adrel much more easily than he would have under any other circumstances. Even if Nic hadn't wanted to experiment with this—just in case she needed to fly him to safety on short notice some day—she'd been reluctant to trust such a critical negotiation to Ratsiel couriers. There was no direct proof that House Ratsiel read the missives entrusted to their communication wizards, but everyone in the Convocation generally assumed Ratsiel knew their business.

It's what they all would do, in Ratsiel's position.

So, it came to be that Nic soared toward House El-Adrel on

sore and tired wings, Gabriel on her back alternating between petting her, worrying about her and Selly in equal measures, and practicing the speech to Lady El-Adrel that they'd crafted. Just as she began her descent to land before the massive gates in the wall surrounding House El-Adrel, however, Gabriel suddenly tensed. With an oath, he swung about on her back, nearly unseating himself and unbalancing her.

"Selly!" he exclaimed. "Nic—I sense her. And Jadren, too, that duplicitous fuck. They're not in the house. They're outside it."

So much for the longed-for setting down on the ground to rest her wings. She circled, hoping to convey inquiry. It would really help to know which direction she should go.

"Sorry, my heart. That way." He pointed to the woods on the far side of the house. "Can you make it? I promise we'll set down there."

She should've known he'd sense her exhaustion, connected as they were. Hopefully she'd never have to hide something important from him. Warbling a reply she hoped sounded cheerful, she made a wide circle around the house environs. No way was she flying straight over it. That was just begging to be shot down by one of the scary-looking mechanisms studding the blindingly bright rooftop of the clockwork house. She'd visited House El-Adrel a few times, with her parents and with school friends, so she had reason to know how well-defended it was.

"Just a bit farther, that direction," Gabriel murmured, stroking the sleek feathers of her neck. "Just a bit longer and Jadren will pay for what he's done. They're bonded," he added.

"I can sense it easily."

She hummed a question, wanting to convey caution. Not having words wasn't ideal.

"Fastest way to sever that bond is death," Gabriel said, as if answering her. He shimmered with violently sharp, silver magic. "Then I'll leave Jadren's corpse on his mother's doorstep. That should explain everything."

Or destroy everything, Nic thought, winging her way to recover their friends and wondering how she could stop Gabriel from murdering Jadren before asking questions—and listening to the answers.

IT WAS SUCH a relief to be outside of that windowless house, beyond the walls, and in real sunshine again that Selly practically skipped with happiness. If she'd been on her own, she'd have run for the sheer joy of being able to. Running, however, was out of the question, as they were forced to keep to the tangled undergrowth, not daring to risk the roads.

Also, Jadren wasn't up for it. His breathing still sounded too harsh and, when she asked if he might have more gadgets inside still impeding his healing, he'd only said it was likely and hadn't summoned even a hint of mockery. He looked pale, his skin greasy with sweat and hair soaked with it. But every time she glanced at him, even out of the corner of her eye, he snarled at her and told her to watch where she was going.

It was good advice, as she'd already snagged the thin silk robe on a twig, tearing it badly, and her feet were bleeding in several places, even tough as they were from all her time running barefoot in the wild sanctuary of the marshes. They were too close to the house still to explore the bag of supplies to assess what Fyrdo had put in there. The bag wasn't terribly heavy, which didn't bode well for food stores. At least Jadren had capitulated on letting her carry it, though he'd taken possession of the machete, threading it onto his belt with stolid determination, along with a dagger. His magic had worn thin again, no doubt consumed by trying to heal whatever horrible devices remained implanted in him, and he was hardly in any shape to fight anything off—physical or magical. It was all he could do to keep walking.

She had precious few arrows and, while it was a waste to use the enchanted silver on squirrels, she highly doubted they had enough food in the bag to fuel them for the days and days it would take to walk to House Phel. She'd have to keep Jadren fed to keep him going; she'd have to feed herself so she'd have magic to give him, so he could heal. Though he'd gone back to refusing magic from her. She didn't really understand why as that was the purpose of the bonding, but Jadren was firm on the subject and wouldn't be moved.

Once they got safely back to House Phel and Wizard Asa fully healed Jadren, then she and Jadren could talk. They were bound together now, irrevocably, so they'd have to agree to work together. Besides, he'd promised to bed her and he wouldn't go back on that. She had a feeling that if she could get him to let her through those defenses, if he gave into his obvious desire for her, embraced their partnership, and trusted her even a little, then he'd be able to let go of whatever fears plagued him so.

Jadren halted in his tracks, tensing. "Someone's closing on us. A wizard."

Shit. Selly swallowed, bearing down on the terror welling up in her. "Jadren?" she asked through a suddenly dry throat.

"No, I can't tell who it is yet. Shh."

"Not that," she persisted, lowering her voice, "will you promise me something?"

"Not now. Be—"

"It *has* to be now." She moved in front of him, forcing him to look at her. As he had been recently, he met her gaze with haunted regret, his magic reaching for her even as he physically stepped back. "If it's them," she continued, "I want you to kill me."

"What? No."

"Jadren." She put a hand on his breast over his heart, not letting him run from her, from this. "If your mother recaptures us, she'll make sure we never escape again. I'm not asking for me—though that is a nightmare I don't know if I can endure again—but for you. She'll use me to keep you alive for more of her experiments and as leverage against you. If it's them, you need to kill me." She nodded at the machete on his belt. "You can make it fast."

He stared at her, jaw muscles working, his wizard-black gaze furious and agonized. "Don't ask me this."

"I am asking." She held his gaze steadily. "I'll never ask anything of you again, if you'll promise this."

His lips twisted wryly at that. "A positive outcome—if we survive, I'll be spared your many demands."

"Yes, you will," she replied gravely, not taking the bait.

"I'll try." Sidestepping her, he held up a hand to fend her off. "That's the most I can promise. Don't ask me for more than that," he added harshly. Then he spun, searched the sky, and let out a bark of a laugh. "Dark arts fuck me. I should have known."

"Who is it?"

Jadren cast her an oblique look, seething with dark emotions. "Your life is safe, sweet Seliah. Mine..." He laughed again, looking to the sky. "Well, it was always worthless anyway."

"Don't say that! I—"

"Selly!" Gabriel's voice rang through the trees. A flash of silver and Nic in her alternate form landed in a small clearing ahead, Gabriel improbably on her back. He leapt to the ground, rushing toward them.

Selly exclaimed in wordless relief, ready to embrace her brother. But his trajectory changed. As he ran he extruded a silver sword of moon magic, his expression fierce and terrible, magic palpably streaming from him as he charged at Jadren.

It happened before she could react, her mind dully far behind what her eyes reported. Gabriel—a violent storm of motion unlike she'd ever seen from him—pierced Jadren through the heart, pinning him to the tree behind him.

She might have screamed. Absurdly, Jadren laughed a third time. He looked down at the sword impaling him, the bright blood darkening his black shirt, then raised his gaze to

Gabriel's. "Fairly done, Lord Phel." He twitched a hand as if to salute, but couldn't lift it. It fell weakly to his side. He said something more, words too quiet for her to hear, then collapsed, like a wax doll, held upright only by her brother's sword.

Now she screamed.

~ 22 ~

S ELLY'S SCREAMS DROWNED out everything, all sense, all rationality. Gabriel heard them, but couldn't seem to look away from Jadren's unnaturally pale face, his hair bright against the waxen skin, darker blood spattering him. Jadren's last words echoing in his mind.

Then Selly pushed past him, reaching for the sword to pull it out, crying for Jadren to wake up. It broke Gabriel's heart and he pulled her away, lest she harm herself. She turned her fury on him, a whirlwind of fists and feet, flailing at him and screaming denials, hurling curses at him. He tried to contain her, but that had never been easy when she was crazed like this, especially without hurting her. With a despairing heart he realized she'd lost her mind again, not knowing him or that she'd been rescued. They'd brought her back from the mists of insanity only to lose her again. He wrapped his arms around her, talking to her soothingly, urging her to silence. They weren't that far from House El-Adrel and he'd just killed the lady's son. They were far from out of danger.

Something butted him from behind, hard enough to make him stagger. Nic, her faceted eyes flashing with demand. Oh, right. Grateful that he didn't need to spare a hand to touch Nic, that their bond let them work together without having to physically touch, he drew on the silver webbing that connected her to him, pulling her through to her human form, making sure she would manifest wearing clothing appropriate for trekking through the woods. Including boots. He'd once forgotten to give her shoes and she'd hid the fact from him, both pieces of that particular incident enough to make him grind his teeth.

Nic appeared fully shod in good boots, glaring at him in purest fury. "Put her down!" she snapped.

He was so shocked, so taken aback, that he did so. Selly immediately stopped fighting, hurling herself at Jadren's bloody corpse, sobbing as wildly as she'd been struggling a moment ago. "Help me," she cried to Nic, tugging ineffectually at the embedded sword.

"Oh, honey," Nic said, going to her and stroking Selly's shorn hair, kissing her tear-drenched cheek. "I'm so sorry. So very sorry."

"He tried to kill him," Selly sobbed. "Gabriel, he—he…" she broke off into heartbroken weeping.

"I know, my darling. I know." Nic glared daggers at him, a keen-edged counterpoint to her softly soothing voice. *How could you?* She clearly demanded with her gaze. "I thought we were going to wait for explanations," she said aloud.

"*What* explanations?" Gabriel demanded, feeling supremely and unfairly abused. "He bonded her and look at Selly, she's clearly out of her mind again. We don't know what all he did to her, but there's no doubt he deserved to die." Though a niggle of doubt did worm into his heart. Those last words…

"My only regret is that he died so quickly."

"I am *not* out of my mind!" Selly stopped struggling to withdraw the sword and faced him squarely, burning with righteous rage, her silvery magic boiling in a way he recognized very well. Tears flowed down her cheeks, her short hair waving in wild, uneven curls. She looked older somehow, no longer the little girl in a scrawny, coltish body. "Jadren *saved* me," she said, dashing away the tears. "He sacrificed everything for me. He bonded me because he had to get us out of that place."

Uneasy, Gabriel did his best to assimilate that information. Behind Selly, Nic stood with arms folded, emerald eyes hard, clearly conveying an "I told you so" of epic proportions. Unable to face her righteous judgment, he focused on Selly, searching for words. He had nothing.

"That's right," Selly snarled. "You tried to kill the man who saved me. Now pull out that sword so he can heal."

"Selly..." Nic wrung her hands, regret dampening her magic. "The sword pierced Jadren's heart. He's dead."

Behind him, Jadren coughed, a wet, horribly hacking sound. "Not quite," he grated out.

Feeling as stunned as the expression on Nic's face, Gabriel turned in slow disbelief. Selly let out a glad cry, spinning around and embracing Jadren, showering his face with kisses. It wasn't easy, what with the sword embedded to the hilt in his chest, but she nimbly dodged it.

"Off, you feral creature," Jadren said, his voice weak. "Make yourself useful and pull this fucking thing out of me."

"Right! I've been trying." Laughing and crying at once,

Selly fastened her hands around the hilt, braced herself, and pulled, budging the sword only slightly.

"How are you alive?" Gabriel asked wonderingly, not quite believing his eyes. Nic came up beside him, her magic similarly besieged.

Jadren flicked him a feeble grin. "Can I pause the questions and say it's a long story? I'll tell, but we really need to get out of here and I'd be obliged if you'd take me with you, *sans* stake through the heart, if it's all the same."

"Gabriel," Nic said, prompting him.

"Ah. Allow me." Edging Selly gently aside, Gabriel grasped the sword, firming his grip. "I've never withdrawn my weapon upon request from a man I tried to kill."

"Funny," Jadren commented drily, gaze flicking to Selly, "it's been happening to me a lot lately. Must run in the family."

"This will hurt," Gabriel warned him, then felt foolish. What could hurt worse than having a sword cleaving your heart?

Jadren sighed philosophically. "You have no idea."

JADREN PASSED OUT cold, something that distressed Selly to a bewildering extent, and further confused Gabriel. She kept saying he couldn't draw on her magic to heal, which made no sense, as Jadren wasn't a healer and healing magic didn't work on the wizard practicing it anyway. Nic, however, gave him a stern warning look, so he didn't argue with his distraught sister. Instead, as instructed, he hefted Jadren's wiry form over his shoulders and started walking.

Nic and Selly followed behind, keeping up with his brisk pace, and Selly calmed enough to tell the whole story. Though they were braced for pursuit, no one came after them. Somehow Jadren's father had managed to disguise their escape and buy Jadren and Selly enough time to get cleanly away. Gabriel had no idea how the man could have done it. He remembered Fyrdo from when he and Lady El-Adrel brought Jadren to House Phel. An older, more genial version of Jadren, he hadn't seemed like the heroic sort. But he'd also embraced his son with real affection, Gabriel recalled, something that seemed to be a rarity in the Convocation.

Gabriel understood that much of being a father—he already loved the unborn child Nic carried with an intensity he'd never before experienced. The part he didn't understand was how Fyrdo had apparently stood by all those years while his son was repeatedly tortured. He couldn't imagine it without feeling ill, so he set it aside. Along with what Jadren had said to Gabriel when they both thought he was dying.

What mattered was getting Selly—and Jadren—safely across the border to House Refoel lands. It would be a long walk.

ALISE, HAN, ILIANA, and Asa met them at the border with horses and a brand-new elemental powered carriage. That they were there at the precise location didn't surprise him. Alise had sent a small spirit scout to ascertain their path and progress to the border crossing. Being a house dedicated to healing, Refoel didn't guard their borders and Nic said that Alise's Elal magic could handle any defensive gadgets El-Adrel might've buried on their side. The carriage, however, was a surprise, and Nic met his questioning gaze defiantly.

"I ordered one from a nearby depot and Alise picked it up on the way. I know you didn't want anything from House Elal, but we *need* this. If you're going to be stubborn about it, Alise can swap out her own elemental for the bottled one it came with, but Selly and Jadren are riding from here."

"I wasn't going to argue," he replied mildly, grateful that Han and Asa possessed the strength to lift Jadren carefully from his shoulders, carrying the wizard gently to the carriage. Iliana and Selly followed behind, arms around each other, Selly's dark head inclined against Iliana's bright one. Asa was already stabilizing Jadren with his own native healing magic, while Han and Iliana stood ready to bolster him with theirs. Stiff, tired, and grateful to be relieved of the physical burden of Jadren, along with the temporary reprieve of passing the responsibility for saving the man to Asa—the rest of the guilt would likely never disperse—Gabriel rolled his shoulders. Not quite ready to address the gulf between Nic and him, he chose the lesser battle. "Was it expensive, the carriage?"

She huffed out an annoyed breath. "Double wholesale value. It nearly broke my mercenary heart to pay that price. I may have shed a tear." She eyed him in return. "You're worn out."

"As are you." He was very aware of how much she'd given to the flight and the subsequent walk out of El-Adrel lands. They were incredibly lucky House El-Adrel lay so near the Refoel border. Neither of them could have gone much longer. Bracing himself, he decided he might as well brave her anger. "How much do you hate me?"

"Oh, Gabriel." She smiled at him, though it lacked her usual vividness. "I could never hate you." She came to him and wrapped her arms around his waist, leaning her cheek against his chest over his heart. He folded his arms around her gratefully, holding her tenderly, bathing in the rose-infused heated wine of her magic, as always offered so generously. "One could hardly fault you for your assumptions or actions. Jadren *did* unlawfully bond a familiar of your house. Convocation law is on your side, even if he had died."

"I'm not comforted in the least to be finally on the right side of Convocation law," he replied drily. But that, too, could be set aside for another day. "Why do you suppose he isn't dead?" Selly had been vague on that score, including why she'd been so convinced the sword hadn't killed Jadren.

"I suspect that whatever the reason is, that's why he never attended Convocation Academy or released his MP scores." She tipped back her head to look at him. "There are tales of hopeful monsters arising at times."

"Hopeful monsters?" he repeated, bemused by the odd phrase.

"New variations in magic types and wielders," she supplied. "Non-standard or never-before-cataloged magic potentials. Sometimes the people born with those don't survive childhood or they go insane from the magic, unable to turn it in a productive direction. Others live normal lives, but essentially as magical duds. Hard to say which is worse."

"I think one is clearly worse than the other."

"You would. Still, the other possibility is that the new variant leads to the person being a powerful wizard. Or familiar," she added hastily, anticipating his correction. "They might be a monster, but they win that particular lottery and become something never before seen. If Jadren is able to magically heal himself to the point that he cannot die..." She trailed off meaningfully.

It gave Gabriel a headache to contemplate. "Quite the weapon, then, for House El-Adrel, is what you're saying. I'm surprised they risked inserting him in House Phel in the first place, if he's so valuable."

Nic shrugged a little, raising her brows. "What risk? He can't be killed."

"Lord Phel?" Asa called. He stood in the carriage doorway, dark face serious. "Wizard Jadren is stable enough for travel. I'd like to get him back to the House Phel infirmary as quickly as possible."

"Go," Gabriel told him. "Nic and I will follow on the horses. Do you mind?" he asked Nic belatedly. "If you're too tired to ride, you could go in the carriage with them."

She slipped her hand into his, interlacing her delicately boned fingers and robust magic with his. "My place is with my wizard," she answered firmly, waving as Alise instructed the air elemental to return to House Phel and the carriage sped off. "I imagine you want to debate what to do about the bonding."

He sighed in agreement, leading her to Salve to give Nic a boost into the mare's saddle. "Selly seems bizarrely emotionally attached to him, especially in so short a time. Is it the Fascination?"

Nic settled herself into the saddle, taking up the reins, watching him with a thoughtful gaze as he mounted Vale. "I don't think there's any way of knowing. Is the Fascination real? If so, is it only induced by the Aratron potion my father devised and abused? Did House El-Adrel have access to that potion to administer it to Selly?" She shrugged. "It could be she truly cares about him."

"I doubt that," Gabriel commented sourly, though what Jadren had said to him in those final moments couldn't be shaken so easily. "It would have happened too fast."

"I don't think there's a timeline for such things."

"They suffered through an intense trial together," Gabriel argued. "That creates an emotional attachment of its own. Like warriors in battle. It fades once the fight is over." He wanted to believe that.

"What did he say to you?" Nic asked, her expression knowing when he glanced at her in surprise. "I saw your face. What did he say when you both thought he was dying?"

"That true love makes fools of us all in the end," Gabriel answered on a sigh.

"Ah," Nic breathed. He imagined she remembered, also, how Jadren had snarled at them for being stupid in love, embracing upon their reunion while the hunters bore down on them. "So he does love her."

"Or *thinks* he does," Gabriel corrected darkly. "Either way, it might be difficult to convince them to allow Alise to sever the bond. Do you think she can do it without their cooperation?"

"You would do that to them?" Nic asked in considerable surprise, and perhaps a hint of censure.

"I'll do what I have to do to protect Selly," Gabriel returned. That wasn't a question. "If possible, I'd like to prevent Jadren from knowing about this trick. I think it would be unwise to trust him with that secret. He might tell El-Adrel."

"And here I thought you wanted to broadcast it to all the world and free the familiars from tyranny at last!" Nic punched a fist into the air, giving him a bright smile.

"You shouldn't mock me," he told her, fighting not to laugh.

"Why, will you punish me for it, wizard?" She gave him such a heated look that he considered pulling her from Salve's back and demonstrating exactly how he'd take revenge.

"Later," he promised.

"Good," she purred, looking immensely pleased with herself.

"As far as broadcasting the bond-severing to all the world," he continued, firmly ignoring the fantasies she was deliberately conjuring for him. "I've been thinking on the perspective you offered. It's a potent weapon. If we're going to overturn the Convocation, then we need to use this weapon wisely and judiciously. You're right—if the Convocation discovers this too soon, they'll move to destroy anyone who knows."

"While you know I love to hear that I'm right," she said, producing a smile that fell short of saucy, "I feel I should point out that my father will know. He can't fail to notice Maman has been severed from him."

"You were the one to point out that Lord Elal has been oddly silent since we sent him home, even given the wound I gave him."

"Knowing him, he's plotting his next move," Nic commented darkly, gazing into the distance. "We likely won't know what it is until it hits us."

"Then we need to plot our own next moves. Form a strategy."

Nic flashed him a brilliant, and very real smile this time. "My favorite thing."

"Your *favorite*?" he teased.

"Well..." She pursed her lips, raking him with a lascivious gaze. "Top five, anyway."

That did it. He halted Vale, leapt from the gelding's back, and came around to lift a laughing Nic off of Salve. "Gabriel, my only love," she exclaimed, pretending to be shocked. "Here, in the Refoel wilderness?"

"Yes." He claimed her mouth, sinking into her. "Whatever it takes to crowd planning war out of your top five."

"Oh, my darling wizard," she murmured, yielding utterly. "You say the sweetest things."

~ 23 ~

JADREN AWOKE IN the House Phel infirmary. For a disorienting moment, he thought it was still the days after Seliah had been treated, when he'd collapsed after draining her stagnant magic. Then he became aware of how much his body hurt, particularly his heart, which sent a stabbing double ping of agony with each one-two beat. Gabriel Phel and his fucking sword.

A cool hand smoothed his brow and he opened his eyes to see Seliah sitting beside him, looking hopeful and worried. She'd cleaned up, and had her hair neatly trimmed so it wreathed her pixie face in adorably springy black curls. But, despite the youthful delicacy of her fine-boned features, she no longer looked like the waifish gamine of a girl he'd first met. Seliah had a woman's confidence to her now, a sensual ripeness in the way she caressed his forehead, and he was abruptly reminded of the promise she'd extracted from him.

Good thing he'd been clever enough to build a loophole into it.

"Hey," Seliah said softly. "How are you feeling?"

"Why do people always ask sick and injured people that question?" he returned. "Obviously we feel like total shit, or you wouldn't ask. And you're the ones who know exactly how fucked up we are."

"Definitely better," she said, smile deepening. He was really losing his touch.

"You're going to live," Asa said, his darker-skinned face coming into view behind Seliah, wizard-black gaze penetrating. "How, I don't know. With the amount of metal I've extracted from your body, not to mention your heart, you should be dead several times over."

"Yeah, about that. I—"

Asa held up his hands, stopping him. "I really don't need or want to know. What's relevant at the moment is that I've done what I can to restore your heart, but it was well and truly shredded."

Jadren winced. No wonder every beat hurt.

"Exactly," Asa said, as if Jadren had commented. "Selly claims you can finish the fix on your own, so I revived you far sooner than I normally would have so you can avail yourself of your familiar's magic."

His familiar. Seliah. She beamed at him, foolishly happy. The possessive longing for her nearly took his breath away. Well, that and the fact that his literally shredded heart was leaking blood instead of pumping it. His mother would be fascinated by this new data on what he could survive. Not that he had any intention of letting her find out. He rolled his head away from Seliah's touch. "Leave me alone, poppet. I need to sleep."

"You need my magic," she insisted, wrapping her hands around his. Sadly, he was too weak to resist.

"You need her magic," Asa confirmed wearily. "Otherwise you'll kill me with trying to keep your heart working."

"No one asked you to," Jadren pointed out dourly.

"Incorrect. Lord Phel's orders."

"I wish the Phel family would decide whether they wanted me alive *before* they tried to kill me," Jadren complained.

Seliah canted her head, amused. "I feel you have only yourself to blame."

Likely true.

"Take my magic, Jadren," she said in a quietly urgent voice. "Heal yourself. The rest can be worked out later." She regarded him so seriously that it was clear she understood his reservations. Perhaps she even understood that he would leave, and why he had to.

With a resigned nod, he closed his eyes and gave in, opening himself to the sweet rush of her magic, moonlight on water, rain across the moon, purely, brightly argent, the cooling wave of it bathing his aching heart in such an immediate cessation of pain that he moaned involuntarily.

And fell back into oblivion.

ASA KEPT HIM in the infirmary for another day, threatening to strap Jadren to the bed if he attempted to get up for anything more than visits to the necessary. Seliah hovered, undaunted by his snarling insults and taunting, smiling as if he was reciting love poetry instead. She only left his side when ordered to by Asa, at which point shed give Jadren a kiss he couldn't dodge, smile, sweetly, and promise to return before he could miss her.

He missed her before she even disappeared from sight. He had to get away from her, and soon.

A steady stream of visitors, all wishing him well, further befuddled him. He'd known from the beginning that House Phel was a cesspool of idealists, all of them merrily making friendships and alliances, all so happy and convivial, but he'd never imagined they'd turn it on *him*.

They all seemed sincerely pleased to see him recovering, obeying Asa's injunctions to avoid distressing news, and keeping to irritatingly idle chatter. Tall, blond Han spoke cheerfully of the weapons training they'd work on once Jadren was up and about, while pretty freckled, redheaded Iliana regaled him with tales of the creature that lurked in the workshop watery abyss, which sounded improbably like a giant pink seahorse. Even Alise, who he'd treated with rather merciless condescension, spent time chatting with him about carefully neutral aspects of wizardry, drawing out his opinions on potential product lines for House Phel.

Nic visited also, inquiring after his needs, not lingering long, though she gave him searching looks and reassuring smiles. Gabriel Phel did not visit, not until the hour before Asa had decreed Jadren would be allowed to leave the infirmary—after the evening meal and a final infusion of healing magic, from both Seliah and the Refoel healer. The infirmary was quietly deserted when Phel arrived, Jadren impatiently waiting through the ticking minutes until he was free.

"Well, I suppose this was inevitable," Jadren observed drily as Lord Phel entered and set up wards for privacy. "Come to try to execute me again? I'd request something less painful, but that wouldn't be as satisfying for you, I imagine."

"Tempting as the invitation might be, I'm not going to kill you," Gabriel replied, snagging a chair and bringing it to Jadren's bedside, straddling it backward. "If I even could," he added, a question in his voice.

"Well, not for want of trying anyway," Jadren said consolingly. "And not that I blame you," he continued in a more serious vein. "Lord Phel, I never planned to bond your sister as my familiar. I know you have no reason to believe me, but I didn't want this for Seliah."

The silver-haired wizard looked taken aback by that confession. "What did you want for her—or, rather, what *do* you want?"

Good question. "Better than me," Jadren answered with brutal honesty. "I harbor no illusions about my ability to function as anything resembling a healthy human being. Seliah deserves a decent life. She's had a shit deal so far and an even shittier one because of me. The one upside of her being bonded to me is that it gives her better legal status. She doesn't have to attend Convocation Academy now if she doesn't want to. No other wizard can bond her." He wrung out a smile at Gabriel Phel's dubious frown. "I plan to leave," Jadren clarified. "All I need from you is your permission, releasing me from my contract. You all have the ability to tap Seliah's magic here. She'll let you do it, so you can keep her sane and healthy. I relinquish all claim to her. I'll disappear and never be seen again."

"Why would you do that?" Gabriel sounded sincerely bewildered. "I'm looking for the trick here and not seeing it."

"No tricks. Not this time. I never planned to keep her."

"But you won't be able to bond another familiar while she lives."

"I don't want to," Jadren assured him. "Believe me, it's really better for everyone if I don't have access to that level of power."

Bemused, Phel studied him. "I have been repeatedly told that all Convocation wizards crave as much power as they can possibly get."

"Not me," Jadren said, too quickly. "All I want is a place where I can be alone, where no one will bother me." Like a cave in the mountains. No, too cold. Maybe the desert. Definitely not a swamp which Seliah could navigate with her preternatural abilities and find him.

"After what you've apparently endured all your life," Phel said slowly, "I can't blame you for wanting to be left alone."

"Save your pity, Phel."

"Fair enough." He considered. "What about what you said about true love making fools of us all?"

"You can't trust what a man says when his heart is being carved out of his chest."

Gabriel blinked at him. "Figuratively or literally?"

Jadren only laughed. *Both*, he didn't say aloud.

"If you truly love Selly," Phel began, "then—"

"She prefers to be called 'Seliah,' you know," Jadren said, interrupting before that could go too far down a painful path.

Phel paused, frowning. "What?"

"'Selly' is her childhood nickname," Jadren explained. "She prefers 'Seliah' now. You should respect that."

"I didn't know."

"Well, now you do." Jadren twitched restlessly, ready to be out of the bed, the house, and Seliah's life. "So, are we agreed? I disappear, you let me go, and we're done with each other."

"What will you tell Selly—Seliah?" Gabriel asked, correcting himself. "Regardless of all else, she won't be happy about this. She'll want to go with you, most likely."

"I'll handle the disappearing part. You handle keeping her from thinking she needs to look for me."

Gabriel considered. "I'm thinking Nic would say this is a terrible idea."

Once, Jadren would have made a cutting remark about listening to what familiars thought. Now he only regarded Phel with somber urgency. "You and I both understand that I'm no good for Seliah. Let me do this one thing for her."

"All right." Gravely, Gabriel held out a hand. Though it wasn't a Convocation custom, Jadren made a concession for Phel's country manners and shook it.

"Deal." Jadren rubbed away the magical residue from Lord Phel, the moon and water sensation too reminiscent of Seliah. He hesitated. "I don't have to ask you to take care of her."

Gabriel Phel raised one dark brow. "If you're leaving, what does it matter to you?"

"It doesn't," Jadren answered hastily, hearing the lie in his own words. "She's a good person. Too innocent and sensitive still. She thinks she's tough, and she is in some ways, but she needs to be protected from her own worst impulses."

Phel nodded, expression neutral. "I suppose you need supplies."

"That would be good," Jadren admitted. "And, ah… could I keep the machete?"

"Seems I recall you won it fair and square."

"The reverse," Jadren corrected. "I lost and you gave it to me anyway."

"Ah well." Gabriel grinned, clapped his hands to his knees and stood. "Keep it. Use it well." He put the chair back where it had been, one of the many small tells that showed he wasn't the arrogant high-house lord he pretended to be. Jadren liked him all the better for it, not that he'd ever tell the wizard that. "Also, Wizard Jadren…" Phel paused, hand on the back of the chair, studying him with an opaque expression. "You have a place in House Phel, should you ever want it."

If Jadren hadn't been lying down, he'd have staggered. He had no words, opening and closing his mouth over nothing, several times in a row. "What's the catch?" he finally managed.

Gabriel shook his head. "No catch. Everyone deserves a place of refuge, somewhere they can be safe. Seems to me you don't have one in your birth house, so I'm offering House Phel, should you ever want it."

"You're a fool," Jadren informed him. "Lady Phel would have your head for offering this."

Gabriel smiled faintly. "I think you'd be surprised. Nevertheless, the offer is there. Do what you will with it."

"What about Seliah?" Jadren asked.

Phel shrugged, smile going enigmatic. "I've been forcibly

reminded that Seliah is a grown woman. She can make her own choices." He turned to go. "Something for you to keep in mind, too."

With that, he dropped the wards, and left.

~ 24 ~

S ELLY HAD SPENT Jadren's convalescence in a frenzy of preparation.

And anticipation. The happy fantasies of how she and Jadren would spend the coming night had her simmering with impatient desire. He'd made a promise and she knew he'd keep it. No matter what else Jadren was or did, he kept his promises. Once he got over whatever worried him about bedding her, that final barrier between them would crumble. He could begin to heal, perhaps even trust. They'd learn to work together as wizard and familiar, be like Nic and Gabriel, perhaps even have a proper wedding, which would please her parents. She was fully confident she could talk Jadren into it.

At this point, she knew Jadren better than he knew himself. He wanted to pretend he didn't have a soft heart inside that jaded façade he presented to the world, but she'd seen it for herself. They'd been through the worst together, so they could get through anything. If nothing else, Jadren desired her, even if it was despite himself.

Regardless, they were bonded and he was hers. She intended to demonstrate just how much he'd enjoy that. She hadn't forgotten all the delicious, seductive things he'd said to her, beseeching her to say yes to him pleasuring her. She was saying yes now.

The biggest challenge had been the setting. The bedroom her well-meaning family had set up for her in the central and oldest part of the manse was ridiculously childish. Not at all the setting for the kind of sex she intended to indulge in with Jadren. And he didn't need the reminders of her childhood giving him scruples. The problem was that his suite in the north wing with the other wizards of his status was offputting-ly sterile, uncomfortably reminiscent of the coldest aspects of House El-Adrel. Daisy, still acting as chamberlain and minding which minions got which rooms, had given her daughter a spare key, and Selly had gone to explore the rooms that Jadren had picked out, on the highest floor. Though others had warned her Jadren might've warded the rooms, he hadn't.

Once she saw them, she knew why, too. There was noth-ing in there worth protecting. Oh, he'd had it furnished in style, but none of it reflected what she knew of Jadren. The place looked like something out of an ad for a fancy inn in Convocation Center. Just another of Jadren's covers, him presenting to the world an image that had nothing to do with who he truly was.

She placed the bag of metal gadgets there for him—both the one he'd told her to keep as they were escaping, and the others Asa had collected from Jadren's healing flesh. She'd given him his weapons in the infirmary, which had made him smile, particularly the machete, which he seemed attached to. Her long tail of hair had been in the bag, too—hopelessly tangled—and she'd planned to throw it away, but Jadren said it was traditional to keep it, so she set that with the brass gadgets. The detritus from both of their bodies and their sojourn in House El-Adrel didn't match the sleek formality of the rooms, but Jadren could deal with that later, when he was ready.

Selly locked the door behind her, knowing this wouldn't be the place for their reunion.

Instead, she threw herself into redecorating her simple set of rooms, her mother willingly assisting and happily chattering about wedding plans. Her parents still didn't quite understand the wizard–familiar relationship, or how bonding worked, so Selly had simply represented herself as engaged to Jadren. It wasn't a lie, especially in light of the fact that their true relationship went much deeper than that and was far more permanent. They moved out the toys and dolls, enlisting Wizard Dahlia's help with bed linens and upholstery that looked less girlish and bit more in the style of Jadren's rooms in House El-Adrel.

When Selly fetched Jadren, promising to give him an infusion of magic in private so that Asa would release him, she actually blushed at the healer's knowing look. "Go on, you two," Asa said genially, waving them away. "I remember what it's like to be freshly bonded." He looked briefly downcast.

To Selly's surprise, Jadren hesitated, then clapped the Refoel wizard briefly on the shoulder. "They executed your familiar after all, huh?"

Asa opened his mouth, clearly taken aback.

"I can sense it," Jadren explained with compassion. "The bond is gone. The only way that happens is death. Sorry, man."

Asa hesitated a moment more, seeming about to say something, then simply nodded. "Thank you. It's been... a difficult time."

"Bright side is there's more where she came from." Jadren grinned at her. "Plenty of familiars in the sea, right, poppet?"

She rolled her eyes at him, making him laugh. But she wondered. It didn't seem at all like something Gabriel would do, executing Laryn, particularly as she'd been pregnant. Selly had been too busy being giddy over Jadren the last few days to think about Laryn, however. She knew Sergio was dead—hooray!—and Sabrina returned to House Sammael in abortive attempt to ransom them—alas—but no one had mentioned Laryn. Asa gave her a warning shake of his head behind Jadren's back. Fine, she'd ask Gabriel later. Much later. Tomorrow.

"Come on," she told Jadren. "I have a surprise to show you."

"I'm pretty sure I've seen all of your surprises already," he drawled, but went with her obligingly enough.

When they arrived in her rooms, she made him close his eyes. Though he scowled at her, he did so, allowing her to draw him inside. Closing the door behind them, she took one last assessing look around. Everything was in place. The glowing candles. Flowers. Wine—the best House Phel had.

The bed turned down invitingly.

"Ta da!" she said. "You can look."

Jadren opened his eyes, taking his time absorbing everything, then he raised an auburn brow at her. "Looks like you've thought of everything."

"I tried." She fidgeted, anxious now, unable to tell if he was pleased. "Would you like some wine?"

"Yes. I'll pour."

She waited while he uncorked the bottle, relieved that he didn't comment on what was probably not a very good vintage. He poured, then turned and extended a glass to her, an opaque look in his wizard-black eyes. "Is everything all right?" she ventured, taking the glass.

"Why wouldn't it be?" he smiled, an odd twist to it, as he lifted his own glass to his lips. "Drink your wine, sweetling."

"Wait," she said before he could drink. "We should toast."

He took a breath, expelled it. "What shall we toast to?"

She lifted her glass. "To us."

Jadren paused long enough that she thought he might refuse. Then he lifted his glass and clinked it to hers. "To you."

He drank down his wine before she could object to the alteration, tipping back his head so the corded lines of his throat showed as he swallowed. "Don't you like the wine?" he asked, tipping his head at her untouched glass. "It's bad luck if you don't drink everything in your glass. The good wishes of the toast might not come true."

"I didn't know that." She drank, making herself swallow it all. Finishing, she smiled at him. "More wine?

He laughed and took her glass, setting them both aside. "A hint, poppet—you don't need to get a man drunk to seduce him. Just take off your clothes, lie back, and spread your legs. That does the trick every time."

He was nervous, she decided, and she refused to let him bait her. "All right." She smiled at his suspicious frown, then triggered the fastening on the Ophiel gown Wizard Dahlia had made for her. As promised, it slithered off of her like a fall of water, pooling around her feet and leaving her naked. Jadren goggled at her in shock and obvious desire. It shot through his magic, like lightning, galvanizing the connection between them and heightening her already aroused senses. As he seemed rooted to the spot, eyes traveling over her with glittering intensity, she sidled closer, stroking her palms over his chest. "What's the next step, again?" she purred. "Lie back, I believe. The bed is through here."

She took his hand and pulled him along—except he didn't budge.

"Seliah," he breathed when she looked back at him in question. Slowly he drew her closer to him, skimming his soft wizard's hands over her arms, then down to settle on her hips. "Thank you for this gift of yourself. I want you to know that, as much as I'm capable of it, I appreciate this. All of this."

"You don't have to thank me," she replied softly, slipping her hands behind his neck. "Just kiss me."

For a moment she thought he wouldn't, but then his mouth closed on hers in a kiss unlike any other they'd shared before. Deep, dreamy, drugging, the kiss seemed to last an eternity, to promise even longer, sweeping her up with erotic intensity beyond what she'd known to imagine. In truth, she grew woozy with it, bemused to find Jadren carrying her to the bed and laying her gently upon it. Befuddled she blinked up at him. "Jadren?"

He caressed her cheek. "Everything is fine, love. And soon to be better. Sleep now."

SHE WOKE HOURS and hours later, morning sun pouring in her windows, the candles all cold pools of wax, the flowers wilted.

A note on her pillow.

Dread in her heart, she unfolded the fine paper, reading the crisply inked, meticulously even words.

NO, I DIDN'T FUCK YOU SENSELESS. THAT WAS THE POTION I PUT IN YOUR WINE. I SAID AS SOON AS YOU'RE SAFE, I'D TAKE YOU TO BED. YOU'LL NEVER BE SAFE WHILE YOU'RE WITH ME, SO... I'M GONE. DON'T BOTHER LOOKING AS I WON'T BE FOUND. DON'T SHED ANY GIRLISH TEARS OVER ME. JUST GO ON WITH YOUR LIFE. IT'S THE BEST REVENGE AND YOU DESERVE THAT MUCH. ~J

She sat up. Read the note again. "Girlish tears," she muttered. "You should be so lucky that I'd weep over you, Jadren El-Adrel." She started to ball up the note, but stopped herself, refolding it back into the precise, straight lines. "You're be the one crying when I catch up to you," she vowed. "And then we'll see about the best revenge."

Selly and Jadren's story will continue, I promise!

Selly promises, too.

Look for Rogue Familiar coming 2/23/23!

Preorder links available here.

jeffekennedy.com/shadow-wizard

TITLES BY JEFFE KENNEDY

FANTASY ROMANCES

BONDS OF MAGIC
Dark Wizard
Bright Familiar
Grey Magic
Familiar Winter Magic (In Fire of the Frost)

RENEGADES OF MAGIC
Shadow Wizard

HEIRS OF MAGIC
The Long Night of the Crystalline Moon
(also available in *Under a Winter Sky*)
The Golden Gryphon and the Bear Prince
The Sorceress Queen and the Pirate Rogue
The Dragon's Daughter and the Winter Mage
The Storm Princess and the Raven King

THE FORGOTTEN EMPIRES
The Orchid Throne

The Fiery Crown
The Promised Queen

THE TWELVE KINGDOMS
Negotiation
The Mark of the Tala
The Tears of the Rose
The Talon of the Hawk
Heart's Blood
The Crown of the Queen

THE UNCHARTED REALMS
The Pages of the Mind
The Edge of the Blade
The Snows of Windroven
The Shift of the Tide
The Arrows of the Heart
The Dragons of Summer
The Fate of the Tala
The Lost Princess Returns

THE CHRONICLES OF DASNARIA
Prisoner of the Crown
Exile of the Seas
Warrior of the World

SORCEROUS MOONS
Lonen's War
Oria's Gambit
The Tides of Bára
The Forests of Dru

Oria's Enchantment

Lonen's Reign

A COVENANT OF THORNS

Rogue's Pawn

Rogue's Possession

Rogue's Paradise

CONTEMPORARY ROMANCES

Shooting Star

MISSED CONNECTIONS

Last Dance

With a Prince

Since Last Christmas

CONTEMPORARY EROTIC ROMANCES

Exact Warm Unholy

The Devil's Doorbell

FACETS OF PASSION

Sapphire

Platinum

Ruby

Five Golden Rings

FALLING UNDER

Going Under

Under His Touch

Under Contract

EROTIC PARANORMAL

MASTER OF THE OPERA E-SERIAL
Master of the Opera, Act 1: Passionate Overture
Master of the Opera, Act 2: Ghost Aria
Master of the Opera, Act 3: Phantom Serenade
Master of the Opera, Act 4: Dark Interlude
Master of the Opera, Act 5: A Haunting Duet
Master of the Opera, Act 6: Crescendo
Master of the Opera

BLOOD CURRENCY
Blood Currency

BDSM FAIRYTALE ROMANCE
Petals and Thorns

Thank you for reading!

ABOUT JEFFE KENNEDY

Jeffe Kennedy is a multi-award-winning and best-selling author of epic fantasy romance. She is the current president of the Science Fiction and Fantasy Writers Association (SFWA) and is a member of Romance Writers of America (RWA), and Novelists, Inc. (NINC). She is best known for her RITA® Award-winning novel, *The Pages of the Mind*, the recent trilogy, *The Forgotten Empires*, and the wildly popular, *Dark Wizard*. Jeffe lives in Santa Fe, New Mexico.

Jeffe can be found online at her website: JeffeKennedy.com, on her podcast First Cup of Coffee, every Sunday at the popular SFF Seven blog, on Facebook, on Goodreads, on BookBub, and pretty much constantly on Twitter @jeffekennedy. She is represented by Sarah Younger of Nancy Yost Literary Agency.

jeffekennedy.com

facebook.com/Author.Jeffe.Kennedy

twitter.com/jeffekennedy

goodreads.com/author/show/1014374.Jeffe_Kennedy

bookbub.com/profile/jeffe-kennedy

Sign up for her newsletter here.

jeffekennedy.com/sign-up-for-my-newsletter